The
Stolen
Hours

Karen Swan is the *Sunday Times* top three bestselling author of twenty-four books and her novels sell all over the world. She writes two books each year – one for the summer period and one for the Christmas season. Previous summer titles include *The Spanish Promise*, *The Hidden Beach* and *The Secret Path* and, for winter, *Together by Christmas*, *Midnight in the Snow* and *The Christmas Postcards*.

Previously a fashion editor, she lives in Sussex with her husband, three children and two dogs.

The Stolen Hours is the second of a five-book historical series called The Wild Isle, based on the dramatic evacuation of Scottish island St Kilda in the summer of 1930.

Follow Karen on Instagram @swannywrites,
on her author page on Facebook,
and on Twitter @KarenSwan1.

Also by Karen Swan

The Wild Isle series
The Last Summer

Other books
Players
Prima Donna
Christmas at Tiffany's
The Perfect Present
Christmas at Claridge's
The Summer Without You
Christmas in the Snow
Summer at Tiffany's
Christmas on Primrose Hill
The Paris Secret
Christmas Under the Stars
The Rome Affair
The Christmas Secret
The Greek Escape
The Christmas Lights
The Spanish Promise
The Christmas Party
The Hidden Beach
Together by Christmas
The Secret Path
Midnight in the Snow
The Christmas Postcards

The Stolen Hours

Karen Swan

MACMILLAN

First published in paperback 2023 by Macmillan
an imprint of Pan Macmillan
The Smithson, 6 Briset Street, London EC1M 5NR
EU representative: Macmillan Publishers Ireland Ltd, 1st Floor,
The Liffey Trust Centre, 117–126 Sheriff Street Upper,
Dublin 1, D01 YC43
Associated companies throughout the world
www.panmacmillan.com

ISBN 978-1-5290-8442-9

1 3 5 7 9 8 6 4 2

A CIP catalogue record for this book is available from the British Library.

Map artwork by Hemesh Alles

Typeset in Palatino by Palimpsest Book Production Ltd, Falkirk, Stirlingshire
Printed and bound by CPI Group (UK) Ltd, Croydon, CR0 4YY

Visit **www.panmacmillan.com** to read more about all our books
and to buy them. You will also find features, author interviews and
news of any author events, and you can sign up for e-newsletters
so that you're always first to hear about our new releases.

For Clare Boret
As generous as she is loyal

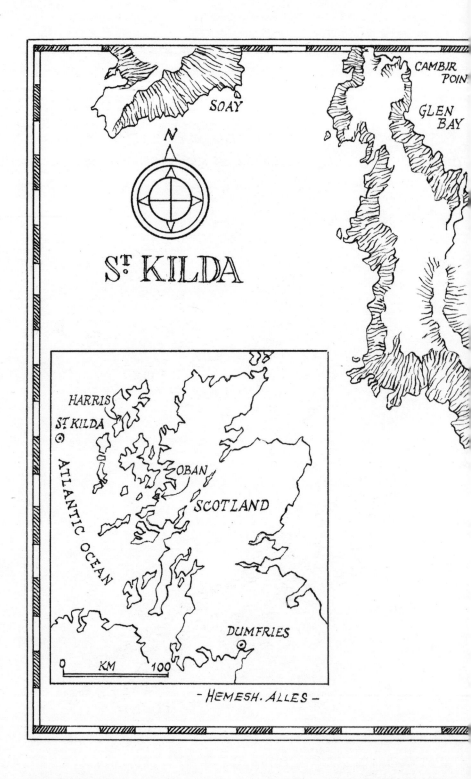

SOAY

CAMBIR POIN

GLEN BAY

N

S.^T KILDA

HARRIS

ST. KILDA

ATLANTIC OCEAN

OBAN

SCOTLAND

DUMFRIES

KM   100

— HEMESH. ALLES —

BORERAY

AMAZON'S
HOUSE

CONNACHAIR

MHAIRI'S
HOUSE

AN LAG

OISEVAL

EFFIE'S
HOUSE

FACTOR'S
HOUSE

AM
BLAID

COFFIN
CLEIT

STORM CLEIT

VILLAGE
BAY

HARRIS →

RUIVAL

DUN

0·5   1
KILOMETRES

Dear Reader,

Thank you for choosing to read *The Stolen Hours*, the second instalment in my Wild Isle series. Set on the distant and remote Scottish island of St Kilda, the action centres around a pivotal moment in time when, in the summer of 1930, the villagers were evacuated to the British mainland, thus ending over two thousand years of human settlement there.

The series is rooted in historical fact and accuracy but the characters, and the challenges they face, are wholly fictitious. Each book centres on a different young woman from St Kilda – all friends, all neighbours – but their stories are threaded together by a central mystery. *The Stolen Hours* focuses on Mhairi MacKinnon, whereas *The Last Summer* is concerned with her best friend Effie Gillies, and while each book can be read in isolation, I would strongly recommend starting with *The Last Summer* if you possibly can, in order to best pick up the clues that are subtly spooled out over the course of the series.

However if you can't, or you simply need a brief recap on events in *The Last Summer* – many of you have, after all, waited a year for this sequel – it is, in short, a love story that defies distance, social standing and a dangerously jealous man. You'll get peripheral glimpses of Effie's struggles and her startling new romance in *The Stolen Hours*, of course, but what you really need to know is that when the islanders left St Kilda, Frank Mathieson, the landlord's factor, went missing, only for his body to be discovered later on the island – begging the question of what happened on their last night there.

By the end of *The Last Summer*, Effie – who had been the target of Mathieson's unwanted advances – finds Scotland Yard collecting evidence against her.

Those who have read the book will likely not yet have forgiven me for the cliff-hanger on which it ended, and while some questions are answered in Mhairi's story, yet more are asked, as it transpires that Effie might not have been the only person with a motive to murder the factor.

Welcome back to St Kilda . . .

Happy reading.

Love,

Karen

Glossary

Characters

MHAIRI: pronounced Vah-Ree

CRABBIT MARY: Donald McKinnon's wife, crabbit meaning irritable or angry

BIG MARY: Mary Gillies

BIG GILLIES: Hamish, Mary and their children (as opposed to Effie and her father Robert Gillies; Robert and Hamish are brothers)

Dialect

BLACKHOUSE: a traditional, single-storey, grass-roofed dwelling

BLOODS: youngbloods; local youths

BOTHY: a basic shelter or dwelling, usually made of stone or wood

BROSE: a kind of porridge

CLEIT: a stone storage hut or bothy, only found on St Kilda

CRAGGING: climbing a cliff or crag; a CRAGGER is a climber

CREEL: a large basket with straps, used for carrying cuts of peat

CROTAL: a lichen used for making dye

DREICH: dreary, bleak (to describe weather)

DRUGGET: a coarse fabric

EEJIT: fool; idiot

FANK: a walled enclosure for sheep, a sheepfold

HOGGET: an older lamb, but one that is not yet old enough to be mutton

LAZYBEDS: parallel banks of ridges with drainage ditches between them; a traditional, now mostly extinct method of arable cultivation

PARLIAMENT: the daily morning meetings on St Kilda, outside crofts five and six, where chores were divvied up for the day

ROUP: a livestock sale

SOUTERRAIN: an underground chamber or dwelling

STAC: a sea stack – a column of rock standing in the sea – usually created as a leftover after cliff erosion

SWEE: an iron arm and hook fitted inside a chimney for hanging pots above the fire

TEA AND A PIECE: tea and fruit cake

TUP: a ram; a ewe that has been mated with can be called TUPPED

WAULKING: a technique to finish newly woven tweed, soaking and beating it

I had reached the boundary wall of the croft when I heard my mother's voice sharply calling me back home to fill the water pails. I turned, automatically, to obey, and I could see the village with its outline already dimmed grey in the early winter dusk, and, for a moment, I fancied that it had changed. Of course it hadn't. A village can't change overnight. But a boy can.

Finlay J. MacDonald, *Crowdie and Cream:*
Memoirs of a Hebridean Childhood

Prologue

5 September 1929

The North Sea

Mhairi screamed as the two men fought, fists flying, a stink of whisky and smuts filling the tiny cabin. The whaling ship pitched again in the darkness, flying down a glassy cliff and smashing them both heavily against the wall. The strap lashed at her waist kept her in place on the mattress, but if it saved her from being thrown about like a rag doll, it also unwittingly kept her a prisoner here, unable to escape.

Getting back to his feet, Donald got another few punches to the whaler's kidneys, jabbing him hard and fast three times.

'Aye, okay! Okay!' the man shouted, shielding his head with his arms, his body in a protective crouch.

'Next time I'll break your legs, do you hear me?' Donald shouted – his body flexed, fists pulled, jaw balling, eyes blazing – as he waited for the man to stagger off and disappear from his sight. It was several moments before he was satisfied that it was safe enough to turn back to her.

He looked in, seeing her wide-eyed terror, hands splayed on the walls either side of the narrow bunk. 'It's all right, Mhairi. He's drunk, not suicidal. He won't be back.'

1

'But what if there's others?'

His jaw balled again. 'There won't be.'

'But how can you be so sure?' she argued.

'Because I can. I will be right outside. Now try and sleep. We'll be there in a few hours.' His eyes grazed over her, as if checking for injuries or anything he should have to report to her father, little knowing that what wounds she had could not be seen. He looked at her again with a quizzical expression as if sensing still her earlier hostility, an argument between them still unarticulated and yet fully palpable. '. . . G'night then, Mhairi.'

He stepped back and closed the door firmly. She stared at it for several moments, her eyes on the handle, dreading that it would turn again. She didn't share his confidence that the night would be uneventful; if today had shown her anything, it was that she could trust no one.

She couldn't lie here and just wait. She couldn't sleep. She would need to be alert . . . She would need a weapon. It had been sheer luck that Donald had disturbed the whaler this time, but she couldn't rely on him again.

There had been an axe on the wall, she had noticed, on her way down here. There was scarce room to swing it in here but it might be enough to make the next drunk think twice.

She waited for the boat to pitch and drop again. There was always a moment of suspension in the trough of the waves when moving about was slightly easier, and she timed it so that she could stand and get to the door in the lull. She braced, her feet wide, as the boat slammed down, still throwing her against the cabin wall and slamming her shoulder, but in the next moment she was level again. She put her eye to the spyhole and looked out; she would need to check the corridor was empty before . . .

She frowned as she saw Donald was still in the passageway. He was standing directly opposite between two vertical steel beams, his arms looped through narrow openings. He had a booted foot wedged against her door, his head nodding forward as he tried – inconceivably – to sleep.

She watched his body sway with the motion of the sea, relaxing into it rather than resisting it. Was he really going to stand there all night?

Another slam! She was thrown back down again, making her groan. It was bad enough in here; she couldn't imagine how hard he was being knocked about out there . . . She remembered his bruises after the outward journey, that nasty cut to his lip. Had he done this before? Stood sentry at her door then too, guarding her, the only woman on a ship full of men?

She watched him again trying to sleep, pale-faced with reddened knuckles, his body battered, eyes closed but one ear open. She still felt angry with him; she would never forgive him for what he'd done, but as always with him, she felt safe now. Protected.

He was a flawed hero, her chaperone.

Chapter One

Four days earlier

Hirta, St Kilda

Dusk was falling when the whale exploded, the sudden gush of scarlet plumes still vivid against a darkening sky. Mhairi MacKinnon looked up from where she was stacking the peats and watched the blood stain the pale sea, the drifting seabirds harried into an ill-tempered frenzy and wheeling sharply on the currents above. They had been pecking away fruitlessly at the carcass for the couple of days since the fishermen had fixed it to the buoy at the neck of the bay. They would pick it up any day now, on their way back to the whaling station on Harris.

It couldn't come a minute too soon. With no winds to speak of for once, the late summer skies stretching endlessly blue, the nauseating smell of rotting meat had settled over the isle, getting into the villagers' hair and clothes and driving her ma spare; but now, released from its blubbery walls, a noxious stench would be carrying over the water in an invisible cloud, like one of those rain bombs that some-times peeked over the Mullach Bi ridge and disgorged its contents with sudden violence.

5

Mhairi glanced back down the slopes towards the village. She wasn't far past the dyke headwall and could easily make out the womenfolk standing by their cottage doors, watching the spectacle, the dogs tearing down to the beach, swiftly followed by the men. They would pull the smack into the water and salvage what they could of the haul for themselves. The tethered carcass was officially the property of the Norwegian whaling company Christian Salvesen – the St Kildan landlord Sir John MacLeod had leased the anchorage to the whalers – but it would soon sink now and the only winners would be the islanders, compensated with a dinner of novelty meat on their plates tonight. The usual diet of salted fulmar, guillemot porridge or gannet eggs was limited to say the least.

She stepped into the curved embrace of the stone cleit and lifted the last of the peats into the creel. These cuts had been made in the early spring and stored over the summer in the ancient stone structure that had been part of her family's meagre dowry for generations. There were over two thousand cleits on the two-mile isle and they scattered the landscape like giants' marbles, constructed in such a way as to keep the rain off but still allow the wind to blow through and dry the contents. The villagers had been told by the well-heeled visitors who stepped ashore from steamers and sloops that they resembled grassy-topped beehives, but as there were no bees on St Kilda, no one quite knew what that meant.

Every family had dozens of cleits sited all across the isle. Some were used for storing fulmar oil or feathers, others for salted bird carcasses, butter or the peats. Often the sheep would trot inside for shelter when the rain came and occasionally someone would get a fright as an inquisitive bird checked its curiosity and flew out at them amid a flapping of wings.

Straightening up again, Mhairi swung her arms above her head to stretch her spine, watching the men dragging the boat to the water's edge. Norman Ferguson was in the vanguard with his usual broad-shouldered vigour; Donald McKinnon and Mhairi's eldest brother, Angus, behind him; Flora's father Archibald grabbing the oars; her best friend Effie and Effie's uncle, Hamish Gillies, bringing up the rear. Their ages ranged from seventeen to forty-six but they worked in seamless synchronicity, well used to getting on the water quickly. The only person out of step was the factor, Frank Mathieson. The landlord's 'man on the ground', he was over for the second of his two annual visits, this one being the delivery of their winter provisions and collection of the rents. Everyone had been on edge all week as he queried feather weights, fulmar oil grades, the handle of the signature tweeds . . . a perpetual crease between his brows telling them that nothing was ever quite right.

She watched as the villagers heaved the boat off its mooring stones and got it afloat, Mathieson walking three easy paces in the shallows and stepping inside like he was the laird himself. Within three pulls, the boat was cutting across the water like a blade over blue silk.

Slipping the creel straps over her shoulders again, she walked back down the slope to the village. It was built along the southeasterly curve of the horseshoe-shaped bay, a single row of low stone cottages interspersed by the gentle ruins of their older and darker grass-roofed forebears, the black-houses. Some of the villagers still used theirs as animal byres or food stores, but it wasn't unknown for them to be re-inhabited for short spells too if a family disagreement escalated. Norman Ferguson would, on a fairly regular basis, carry his fireside chair and a blanket to their old blackhouse, where he would stay in petulant sulks before his long-suffering wife Jayne would go over and fetch it, and him, back home again.

A wide, flagged path known as The Street was laid in front of the houses and bounded by a low wall, with long allotments on the other side narrowing down to the shore. They weren't able to grow much there, beyond a few potatoes and some barley, for the sea spray and the wind conspired against them to render the soil poor; more successful were the raised lazy-beds in stray patches around the glen and some small walled enclosures between the back of the cottages and the dyke. They had no trees for fruit, timber, firewood or shade, but they had their sheep and a few milking cows, and of course the dramatic, vertiginous sea cliffs on the other side of the glen's grassy plains housed one of the world's greatest colonies of seabirds. They would never want for meat or eggs on St Kilda, only variety.

She passed her younger siblings playing tag-toe in the grass, Wee Murran, just turned five, hooking an arm around her legs and using her as a turning pivot as she approached their home. Patiently, she waited momentarily in her role of totem as Red Annie tore past her too, screeching with six-year-old delight. Mhairi could remember that feeling of the giddy joy of a full belly and a setting sun as another day collapsed into quiet night; it hadn't been that long since she too had played games before bed, sitting in a tight circle with Effie, Flora and Molly and plaiting each other's hair, chatting non-stop in high, spirited voices. But at eighteen years, those heady days of girlhood were behind them now – the village needed every set of strong hands and legs it could get.

She came through carrying the night's peat and set it down next to the open fire. Her father would throw it on before bed to smoulder through the night and be easily reinvigorated before breakfast in the morning.

Her mother kneaded the dough in a brisk manner, slapping the flour so that small dust clouds enlivened the dark space. She was a striking woman and Mhairi had inherited her fiery red hair and pale grey eyes, distinct from the sea-blue hue of most everyone else on the isle. The flames in the open fire flickered weakly, the oil lamp hanging on its hook on the rough wall, as yet unlit; her father had a rule that it couldn't be lit till the sun dropped behind Ruival, the mountain on the opposite side of the bay. On the deep windowsill sat several fulmar eggs, nestled in hay for safekeeping, and the small slate that still bore the traces of her twelve-year-old sister Christina's reading lesson this morning. The cottage managed to be both cluttered and bare all at once – they had a simple iron stove and a swee arm above the fire for boiling the bigger pots. Chains hung down inside the chimney for smoking the meats; water was collected from the burn. They sat at a table made from three different types of driftwood and set with two old pews rescued from the kirk, from when the minister had first arrived and found the facilities lacking. Her father had his own high-backed chair beside the fire, her mother preferred a low stool, and there was a potato crate stuffed with hemp sacking for feeding the baby at mealtimes. Cooking utensils and farming tools hung on the walls, horsehair climbing ropes were looped over the rafters, and every crevice and nook was filled with something of use: butter pats, brushes, carding boards . . . The washing scrubber was propped in one corner, the spinning wheel tucked in the other, a loom stored in the loft space.

In all their neighbours' houses, the looms would soon be coming down as the nights drew in. The men of the village took on the weaving of the tweed in the winter evenings but Mhairi's father, Ian, was the village postmaster and that meant he had his own special duties, distributing the letters that arrived and preparing for sending those the villagers wrote. The post office was a flimsy wooden structure that had been built on a small knoll adjacent to their cottage, and after every storm he would have to check it was still standing. In a community of only thirty-six people it was sometimes hard to believe he could be kept so busy, often working late into the night – and yet, for reasons none could fathom, a stamped St Kildan postcard had become desirable to people on the mainland. The sacks that came over with the passing trawlers and whalers were always bulging and demanding of urgent attention before the next load arrived.

There was no room for a loom to come down, anyhow – with eleven of them in all, and as the largest family left on the isle, they were packed in like herrings. Her parents had the box room, and baby Rory, approaching eleven months, slept in one of the kitchen drawers, the door left open between them. Mhairi, as the eldest girl, had her own narrow cot in the bedroom but the large curtained bed was shared between Christina, twelve; Euphemia, ten; Red Annie, six; Murran, five; and Alasdair, three, all sleeping top and tail. Her elder brothers – Finlay, nineteen, and Angus, twenty-two – slept in the byre both by necessity and by choice. Once married, they would each be able to move into one of several cottages that had remained empty after Dougie McDonald and his family had left for Australia a few years earlier, but they weren't spoilt for choice for brides – the only girls of marriageable age on the isle currently were Effie Gillies, Flora MacQueen and Molly Ferguson, and none of them would suffer her doltish brothers. Molly was wholly enamoured with Flora's brother David, while Effie would only break their spirits and Flora their hearts.

'Hallo.'

Mhairi looked up. Talk of the devil herself.

'Are you coming to the beach?' Flora asked from the doorway, holding an oil lamp. She stood in a wasp-waisted silhouette, the sky behind her an astral purple.

'Aye.' Mhairi reached for theirs on the windowsill. It would be dark by the time they returned; the evenings were already drawing in.

'Tell your brother to take some of the pulp for the dogs if he can,' her mother called after them as they left.

They walked together down the Street, past the quiet industry in the open-doored cottages as the households readied for another night. Tin baths sat before dancing fires, the youngest children pulling on their nightshirts, older ones coming back from the burn in the half-light with cleaned dishes. Mad Annie was sitting fireside with Ma Peg, the two women knitting as they talked, not even seeming to notice the way their hands flew in rhythmic sequences, spewing out perfectly turned socks.

'I got a letter.'

Mhairi looked across at her friend, hearing the pink-tinged note of coyness in her voice. 'From whom?'

Mhairi had never received a letter. Was that not ironic for the postmaster's daughter? In truth, she had never written a letter either, for she would first need someone to whom to send it, and everyone she knew lived here, upon the isle.

'Mr Callaghan . . . James.'

Mhairi gasped at the familiarity of using the man's given name. She remembered him well, of course. He had been on the isle for three days a few weeks back – a friend of one of the fishing company owners, he had been hitching a ride from Greenland when a storm had driven them into the bay for a few days. It had been clear Flora had caught his eye – but then, she caught everyone's eye. Certainly no passing flirtation had ever been followed up with a letter before.

'What did he say?' Mhairi watched the smile curve her friend's mouth, the light that gleamed in her eyes surprisingly soft.

'That he can't stop thinking about me and he would like to know me better.'

'And how's he going to do that?' Mhairi scoffed, jerking her chin towards the horizon where distant waves were already swelling up, readying to cut them off from the mainland till next spring. She felt a barb of envy catch and snag on her innards, like a bramble dragging on her skin.

'He wondered if we might write.' Flora spoke the words simply, but Mhairi knew this was an earthquake beneath their feet. Rich, handsome strangers would occasionally visit these small islands and she and her friends were of an age now to be excited by the prospect of them. But no matter how handsome or courteous they might be on these shores, they would always climb aboard their boats and sail away again, the flirtations with a pretty Wild Isle girl already forgotten by the time they docked back home. She remembered, as a very little girl, listening to one of the navy men who had been stationed with them during the Great War explain that back on the mainland, the maidens of St Kilda were regarded almost as mermaids or selkies – notable beauties but simply too distant to be real. Flora's beauty was an uncommon thing and Mhairi didn't doubt a man could sail the world and never see another face as captivating as hers. But still, they never wrote.

Until now.

Mhairi looked out to sea, not liking the sensation in her stomach. She had a sweet, gentle nature – 'selfless', that was what everyone always said of her – why should she resent her friend's happiness? But she did. Like the stench coming from the rotted, stinking whale, it was rancid and bitter, making her recoil.

'You liked him,' she said quietly as they stepped onto the beach and stared out at the inky water. Lights bobbed in the bay like dropped stars as the men – and Effie – worked on the eviscerated carcass, making their quick cuts against an encroaching sea.

'He was a gentleman. He talked to me. Most only look at me.'

'He looked at you too.' She studied her friend's profile – long black hair flowing in the evening breeze, full lips and a straight nose, sweeping brows that offset dazzling green eyes.

'Aye. But he talked to me. And now he's written.'

Mhairi swallowed. No one ever looked at her, not like that; her cheeks were too flushed, her hair too bright, her hips too round, her hands too rough. 'What else did his letter say?'

'He told me some things about his life – that he's a businessman, but an explorer at heart. His father was an industrialist.'

'What's that?'

'I don't know,' Flora shrugged. 'He has a wee sister and a nephew and nieces. He lives in Glasgow when he's not travelling.'

'What does he explore?'

'He didn't say. I'll ask him, shall I, when I write back?'

'You're going to write back?'

'Or is it a daft question? I don't want him thinking I'm simple.'

'The last thing you are is simple,' Mhairi scoffed. Her mother called Flora 'the minx', for she had learnt at an early age that her beauty marked her out as different, special and rare; and she had learnt how to use it to her advantage, be it shirking duties or escaping the minister's rod.

'I want him to think well of me.'

Mhairi heard the rare self-doubt in her friend's voice and relented. 'How could he not?'

The sun had dropped now behind the westerly ridge and she gave a small shiver as the blackening breeze whispered over her skin. She turned towards Flora, who instinctively leant in and lit her lamp, her beauty striking even when she wasn't aware of it.

Effie and the men had finished their work and were heading back now, the boat drawing closer and lights beginning to pool dimly on faces, the sound of the oars rolling in their cups coming to their ear. Mhairi set down her lamp and began tucking in her skirts, exposing her bare feet, as behind them came the crunch of footsteps and the murmur of voices. Others were joining them on the beach to help: Norman Ferguson and Donald McKinnon jumped out first, thigh-deep in the water, and helped haul the boat in, steadying the prow against the breaking waves as Hamish Gillies and Effie began handing over heavy pails.

Mhairi, wading into the shallows, took the first and handed it back to Flora, who in turn handed it to Mary McKinnon. Mhairi knew better than to look down at the great slabs of pink glistening flesh slipping against itself, blood slopping over the sides. Flora was less restrained, giving a cry of complaint as the buckets were handed over, the men jumping out at last when all was delivered and hauling the boat onto the beach. The factor was the last to disembark, again, making dry land with just a couple of steps; but unlike the islanders, he wasn't used to going barefoot and the stones hobbled him, drawing smirks from the men and Effie.

'Was there much there?' Lorna MacDonald called, running down. Their resident nurse, she had been changing a dressing on Old Fin's leg.

'Aye, no bad,' Hamish Gillies said, bending over and looking through the pails. 'Given she was already half under by the time we got to her.'

'Ma wants some slops for the dogs,' Mhairi said to her eldest brother.

'Well, slops we've got,' Angus said, handing her a bucket of eviscerated flesh. Mhairi made the mistake of glancing into it and felt her stomach flip-flop.

'The stench,' she grimaced, slapping a hand over her nose and mouth. 'It's not usually so bad.'

'Ach, it's not the meat. It's that black gunk the factor insisted on bringing back,' Norman Ferguson muttered, shooting a dark look in the senior man's direction.

'Black gunk . . . ?'

'Intestines,' Norman muttered.

Flora slapped her hand to her mouth as the bucket of offensive 'gunk' was passed by her. Mhairi felt her eyes water. It was unlike anything she had ever smelt before – salty but also tobacco-y, faecal, the mustiness of old paper, the sharp tang of sour milk. The beach at low tide . . . She couldn't pinpoint it.

'What the devil made you bring that back?' Flora gasped, scrunching up her beautiful face and having to turn away. 'Oh! It's awful!'

'That black gunk, as you call it,' the factor said testily, unimpressed by the young women's histrionics, 'is in fact well known to be a remedy for gout.'

'Gout?'

'Aye, and my poor mother is much afflicted by it.'

'What's gout?' Mhairi asked.

'Isn't it known as the rich man's disease?' Donald McKinnon asked with narrowed eyes, clearly unsympathetic to Frank Mathieson's mother's plight.

'Aye,' Lorna confirmed.

'It's gout and it's very painful,' the factor said thinly. He and Donald McKinnon had still not recovered any good humour following a bitter argument earlier in the week over the price he would give for their black puffin feathers.

'And how does that help?' Flora grimaced, holding her nose. 'Please don't tell me you have to touch it.'

Frank Mathieson gave a smile. 'More than that, Miss MacQueen, you have to eat it.'

'Eat it?' Flora looked so aghast, the factor laughed.

'Indeed. Though it will be a year before it's ready.' He looked around at the quizzical faces. None of them had seen the like before. He sighed, seeming wearied by their ignorance. 'With the right conditions – constant exposure to the sun and the sea – it will harden and grow paler, sometimes white if left long enough. Then, and only then, can it be sliced into thin shavings and sprinkled on your food.'

Flora looked like she was going to throw up. 'And that's what you're going to do?'

'Aye. But I will need someone to help me first. Someone must cure it for me, every day, till I come back in the spring. I can't transport it in this state. It must harden first. Who will help me?' He looked around at the gathered group hopefully, but none there was minded to do him any favours and they stood impassive and silent. He saw the scorn in Donald and Norman's eyes, the scepticism in Hamish's. What did any of them care if the factor's mother was ailed by the rich man's disease? They themselves had to deal with much harder than that.

He looked at Effie, but she was scowling too. 'Well, I see I can't appeal to your better natures. Let me then induce you with payment. One shilling?'

At that, Effie's hand shot up. 'I'll do it,' she said quickly. Her brother John had died three years back, and with her father too aged to climb the ropes any more, it was down to her to provide for them both. The other villagers pitched in where they could but Effie's pride wouldn't accept charity and she fought like a tomcat for every man's privilege, which caused problems of its own. But no one would deny her this; there was nothing improper in a girl doing this work.

The factor shook his head, though he had looked to her in hope only a moment before. 'No.'

'No?' she gasped.

'You're busy enough, Miss Gillies, for you already have your extra duties with the bull, do you not?'

'But I could still—'

'No. It would not be fair on your neighbours that you should acquire all these favours for yourself.'

Favours? Mhairi gave a snort of disbelief, but he appeared not to hear. She watched the indignation stain her friend's cheeks, her eyes a blazing blue.

'It is not heavy work, but I concede it will be odious on account of the smell, which is why I am happy to pay.' The factor swung his gaze around their faces. 'Miss MacQueen?'

Was he in a playful mood? Amusing himself at everyone's expense. Flora merely arched an eyebrow. 'My mother would not allow that near the house,' she said tightly, but none were fooled that it was her mother who would take exception.

'Miss MacKinnon, then, how about you?' The factor's keen gaze came to settle upon Mhairi suddenly. 'Would you like to earn some extra pennies for your large family? Or perhaps

I could strike an arrangement with your father and take it off the rent? You have little need for coins, of course.'

Mhairi's mouth parted. She caught Effie's eye and saw the accusation of betrayal in her gaze – but was this her fault? It was true that Effie was the sole provider for her and her father, but Mhairi's own father had eleven mouths to feed, and anything that could reduce the burden on him . . . She'd over-heard her parents talking late one night when they had thought all the children asleep; they'd never had too much of anything before, but increasingly it was becoming hard even to have enough.

'Take it, Mhar!' Angus said roughly as she hesitated.

She nodded, casting her gaze down to the ground.

'Good – so it is agreed.' The factor picked up the offending bucket and looked down at it with a smile. 'I'll bring this up and show you what to do, Miss MacKinnon. I don't doubt your parents will be grateful.'

Angus came over to her with a scowl, holding out another bucket for her to take. He was tall and well built, with huge hands and a thick beard that could have belonged to a man ten years older. Physically imposing, her brother still wasn't beyond using his size to intimidate her when he felt it was warranted. 'What were you hesitating for?' he scolded. 'If Father was to hear that you almost passed up on a shilling . . .'

'I didn't. I wouldn't.'

'You took your time deciding though. Are you too precious to do the work, is that it?'

Effie passed by, carrying two buckets that looked like they weighed more than she did, her gaze dead ahead, and Mhairi knew her friend was upset with her too.

She saw how Angus's eyes followed her elfin friend up the beach. 'A shilling's not going to make much difference either way,' she replied crossly. 'Besides, if you really wanted to reduce the burden on Pa, you'd take a wife. But don't think it'll be her. Eff's too smart for the likes of you.'

'Oh, and she has plenty of other choices, does she?'

'There's always a choice.'

'Is there?' His eyes narrowed as he took a step towards her, ever the bully boy. 'And what about you? Who here'll have you, Mhar, or will you be our old maid? Because I don't see you receiving any letters.'

She swallowed as she saw the victory smirk in his eyes. Just as he had when they were children, her biggest brother knew exactly where to strike the low blows. She would never draw a suitor from over the seas like Flora. She was too ordinary for a big love story.

They both were.

He turned on his bare heels and began striding up the beach. She followed after in silence.

Lights glowed from the cottages, dotting the length of the Street, but they betrayed scant signs of life to any passing ships as night fell like a black shroud around their lonely isle. The moon was already on the rise, the waves shushing gently at their backs, as somewhere in the silky depths, a long-dead whale lilted softly to its grave at last.

Chapter Two

Mhairi awoke to drizzle patting on the glass, the horizon smudged from sight through the narrow opening of the bay. The break in the good weather heralded autumn was on its way – early, this year, but it would mean the pungent odour had been washed from the sky at least. She could see the birds were no longer circling the buoy with murderous intent. The whalers wouldn't be happy when they returned and found their precious bounty popped and sunken to the seabed.

She rose from her narrow cot and pulled a knitted shawl over her nightdress, her long hair held back in a loose braid. Her little brothers and sisters were still fast asleep, snuffling and whimpering through boisterous dreams, limbs twitching sporadically, the room stuffy and airless.

'Time to get up,' she said gently, knowing how rude daybreak could be to little growing bodies. She touched the nearest pair of legs – Red Annie's – as she passed. The child startled as if prodded by a poker.

Mhairi could already hear their mother setting the pans atop the stove, the scraping of the hearth shovel against the grate as she walked through to the main room.

'Good morning,' she mumbled, glancing through the open door to see Old Fin shuffling down to his allotment in search of fresh kelp, for the tide was out. An incipient dampness in the air made the thin cotton of her nightdress feel limp and she pulled the shawl a little closer.

'Are they awake?' her mother asked, not even glancing up as she set the teacakes upon the hot plate.

'Aye.' She moved around her mother and poured them each a cup of the weak tea that was brewing in the pot.

'Ta.'

Mhairi stood at the doorway and looked out over the bay; she always enjoyed these first quiet moments of the day, her large, loud family stirring in muted dribs and drabs. All the hard-edged brightness and solid saturated colours of yesterday had smudged and leached overnight, leaving the landscape soft and as if unfinished, a tender sea mist drifting like a wraith through the valley and pulling in the walls of their world. She could scarcely discern the factor's house or the featherstore at the far end of the Street, and distant figures were mere grey blots. Voices were still hushed at this hour and it was only the lowing of the cows that carried on the breeze.

A scrabbling sound startled her from her thoughts and she stepped out, looking up to find her brother Fin standing on the ridge of the thatched roof of the byre beside them. Tall and lanky, dressed in his brown woollen trousers and work shirt and barefooted, his arms were outstretched, ready to catch the length of heather rope coiled in their father's hands.

Winter would be upon them before they knew it and repairs couldn't be shirked if they were to weather the storms. The winds here could be particularly ferocious, funnelling down the slopes at speeds that lifted rocks on the beach and tore the roofs from the houses; very often the villagers would be left deafened for days afterwards. MacLeod had done his landlord duty by having metal straps affixed up and over the zinc roofs of the new houses – built forty years ago now – but the old blackhouses and byres were being tacitly left to fall into ruin: acceptable for some of the families perhaps, but the populous MacKinnons needed all their spaces to be habitable. She watched as Fin caught the rope and, straddling the ridge comfortably, began knocking it into position across the old fishing net that would have to do for this winter at least, their plea to the factor for new thatch having fallen on deaf ears.

She stepped back indoors. Porridge was bubbling on the stove, her mother flipping the teacakes and the sound of squealing from the bedroom making it clear her siblings were fully awake. The broiling pot, filled from the burn last night, was hanging on its chains above the fire, the water beginning to bubble, ready for the blankets she'd soon pull off the beds.

The bedroom door opened and Wee Murran and Alasdair staggered through, eyes puffy with sleep. Alasdair reached for a teacake cooling on the side.

'Hands off,' their mother said, smacking the back of his hand lightly. 'Wash hands and faces first.' She pointed towards the bucket in the corner without looking at it; the baby was beginning to cry. Mhairi went over and lifted him from the bottom drawer, holding him close and kissing the top of his head.

'We'll get that first batch of cloth dyed today,' her mother said, lifting him from her arms and stepping back so Mhairi could take over the breakfast. 'So fetch some crotal in, will you, once they're all fed?'

Mhairi nodded as her mother went through to the bedroom to nurse the baby.

Alasdair reached for a teacake again with dry, unwashed hands. 'Uh-uh-uh,' Mhairi said, pointing towards the bucket like her mother. 'Clean hands. Pure heart.'

He scuttled off and she noticed a large hole in the elbow of his jumper; a patch is better than a hole, her mother always said, but this was too large to patch – she'd need to unravel it and knit it afresh tonight. She began doling the porridge into chipped earthenware bowls, the water in the pot beginning to roll and tumble – time to strip the bed blankets – a new day begun just like all the rest.

The rain had closed in by the time the villagers gathered at the pier, the mountaintops sliced off by thick clouds and the sheep bleating in protest at their heavy coats. Mhairi stood beside her friends, waving dutifully as the factor was rowed out to the landlord's steamship now laden with their annual rents. Bolts of tweed were stacked in the hold, hessian sacks filled with feathers ready to stuff pillows and mattresses, barrels of fulmar oil robustly secured against the North Atlantic swell, knitted woollens folded. Everyone had met their obligations but Frank Mathieson had managed to convey 'only just' with stern, disappointed looks as the men shook hands with him. Flora had muttered to her that most of the villagers who'd gathered to wave him off were only there to see with their own eyes that he was actually leaving.

'Good riddance,' Norman Ferguson said with a hardened tone as he replaced his cloth cap and pushed his way back through the crowd, still in sight of the factor. It was a deliberate and defiant last snub. They would be free of him now till spring, late April at the earliest. Mathieson's departure always heralded the official onset of isolation. It might not be today, or tomorrow, or the day after that, but any day now – any moment – the wind would change, the waves would rise and their world would shrink down to this two-mile rock; no more visitors would come by on sloops and yachts but only the whalers and the trawlermen who fished the deepest, wildest waters, and they were always a crude, rough lot.

This moment of departure was always a double-edged sword. No one much liked the factor but if he took with one hand, as on this visit, so he gave with the other, and on his return he would bring back whatever essentials they begged for over the winter. If they didn't want him here, they also didn't *not* want him here, for their very survival perpetually hung in the balance. Last winter had been especially harsh and long, with weeks of snow and gales destroying their meagre harvest so that an SOS had had to be launched on a St Kildan mailboat, washing up on the shore of Benbecula five days later. An emergency supply of oats and potatoes had been raised and sent over with a passing trawler. No matter how pleased they were to be rid of the factor in this moment as they watched him slip into the mist's murky embrace, they would still be giving thanks on the beach when his smack rounded the headland of Dun eight months from now.

'What comes with the wind, goes with the water,' Flora murmured. She had been holding her body stiffly but she softened again, sinking onto one hip as the dinghy became steadily more obscured, before disappearing altogether.

'A storm's coming,' Jayne Ferguson said, seemingly sniffing the wind as she stood just behind them. Mhairi hadn't even realized she was there, but she turned her face to the sky and allowed the dew to settle on her skin for a few moments, listening to the birds and the breeze.

'Then here's hoping it catches up with him,' Flora said, as she whipped out a cold smile and spun on her heel, flipping her long skirt around her legs like she was going to launch into a polka. 'And may he be tossed around like the devil's dancing with him.'

They all turned back towards the village. All but one.

'Are you coming, Eff?' Mhairi asked, pressing a hand to her friend's slight shoulder, seeing how she was still staring into the mist as if daring the boat to reappear.

'Huh?' Effie looked at her blankly, her thoughts several beats behind her ears. '. . . Aye.'

'Don't worry. We're free of him for another eight months,' Mhairi smiled, looping her hand through Effie's arm and clutching her close. 'Did you come to an arrangement on the rent reduction?'

Effie shook her head. 'He says the tithe remains the same, regardless of the number of occupants.'

Mhairi was aghast. 'He didn't say that?'

Effie just shrugged, but her face was pinched and for once she looked cold in the dreich conditions. It had been three summers now since her brother John had died in the climbing accident and Effie, at seventeen, was now the age he had been when he'd 'gone over the top'. She had to fight almost every day to be allowed to earn on equal terms to the men – doing what were considered to be the 'male' jobs of cragging, fishing, sheep-plucking and weaving – to save her aged father from the indignity of relying on their neighbours' charity.

'I'm sorry.'

'It's all right. I'll catch some extra birds when the gannets come in the spring.' Effie said the words carelessly, but the annual hunt on Stac Lee – a rocky sea tower that sat between here, Hirta and the isle of Boreray five miles east – was a treacherous expedition and involved leaping from the dinghy onto wet rock and catching a fixed rope. No woman had ever been allowed to attempt it before.

Flora, just ahead, broke off from her conversation with Jayne and pivoted round to face them, walking backwards with a jaunty step. It seemed that with every oar-stroke that drew the factor further away, her mood brightened. And Mhairi knew why.

'You wrote back to him, then?' Mhairi said lightly as Flora grabbed at a stalk as she passed and drew it distractedly through her palms, humming a jaunty tune. She broke off in the next instant.

'I did,' she beamed, luxuriating in the triumph of her swift reply. It might have been weeks before another trawler dropped anchor and the next mail bag could be sent off. As it was, Flora had burst into the post office just as Mhairi and her father were closing up the sack, ready for the post to be taken back over to the mainland on the factor's crossing. She had clearly been taken aback to find Mr Mathieson in there too, talking intently with Mhairi's father, and in her ensuing freeze had only brought more attention to the letter in her hand. The factor had taken it from her and made a point of reading out Mr Callaghan's name as he passed it over to Mhairi's father.

'Are y' courting a fine gentleman, Miss MacQueen?' he had teased, oblivious to having hit upon the truth of the matter, and his humour at the very idea of it had cast Flora into a sour mood. But he was gone now, and the letter with him. Mr Callaghan – James – would be getting his reply sooner than he could ever have hoped.

'And what did you say to him in the end?'

'Who's *him*?' Effie asked, looking bewildered.

'Mr Callaghan, who was here last month.'

Effie gasped, her eyes widening as she recalled the well-dressed visitor. 'He wrote you a letter?'

Flora's smile broadened. 'Yes. And I answered all his questions.'

26

'Which were?' Mhairi pressed.

'Mhairi, did your father never tell you letters are supposed to be private?' Flora pouted, becoming uncharacteristically coy as she heard the curiosity in her friends' voices.

'Flora!' Mhairi exclaimed impatiently.

Flora laughed, delighted to have their rapt attention. 'Fine. I'll tell you one of the questions, then,' she sighed, casting her eyes to the cloud-wrapped hills. 'He asked me what one thing I wish for from the mainland.'

Mhairi felt as if her heart was being squeezed, for she knew very well what Flora wished for: a new life there. She and Effie were wedded to this rock but Flora, ever since she was a girl, had been like a tropical bird blown here off course and desperate to fly away to her true home.

'And you said?' Effie pushed, as Flora allowed a dramatic silence to open up.

'A red lipstick. Just like Jean Harlow's.'

Jayne laughed like she was being tickled. 'Oh, Flora,' she sighed, tutting lightly. 'Of all the things . . .'

Flora frowned. 'What? What would you have wished for, then?'

Jayne shrugged in her lackadaisical way. 'Some chickens?'

'Chickens?' Flora spluttered. 'When you could have anything?'

'Aye. It'd be nice to get my eggs from outside the door, and not off a cliff.'

'I'd have said a new rope,' Effie said thoughtfully. 'And a feather cushion for Father's chair.'

Flora shook her head disappointedly at them. 'Mhairi?' she asked hopefully. 'How about you?'

Mhairi's mouth opened. She had been about to say a love letter, but that would be copying her friend's path. But she could think of nothing else. In truth, the idea of the mainland had always somewhat frightened her; her mother had been over once and had come back deploring the crowds, the noise, the 'cars that could flatten you' . . . Besides, everything Mhairi wanted, she already had. She had never seen the point in wishing for things that could simply never be. But she could see the agitation in Flora's eyes – the need for someone to want more the way she did.

'I'd have wished for a dress,' she faltered.

'What kind of a dress?' Flora enquired, her eyes brightening at having found an ally.

'A . . . light blue one.'

'Wool?'

Mhairi shook her head. 'Hemp? For the summer.'

'Cotton, then,' Flora said with authority.

'Yes, cotton,' Mhairi agreed.

'Long?'

'To there,' Mhairi said, pointing to her knees. Her own skirt – navy drugget with green stripes – fell to just above her ankles and was paired, as always, with a white blouse, her hair held back in the wind by the red plaid scarf all the women wore. Effie alone broke with convention, wearing her late brother John's old breeks and jumpers, arguing that it wouldn't be seemly to crag in skirts and somehow manipulating the social mores to her own advantage. It was always very peculiar to see her in a skirt at church on Sundays.

Flora beamed, seeming delighted by the thought of such an airy garment, and Mhairi smiled too, aware that she had opened a small window of want inside her soul. Until this moment she had never given a second thought to such things – but now she realized she must have noticed and remembered some of the female visitors' outfits, to be able to be so precise in the details she had just given. It would be lovely, in the hot days of summer, to wear such a thing. She felt a tiny pang of sorrow at the knowledge that she never would.

They peeled off, one by one, as they passed their crofts: first Jayne, then Effie. Flora's was just past Mhairi's.

'What's going on?' she asked her mother as she walked back into the house. Several of the men – Hamish Gillies, Norman Ferguson, Donald McKinnon and Archie MacQueen – were gathered around the tiny post office, talking heatedly to her father inside.

'Not what. Who.' Her mother was sitting at the spinning wheel, the yarn spooling on a cone as her foot pressed rhythmically on the treadle. It was quiet inside the cottage. Mhairi's brothers and sisters were at their lessons with the minister's wife, Rory was slumbering again in his drawer and Alasdair was napping on the box bed. The woollen blankets were drying in front of the fire, the mist making it too wet to hang them outside today. 'Mathieson has ruffled too many feathers this time. Norman and Donald are staging a revolution, from what I can gather.'

'Why? What's he done now?'

Her mother gave a bored shrug. 'What does he ever do? Scold? Mock? Rile?'

Mhairi saw the small pan of water simmering on the stove – set in anticipation of her return – and reached for the feathered lichen she had picked earlier, now bulging in her pockets. She tossed it in and stirred gently, seeing how the sea-green pigment bled into the water; in a strange alchemy, it would stain the wool a warm golden-brown hue. The great tufts of raw wool she would be dyeing today were already soaking in a large shallow tub set on the grass on the other side of the street wall.

Mhairi took the small pan outside and slowly poured in the lichen water, letting it steep and make a dye bath, swirling it through. She knelt on the grass and began to lightly knead the wool, making sure the dye was evenly dispersed. The men's voices carried over the wall, notes of agitation speckled with frustration, despair and anger.

'—not prepared to show us any respect,' one was saying. Norman, she'd have guessed. '. . . go so far as to call it contempt. He thinks we're fools, that we have no other options.'

'We don't,' another scoffed. Archie MacQueen?

'That's where you're wrong. I met a man, McLennan, on my visit to Harris in the spring. He said he'd take my extra oil for a shilling and ten a pint. A shilling and ten! Mathieson only gave us a shilling four.' Mhairi couldn't see from her crouched position behind the wall, but she knew it was Donald McKinnon talking – he was the only one who'd left the isle this year. 'I've been holding back my surplus specially; hid it up on Oiseval to make sure Mathieson didn't catch wind of it. I've got nineteen pints over to sell. And if McLennan takes the extra feathers too and gives me more than seven shillings a stone for them, what sense would it make to keep selling to the factor?'

'Because he's the factor.' Mhairi recognized the sternness in her own father's voice.

'Aye. The landlord's man, and I'm not saying we cheat him. We give him what MacLeod is due in rents, not a feather more, not a feather less. But if we can harvest more than our rent obligations, it's up to us how we manage our own profits. He's relying on us being too dim or too lazy to take our goods elsewhere – but I'll go.'

Mhairi heard some tuts and heavy sighs at this fighting talk, then a long silence.

'Well, that's all well and good in principle but it's too late now anyway, there's no time,' Archie MacQueen said gruffly. 'Mathieson's gone with the rents and this year is done.'

'No. It's not. The whalers will be back any day now. Any minute. They'll take me – I've already approached the captain.'

'Go now?' Hamish scoffed. 'And then what? It's the getting back you need to worry about! You could get stranded there, and what would your Mary have to say about that?'

'I don't doubt she'd be pleased,' Donald snorted back.

Mhairi heard some of the men chuckle. She didn't stop turning and pressing on the wool in the tub, but she was intrigued by the conversation. The idea of earning money had always been redundant on St Kilda, where barter was king, but in recent years the old ways had begun to change. The tourists brought with them coins for postcards, gull eggs, socks, photographs with the villagers, climbing exhibitions . . . And though there was no shop on the isle in which to spend them, there were plenty on the distant neighbouring isles of Harris, Lewis and Uist, a ten-hour boat ride away.

'Can you be sure this McLennan will do business wit' you?' Norman Ferguson asked. 'It's a long way to go to find he's no better than Mathieson.'

'It's a risk, I don't deny it. We agreed a price in principle but I made no firm assurances of delivering the goods. I wanted to give Mathieson the chance to do a fair trade first. It felt the honourable thing to do. I tried negotiating with him and told him what I believed was the true market value – and he just laughed in my face.' There was a slight pause. 'So I've kept back my surplus and, because of his own greed, he'll miss out on all the extra commission. Now he gets only exactly what he's owed. I'll make a profit and you can too. If you've anything going spare, I'll take it and sell it for you there too.'

Mhairi sat back on her heels, interested now and listening as the men considered the enterprise. Trips to the mainland were usually only ever made in cases of medical emergency. Going there purely to make money was – her mother had been right – revolutionary. She raised her head just above the parapet to see the men standing with bent heads, hands stuffed into their trouser pockets. Her elder brothers were looking at their father with expressions both anxious and intrigued.

'There's no doubt we need to be able to help ourselves better, father,' her brother Fin said quietly. 'We've several ells of tweed lying spare. With what we could get for that, we could buy some more tools. A peat spade would come in handy. If we were to have another winter like the last, well . . .'

His voice trailed away but they all knew what he'd been going to say – they might not get through it.

Their father nodded, knowing it was true; but he still looked barely consoled, much less convinced. If Mhairi had been hoping for fanfares last night when he learnt of her new earnings turning the slops, she had been sorely disappointed. A shilling couldn't fill eleven bellies and even these new profits would provide scant comfort. But her brother was right – a spade was a spade. It all helped.

'Hey!' Angus barked, spotting her eavesdropping. 'We've a spy among us.'

The men followed his line of sight and Mhairi straightened, her vivid red hair impossible to miss above the mossy wall.

'I'm not spying, I'm dyeing,' she said flippantly, holding up a limp length of wool.

He swatted a hand in her direction. 'Scat! This is men's business.'

'No it's not,' she sneered. 'If it were, Effie would be among you.' Her eyes gleamed with mischief, for she knew perfectly well how much Effie's insubordination challenged the men's – and especially Angus's – masculine principles.

Angus's eyes narrowed, last night's argument still festering, a shadow quivering between them.

'Perhaps Angus should go with you, Donald?' she said slyly, still smarting from his cruelty over Flora's letter, and her own bleak prospects. 'He could find himself a wife there and bring her back. Coins might buy spades but we still need hands to do the work.'

Her father looked to Donald with a revived interest she hadn't anticipated. 'The lass has made a good point there. Are there womenfolk in need of a husband?'

'On Harris, undoubtedly, but not at Bunavoneader specifically,' Donald shrugged. 'There's just the whaling station and McLennan's farm a few miles off; this wouldn't be the time for any extended visits. If I can, I'll be there and back within a few days.'

'Well, this McLennan fellow then . . . has he a daughter?' her father asked in a faintly bemused tone. And yet not. A tinge of desperation frilled the words.

'A daughter? No.' Donald shook his head. 'But he has a son.'

'A son?' Angus crowed, shooting Mhairi a delighted look. 'Well, then perhaps he might be in need of a wife! How old is he?'

'A year or two younger than me, I should say.'

'Father! Are you thinking what I'm thinking?' Angus not-so-subtly jerked his head in her direction. 'It's not just me and Fin as you need off your hands. Mhairi's marriageable now and what real options does she have here, since poor John Gillies died? David MacQueen's set on Molly, and it's clear Mhairi only sees Euan as a brother. A farmer's son on Harris is not to be sniffed at.'

Mhairi felt her stomach drop to the ground as she saw her father's look of interest. 'A farmer's son is no good!' she protested. 'If they've a farm, then he'll be wanted to stay on there and take over when the time comes. He wouldn't come all the way here!'

She saw the furrow in her father's brow as he took on board the point; but he looked contemplative, and she felt her heart pound dully at this sudden turn in the conversation. A silence breathed. Surely he wasn't seriously considering the idea?

'It might mean one less pair of hands, but it would also be one less mouth to feed,' Angus argued – just to win. 'You said yourself, just yesterday, that you can't support us all past this winter.'

'Then it should be you looking to reduce the burden,' Mhairi said hotly, feeling her temper fray now – the famous 'red flash' her family forever teased her over. 'You're the eldest son!'

'And I am actively looking to take a wife,' Angus agreed, growing calmer in the face of her agitation. 'If an arrangement can't be made this winter on the isle, then I'll travel to Skye come the spring tides.'

Spring it would be, then, for Mhairi knew neither Flora nor Effie would ever accept him. Flora most especially, now she'd received her letter from Mr Callaghan, for it had watered the seed of her long-held idea that she was destined for greater things than being a St Kilda wife.

'There may be some wisdom in the idea nonetheless,' her father said thoughtfully, and Mhairi could almost see the relief climbing onto his features at the prospect of his eldest son and daughter each married off in the spring. 'Harris is just over there, after all, and you would have an easier life there, lass.'

'No, Father,' she said quickly. 'I couldn't even think on it. I could never leave Hirta.'

'You might think differently if you saw the way of things over there,' Donald said.

Mhairi glowered at his interference. 'I don't want to!'

'But is there any harm in at least looking into it?' Angus asked, with a mildness that didn't match the gloat in his eyes.

Her father looked back at their neighbour. 'Mhairi and I could travel with you, Donald, and meet this McLennan and his son for ourselves. They might even know of a suitable wife for Angus, possibly Fin too. We could then decide for ourselves whether there's an arrangement to be made.'

Mhairi couldn't speak, such was her horror at the idea – to marry a stranger? To live far from here, on the Other Side? She needed to speak to her mother, to get her to see it was sheer madness. She jumped to her feet.

'What do you recall of the man, Donald?' Angus asked with an interested expression.

Donald gave a shrug, rolling up his sleeves even though the breeze was growing cold. 'I only know the old man, but he seemed solid and respectable so far as I could see. Plain-speaking and strong. No oil painting. No stranger to hard work for sure.'

'He sounds almost like one of us.' Angus shrugged, a glint in his eyes.

Her father gave a nod as though the matter was settled. 'I'll tell Rachel to get us packed for a voyage.'

'Aye, then,' Donald nodded. 'Best to be ready. The whalers won't be stopping long once they find out this one popped; they'll want to get the other kills back all the sooner. They'll no' wait around. Time's running out on them.'

35

Mhairi watched, aghast, her mind scattered with panic as the men, with a plan agreed, all ambled off and went their separate ways – as if they'd just agreed to lift the potatoes. As if they hadn't just taken a sledgehammer to her life and smashed it wide apart.

Chapter Three

'Is it true? Are you going with the whalers?' Effie panted, her red cheeks suggesting she'd raced from Mullach Mor as she burst into the bedroom. There was a feather in her pale hair and the two dead fulmars roped to her shoulder swung a half beat behind her. Poppit, her brown patched collie, lay down on the street outside the window. All the other dogs slept in the byres and never entered the houses, but Poppit was no mere sheepdog and was never more than two strides from her mistress.

Mhairi bit her lip as she stared down at her scant belongings on the bed – clean undergarments and a fresh blouse – folded atop a bolt of tweed that would be wrapped and tied for the voyage. 'Aye,' she said stiffly. 'We're to Harris for a look-see. There and back.'

'But . . . but why?' Effie gasped, sounding incredulous.

Mhairi's shoulders dropped. 'There's a man I'm to meet. Father needs me to marry. He can't keep feeding all of us.'

Effie looked shaken. They were all coming of age – Effie not even a year behind her – and it was their duty to marry; they knew they must reduce the burden on their parents and bear the children that would ensure the community's future, but their girlhoods still sat upon them like a morning dew.

'But . . . can't it wait till spring?' Effie asked, her voice lacking its usual staunch conviction. 'Mathieson's gone, the weather's going to turn . . . I don't understand why it has to be now.'

'Donald McKinnon's made an agreement with a man on Harris. He says he can get more than the factor would pay and he wants to go immediately so that we can use the extra money to buy tools to get us through the winter. And this man – McLennan – he has a son, near his age, he thinks. Father's convinced this would be an opportunity to meet him and see whether he's suitable for me to marry.'

'A complete stranger?'

'We're just to meet for now. But if we like the look of one another, then we could wed in the spring.'

Effie's eyes narrowed. '. . . And he'd come to live here?'

Mhairi didn't reply immediately. She didn't want to reveal that this stranger was a farmer's son, that he was tied to the land there. They had both always known that Flora would leave here – but Mhairi too?

'It's just a look-see,' she repeated flatly. Her voice was calm, but Effie's incredulity at the situation matched her own. She couldn't have known, as she rose from her bed this morning, that she wouldn't be falling back into it tonight. She had awakened to just another day of island chores – no sense of impending calamity or doom – but before nightfall she would be on the water in search of a husband. Donald McKinnon's prediction that the whalers would be back imminently had been horribly accurate; the dogs barking on the beach as she had walked to the cleit to get the night fire's fresh peat had set her stomach churning, long before the ship nosed the headland.

'I'm sure it'll come to nothing,' she said, pulling up the

short ends of the tweed and tucking them in. 'Or you never know, it might be love at first sight. Perhaps I'll take one look at him and never come back.' She raised a smile but it didn't quite travel to her eyes.

'Don't even jest!' Effie gasped, looking utterly horrified. 'You know there's no such thing.'

Her smile died. 'I know, but I have to do this. We're too many here, Eff. Have you not seen how thin Father has got? I'm a burden to him.'

'Not as much as your brothers are!' Effie replied hotly. 'They're the ones as should be getting married off, not you!'

'Oh, so then will you marry one of them for me?'

Effie's mouth dropped open and this time Mhairi smiled with genuine amusement. 'Don't worry, Eff, I'd never condemn you to that fate! I'd honestly wed this stranger before I saw you shackled with Angus.'

'I don't see why we have to marry at all,' Effie said bitterly, scuffing the floor with her bare foot.

'Ahem! Some of us want to get wed!' a voice intruded.

They both turned to find Flora peering in at the window. She had wound some pink thrift flowers into her dark braid. Like Mhairi, she and her mother had been spinning and dyeing the tweed all day, but unlike Mhairi, her hands weren't stained yellow. In all her shock at the men's conversation earlier, Mhairi had forgotten to lift her hands from the lichen bath.

'Don't tell us you've had another letter,' Mhairi quipped, feeling a sickness in her stomach at the divergence in their fates. For everything bright upon Flora's horizon, there was only darkness along hers.

Flora spluttered with surprise. 'My reply only left here this morning!'

'Aye, but such are your passions for one another, we wouldn't be surprised if he sends another one by carrier pigeon.' Effie fluttered her hands above her heart.

'Or carrier gannet, at least,' Mhairi rejoindered.

Flora laughed, enjoying their teases, but her sharp gaze came to rest on the tweed bundle on the bed and her smile faded too. 'It's a nonsense, this. You should just say no.'

'Right!'

'They can't make you go.'

But they all knew perfectly well that wasn't true. The men would carry her onto the ship if need be.

'For Father's sake, I have to. And anyway, as I just told Eff, it's only a how-do-you-do. I'm not going to marry him on sight. We'll see if we like the look of one another first.' Even to her own ear she sounded calm, implacable, but there was a tremor in her hands and a sudden shrill laugh escaped her, betraying her nerves. 'He doesn't even know about me yet! He has no idea we're leaving here to go over! The first he'll know of maybe getting a wife is when we knock at his door. Poor man, he's in just the same bother as me.'

'Mhairi!' her mother called through from the other room, appearing at the door a moment later and looking unsurprised to see Effie and Flora variously grouped around her daughter. 'Donald says the captain's heading down to the jetty now. He's in a fearsome temper to have lost the whale so don't tarry, get yourself down there – and no mischief, girls!' Her mother pointed a knowing finger at Mhairi's friends. 'This is a serious business.' A solemnity came into her voice and the women's eyes all met as they stood in silence for a moment. This was simply what had to be done. Needs must.

Mhairi knotted together the long ends of the clothing bundle and lifted it into her arms with a hard swallow. 'Is Father back then?' she asked, following her mother outside. Poppit sprang up as Effie came out too, and Flora wandered over from where she'd been leaning on the sill.

'He's on his way. Fin says they've been having a terrible trouble getting one of them up.' Several of the sheep had dropped onto a plateau on the north side of the isle and were stranded. Retrieving them on the ropes was usually a straight-forward job, but a cloudburst had soaked their fleeces and doubled their weight.

'It'd be easier just to push it off,' Fin himself said, wandering outdoors, one hand stuffed in his pockets. He looked down to the bay where the whaling ship rocked. Stocky and covered in soot and guts, it lacked the elegance and streamlined finesse of the yachts that moored in the summer months as the rich sailed the northern seas in search of dolphins, auroras and polar bears. This would be Mhairi's first time ever on the deep water; the women rarely even got in the smack. She was nervous, she couldn't deny it.

She frowned at Fin. 'Why are you back and not Father?'

'We didn't know the whalers were back. We couldn't hear the dogs all the way over there and there was no need in all of us staying up there, so he sent me back to help Old Fin with his bad leg. But it was only the one sheep left stranded that he had to fetch. He'll be heading back already.'

'Get down there, Mhairi,' her mother said, looking anxiously up the hills for sight of him. 'There's only this one chance now. Look, Donald's pacing down by the jetty already. He's all loaded up for that McLennan fellow.'

The girls all looked at one another in alarm and Flora and Effie moved as one, enveloping Mhairi in a pincer movement, their arms overlapped, heads resting on each other's shoul-ders, fingers gripping tightly.

'Don't fuss now,' Mhairi said, her voice cracking. 'I'll be back in a couple of days.'

'Uh-huh,' Effie agreed, but with her eyes squeezed shut.

'Tell him you cry when you're happy. And . . . that you can whistle better than a boy . . . And that you can read palms!' Flora whispered hurriedly. 'They hate all that.'

'Palms. Right.' She pulled out of the embrace, the three of them looking at one another with a sense of curious surprise. They had grown up here, side by side. Not a day had ever passed when they hadn't seen one another, when they hadn't played or talked or fought. So the idea of saying goodbye . . . especially so suddenly like this . . .

'Mhairi.'

Her mother's nervous caution drew her from their bubble and Mhairi turned to her with even more trepidation. 'Go now and don't fret,' her mother said, not quite able to hold her gaze, instead fussing with the shawl over her shoulders, patting her shoulders and arms anxiously. 'I know it's sudden but the essence of a game is at its end, that's what your father always says. So you may be pleased yet.'

'Aye,' Mhairi demurred.

'Either way, you'll be back in just a few days and we can talk about it at length then, when we know what we've got. Now take your father's things, I'll send him straight down to you.' Her mother picked up the other tweed boll left resting on the wall.

'Mother—'

'And there's some food packed for the journey too. Some teacakes and smoked puffin. You'll be fine. Your father will take care of you. He's done the trip many a time, don't worry now.' She was still patting her shoulders, smoothing her sleeves . . . Fussing. Fretting.

'I won't,' Mhairi said quietly, wishing her mother would meet her eyes at least once.

'Go then.' Her mother stepped back just as Alasdair came staggering out, chased after by Wee Murran, and her mother scooped up the toddler to safety, grateful either for the distraction or someone to hold.

Mhairi turned and made her way down the Street, the neighbours calling after her as she passed by.

'Tell your father not to forget my black twist!' Robert Gillies, Effie's father, called.

'Check his teeth!' Mad Annie cried from her door. 'They'll tell y' what sweet words hide.'

Mhairi turned back once and saw her mother with a hand pressed over her mouth, but she quickly waved instead as she was caught watching, the two of them too distant now to see one another's tears shining. Already Mhairi longed for the quiet boredom of this afternoon, the quiet ritual of their day as they had moved around one another almost in a dance, performing the chores that kept their family life moving through every sunrise and sunset.

'I'm fair sorry for you, lass. Marriage is bad enough fishing from a small pool as I had to do, much less like this with a stranger,' Mary McKinnon, Donald's wife, said with a pitying look as they passed one another at the featherstore. The doors were open and the double-height space that had been filled only yesterday was now almost entirely empty after the factor's rent collection. Hamish Gillies and Archie MacQueen were inside, rummaging through some spare bags of wool and a spoilt ell of tweed, looking for anything that might yet be taken to Harris to yield coins and ultimately more comfort for the coming winter.

'Well, I think I knew it would always be this way.' She gave a hopeless shrug as Mary nodded in sympathy. Commonly known as Crabbit Mary, she rarely seemed content with the institution herself and wore a frown in all weathers. 'It's just the suddenness that's taken me by surprise.'

'Aye. Well, my pig-headed husband never has known when to keep quiet. Once he gets fixed on an idea . . .' She tutted disapprovingly, her gaze flitting over Mhairi's shoulder towards where he was working on the jetty.

'I'm sure the man he's introducing me to will be a good sort, though. He wouldn't have recommended him otherwise.'

It was intended as a question. Mary placed a hand on her shoulder and her mouth parted in ready reply, but for once, she didn't offer her opinion. Her gaze fell to her husband again, then she looked back at Mhairi and squeezed her shoulder. 'Good luck, Mhairi. I do wish it could ha' been different for y'.'

She turned and carried on up the path. Mhairi stared after her, feeling distinctly discouraged by the encounter.

'Mhairi! Hurry now! We've not all night.' She turned to find Donald staring, his hands on his hips, his piercing blue eyes peering from between a dark fringe and a thick beard. He had plenty of hair and was in sore need of a trim. 'What are you looking like that for? What did she say to you?'

'It's what she didn't say.'

'Och, pay no heed to her,' he said with a roll of his eyes. 'Get down here.'

She didn't stir. 'I don't think she thinks this McLennan fellow is a good man.'

He scowled. 'She's no business saying anything of the sort when she's never met him.'

'. . . I don't think I should be doing this,' Mhairi said quietly, looking down at the boat bobbing on the water several feet below.

Donald watched her for a moment, seeing the stubborn set of her jaw. Then he walked up to her, looking around to make sure no one was standing near. 'Now see here, Mhairi,' he said in a low voice. 'My wife is . . . well, you'll know what she is. She's a discontented woman. And she's never so bad as when her monthly comes, which it has. Again.' He looked to the ground, scuffing a stone with his booted toe, his mouth set in a flat line. 'It's no secret she wants a baby and till God grants us that good grace, I don't think she'll ever be happy. So don't take to heart anything she said to you. Right now she'd say none of us should ever wed, that it's all a fool's errand; but she'll be right enough again in a few days, when the disappointment passes. All you need to focus on is helping your father, do you hear?'

Mhairi nodded, taken aback by his candour. His wife's monthlies weren't words she had ever expected to hear from him. He'd scarce said more than a few dozen words to her in her whole life.

'Where is your father, anyway?' he asked, stepping back and looking up to the village as they waited.

'Coming. He'll be here directly, Fin says. I've got his things,' she said, holding up his bundle.

Donald took it from her without ceremony, throwing it down into the floor of the boat. 'You'd best get in then,' he said. 'Cap Ferg's in no mood to hang about . . . Go on now.'

She pulled her red shawl up over her hair and went down the jetty steps carefully, feeling uncommonly hesitant now she was in her boots. Footwear was never worn on the isle save for Sundays, deep winter and when visitors arrived on the boats, but what had seemed natural to the islanders for centuries inspired such open surprise from the newcomers that a sense of shame had crept in.

She hesitated as she saw how the small boat rocked with the slapping waves but Donald jumped down, grabbed hold of one of the mooring rings and steadied it with his foot. 'Here,' he said, holding out a hand to balance her as she stepped down.

She took it and was immediately stabilized. All the men – and Effie – had exceptional balance and strength from a lifetime of cragging and fowling. She crouched low and grabbed the boarded seat, able to taste the briny tang of the sea as she transferred from one element to the other, land to water, home to Over There. Clutching her tweed sack, she looked back to shore. People were coming and going from the cottages, sweeping out the day's dust, bringing in the peats, calling for the children as they played between the cleits. Her mother had gone in, no doubt to feed the wee ones as the bathwater was heated. Mhairi's feet were only moments off the soil and life was already continuing without her.

The smack rocked again as Donald, taking his foot off the side, began to pace the pier. 'Come on. Come on,' he muttered to himself, a low growl in his voice and fingers flexing.

Hamish was striding towards them, a few bags of wool clutched in his giant hands. 'Take these for me, Donald. See what you can get.'

Donald frowned as he took possession of them. 'Are these . . . ?'

'Aye. From the lambs as and when they died. Mary was collecting enough for the bairn. But it wasn't God's will . . . so I reckon we've a duty to do all we can for those as are wit' us. We've no use of a baby blanket now. It's tools we need.'

Mhairi watched the exchange between the men, recognizing the faint sliver of emotion that belied their words. Mary Gillies – Big Mary, she was called, on account of their large family

46

outnumbering their relatives Effie and her father, the Little Gillies – had lost her unborn baby soon after Easter, and though she had her other five, she had taken the loss hard. Mhairi's own mother had lost four babies, Flora's mother two. It was not unusual but nor was it ever easy. Familiarity, in this instance, truly bred contempt.

The boat rocked as the sacks of lambswool were thrown down at her feet. The sound of a whistle pierced the crystal-line evening and both men startled, looking concerned. Shouts carried from the ship, though Mhairi couldn't make out what they were saying; she could only see someone aboard waving their arms.

Donald looked back towards the village, slitting his eyes as he scanned the slopes for signs of her father. There was no sign of movement past the dyke. Had he stopped at home quickly after all?

A sound of frustration escaped Donald. 'What's he doing up there? They'll go without us at this rate!'

'I'll go fetch him,' Hamish said, turning decisively. 'You take her to the boat and get these last bags loaded. Tell the skipper I'll have Ian here by the time you get back. We'll no' hold him up.'

'Aye.' Without another word, Donald jumped into the boat, sitting with his back to her as he grabbed the oars and used one of them to push away from the pier. Mhairi swallowed as she felt open space envelop them, the hull gripped by the shifting body of water. Like the rest of the islanders, she couldn't swim, though the men moved with a confidence on the boats that belied their ability to save themselves.

Water from the oars splashed her as they began to move across the bay, small waves lapping against the sides, ominously close. She watched as her home – the only world she had ever known – began to recede and grow small, faces lost to silhouettes in the fading light. She could just make out Hamish Gillies running along the Street, faint shouts carrying as her father's name was called.

Donald rowed with unusual power for a solo oarsman but he didn't seem to even think of asking for her help. Desperation fuelled him. His row with the factor had simmered for days and he wanted his profit; he wanted to get through this winter as best he could. They travelled quickly, aided by the ebbing tide, and she was surprised when a rope was thrown down, landing in the water beside them with a hard splash.

'Grab it!' Donald ordered, rowing with one arm now to turn the dinghy and bring them alongside.

Mhairi did as she was told, reaching out an arm and grabbing it. She looked up to see one of the whalers holding the other end and he began to walk back along the deck, towing them with him. Mhairi stared up at the brutish hull of the whaling ship towering above them, noticing a red smear along the prow, smudged over the letters *Polar Star*. The stench of rotting flesh was unmistakable and the chimney was already puffing black smoke.

The ship was moored near the buoy where the whale had been tethered only yesterday. Donald quickly fixed the back of the dinghy to the buoy with the small rope on board.

'Give me that.' He took the ship's rope from her hands before he had finished asking for it and tugged down hard so that the nose of the boat was pulled round and they sat parallel to the starboard side, where a ladder was fixed. Mhairi stared at it, seeing that the first rung was above her head. How was she to pull herself up? If she fell . . .

Donald, holding the rope firm, saw her hesitation. There was no time for it. 'Here.' She could hear the impatience in her neighbour's voice as he dropped the rope and stepped towards her, lifting her up in a fluid movement. 'Grab the rung.' The front of the boat began to drift away from the side of the ship now that the rope was released, but she got a hand to it and climbed up quickly, in spite of her ungainly boots. The whaler grabbed her roughly by the arm as she neared the top and helped haul her over. It wasn't the elegant embarkation process she had seen the rich summer visitors perform, but whaling ships weren't built with women in mind. She felt the fabric of her thick skirt catch and tear on a bolt.

The wind was sharper on deck, flapping her clothes, and she had to place a hand to her head to keep her shawl from flying off. The fisherman looked at her for a long moment, like he'd never seen a female before, then leant over the rail and called down to Donald.

'What are y' sending her up for? Y' said it was the wool you wanted loading?'

'Aye. But she's coming too now,' Donald shouted back, holding up the first of the sacks to hand over.

'Ha – no!' the fisherman scoffed. 'No women on this trip!'

'The skipper agreed to take three of us for a bottle of whisky!' Donald shouted up again.

'Well, he hasn't told me about it!'

'Then ask him now and he'll tell you!'

'I've no time for running errands. He wants away. There's no lasses on this ship and that's all there is to it.'

Mhairi looked around. There were three more whalers standing smoking up front, watching in sullen silence, woollen hats pulled down low over their brows, their beards so thick birds could nest in them. The whaler took Mhairi by the arm and led her back to the rails. 'Back down with you.'

'For pity's sake, man!' Mhairi could hear the frustration in Donald's voice. 'Speak to Ferg and you'll see. It's agreed.'

But the whaler was done discussing it. 'C'mon, get!' He pulled roughly at her arm, urging her back over the rail and down the ladder, just as two of the sacks of wool came flying over the bow rails. The man ducked in surprise, before recovering. 'This is no place for the likes of you.'

Mhairi gave a yelp of fear as he grabbed at her and made as if to lift her back over himself.

'Take your hands off her!' Donald's face suddenly appeared at the rail, the two tweed bundles looped over his opposite shoulders. The fisherman instinctively stepped back, pulling Mhairi with him as Donald leapt on deck, looking furious. 'Where is he? I'll get him myself.'

'The bridge,' the fisherman muttered.

'Leave her be. If you won't listen to me, you can listen to him.' Donald strode off towards the bridge.

The fisherman released her arm as Donald pushed past and Mhairi turned away from the men's prying eyes, determined to hide her fright. It was an inauspicious start. She'd not anticipated such a hostile welcome, at least not on this leg of the journey; she'd been more concerned by the response of the stranger who, this very moment, was going about his business with no idea she was setting sail for him. Would he be as ill-disposed towards her too? She instinctively knew Flora would never have received any such response.

She waited there, not daring to move as she stared down at nothing and heard men's voices in the distance, raised even over the clamour of the puffing chimney. Down below, the small dinghy swung away from the hull, still tethered to the buoy and rocking gently with the waves. From this elevated vantage point, she looked for signs of the giant whale that had floated there for three days, growing ever larger in death and bestowing a posthumous revenge on man with its 'unholy stink', as her mother had complained – but the depths below were clear, the local fishes doubtless fattened on the blubber feast.

'It's settled.' She turned to find Donald striding back towards her a few minutes later, his mouth set in a grim line that suggested a fierce argument. 'She's staying. He wants to see you.'

The whaler muttered a profanity under his breath but sidled off.

'What did you say to him?'

'Nothing that calmed him down. Ferg's opened the whisky already, smarting over their lost prize. There's no getting through to him now,' Donald said dismissively.

'But why's he so cross? I don't understand.'

'Because he's convinced we could have saved the bones, even if not the oil. He says they can fetch over three thousand pounds a ton.'

Three . . . ? Mhairi blinked at him. She couldn't fathom such a sum of money. She knew animal spoils paid the rent – puffin feathers supplied the upholstery trade, fulmar oil was used for lighting, but for a whalebone to reach such a figure . . .

'I put him straight. It was too far out to haul in for flensing, and in our smack we'd have been sunk. We did what we could but they left it too late.'

A sudden loud blast from the chimney made them both jump, and they turned back to see the men in action now – one was clambering the rig to the crow's nest; two others were winching the anchor chains. Still one was smoking, leaning on the rails on the bridge and staring down at them with a mutinous expression.

'Wait . . .' Mhairi murmured as there came a sensation of moving, the bubble and churn of water being displaced.

'What the . . . ?' Donald looked confused as the ship began to swing. 'Hey!' He ran back towards the bridge and this time Mhairi followed after. 'What are you doing? We're still waiting on one more!' Donald shouted up.

'We're done waiting. You've had long enough.'

'But we agreed passage for three!'

'Aye, and I'm telling you I'm done waiting. You've left it too late, isn't that so?' Sarcasm tinged the captain's words.

'But she can't travel without her father!' Donald yelled. 'She needs to be accompanied.'

'Aye, and she's got you.'

'I'm not her chaperone!'

'Why not? You're a married man. Just as respectable as her father, just as old.'

That wasn't true – Donald was maybe nine, ten years her senior, but the captain clearly wasn't interested in either facts or propriety and stood up, giving a deep, defiant shrug and dragging so hard on his cigarette, the tip glowed in return. 'You'd best take her down to the bunk. It's not safe up here.'

'No, please, Captain Ferg!' Mhairi called up desperately. 'My father's almost at the jetty! If you could just wait . . .' She looked back to shore – surely he was there now? – but a sharp gust of wind caught her, blowing back her shawl from her head and setting her red hair free.

The captain recoiled. For several seconds he couldn't speak at all. But when he did, he was directing his words to Donald. 'What the hell were y' thinking, bringing her sort aboard?'

Her sort? Mhairi knew the fishermen were a superstitious bunch; her mother had raised her to know that they commonly believed that encountering a redhead on the way to a boat

52

was deemed unlucky enough to send the fisher straight back home again. It was why she always kept indoors when the visiting fishing boats were heading off.

'None here passed her on the way to the ship,' Donald shouted up, seeing how the burst of activity that had only moments ago enlivened the deck, had fallen still again, all eyes upon her as her flaming hair streamed like a pennant in the wind.

'But you did. You came in the boat with her.'

'Aye, but I'm not a fisher! I'm not one of you!'

It was pure wordplay. Mhairi heard the note of desperation in Donald's voice and knew what he feared – if she was thrown off, he might well be too. His opportunity for small profit would be gone; there would be no other boats stopping here in time. But she didn't care about his ambitions. It was he, after all, who had put her in this position in the first place, and if her father wasn't even here to visit with her . . .

'Let me off! I'm getting off!' she said quickly, making to move away, but Donald grabbed her arm and held her firm.

'It's too late,' he growled, with his eyes on the skipper. 'It's too late, Fergus, you hear? If it bothers you so much that she's aboard, then you'll all have to abandon passage tonight and wait till sunrise. Can you risk that delay?'

There was a tense silence as the ship still swung on its axis, the prow nosing towards the gap between Dun and Oiseval. Momentum was already underway, but not yet unstoppable. They could still stop this charge to deeper water and send her back on the smack.

Mhairi felt her very future sway. Which way would it fall? Would she be sent back home, her fate postponed till the arrival of the westerly winds and spring tides? Or would the men stare down certain doom and risk everything for profit – dragging her with them?

The captain paced once, twice, conflicted, before throwing a pointed finger in her direction.

'Get her below deck!' he cried finally. 'I don't want sight of her till we dock, do y' hear?'

Donald's grip relaxed on her arm at the 'good news'.

'I don't want to be here!' she repeated.

But the captain hadn't finished. 'I mean it, McKinnon – she's to stay hidden. If she comes up even once, I'll throw her overboard m'self.'

'Understood,' Donald said, pulling her quickly along the deck and past the men, who stared at her now with a look akin to fear. None would meet her eyes, and Mhairi bridled that they should regard her as a curse! If they were scared of her, it was nothing at all to what she felt of them.

He pushed her ahead of him down a metal staircase into the belly of the boat. The heavy smell of grease and coal, of smuts and guts, turned her stomach as they staggered down the narrow passage, the boat picking up speed and making the water churn.

'How dare you! You had no right to do this! None at all!' she cried as Donald opened every door he passed, looking for somewhere she might be stowed, desperate to hide her lest any more of the men should be spooked. 'Wait till my father realizes what you've done! He'll have your guts for garters!'

But he didn't reply. Was he even listening?

'Here,' he said, pulling one door open and standing back to reveal a horizontal space so narrow there was no floor room on which to stand, only a bunk that ran the length of it. He shrugged off the tweed bundles and tossed them onto the thin mattress. There was no pillow or blanket, just a small porthole giving onto the now-black sea.

'In case of heavy weather,' he said, pointing to the woven straps that lay loose across the bed, suggesting the occupant be tied down. '. . . Go on. *In*,' he commanded when she wouldn't move.

She climbed onto the bunk in silence, glaring back at Donald in silent fury. His ambition had blinded him; he knew he should have taken her back off but he didn't trust the skipper to wait for his return. His profit would come before her reputation. Couldn't he see this entire situation was all his fault? But he seemed to see nothing. It was as though she was invisible.

'You heard the skipper. Stay put – I don't doubt he'd be true to his word and throw you over. I'll come for you when we make landfall,' he said, simply giving a terse nod and closing the door on her.

'But where are you going?' she cried as darkness washed down, the lights from the passage blocked out. 'Donald!' Footsteps receded down the passage.

'Damn him!' she cried, pressing her face to the glass, trying to catch a last glimpse of the village as they steamed out of the bay, but they were on the starboard side now and all was black, the grassy slopes of Dun sitting silent and still and offering no view at all.

She had never been confined in a space like this before. She had never known how it felt to float in deep water. She couldn't understand how the room could be both steamy and clammy and coolly damp at the same time. Her eyes adjusted quickly to the dimness as she took off her boots and reached for her bundle, unwrapping the tweed cloth and placing her clothes beside her. She draped the fabric over the length of her and placed her father's soft parcel under her head. She lay down stiffly, her body recoiling to the industrial sounds of heavy machinery, so foreign to her – the clamour of hissing pistons and the clanking of the anchor chains sounded like the minister's depictions of hell. She closed her eyes, yearning already for the feel of lush green grass against her bare soles, the smell of peat smoke in the air . . . She could well imagine her mother's dismay, her father's consternation, standing on the jetty at this very moment as she was ferried away from them. Donald McKinnon would have a rude welcome on his return, she knew that for sure. He'd regret his haste then.

It was the only thing she had to look forward to.

Chapter Four

The sudden, precipitous pitch downwards meant she awoke with a gasp – only to find herself staring back at a giant eyeball, unblinking against the glass. With a scream, she pushed herself against the far wall, her heart catching in her chest as she struggled to make sense of what she was seeing, to remember where she was, and why.

The limpid light told her it was dawn, a tired sun inching slowly above a pale sea. Had she . . . had she slept all night? She felt her body lilt and sway with the sea's locomotion and realized she'd been rocked asleep – until now. Another sudden dive downwards sent her face-first against the window, bumping her head hard, but still the whale didn't blink. She couldn't see past the giant eye but the waves must have grown more mighty and wild, for the ship pitched and dived now in a rolling rhythm – four counts up, three down. She felt her body leave the scant softness of the mattress on the bench and she scrabbled for the straps, tying them fast around her and feeling a scrap of comfort as she was secured in place.

A shout came from outside the door. A curse. A groan. One of the whalers thrown about as he tried to navigate his way down the passage?

Heart clattering, she lay as still as she could, staring up at the ceiling and counting the metal rivets above her head.

She longed for the symphony of snuffles that came from her siblings in the box bed; the scraping of the hearth as her mother prepared for breakfast, the creak of the swee being swung, her father's morning cough . . . But the eye continued to look upon her, on and on, only inches away.

She swivelled her gaze across to meet it; it was the size of her head and the whites were reddened, as if the pain of the animal's death remained in that now-unseeing stare. She tried not to think about its final moments as the harpoons struck; she tried not to imagine the terror of the hunt. It seemed to her it must have been a one-sided quest for, in spite of its size – and it had been one thing glimpsing the whales out in the bay, but eyeball to eyeball, it was a colossus – there was something gentle about the animal. It was grotesque to think of such quiet majesty being dragged alongside a boat like this. It felt like an affront to nature, a subversion of the natural order. Surely if anything was to incur the wrath of the sea gods and sink them, it would be not her red hair, but this abhorrent sight?

She turned on her side and gazed sadly upon the wretched beast, pressing her palm to the glass now. The two of them were lashed to this boat, both prisoners in their own way, both facing a wretched fate at their destination. She had no more power over her destiny than this poor creature – a woman in this world had no more prerogatives than the dead.

The knock at the door was brief and notional, Donald peering in a moment later with a queasy demeanour. 'We're arrived,' he mumbled. 'You can come out now.'

Mhairi watched as he swallowed hard, looking like he was trying to keep the contents of his stomach down. An excellent cragger and formidably strong, he was nonetheless no more a sailor than she.

'What happened to your face?' she frowned, shocked by the sight of him. There was blood in his beard and a deep cut on his lip, what looked like the beginnings of a bruise around his eye. Had he wrestled the whale himself? He looked like he'd gone ten rounds with a boxer.

'Nothing.'

She rolled her eyes, guessing that meant he'd been drinking with the crew. The reverend took a dim view of drinking back home but that didn't mean the men would pass it up when it was on offer elsewhere. 'Well, you look like you've been carousing all night,' she muttered, untying the straps holding her in place and moving stiffly onto her knees.

He made a noncommittal sound and she guessed that meant he had a sore head from the whisky too.

She quickly rewrapped her clothes in the tweed cloth, then jumped down and, putting her boots back on, followed him back along the corridor. He turned back to her at the bottom of the steps. 'Cover your hair,' he said brusquely. 'I want to get off this ship with less bother than we had getting on it.'

She supposed that was something they could agree on. There was a dank steaminess still, in the passageway, though the clank of pistons had stopped and she could hear men's shouts outside as they carefully climbed the staircase to the deck in their heavy boots.

She blinked several times as they stepped out into the harsh sunlight and she took in her new surroundings. The landscape wasn't as foreign as she had feared; the granite mountains were lower, rounder and more distant than she was used to – back home they squared up like a fighter's raised fists but here they rippled back in horizontal layers, showing the backward spread of land towards the horizon. There were still the same brawny heathered grasslands, and boulders and rocks dotting the ground in lieu of her familiar cleits, and sheep speckling the slopes; but the skies were notably empty and quiet, with none of the crying cacophony of the gannets, fulmars and guillemots which inhabited the sea stacks and sheer cliffs in colonies of hundreds of thousands. It was close to home, without being home. There was a bleakness to this place that Hirta lacked. In Village Bay, remote though they were, there was life – here only industry. She could see no women or children, no dogs, no clean washing drying on lines.

She turned on the spot and saw that the rocky bay encircled them in a deep U, another vessel moored further along the quay, a few men working on the deck. No sign here of the world-famous white sand beaches. There was a smattering of tall double-storey timber buildings set along the shore immediately beside the jetty, with some smaller buildings – workers' cottages – just behind. Her eye came back to the tall brick tower straight ahead, pointing skywards with smoke puffing from the top. The smell was unmistakable and she could guess exactly what was happening inside – the whale was being rendered down, the blubber boiled to extract the precious oil, the meat and bones cooked separately.

The sound of machinery gearing up, of cogs grinding and cables straining, caught her attention, more foul shouts emanating from men just out of sight from where she stood. She followed Donald over to the railings and peered down. What she saw made her cry out.

Not one but two whales were being winched up the slipway, a river of blood streaming behind them and harpoon bolts protruding from the giant bodies. She stared in horror at the bright gaping wounds already slashed through the thick blubber; she couldn't tell which of them had stared in sightlessly at her bunk, the hours they had spent side by side in desperate silence as the ship plunged and reared through the dawn ocean. Out of the water they seemed greater still in size, a scale that wasn't comprehensible. Even just lying on their sides, the whales were twice the height of the men, their lengths almost that of the ship, giant tails that could once have raised a tidal wave now lying still in the water.

Her hand flew to her mouth, tears gathering at her eyes as she saw the men gathered with their knives, ready to butcher or flense, cusses falling from their lips like they were prayers.

'Away,' Donald muttered, steering her away by the elbow from both the sight and the sounds. 'And keep that shawl up.'

Head bowed, she followed him down the gangway and onto the jetty. There was no sign yet of their precious cargo from St Kilda, the whalers' efforts concentrated entirely on their own harvests. They hadn't even noticed the two visitors emerging with their heads bowed as though in shame.

'You stand there,' Donald said, pointing to the low stone wall. 'Keep your back turned, raise no fuss.'

Mhairi turned her head indignantly at his words – any fuss, such as there was, had not been of her bidding – and stared at the nearest building, fifty yards from where she stood. A row of what looked like stiff black stockings hung on hooks, drying in the salt air and wind. They weren't stockings, she knew that; it just seemed incomprehensible that something so dense and mighty could be reduced to strips and slivers. Her gaze scanned the workers' buildings as she tried not to hear the sounds behind her – the clean whistling swing of steel blades, the sloppy wetness of blubber being cleaved, the rolling of wheels over cobblestones as the meat was thrown in carts and brought up to the boiling house. It felt like her body protested at every sense – the sound, smells, look and feel of it all. Her mother had boiled up some of the whale meat salvaged from the bay the other night, but their spoils had lacked this bloodthirsty theatre. If she were to live here, would whale meat be to the Harris man what the fulmar was to the St Kildan?

Donald threw down several sacks by her feet, off again in the next instant, striding back up the gangplank and into the bowels of the ship, hauling off the surplus goods he had been so determined to bring over. Mhairi watched impassively as the fare piled up around her: several casks of fulmar oil, the second quality tweed, Donald's finest lambswool, the black puffin feathers.

'And how will we move all this? Where will it go?' she asked him, surrounded now by their goods.

Donald glanced back at her like she was stupid. 'McLennan will come,' he frowned.

'But he doesn't know you're here.'

'No. He doesn't know *you're* here,' he corrected her. 'I sent him a message telling him to expect me on the *Polar Star*.'

'When the factor left?'

'Aye.'

An unfamiliar sound made her turn and as if on cue she saw a man approaching them on a horse-drawn cart, reins slack in his hands and a pipe dangling in his mouth. His cap was pulled down low so that his face was almost obscured in shadow, but she could discern grey whiskers and a loose dark cloth suit that had been patched many times. He wasn't a young man but there was vigour in his movements.

'So you made it then,' he said by way of welcome as he jumped down.

He came only to Donald's nose but the two men shook hands, maintaining strong eye contact. On St Kilda, a handshake was a token of honour and merit and she had grown up hearing her father tell her brothers that a handshake said more about a man than his words ever would.

'Aye, though the crossing grew rough.'

'Aye,' McLennan nodded, taking note of Donald's various injuries. His gaze slid over to the goods piled up in an assorted heap. 'You've brought a full load with y', I see. This will need some sorting through.'

'I've more with me than I intended . . .'

Mhairi rolled her eyes, turning away slightly. Little did this man yet know.

'. . . Some of the others were keen to rid their surplus too.'

'Aye, I don't doubt it,' McLennan murmured, putting a hand into the lambswool and pulling out a fistful. He pulled apart some of the fibres and rubbed them between his thumb and fingers before he let it fall again and raised his attention suddenly to her, as though she was the next product to be inspected. Up close, she could see that his gaze was sharp and keen, small dark eyes hidden beneath the peak of his cap. 'And this is your wife you've brought with you?'

Donald gave a wry smile. 'No. She is my neighbour's daughter. Mhairi MacKinnon. No relation,' he said quickly.

The farmer looked behind her, then around them, seeming baffled. 'Is she sick?'

'No sir, I'm quite well.'

McLennan's eyes rested upon her a moment, as though surprised she had a voice. 'Then where is your neighbour?' he asked, looking at Donald again.

It was Donald's turn to roll his eyes. 'The skipper wouldn't wait,' he tutted. 'He lost a whale in the bay and was in no mood to lose any more. We had to travel without him.'

'She travelled across here with all of them' – McLennan nodded his head towards the whalers on the slipway – 'and only you as her chaperone?' He chuckled. 'Then I think I understand how you got so battered.'

Mhairi looked between them, none the wiser as to what they meant.

'I assure you, she was far more of a threat to them than they were to her,' Donald muttered as he reached up and pulled down her shawl.

McLennan's expression changed as he saw her fiery hair blow free in the breeze. In spite of herself Mhairi looked down at the ground. She loved her hair – her mother's hair – but it made her both conspicuous and the object of superstition, and she was never comfortable with many eyes upon her. '. . . I'm amazed they let her aboard.'

'It was a battle,' Donald admitted.

'What brings you here then, lass?' he asked, speaking to her directly at last when it was the very question she wished he had directed to Donald. She looked to her neighbour for help – this had been his idea, after all – but he stood mute, for once.

'Well, sir,' she swallowed, feeling her cheeks burn. 'My father, as you know, was supposed to accompany us here. He wished to meet you and talk with you after Donald . . . he . . . he said you had a son who might be in want of a . . .' She couldn't bring herself to say it, that final word that confirmed she was in effect for sale.

A faint gleam alighted in the man's eyes as he grasped her meaning. He looked her up and down like she was a brood mare at a sale. 'I see. How old are you, Miss MacKinnon?'

She swallowed again. 'Eighteen, sir.'

'My son is six and twenty.' He looked at her through narrowing eyes. 'Do you speak English?'

She nodded. 'Very well. The minister taught us since we were bairns.'

He looked pleased by that, rolling his lips together as he continued to scrutinize her. 'Turn around,' he commanded. Eventually he looked back at Donald again. 'You'll be tight for getting back. The swell's rising up already.'

'Aye. But we had a deal, and I'm a man of my word.' He gestured with his foot again at the sacks on the ground.

McLennan nodded distractedly, his attention coming back to Mhairi. 'The *Endurance* is scheduled t' leave for Rockall tomorrow on the tide.' Rockall was the whalers' hunting ground, 163 miles west of St Kilda. 'Y'll need a bed – beds,' he corrected himself. 'For the night.'

'Aye. We'll ask over there.' Donald thumbed towards the whaling station.

'No, you'd best come with me. That way Miss MacKinnon here can see how fine my son looks and we can see how fine she cooks.'

The men chuckled as if it was all amusing and began loading the cart. Between them it didn't take long and a few minutes later they climbed aboard, Mhairi finding herself wedged on the bench between the two of them. McLennan wordlessly shook the reins and pulled the horses round, Mhairi staring over at the butchery on the slipway and the sea running red at the shoreline. The whales had been carved open, viscera reaching down the lower slopes, predatory gulls already wheeling overhead.

She looked away, rigid and stiff as they travelled in silence, the cart rolling and lurching over the rough track, the whaling station now at their backs. The farmer's thin legs pressed intermittently against hers, Donald's too, as the wheels rolled through potholes and ruts. She clutched the tweed bundles to her stomach, finding comfort in their softness and the smell of home. They trundled over undulating land, the sea to their right side, heather and gorse dotting the moors. She longed to see a tree, her first; she had seen pictures in books but it would be something to see the songbirds darting in and out of the branches, to find a nest or see boughs sprinkled with blossom or berries.

After half an hour, she saw some stone-walled pens up ahead and a couple of cows grazing in a field. Donald jumped down to open a gate into a yard – 'Hollow Farm' was etched into a slate upon the crossbar – and she took in the sight of a solitary thatched stone croft nestled in a dip. It was denied a sea view by a grassy bank – that likely kept the wind off too – and the roof was so low the house looked like it was kneeling. It was similar to the blackhouses back home but far deeper, with seemingly an extra room too.

This was no step up, though. The door was splintered along the bottom and one of the window panes had a hole big enough for a wren to fly through. Even from a distance she could see the dark thatch was old and rotted and in urgent need of full replacement. She had never thought she would consider her brothers Angus and Fin diligent, but they wouldn't have allowed their home to fall into such a pitiful state of neglect. Rounded stones hung as weights from the heather nets thrown over to keep the thatch in place.

McLennan pulled back on the reins and, despite their slow pace, they juddered to a halt. The men jumped down, the farmer readjusting his cap as he went to unbuckle the horse from the cart. Mhairi helped her neighbour with the sacks but her eyes were darting everywhere, noticing more signs of decay and gentle ruin – the clean-picked bones of what must once have been a sheep lay in the long grass near a stone wall; a window in the gable end was boarded up. There were several stone outbuildings round the back but one further off, clad with tin walls, had a tree – her first tree! – growing through the middle of it. Mostly, though, she was looking for *him*, the man she had come here to meet.

McLennan walked into the house, motioning for her to follow. Donald was too invested in unloading his sacks to notice and she left him to finish on his own. She stepped warily into the cottage. It had a dank stillness, so unlike the fresh, flickering life in her own home, where children ran about, her mother knitted and the aroma of brose or roasted puffin filled the air. Curtains hung at the windows, mildewed; they needed to be boil-washed and scrubbed . . . But then she saw the vast black iron range that spanned the width of the wall.

'Is it a Modern Mistress?' she asked, her eyes wide. The company ran an ad in the newspaper which would come over with the post – often days or weeks out of date – and would be passed around each family like treasure; for those who couldn't read, the pictures sufficed, or Lorna would oblige with reading for them. Mhairi knew her mother had pored over the illustrations of the Mistress. It was the stuff of her dreams and here one was, unlit and taking up space like a hibernating dragon.

'Aye, it can keep two pots boiling and four simmering on top; and the fire in the middle there heats an oven at this end and a water boiler at the other. And there's a tap there for filling the pans,' he said, pointing to the wall.

'The water comes into the croft?' She couldn't keep the disbelief from her voice.

'It does. And we've electricity too.' To prove it, he pressed on a toggle on the wall and the lamps instantly lit up. 'And the floor's congoleum.'

Mhairi bent down and pressed a hand to it. At home they had stone flags, which were themselves a step up from the compacted earth floors of the blackhouses, but she also knew from the ads – *Every housewife's dream!* – that congoleum, a new material, was easy to clean to a shine. Not that anyone had, recently, for her hand came back sticky and dirty.

'And do you . . . eat here?' she asked, trying to discreetly clean her hand on her skirt. There were no cream pans or milk churns that she could see, no eggs on the windowsills.

'Most days we eat with the whalers,' the farmer said, taking off his cap and setting it on a hook. 'Sheila's a fine cook.'

'Who's Sheila?' she asked, relieved to hear there was at least one other woman in the area. She watched as he picked up a cooking pot, swirling a hand around it to clear it of dead flies, spiders and cobwebs.

'The foreman's wife.'

'What does she cook?' she ventured, worried about what the answer might be – whale broth? Blubber chops?

'Mutton stew, most days,' he said, frowning at something inside the pan. He cleared his throat and spat, scrubbing it clean with his fingers. 'There y' are,' he said, passing it over.

Mhairi tried not to wince as she took it from him. Was she to clean it?

'There's some tatties, neeps and cabbages round the back. You pull them up, I'll get the heat and water going on this first. We connected it a year back.' And he turned his back to her as he opened up the stove door.

'Where are you going?' Donald asked, looking up as she passed him outside a moment later.

'To dig for dinner,' she said over her shoulder. 'I'm cooking. Apparently.'

She rounded the house to find herself facing onto a small pasture with two cows grazing. At the back of it was a byre. There was a small timber hut to the left with a fenced dirt yard before it; to the right was the allotment, barely protected by string and stakes marking the plot. Further back, beyond a tumbledown stone wall, a couple of small fields had been cultivated – one had a giant haystack gathered in it but in the other, someone was walking up and down behind a horse and plough. Was it him? She realized she didn't even know his name.

She began to dig.

Both men were sitting around the small square table when she came back in, her hands soiled, fifteen minutes later. She walked over to the tap, stopping before it. She had never used one before.

'Go ahead,' the farmer said. 'Turn it. It won't bite you.'

She did as she was told, startling a little as water spurted violently for a few moments before beginning to run clear. She smiled back at the men, delighted by the contraption as she washed her hands. Instinctively they both smiled in return.

'So what am I cooking?' she asked, drying her hands on a cloth.

'We'll have a stew,' McLennan replied. 'There's some salted mutton on the cold shelf.'

It was a test, then. Her stew would be matched against that of the skipper's wife. Well, she wasn't fazed. Her mother had taught her well, the two of them standing side by side as they cooked and went about their chores, talking and singing together, sometimes more like sisters.

She set to work, the men talking business behind her. Gradually it dawned on her that they appeared to be in mild disagreement; Donald kept repeating a number and McLennan kept talking a lot about 'different factors'. She didn't listen in in any detail – she was too concerned with her own task – but after a while she heard them get up and go outside. A glimpse through the filthy window and she saw them rummaging through the sacks, Donald's jaw clenched.

She got the stew simmering and, for want of anything else to do, began moving around the space, first cleaning out the cobwebs and then sweeping the floor, humming lightly to herself. She took down the curtains and, crouching on a low stool, set to washing them on the scrubbing boards, scouring out the mildew.

'Have you a drying line?' she asked the farmer as she joined the men outside, holding the curtains in her arms.

If McLennan was surprised to see her initiative in cleaning his curtains for him, he didn't show it. 'Over there,' he said, and he jerked his chin to the grassy hump forward of the cottage where the land rose up.

She climbed up, feeling the sea breeze catch her hair and lift it off her neck. A small brown songbird with yellow flashes on its wings – Effie would have loved it – was sitting upon one of the wooden posts, chirruping loudly and only flying off as she drew near. It was the first beautiful thing she'd seen since arriving here.

She began to peg the curtains to the line but her eye was drawn to the view out to sea. Whereas the whaling station was settled in the crook of the bay, an arm of land encircling it and providing a buffer from open water, here – several miles down the road – it looked straight out onto open water and the sight of St Kilda, a faint smudge on the horizon, made her hands drop. None of its majesty could be discerned, not the scale of its cliffs nor the throng of birdlife, but its wildness and splendid isolation had never been more apparent. The archipelago was but a blip on an otherwise unbroken grey line, nothing around it but wind and sea.

She tried to imagine them – her mother and father, her big brothers and the wee ones too, Flora, Molly and Effie, Mad Annie and Ma Peg . . . everyone she cared about, moving on the land and through the days, the way they always did. From here, their lives would look as inconsequential as ants crawling on a stone. There was no sense of the power of their sunsets, the aquamarine tint of the bay on a sunny day, the thrill that came from climbing a rope or receiving a letter . . .

'Mhairi!'

She turned round, startled as the voice rudely intruded on her thoughts.

'I thought you were asleep standing up,' Donald scowled up at her, his hands on his hips. He looked irritable and impatient, with heavy bags under his eyes and that bruise beginning to darken; the blood had thickly congealed on his beard too. He was beginning to look like he'd been in a fight. 'I've been standing here calling you.'

'What is it?' she sighed, turning back to him, her skirt flapping against her legs as a gust of wind jettisoned past.

'He's here.' Donald jerked his head back towards the cottage and she saw a tall young man standing by the unfastened cart, watching her. His hands were in his pockets, shirtsleeves rolled up, light brown hair the colour of that songbird.

The second beautiful thing she had seen here today.

Chapter Five

She walked carefully down the small slope in her boots, rueing the slippery leather soles. The wind was making mischief all of a sudden, as if it knew about the importance of first impressions, flurrying about her in a squall and making her red hair dance like flames. She wished now she had thought to pull her shawl back up after Donald had tugged it down on the jetty but she hadn't, and now here she was, meeting this man, looking like a banshee.

She felt the younger man's eyes on her as she approached, skirt flapping, and was certain her cheeks must match her hair. She forced herself to meet his eyes but could only hold the gaze for a second, no more.

'Pleased to make your acquaintance Miss MacKinnon,' he said after a pause, as if he was waiting for her to look at him again before he spoke. His voice was slow and low; she could imagine how it steadied the horse and scared the sheep.

'The pleasure's all mine, Mr McLennan,' she murmured.

'You can call me Alexander.'

Alexander. So that was it. Yes, she thought, he did look like an Alexander – fine-boned, deep-set eyes but with high colour too. He wasn't like Donald and the other St Kildan men: barrel-chested, strong-armed and blessed with thick heads of dark hair and bushy beards. He was tall, lithe and athletic from working the land; he looked in possession of both vigour and keen intelligence.

But apparently not a wife. 'Mhairi.'

'You've come a long way, Mhairi.'

Her eyes flitted up to his in alarm, anticipating the next words – *to find a husband* – but he was polite enough to spare her blushes and she glanced across at his father and Donald, both men watching the introduction with silent interest.

Were they pleased with the potential match too? It crossed her mind to wonder what Flora would think of him. She had her fancy gentleman in his tailored suit, but Mhairi had never dreamt of a man like that; his life would only take her away from her own and she had never had the wanderlust of her friend, none of her desire for more. The only 'more' she wanted was more of the same, her mother's life – a husband, a home, children, a peat fire burning and the view over Village Bay from sunrise to sundown. Was Alexander the kind of man to write her a letter, she wondered? She remembered her envy, the bitterness in her craw, as Flora had preened over her reply like a cat licking its paws.

'Tis a pity y' father couldn't make it over too,' he continued. 'I should have liked to meet him.'

'He's the postmaster,' she said proudly.

One of his eyebrows flickered ever so slightly. 'Is that so?'

Mhairi wondered whether to explain the importance of a role like that back home. Her father was the first and last point of contact between the villagers and the outside world. They depended upon him – him and Lorna – not just to safely deliver the letters but also to write and sometimes to read them too. She wouldn't have said he was as important as the minister, of course – the reverend's role as spiritual guardian overarched everything – but he was second in command, certainly.

'I thought all roles were shared between the community over there,' he said. 'What is it you call it?'

She hesitated for a moment, not quite sure what he was referring to. 'Oh, you mean the parliament?'

'Parliament, aye, that's it.'

'Aye, Father does his share of the cragging and fishing too, he just doesn't weave. He has his post office duties instead.'

'And do you ever help him with those duties?'

'Only when the sacks are full. He has an assistant, Lorna. She's a nurse from Stornoway and very clever. She translates the English letters into Gaelic, and the other way back. Father doesn't have much English.'

'But you do?'

'Aye. We learnt in school from the minister. I don't have to much think about it.'

A smile curved the corners of his mouth; he seemed pleased by her answers and she grew a little taller, feeling clever for something she'd never much considered before now. It was no more bother for her to speak English than it was to breathe.

She watched as he too now glanced over at their witnesses, as though remembering they were there.

'Would you care to see the farm, Mhairi? I could show you what we have here?'

It had begun, then, the business of their transaction – what she could offer, what he could in return.

'. . . We've no post office, to be sure, but if you like pigs, you're in for a treat.'

She grinned. She had never seen a real pig before. 'Aye—'

'The tour will have to wait, I'm afraid,' Donald said, stepping in and piercing the bubble that had begun to seal around them. 'We've to get to the store and buy the equipment we need before the *Endurance* sets sail tomorrow.'

Alexander looked back at her, as if surprised by the news they were leaving again so soon. 'Then 'tis a fleeting visit indeed.'

'An introduction was all that was intended by my father on this occasion,' she murmured, unable to meet his eyes again as she was reminded that without the formality of her father's presence, she was in effect having to broker any arrangement directly. Donald was her chaperone, of course, but he was patently more interested in his own business than hers.

'Well, as your time here is so short, can Miss MacKinnon not stay here with me while you go?' Alexander suggested.

Donald's eyes narrowed, as if his propriety had been offended. 'Absolutely not. Her father would have words to say about that. None of them good.'

Alexander gave a small shrug and stepped back. 'Then I wouldn't want to prompt them.'

Mhairi felt both relieved and disappointed. She threw Donald a furious glance.

'It's a couple of hours there and back to the store, you say?' Donald asked, looking back at the old farmer.

'Thereabouts,' McLennan replied, the languor of his body language at odds with the tension in her neighbour's. What exactly had transpired between them? Donald was in a filthy temper and she wished now she had paid more attention.

'By foot, aye,' Alexander said, stepping forward again. 'But if you take the pony and trap, you'll be there in half the time.'

'They're not accustomed to horses,' McLennan said, dismissing the notion.

'I was only thinking it would mean we'd have more time to get to know one another before they leave. 'Tis a pity to spend half the day on the road when they must leave

75

again tomorrow.' His hands were stuffed in his pockets again, the arms stiffened straight.

'They're not accustomed to horses,' his father repeated, 'and you've to finish the field, remember. You only came back for the other bit.'

'. . . Aye.' Alexander looked back at her disappointedly, his gaze falling down the length of her. 'Well, just be aware, Mhairi—' and he reached down, towards her.

The sudden touch against her bare thigh made her jump and Donald sprang between them like a cat.

'—There's a tear in her skirt. I thought she'd want to know.'

Mhairi looked down in horror. Sure enough, there was a rip in the heavy fabric, the pale skin of her thighs winking through. How . . . ? Then she remembered the way the whaler had roughly hauled her aboard last night, the momentary pull on her skirt as she had been manhandled over the railings.

Without hesitation, she unknotted the red plaid shawl on her shoulders – she wouldn't be needing it here, either for the winds or the superstitious fishermen – and tied it round her waist, pulling down on the longest point to cover the tear. When she looked up, all were staring. Did they think her rough – uncouth – to have arrived here on their doorstep, in that state?

'Just follow the road,' McLennan muttered. 'Bear right at the fork, keep the water to that side and you'll see the store ahead soon enough. It's away on its own.'

Donald nodded and together they began to walk.

'You could have told me!' she hissed as they got to the gate.

'I hadn't seen it!'

'How could you not see it? It's a huge gash down the side of my skirt!' She saw Alexander was still watching from the house and she gave a wave.

Donald didn't. 'Well, believe it or not, I don't spend any time looking at your skirt!'

They lapsed into a cross silence, arms swinging, both of them awkward in their boots. The road rolled back in its undulations towards the whaling station, the ships' rigging and masts peeking above the small hillocks until presently they came to the fork that peeled right. There the road meandered through the glen, facing onto distant purple hills. Occasional trees speckled the landscape and she saw sheep on the moorland, far bigger and brighter than the ones they had back home.

She listened to the birds, noticed the flowers, but the urge to speak began to rise like bubbles. She wanted to stay angry with Donald – his brusque manner and the offhand way he interfered with her life entitled her to some indignation, she felt. On the other hand, she needed to get some perspective, or someone else's perspective. She felt distinctly off balance and unsure of how any of this was going. Was she making a good impression, or bad? Did Alexander like her, or was he simply bemused to find that a woman had arrived from over the water to discuss potentially becoming his wife? He had taken it in his stride, certainly – she wasn't sure she'd have been so composed if it had been the other way round – but there seemed to be a natural disposition between them. He was attractive to her eye and the way he looked at her made her think she might be attractive to his. There was something in his manner – so direct, so . . . manly – that made her nervous, butterflies taking wing in her stomach. She realized her leg was still tingling from his touch. No man had ever touched her leg before.

'So you must be pleased with how it's going,' she said finally.

He grunted in reply as they marched on, arms swinging like soldiers.

'Ha! And to think you said he was no oil painting!'

There was a silence. Clearly this was going to be a one-sided conversation. Then Donald frowned. 'I said his father wasn't. I'd never met the son.'

'Well, you have to admit he's fine-looking. I'm lucky Flora's not here or he wouldn't even know my name.'

'What do you mean?' His frown deepened as, after a moment, he seemed to understand. '. . . Don't be ridiculous.'

Ridiculous? She rolled her eyes. What would he know about being friends with a girl like Flora – to be by her side was to be invisible, all day, every day. 'What did the father say to you that's got your goat?' she muttered.

She saw his jaw clench. His anger was real.

'Did something happen?'

'You could say that.'

Immediately she felt troubled. 'Does he not want the goods?'

'No, he wants them. Just not at the price we agreed.'

'. . . Why not?'

'The market's "moved", apparently. There's a glut of wool, they've not so much call for fulmar oil now the electricity's coming in, and the spoilt tweed is no good for anything but sacking or bedsheets.'

'That's not true!' Mhairi gasped.

'I know, but we're here now and that's what he's saying. He's got me over the barrel. He knows I need to sell, that I'll not take it all back again. But can I sell to anyone but him? No, I can't, there's no time. He's not stupid. Why do you think he'll no' let me use the trap? He doesn't want me getting anywhere quickly here and finding a new buyer. And with the factor now gone back, he knows he's my only option . . .'

He bit the corner of his lip, then gave a sharp gasp – he had caught the cut again. Immediately it split open, blood oozing, the scab little more than a thin crust. Mhairi instinctively went to check it with her fingers but he batted her away, shooting her an annoyed look.

'That looks like it needs a proper clean,' she protested.

'It's fine.'

'But it could get infected! Especially with your beard so thick.'

'I said it's fine.'

'Have it your way,' she shrugged.

There was another silence.

'. . . So how much is he offering?'

Donald's sigh told her it was bad news before his words. '. . . A shilling five for the oil.'

Mhairi frowned, certain she'd heard the factor offering a shilling four. Had they really come all this way, just for a penny's profit apiece?

'Six shillings for the feathers and three shillings a yard for the tweed.'

'That's scarce better than the factor offered!'

'But as McLennan said, it's still better.' His jaw clenched, and she wondered how much of his anger was down to wounded pride. He'd stuck his neck out back home, telling all the men of the profits they could make if they held back their surplus from the factor for his man. Only to be double-crossed. He'd been made to look a fool.

'Well, at least his son seems more honourable,' she shrugged.

Donald looked at her at with his usual sceptical expression. 'And how do you make that out?'

'He offered us the use of the trap, for one thing.'

'And touching you the way he did back there – was that honourable too?'

'He was pointing out something that would have embarrassed me in public,' she said defensively. 'He was being kind.'

'Oh, was he? And would he have dared pull that stunt had your father been standing there?' He tutted. 'You shouldn't fall for such games.'

'But . . .' The words failed her. Had it been a game? She had taken it as chivalry, him protecting her modesty. She stared at the ground as they walked, watching her boots kicking up dust with each step. No, she decided, he was just sore because Alexander's father had got the better of him. Pride had come before a fall, like the reverend always said it did.

The store, when they eventually came upon it, was little more than a converted bothy, with the only light coming in through the open door. Inside it was lined with shelves that hugged the walls on three sides and there was a high wooden counter with a short man behind it. He had a grey beard so bushy it made Donald's look like 'bum-fluff' (as her father had teased her brothers). He was sitting on a stool, reading a newspaper, but he stood as they entered, regarding them with an open suspicion that suggested strangers were rare in these parts.

'Good day to you,' Donald said, touching a hand to his cap and radiating more vigour than he'd shown in the past twenty-four hours. Finally they were getting what they'd come for. Or at least, what he'd come for.

Mhairi stood back, seeing how the man startled at the sight of her, as if he'd seen a ghost; she averted her eyes, bracing for another hysterical reaction. Donald saw it too, looking between the two of them in momentary confusion. Should she have put on her shawl after all? He looked like he was more disturbed by her hair than he would have been by her legs.

'You must be Murdo Macaskill,' he said after a pause, drawing the man's attention back to him. 'Hugh McLennan sent me. Said you might have some tools of interest to me?'

Released from scrutiny, Mhairi found herself bedazzled; the tiny store seemed like a treasure trove to her eyes. Shelves were lined with brightly coloured tins and packets. She'd never seen the like – Bovril; Colman's mustard; Lyons tea; Oxo cubes; Cowan's Meadow Cream caramels; Thornton's toffee; Sangster's preserve; McVitie & Price's digestives; Jacob & Co. cream crackers; P. C. Flett & Co. bramble jam; Rowntree's cocoa; National Dried Milk . . . What was it all? If only her mother could see it! And her wee brothers and sisters, the stack of tall glass jars filled to the top with coloured pastilles.

But Donald fancied a different kind of treasure. Not for him brightly coloured foodstuffs – he couldn't take his eyes off the various agricultural and domestic implements propped against the walls. A wooden washing dolly, a potato riddle, a harvest sickle, some coir rope . . .

'Hughie, eh?' The man stood with his hands pressed flat to the counter. 'And what tools might y' be looking for?' he asked, as if, having assessed them thoroughly, he had decided they could be served.

'A dibble, for one.'

The shopkeeper bent down and reached under the counter, placing a dibble on the bench before them. Mhairi watched Donald handle it – little more than a wooden stake, it was used for planting potatoes, the ground having been turned by a crooked spade first. It was such a simple implement, but for a community with no trees from which to harvest the wood, it was indeed true treasure.

Mhairi saw Donald swallow with anticipation as he turned it over in his hands.

'And a potato hook,' he murmured.

The same process occurred – the shopkeeper dipping below the counter and straightening up again a moment later with the desired equipment.

'A foot plough.'

There was a moment's hesitation. 'Do y' mean a crooked spade?'

'Aye, call it what you will.'

The man held his finger up, as if asking them to wait as he lifted a section of the counter and walked past them, outside. He returned a moment later with the crooked spade, passing it to Donald, who handled it like a newborn. Unlike their few rudimentary tools back home, naively carved from driftwood and lashed with chiselled stone, this woodwork was honed and polished, with iron hooks and paddles beaten in the blacksmith's forge.

Donald's eyes lit up as he assessed the tools, envisaging the ease and efficacy they would bring back to Hirta. He looked again at the shopkeeper, almost like a little boy now, his excitement palpable. 'And a peat-cutting spade and a turf spade too.'

The man allowed himself a smile so wry, it only glimmered in his eyes. 'Are y' come to crofting fresh from the city?'

'From St Kilda.'

'Ah.' The man shrugged as though it was one and the same thing: Not Here. He reappeared several moments later with the desired tools and went back behind the counter. Mhairi stared down at the assembled equipment, trying, like Donald, to see it as gold. She remembered James Callaghan's letter to Flora asking her what one thing she would want from the mainland. She had said a red lipstick; Effie had wanted a rope, Jayne some chickens. Mhairi had said a blue dress, but it had been a fib, said on the spur of the moment to complement her beautiful friend's avarice. Now that she was here, looking at all the brightly coloured tins and packets, she knew she would have chosen one of them – any of them – for they had pictures on them that suggested sweetness and flavour, food that wasn't caught off a cliff, and she knew her mother would make a feast with it for their family. Mhairi knew the pleasure of a full belly but rarely the bliss on the tongue.

Donald placed his hands on the counter with a small nod, as though he had agreed something in his head. 'How much for them all?'

Mhairi had heard the coins knocking in his pocket as they walked along the road and she sensed that as much as anything, he was keen to exert this new spending power. Currency had no use back home, but here, she had heard, the customer was king.

They waited while the man did his arithmetic. '. . . Four pound, eighteen shillings and sixpence.'

Donald fell still. Mhairi glanced up after a few moments as a silence lengthened, to find him looking into space with a panicked expression.

'Have you four pounds, eighteen and sixpence, Donald?' she whispered, wondering if perhaps he had misheard.

'Four eighteen and sixpence, you say?' Donald repeated to the shopkeeper.

'Aye. For the dibble, the potato hook, the crooked spade, the peat spade and the turf spade. Four eighteen and sixpence.'

Donald's jaw balled as he looked down at the array of tools and Mhairi understood he was trying to work out which one they could afford to do without – the dibble, for planting the potatoes? Or the hook for pulling them out? The crooked spade for turning over the earth for planting? The peat spade for the tough job of cutting the peats, or the turf spade for stripping the turf beforehand? All were jobs done the hard way – backbreaking and unremitting – but he had come here on a promise to bring back an easier life and, once glimpsed, these tools had him in their grip.

Finally his hand went to the potato hook, his fingers unable to resist stroking the extravagant curve of the metal hook. 'And if we don't take this?'

'. . . Three pound five shilling and tenpence.'

Mhairi knew from the way his head dropped that it wasn't enough.

'And this?' His hand moved to the dibble, touching it like it was a holy relic.

'. . . Three pound, one shilling and eightpence.'

There was a pause, then Donald reached into his pocket and pulled out the lucre, every single last penny set upon the counter.

The shopkeeper counted it and looked up at them. 'You're fourpence short.'

'Fourp . . . ?' Donald looked aghast, then furious. Had McLennan short-changed him? Mhairi saw the anger spot his cheeks, his jaw balling as he let the news settle.

She watched as he looked back down at the tools, clearly deliberating which now to give up. It was one thing to forgo the potato tools; they planted a meagre harvest compared to the number of peats they had to cut to keep the fires going, and that was the most punishing work – the ground hard in the summer and heavy in the winter. To lose any of the spades, when they had come so far to get them . . .

He pressed his hands flat on the counter again and straightened to his full height. 'Is there anything we can barter?'

The man's eyebrows shifted up in surprise. 'Barter?'

'Aye. These tools are badly needed back home and I've not been paid what I was due for the goods we brought over. If I had got what was agreed, I could ha' bought the lot, but I see now not all men are honourable.'

A silence greeted his damning words, his intimation plain. The shopkeeper looked from Donald over to her, and back to Donald again.

'I have a few hours spare. I could help you with any chores as need doing,' he said.

'The chores are all done,' the man muttered dourly.

'Well, there must be something I could do for you,' Donald persisted. 'Is the roof sound? I could make repairs where needed.'

The old man certainly didn't look capable of climbing a ladder.

The shopkeeper's gaze flickered towards her again, this time landing and staying put. '. . . Y' wife might have something to offer me,' he said finally.

Mhairi gasped in horror, stepping back as Donald instinctively stepped forward. 'She has nothing for y',' he said brusquely. 'And she's not my wife. She's my neighbour's daughter.'

Still the shopkeeper stared. 'I'll forgo the fourpence for a lock of her hair,' he said finally.

What?

Mhairi clutched her hair at his words but if she was surprised, Donald was more so. He looked across at her like she was newly revealed and she saw not consternation in his eyes, but hope. The hair that had caused such trouble on their way over here was going to be their salvation now?

'A lock of hair . . .' he echoed, in a voice that suggested it wasn't so much to ask, was it? What was hair, after all? She wouldn't feel its cut, she wouldn't notice its loss. And yet it

85

was her, somehow. The symbol of her being. She was being asked to give a piece of herself to this man, this stranger.

Donald turned to face her as he saw her alarm. 'Will you oblige, Mhairi – for the folk back home . . . ? You have plenty to be sure.'

She shook her head. There was something too intimate about the request. Her father wouldn't approve, she knew it.

'Why do you want it?' Donald asked the shopkeeper, looking him in the eye.

'My sweetheart had hair the same as her. She's been dead thirty years now . . . I have nothing to remember her by.'

Mhairi glanced back at him, remembering his expression as she'd walked in – like he'd seen a ghost.

'A memento, then,' Donald said as if in clarification, but it was a beseechment to her, she knew. Fourpence for a memento would mean tools for their village. Was she to be the one to stand in the way of the collective good? '. . . Mhairi?'

'Very well, then,' she said quietly. What real choice did she have?

The shopkeeper reached under the counter and retrieved a pair of scissors; he pushed them across the counter to her. She picked them up and went to snip a curl – then stopped. She held the scissors out to Donald. 'It should be somewhere the cut won't be noticeable,' she said quietly, sensing her father's consternation if he should find out. 'Underneath, at the back.'

She turned around and lifted her hair off her shoulders. She waited as Donald took the few steps between them and stood behind her. She felt him hesitate as she exposed the back of her neck, a part of herself she had never seen. Her head made a quarter-turn, as if to check on him, and he was spurred to move; his fingers lightly separated a tendril from the rest but as he brushed her skin, she shivered. It was just a reflex, no different to being caught in a breeze, but it made him pause, the scissors caught in a yawn before he tried again, gently twisting the lock free. She heard the snip of the scissors and it made her shiver once more as a part of herself was released.

A moment later, he showed her the cutting in his hands – the curl curved in his palm like a sleeping fox cub – as if reinforcing that there hadn't been any pain, no real loss after all. She looked back at him and after a moment, nodded her approval.

The shopkeeper reached into his waistcoat pocket and pulled out a fob watch on a chain. It had a cover to it and he carefully nestled the lock of hair inside, pushing it into position with his finger. Mhairi watched on, sensing a sort of reverence in the man's silence, his careful movements; but still she felt strangely disturbed – as it was snapped shut and taken from her sight – that there should be a part of her left here.

The shopkeeper nodded that the transaction was complete and Donald gathered the tools from the counter. He tipped his cap and they left the store without anyone saying another word.

'Thank you,' Donald said to her in a low voice as he handed over the peat spade for her to carry, taking the other tools himself. They were weighty, like all true treasure.

'It's fine,' she murmured, looking dead ahead as they began to walk back. She let herself sink into her own thoughts; she felt no compulsion to speak now. Was Donald unsettled by what had passed, too? By his own metric, after Alexander had touched her leg, was this something he'd be happy to relate her father? Because she wouldn't. She had permitted an intimacy to a stranger – but it wasn't the old man she was thinking of; she still felt the heat on her neck from where Donald had swept her loose hair back, but more than that, in the moment when he had looked at her afterwards, it had been with an expression she'd seen many times before – but never once directed to her. It was the look men gave to Flora all the while. For the first and only time in her life, she had felt beautiful.

It was only a shame it had come from entirely the wrong man.

They walked slowly along the road, grooves worn down by the wheels of traps and carts transporting goods from the whaling station over to the village and beyond to the port at Tarbert.

'You don't say much,' she muttered.

'What's there to say?'

'Oh, I don't know,' she sighed, looking around them. 'You might think to point out to me all the new things they have over here that we don't have back home – seeing as this is my first time ever off the isle and all.'

He seemed to consider her words. 'Very well, then.' He looked around them too. 'Do you know what that is?' He pointed towards what she knew to be a tree; disappointingly, there were precious few here, at least on this coast.

'It's a tree.'

'Aye, but do you know what kind?'

'There are different kinds? I thought a tree was just a tree.'

He laughed, and she was surprised by the unexpected sound. She wasn't sure she'd ever heard him laugh before. 'That's like saying a bird is just a bird. Or a dog is just a dog. Or a girl is just a girl. Or . . .'

'Aye, all right, I get the point,' she said, rolling her eyes. 'So what kind of tree is that one, then?'

'It's a rowan tree. They can live to over a hundred years, and around about this time, they grow red berries.'

'Are they berries you can eat, or berries that'll kill you?'

'Happily they're berries you can eat.'

'Ah. That's good to know,' she murmured, looking at the distant specimen, growing on a rock. 'What else . . . ?'

He looked around him some more. At a glance, the landscape was just a sweep of barren moorland, but his eyes narrowed as he scanned for smaller details. 'There,' he said, stopping abruptly and pointing to something near a ridge. 'A red deer. You can just make out the head.'

She stood right by him, her cheek almost on his arm as she tried to see what he was showing her. 'Oh,' she breathed. 'It's got horns?'

'They're called antlers. You only find them on the males. Stags.'

'Stags.'

'And the females are called hinds.'

'Hinds,' she repeated. 'They look sharp, those antlers. Are they dangerous?' It was impossible to gauge perspective at this distance.

He nodded. 'Aye. And you certainly wouldn't want to cross one at this time of year.'

'Why not?'

'It's the rut.'

'The rut?'

He glanced at her. 'Mating season. They're particularly aggressive around now. The antlers alone are probably half your weight, much less the weight of the animal behind them. Plenty of men have been gored by them in the past, and I heard of a farmer here whose dog was disembowelled by one.'

'Ugh!' she grimaced. 'Why so brutal?'

'Because they have to prove themselves; the female has to choose the strongest, fastest, cleverest mate if she wants to pass on the best genes to her young,' he shrugged. 'It's no different for dogs or lions or chimpanzees. Or even humans!'

'Humans?' she laughed. 'Don't be ridiculous. We don't have to fight just to have babies.'

That sound came again of his deep and throaty laughter. 'Oh Mhairi, if that's what you really think, how little you know of men.'

'But it's true,' she protested, feeling her cheeks flame as she sensed her naivete was being laid bare.

'You don't think men compete to get the best women? You don't think a man would go to any lengths to outwit or overpower his rivals to get the woman he wants?' He was staring at her now as if she confounded him. 'There's always a contest, Mhairi – a battle of strength, courage, prowess, wits, you name it . . .'

'Well, I disagree,' she shrugged, sticking her nose in the air.

'Okay then, so tell me this: if there was someone else who wanted you besides Alexander, how would you choose between them?'

'I'd choose the man I loved.'

'Aye, but what would make you love him? Why him specifically?'

She thought of Alexander and his fine symmetrical features: that flirtatious glint, that half-smile . . . 'Well, I suppose if he had nice eyes—'

The laugh came again, jostling her, making her jump. 'No, Mhairi, you would not,' he said, shaking his head with a smile. 'You might think that's what you'd want, but I guarantee you'd choose your mate not on how he looks, but how he makes you feel.'

She swallowed, feeling intimidated by his certainty on what she – or rather women – wanted. 'Which is?'

'Protected. Safe. Adored.'

Now he said it, it did sound good – but Alexander hadn't yet had a chance to make her feel any of those things. There had been no time, yet, to get past eyes. She watched as Donald stopped to remove a stone that had become caught between the loose sole and leather upper of his boot. 'Well, you're entitled to your opinion, but I still say you can tell a lot about someone by their eyes.'

'So by the same token, can you tell a lot about someone by their ears, or their nose too?'

She bridled. Was he mocking her? 'Eyes are the windows to the soul, everyone knows that.'

He glanced at her and she was aware of an edge in their words, of talking at – rather than to – each other. No doubt he didn't like a woman arguing with him; but how could he speak with any authority on what women wanted, when she was the woman in this scenario?

'Besides, it's not a problem for me,' she muttered. 'I won't have to choose and men won't have to fight for me. Alexander's my only option, and now I've met him, I'm perfectly happy with that. I'd marry him tomorrow if I had to.'

'Just because he's pretty?' Donald scoffed.

'If you like,' she shrugged.

But he didn't seem to like, because he threw the stone as hard and far as he could – way out of sight – and they walked the rest of the way back in silence.

Chapter Six

The sun was already hanging low in the sky when the farm-house hove into view. Slanting golden shafts of light picked it out against the moors, and what had seemed so bleak in the morning chill now radiated a bucolic glow. The polished windows glinted, the curtains were dry on the line – still waving to St Kilda on the horizon – and hens were now pecking freely in the yard. The poor condition of the thatch was lost to the shadows and the cottage seemed swollen with contentment, like a freshly risen loaf.

The aroma of the stew drifted out, welcoming them before the farmer heard their boots on the ground and appeared at the door. A pipe dangled from his lip, his cap off.

'Aah, 'twas a successful trip then,' he said, seeing the clutch of equipment in their hands.

'Not as successful as it could ha' been,' Donald said dourly, knocking the satisfaction from the farmer's face as he got straight to the point. No preamble. 'We were fourpence short. You short-changed me.'

Mhairi stiffened to hear her neighbour's aggressively confrontational tone.

'I did no such thing,' the farmer said, narrowing his eyes and straightening up, but he was half Donald's size. The St

Kildan man exuded a brute strength from daily cragging that mere farming alone couldn't challenge.

Donald walked over to the cottage and carefully propped his spades against the wall. There was menace in the slowness of his movements and he turned to the older man with hands already pulled into fists. Mhairi saw them, and she saw McLennan see them too.

'You went back on your word once, changing the amount we agreed for the feathers—'

'And as I told y', that was market—'

'Forces. Yes, I know.' He stood toe to toe with the older man. 'And I'll take the hit because you and I both know I have to. But you'll not dishonour me again. I want every single last one of those four pennies we agreed, McLennan, or there will be a problem between us.'

The farmer smirked. 'Y' might want to consider y' position on that. If y' want my hospitality tonight—'

'We don't need your hospitality. Sleeping out is nothing for the likes of us.'

'And the engagement? 'Twould be a shame to see it falter over a trifling few pennies. Alexander has eyes for the girl. I'd rather not see my son disappointed, but . . .' He shrugged.

'You might have to. I've not made the decision on whether he's suitable yet.'

Mhairi saw the shock on the farmer's face. He looked over at her and she quickly looked at the ground, mortified to have become a bargaining chip in their battle.

'You're not her father.'

'No. But I'm his representative here. And if the sins of the father are anything to go by, I couldn't in all conscience recommend he gives her hand to a swindler, a cheat and a crook.'

'Why, you—' A rush of blood flooded McLennan's cheeks, but Donald didn't stir. It was like watching a fox try to box a bear, and a few moments later, his body sagged. 'Fine. You can have the fourpence then, if such a piffling amount is so important to y', but I'll tell you here and now, there was no malice. It was an oversight and nothing more.' He reached into his trouser pocket and counted out the coins, handing them over with a look of derision.

Donald took them without even looking at the open palm. No thank you, either. 'Mhairi, come here.'

She walked the few steps over to them, dreading what he was going to say next. Was he going to tell her to retrieve their belongings from inside? Would they be sleeping out tonight on principle? Were she and Alexander doomed before they'd even begun?

'This is yours,' he said, taking her hand and giving her the coins.

'Oh, but I don't nee—'

'It's a matter of honour,' he said simply, and she realized it was the only way he'd be able to look her father in the eye again. It was his ambition, after all, that had ultimately put her in that position in the store. She had had to foot the bill through different means, and now she was being compensated.

She took the coins with a single nod, their unhappy triangle standing stiffly in the dying light. It was another moment before she saw a fourth figure standing in the shadows, within the house.

Alexander saw her see him and he walked over to the doorway, a smile flickering on his lips. 'Is everything well?' he asked, standing beside his father.

'Aye,' Donald said flatly. Mhairi glanced at him. He surely

had nothing left to gripe about? She felt desperate for good humour to be restored, and she reached for something to say.

'You have chickens!' she exclaimed, thinking of Jayne's wish.

'Aye,' Alexander nodded, looking faintly bemused.

'I can't understand how I didn't see them earlier.'

'The coop is round the back. Have you ever had a hen's egg for y' breakfast?'

She shook her head. 'Never a hen, only gannet, or fulmar or puffin. I feel always full of eggs.'

'Then let me show them to you,' he said, moving past his father and leading her out into the yard. She watched the birds as they pecked and gobbled around their legs, perfectly tame and unbothered by human presence. There were six or seven pure white hens with red frills cresting the tops of their heads.

'The rooster's here somewhere too,' Alexander muttered, looking around for him. 'Aye, there.' He pointed to a cockerel with a magnificent crown and a plumed tail, standing on the stone wall. 'Y'll never see a short morning with him about.'

'Oh.'

'White Leghorns,' he said as she moved uncertainly out of the way of one particular bird seemingly wanting something specific beneath her foot. 'That one there, she likes to lay her eggs anywhere but the coop. She has me chasin' around after her to find where she leaves them.'

Mhairi laughed at the image. 'Are you successful?'

'Mostly. But I've heard of a trick I'm going to try – a fellow at the market told me he puts golf balls in the coop.'

'Golf balls?' Mhairi queried. She had heard of the game.

'Aye. It tricks the hens into thinking they're eggs and they're reassured that it's a safe place to lay.'

'But where will you find such things?'

'There's a course around the way, by Scarista. There's plenty balls in the rough. The local bloods collect them and sell them back to the players for a handsome sum.' A look in his eyes suggested he wasn't charged.

'Oh.'

'Y' might like to come with me some time.'

Were they making plans now, then? 'Perhaps, aye,' she smiled. She glanced at him to find him already staring, apparently with no intention of looking away again. She felt the blush begin to creep up her cheeks and he smiled a little, seeming aware of the effect he had upon her and oblivious to the fact that they had an audience.

Donald, standing just behind them, shifted his weight restlessly, weary already of his role as unwitting chaperone. Mhairi wished she and Alexander could go somewhere and talk alone, without having their every move scrutinized.

She turned slightly, her gaze falling again upon a bicycle propped against the wall, its silver frame glinting in the sun. It hadn't been there earlier either. 'Is that yours?'

Alexander followed her pointed finger. 'Aye. Have you ridden one before?'

'I've never seen one before,' she laughed, eyes bright. She bit her lip, taking in the sight of the two large wheels, the handlebars, the basket on the front. She had thought only rich people had bicycles.

'It's useful for getting around the farm quickly, and to the store too,' Alexander said, watching her. 'Would you like a ride on it?'

She looked at him in alarm. 'Oh, no, I wouldn't know how!'

'I'll show y'. Come.' He reached for her hand, clasping it casually and pulling her along as though they always did this and it wasn't in fact the first time they'd ever touched.

'You mean now?'

He stopped and stared at her. 'Well, there's no time like the present. Y'll be gone from here again this time tomorrow.' His jaw balled at the last statement. 'When will we see you again after that?'

She heard the distinction – when, not if. She looked at Donald for an answer. Was it when, not if?

'It would be the spring,' Donald replied after a pause, his eyes focused on Alexander's continued grip on her hand. Again the distinction – would, not will. A provisional response. Nothing was confirmed yet.

'Then every moment counts,' Alexander said determinedly, leading her across the yard again. Mhairi glanced at Donald again in surprise, but he didn't stir to stop them.

'Shall we take a dram?' she heard McLennan say behind her.

'I should stay—' Donald rebuffed.

The farmer gave a scoffing sound. 'And what exactly do y' think will happen wit' us thirty feet away?'

She heard the sounds of the two men going inside and felt relief that she had so easily got what she wished for – she and Alexander were alone at last. His hand clasped hers; there wasn't tenderness in his touch, but there was passion. He had purpose and energy and a vital masculinity that excited her.

She watched the back of him as they walked – there was a curl to his hair at the nape of his neck, his shoulders sitting very square. There was a patch near the collar of his shirt that had been mended but not well; she would have done better . . . She felt unlike herself, scattered somehow. Breathless, heady, giddy and nervous.

He released his grip on her and took the bike from its position on the wall. Swinging a leg over the top bar, he sank onto the seat and casually rested his hands on the handlebars. 'Sit here,' he said, indicating the crossbar between his legs.

'What?' she gasped, looking at him as though he'd lost his mind. 'Surely not.'

'It's perfectly safe. Everyone travels like this here. There's no' many cars here yet.'

Was that true? She stared back at him, his body relaxed in inverse proportion to her tension. If she sat where he suggested, would she not in effect be . . . cradled by him?

'Don't y' want to see if you at least have a liking for it?' His stare hooked hers, challenge and excitement in his eyes.

She bit her lip. 'Okay.' Going against her better judgement, she walked over.

He smiled. 'That's it. Face y' back to me. Now put one foot on the wheel and hop up to sit here.' He patted the handle-bars. 'It's quite safe. I'm behind you. Y' can't fall.'

She hopped up, giving a squeal as she felt herself cradled in the metal crux. As suspected, she became acutely aware of how close her hips were to his hands, his arms extending now around her.

'There, it's not so bad, is it?' he asked, his voice almost in her ear so that the hairs on her neck stood on end.

She could only shake her head, her heart feeling like it might clatter its way out of her chest, it was banging so hard.

'And off we go,' he said, pushing with his foot on the ground so that they began to glide. 'We have to get a little speed up if we're to balance,' he murmured as Mhairi gave a gasp of fright – but he held the bike steady, sending the chickens squawking and flapping their wings crossly. He didn't seem to care or even notice them, his body like a protective wall around hers, his gaze dead ahead, breath in her ear as he pedalled. She felt herself wobble on the narrow bar, her stomach muscles clenched tightly for balance, but she was surprised to find she wasn't as terrified as she'd expected.

She was scared, but also exhilarated. Was this really happening – she was riding on a bike with a handsome man? Wait until she told the others what she'd done!

She laughed nervously, squealing occasionally, aware that her hair must be flying in his face as they flew around the yard.

Suddenly, something darted out in front of them—

'Agh!' She heard Alexander's cry of annoyance in her ear, felt his arms brace around her and in the next moment, she flew through the air.

'Urgh . . .' she gasped, lying in the dirt and trying to understand what had just happened. She heard a clatter of metal and saw Alexander throw the bike to the ground.

'Are y' all right?' he asked, crouching beside her. 'The damned cat shot out in front of me. There was nothing I could do.'

Sure enough, a tiger-striped cat padded past her field of vision, proudly carrying a brown mouse in its mouth. If she was troubled by his casual cussing, she was more troubled by the throb in her knee, and she pulled up her skirt to find a large bleeding graze.

He tutted. 'We'd best get that cleaned up,' he said, extending a hand towards her. 'Are y' all right? Can y' stand?' He pulled her to her feet. She found herself vertical again almost as quickly as she'd found herself horizontal.

She put her weight on the sore leg. Only her knee throbbed. 'I'm . . . I'm fine,' she breathed, only now seeing the dirt all over her blouse, the red shawl twisted at her waist and exposing again the tear in her skirt. 'But I look like a toerag!' she exclaimed, giving a defeated laugh.

'Well, a very pretty toerag,' he shrugged.

She looked up at the compliment, realizing how close they were standing, his one hand still holding hers, the other cupping her elbow. He was staring at her intently, more intently than was polite for two people who'd only met this very day. She knew she ought to move away but she felt transfixed by his proximity. 'You know, I thought m' eyes were playing tricks when I saw y' standing up there this morning.' His voice had dropped lower, seeming more intimate now.

She swallowed. '. . . You did?'

'It's not every morning a man finds a beautiful lass in his yard, come t' marry him.'

'I've not come here to marry, only to meet,' she said quickly, needing to clarify. Her pride demanded it, but they both knew it was wordplay. She was searching for a husband.

'And now that y've met me, are y' minded to marry me?' he asked, his eyes steady upon her and leaving nowhere she could hide.

'Well, I'm not minded not to,' she whispered.

A half grin lopsided his mouth and his gaze fell to her lips. 'I'd say it's been a promising start m'self.'

Her heart gathered itself into a skip. 'You would?'

'Aye. In fact it's taking all m' manners not to kiss you right now.'

Mhairi felt as if she was being squeezed, her ribs constricted, heart beating fast. She'd never known attention like this before. It was like standing in a furnace, all artifice stripped away so that all that remained was feelings. Big, hot, bewildering emotions. She had never kissed anyone before, not *kiss*-kissed them; but she knew, with a certainty she could never have anticipated, that he was going to kiss her now—

'Mhairi!'

The sudden bark of her name made them both startle. Donald was standing by the cottage door, with a face like thunder. He crossed the yard in a few strides. He had maybe only a year or two on Alexander, though it was his extra inches in chest and fist size that concerned her. 'Get back from her,' he growled.

Mhairi stepped back instead so that no one had to lose face. 'We were just talking,' she said quickly. 'I fell off the bike and Alexander was checking I was well.'

'Oh, I bet he was.'

Alexander turned to face him, placing his hands upon his hips. It was an open, confident stance which suggested that, unlike his father, he wouldn't be easily physically cowed. 'Will you really stand there and admonish me for trying to get to know the woman you brought over to propose as my wife?' he asked. 'Perhaps your wife wasn't a stranger to you before you wed. You had the luxury of knowing each other's names and faces before you pledged the rest of your lives to one another, did y'?'

Donald's eyes swept him up and down, looking at him like he was something unpleasant he'd stepped in. Slowly, he grabbed the front of Alexander's shirt, tugging up just high enough that the other man had to balance on his tiptoes. 'This is not about my wife,' he said in a low voice. 'I have a responsibility to Miss MacKinnon's father, and if I can't trust you to behave honourably for the few moments y' are alone, then there can't be any moments alone.'

'But Donald, I'm fine, really,' Mhairi interjected, placing her hand on his arm. 'He didn't do anything wrong.'

Neither man looked at her; they were locked on each other only. 'I know what I saw. If I hadn't come out when I did . . .'

'And what? What would have happened? I'd ha' kissed her?' Alexander scoffed, challenging him so that Donald lifted his arm that bit higher still. 'Of course I would! I'd be a fool not to! I've done this long wi'out a wife and I'd rather continue wi'out one if she'll only bring me strife.'

Donald visibly stiffened at his provocative words.

'Hit me if it'll make y' feel better, but if I'm to agree to this, then there must be pleasure. I'll no' apologize for begging a kiss.' Alexander was barely touching the ground now but he refused to break eye contact with the bigger man, and for several seconds, they stood in awkward tension.

Donald released his grip suddenly and Alexander staggered back, arms wheeling as he almost went head over tail over the bike behind him on the ground. He took a moment to recover before looking up again as Donald turned to go.

'But if it's propriety you're so troubled by, then I can kiss her in front o' you and you can watch, I don't mind.'

Mhairi gasped – that was too much! – as Donald whipped around again.

'Or perhaps it's just that you don't want me kissing her at all. Perhaps I'm not the only one wanting to kiss her.'

Donald's fist flew forward, almost unseen, connecting with Alexander's jaw and sending him tumbling this time onto the bike.

'No!' Mhairi cried, running over to him and positioning herself between the two men as if she, somehow, would stop them. She pressed a hand gently to Alexander's cheek as the farmer's son defiantly looked back up at Donald, a tangle of splayed limbs and metal, a smirk on his lips.

'Just you watch your mouth,' Donald sneered, taking her by the arm and steering her back towards the cottage.

'Struck a nerve, have I?' Alexander shouted after them, making Mhairi wince. But he stayed down. If not out.

Alexander returned to the cottage ten minutes after them, clutching several hens' eggs in his hands and moving about as if nothing had happened. He presented them to Mhairi almost as a gift; they were a chalky white – no different to shag eggs, but far smaller.

'They're so wee,' she cooed as he came over to show her by the stove. He stood close as she examined them, his tender gaze roaming openly over her face as she rolled one in her palm, Donald watching from the table in a rigid silence. But whether Alexander intended it as a deliberate provocation or not, Donald said nothing, allowing the moment to pass. He couldn't throw a punch every time Alexander went near her.

She arranged the eggs on the windowsill, nestling them in some hay she had found round the back. With the washed curtains now hanging again and the panes cleaned to a crystal clarity, it was almost a vignette of home. A small bubble of contentment floated up inside her as she poked at the fire, releasing a few small leaping flames. It wasn't happiness, exactly – the thought of leaving her home, her family and her friends still dismayed her – but if she could recreate pockets of her life on St Kilda, she might be able to bear leaving it. They shared the same stretch of sea, after all, just different sides of it; the mountains belonged to the same range that ran beneath the waves; the animals here were cousins to the ones she knew . . . There was enough here that was familiar to keep her going, and in spite of an inauspicious start – and certainly in spite of Donald's dour demeanour – things were going better than could have been expected. She knew she was passing the various tests that had been set, proving herself to be her mother's daughter – a true home-maker and no burden to any man.

Alexander, in turn, was showing himself to be strong, independent and not easily cowed. He was attractive to her eye and seemingly she was to his. He made her feel, in ways no one ever had before, that she was desirable to him, and his provocation that Donald could watch while he kissed her had left her with the distinct impression that a kiss would in fact happen before she left here. In fact, he had almost declared it as a condition. He wanted a taste of his future pleasure before any commitment was made. Just the thought of it made her stomach plunge and roll. When would it happen? Would Donald get any notice? More to the point, would she?

'What have you put in the stew, Mhairi?' Hugh asked as he stirred the pot. 'Something's different.'

'I canna tell you. It's my mother's secret,' she said with a smile, tapping the side of her nose.

'See? She's not just a bonny face; she can cook too. It smells better than Sheila's, do you not think, Father?' Alexander asked.

'Aye, my stomach thinks my throat's been cut,' the farmer replied.

Mhairi laughed.

'I'm beginning to wonder if I'm the luckiest man I ever met,' Alexander said, stuffing his hands deep into his pockets, in what seemed to be his characteristic way. 'I woke up this morning thinking it was a day like any other, but I'll be ending it tonight with a full stomach and a beautiful woman in my bed.'

Donald's head whipped up like it had been yanked with chains and Mhairi saw the newspaper he'd been reading was now scrunched in his palms, which were balling into fists. He looked enraged, but Hugh gave a hearty laugh.

'Calm down, Donald,' he said, patting his guest on the shoulder. 'It's a joke. You'll have to get used to my son's sense of humour.'

'I'll be sleeping in with my father, naturally,' Alexander

smiled. 'Mhairi can take my room, but I'm afraid it'll have to be the settle for you, Donald. Unless you'd rather take a room down at the whaling station?'

Donald's eyes narrowed at the suggestion. They all knew he wouldn't be leaving her alone here overnight. 'The settle's fine.'

'Good, so then it's all agreed. Come, let me show you around, Mhairi,' Alexander said to her, opening the door that led off at the back of the kitchen. She followed him in tentatively, aware of her chaperone's eyes upon her back. There was a double-wick oil lamp hanging from a nail in the wall beside the bed; hemp sacking lined the inner roof, protecting the occupant from any falling loose chaff or thatch, but also creating a soft, pillowy effect. The bed was covered with an old, much-repaired linen sheet and a crudely knitted blanket. There was an enamel pitcher and bowl on a three-legged stool in the back corner, a chamber pot below it, though there was an outhouse round the back; another luxury unknown back home. A red blanket box held Alexander's few clothes – she was welcome to take any should she be cold in the night, he said – and a small coir rug sat in the middle of the floor, offering neither decoration, softness nor much warmth. His was the window she had seen fully boarded up but a frame of light illuminated the edges, providing some relief from what would be pervasive darkness at night.

'If I'd have known you were coming, I'd have changed the sheets, but it's too late in the day now.'

'Oh no, it's fine.'

'They may smell of me,' he said apologetically.

She swallowed. 'That's all right.'

His gaze fell to her mouth before rising to her eyes again. 'Who knows? Perhaps when you have gone and I'm in bed alone again, they may smell of you.'

She blushed, just as Donald cleared his throat loudly from the other room, but Alexander gave her a wink. She could see he was enjoying taunting her accidental chaperone; perhaps it wasn't surprising. She could already see the first shadows of a bruise emerging on his cheek.

'Naturally, this would become our room if you did decide to marry me. Our wedding night would be spent here.' With a wave of his arm, he motioned towards the bed. 'Don't worry, I'd kick m' father out for that, so we could have the run of the place,' he whispered, before walking away with a smile.

Mhairi watched him go back into the kitchen, feeling a small shiver of excitement. Wait until she told the girls about him, the things he'd said, done, the way he'd stood up to Donald. He might not be a fancy gentleman with a townhouse and fine clothes, but he was her sort and he wanted her! She felt that loosening feeling again in the pit of her stomach as she tried to imagine lying in here with him, the two of them shed of their clothes . . .

'Mhairi!' Donald barked. 'Is something burning?'

It wasn't, but she came through, a smile playing on her lips. How much could change in the course of a day! Only last night she had been lashed to a bunk on a ship with a dead whale staring in at her over the nautical miles; yet now here she was in a croft that might soon become her own, with a man who wanted her. She went to the pot and began to stir, daydreaming of him and all the things they could not yet do.

The fire was burning low in the grate, a few last orange flames twisting and leaping above the smouldering ashes, the room suffused with an amber light. Mhairi sat in a wooden chair on the far side; it had a high woven rush back that swooped around her to keep off the draughts as she patched a shirt.

The men were sitting at the table playing cards – gin rummy or some such. The earlier fractious mood appeared to have settled with food in their stomachs and a steady quantity of whisky, the whick of cards accompanied by an occasional low murmur of 'gin', 'knock' or 'undercut'. It wasn't clear who was winning, although the battle seemed to be between the younger men, Hugh more interested in swiping a dram each time he took score.

'You just got lucky,' Alexander sighed, sitting back in his chair and looking over at her again. His eyes had been sliding towards her every few minutes, as if she was something he could drink in and absorb.

'Was it luck?' Donald asked wryly as he gathered the deck and shuffled the cards. 'Want to go again? We can see if I'm on a lucky streak.' Sarcasm coloured the words.

'Very well, though I think we should make it a little more interesting and raise the stakes. It makes the brain work harder when there's something to fight for.' Mhairi glanced up to find Alexander coming in to lean on his elbows, his eyes drilled upon Donald's.

She looked between the two of them nervously.

'And what would we be playing for?'

'Isn't it obvious?' A small smile played on Alexander's lips. 'The winner earns himself a kiss.'

'I'm not kissing you, McLennan,' Donald replied laconically.

Alexander laughed, smacking a palm on the table with amusement. 'I should hope not. That beard must be . . . ticklish.' He reached forward as if to brush his palm against Donald's jaw but the St Kildan swiped at him, catching him by the wrist, eyes blazing.

'Stop your fretting,' Alexander grinned, slumping back in the chair. 'We both know fine it's not each other we want t' kiss.' His gaze slid towards Mhairi again, openly desirous as the whisky played in his blood.

'Hmph, well, I'll not play in this round,' Hugh said, pushing his chair back and getting up stiffly. 'I need t' piss anyway.'

Mhairi watched as the old farmer lurched drunkenly towards the door and out into the night.

'Well that's it, then. The game's no good with two,' Donald said stiffly, setting down the cards.

'Nonsense. We'll play the short version. The first to one run, or one set wins.'

'Nup,' Donald shook his head. 'She's not a bargaining chip.' But he saw the way Mhairi's head jerked up at his hypocrisy – she had been exactly that in the store earlier.

'I don't mind,' she said with a flash of defiance.

'Excellent!' Alexander said, brightening considerably and rubbing his hands together. 'That should make the blood flow.'

Donald shook his head again. 'No. You're not kissing her if you win and I'm definitely not kissing her if I do.'

'But you know y' want to,' Alexander teased through narrowed eyes.

'I'm married.'

'It's just a kiss,' Alexander grinned.

'No.'

Alexander considered for a moment, seeing the determined set of the man's jaw. 'Very well, then – she kisses the winner.'

'What?' Mhairi gasped.

'Aye. That way y' can be sure it'll be a modest peck on the cheek for you, McKinnon, and nothing more. Nothing for y' wife to get bothered about. And the girl's willing, so there's nothing for her father to be bothered about either.'

'I said no!'

'I don't know what you're so exercised about. It's not like I'm going to win. You're the one on a winning streak, remember?'

There was a brief silence as Donald found himself boxed in.

'Come on, man! Where's your spirit?' Alexander cried, slapping the table again. 'You're married, not dead! It's just a game and one little kiss.'

'Yes, go on, Donald,' she rejoindered, enjoying his discomfort. 'There's no harm.'

He looked at her, his jaw balling with tension as he weighed up the options – but Alexander decided for him, grabbing the deck of cards and beginning to shuffle it. He counted out the cards then laid the remainder face down on the table, with one facing up.

'Go,' he said, with a jerk of his chin.

Mhairi watched, her sewing forgotten in her hands, as the men splayed the cards in their hands and looked at what they'd been dealt. Their faces betrayed nothing as they studied, then began to play – choosing a card, setting one down . . . picking up a card, setting down another . . .

There was an intensity to the game that hadn't been there before. Alexander had been right: turning this into a contest and playing to win had raised the stakes. A tension settled in the room, so thick that Mhairi felt she could have bitten down on it.

She watched Alexander, willing him to win – to win her. The number of cards in the 'stock' pile was running down, those in the discard pack rising. Would they have to go again?

'Gin.'

The single word ricocheted off the walls as Donald set down his hand, showing a suit of aces. Alexander's eyes flashed with anger and he inhaled sharply, pushing back in his chair as if he'd just lost his house.

'Well . . . you really are on a streak,' he muttered finally.

Donald just gave a shrug and began idly collecting the cards again, shuffling them repeatedly but without any inclination to deal, as if he was hijacking the game – any game – from here on in.

Mhairi watched Alexander look between her and him. 'Well?' he prompted irritably. 'Claim your prize, then!'

Donald flashed a look at him as he continued to shuffle the cards. 'No.'

'No?' Alexander laughed, sounding disbelieving. '. . . Yes!'

'No.'

Mhairi sighed. Were they to turn this into an argument, too?

'We had an agreement. You have to honour it,' Alexander insisted.

'That was your prize, not mine. I'm quite happy to forfeit, and I don't doubt Miss MacKinnon is too.'

'Miss MacKinnon?' Alexander queried, his eyes narrowing as he leant in on his elbows. 'Why so formal all of a sudden, Donald . . . ? You look so . . . uptight.'

Donald didn't dignify the comment with a reply. Only a twitch of his eyebrow betrayed his disdain.

'She's got you not trusting yourself, is that it? You're worried you'll like it too much?'

'Enough.' Donald's eyes flashed dangerously again.

Alexander gave a laugh. 'The more you protest, the more suspicious I become, Donald!'

'Oh, for heaven's sake,' Mhairi sighed, getting up and crossing the few feet between them. They would argue till the sun came up. She clasped Donald's cheeks in her hands and bent down to kiss him, but the unexpected touch had startled him again and he moved just enough that as her lips brushed against him, they found his lips too and not a bearded cheek.

For a moment, they were eye to eye and she could see a ring of fire around his irises that she had never noticed before. She pulled away quickly, seeing the confusion in his eyes as to what had just happened. 'There, it's settled,' she said briskly, straightening up and running her hands down her thighs. 'Satisfied now?' she asked Alexander, as she turned away and went back to her knitting.

But he made no reply, the game now abandoned as the three of them sat by the fireside in silence, none of them satisfied in the least.

Chapter Seven

In the room it was still dark, a faint, fevered sweat sticking to her skin, but beyond the boarded-up window the cockerel was crowing as if the rising sun was the very devil himself.

Mhairi instinctively knew where she was; she didn't need snuffles from another bed to place her. She listened for a few moments for any sounds outside the door – it wouldn't do to oversleep. But all was quiet in the house, so she rose and washed quickly with the water brought through in the pitcher last night. She made the bed and dressed – keeping her boots off for now – and peered into the kitchen.

Donald was lying on the long pine settle, wrapped in just a blanket. A cushion from the chair was his pillow but it provided scant support against his broad shoulders, with the result that his neck was at a strange angle. Still, he seemed fast off and she stopped to stare for a moment at his sleeping form. So dour when awake, there was a softness to him in sleep, the scowl brushed from his brow and his lips parted and slack. Poor Mary had her work cut out with him, she tutted to herself, for what good was gentleness in his sleep?

She turned to the scant stocked shelves that served as a larder. There wasn't much to go on with, but she reached for the flour and salt. She had got a starter going last night while the men talked and she checked it now, pleased to see

112

it had begun to swell, bubbles forming. It was far earlier to use than she would have liked, but it would need another week before it was fully mature and time was against her. She took a pinch and began kneading a dough on the table, turning, flipping and stretching it the way her mother had always shown her.

She patted it into a cob . . .

'Oh, you're awake,' she said, aware of eyes on her back and realizing she had an audience.

'Hmm.' The sound coming from the bench was more of a growl.

'Did I waken you?'

His scowl was back on. 'You're slapping the bejesus out of that thing. How did you expect me to sleep through?' he grumbled.

'Well, I'm sorry,' she said unapologetically. 'But I needed to get this going. I thought it'd be nice if he woke to the smell of a fresh loaf baking.'

'He?'

'They. You. Everyone,' she muttered.

'Hmm.' He lay back, letting his arm fall across his face, blocking out the light again as she continued to work. When the loaf was in the oven, she wandered over to the window-sill and brought the hens' eggs back over, excited to try them.

She stopped beside Donald on her way past, noticing the cut on his lip again. She had told him to clean it properly yesterday but of course he had done no such thing, and the wound – what she could see of it – was now angry and red. She bent closer, reaching out a hand to see better past his beard, but his own hand whipped down and caught her by the wrist, as with Alexander last night.

'What are you doing?' he demanded.

She blinked back at him, taken aback by his overreaction. No one touched him, it seemed. 'I was having a look at that cut. I told you to clean it up yesterday.'

He pushed her hand away. 'Aye, because I've the time for that, having to babysit you.'

Why was he always so angry? She turned away, hurt by his brusqueness but refusing to let him see. 'It'll get infected if you leave it,' she muttered, heading back to the stove.

Just then, the door to Hugh's bedroom opened and Alexander appeared, wearing his trousers but no shirt, his tousled hair in an appealing state of dishevelment. Mhairi stopped in her tracks at the sight of his bare flesh: tanned skin suggested he was no stranger to working in the sun without a shirt, and his defined muscles showed he was no shirker of hard labour either.

'G'morning,' he said sleepily, rubbing his eyes. 'I thought I heard voices.'

Mhairi tore her gaze away quickly, lest she should be caught staring, but felt the blush rise through her cheeks. Alexander saw it anyway and seemed pleased, brushing past her lightly as he looked over at Donald stretched awkwardly on the bench. 'Were you comfortable?'

'Aye,' Donald said gruffly, pushing himself up into a seated position. He had slept in his trousers and vest, the loop of his braces hanging down, but he was rubbing the back of his neck with one hand; Mhairi could see the night chill from the broken window pane would have hit him directly. No doubt he had a cricked neck. No doubt that would improve his mood no end for the rest of the day.

'Aye,' Alexander grinned, as though he'd guessed as much too, looking back at her. 'And you, Mhairi? Did you sleep well?' He dropped his voice slightly as he addressed her.

'Aye, thank you,' she said quietly, both thrilled and enervated by the intimate tone.

He sniffed the air. 'And what is that I can smell this time?'

'I've made a loaf,' she said. 'It's only a quick one – it won't be too good, the starter needs a lot longer, but it should do us today.'

'Do you bake bread every morning back home, then?' he asked, looking pleased by the idea and coming a little closer.

She shook her head. 'The flour's hard to come by over there. We can scarce grow enough wheat and it's costly to bring over. We mainly try to do without.'

'Without bread?' He pulled a pitying face as he came and stood right beside her. 'So then, that would be something in our favour if you were to come here?'

She wouldn't meet his gaze. 'Perhaps,' she said shyly, turning away to set the egg pan heating.

'Plus we have chickens, remember. And pigs. And bicycles.'

She smiled at the not-so-subtle charm offensive. 'Aye, you do.'

Donald cleared his throat loudly. 'Shouldn't you be getting dressed?' he asked pointedly, standing now too and shaking out the tweed blanket with several angry slaps.

Mhairi rolled her eyes – it really was too early for another of their disagreements – but Alexander merely threw her another grin as he swung his arms above his head and stretched, right beside her, before casually making his way outside. Mhairi watched him go, unable not to.

'Stop flirting with him,' Donald said, in a low voice that offered no sweet intimacies whatsoever.

'I wasn't!' she protested. 'I'm making breakfast!'

'You know perfectly well what's going on between the two of you. What am I supposed to say to your father?'

She turned to face him, incredulous. 'Oh, I don't know – that it turns out I actually like the man you want me to marry?'

'Me?' he scoffed. 'None of this is about me!'

'Oh no? Who was it who put the whole idea in m' father's head?' she whispered. 'Who was it who was coming over here without delay and said he knew a man who had a son in need of a wife? Who was it who turned my life upside down without even giving it a second thought?'

Donald stared back at her, shocked, as though these accusations were completely new to him.

'It was you, Donald!' she said, pointing her finger at him for good measure. 'This proposition might be turning out more fortuitously than I could have hoped, but it so easily could have been worse! It was your careless words that put me here – and now you stand there and scold me for flirting with the man you will all want me to marry regardless?'

She watched the bluster on his face – denials he couldn't quite articulate, realizations only just being realized. 'You always knew marriage was coming, Mhairi.'

'Aye, I did,' she hissed. 'But I would have liked more than a few minutes' notice.'

Donald exhaled heavily. He had none of Alexander's dawn vigour; rather the morning seemed to weigh upon his shoulders like a dead sheep. He rubbed his hands over his face, wincing as he caught the cut again. He checked his finger for fresh blood. 'You need to be careful in your choice, that's all I'm trying to say. It's true, McLennan's an option – but there are other men out there looking for wives too. He's not the only one.'

'Och, that's a fantasy and we both know it,' she said dismissively. 'I've no time to journey the isles looking for just the right one. You heard my father – he needs an engagement sooner, not later. This is the last winter he can manage with eleven to feed.'

'But you need to be sure, Mhairi. Marry in haste, repent at leisure—'

'Ha! That's rich, coming from you!' she scoffed, turning away, but he caught her by the elbow, his stare suddenly stern.

'And what does that mean?'

She didn't reply, but her meaning had been perfectly clear and they both knew it.

She saw the anger flash through his eyes. 'Be careful now, Mhairi,' he warned. 'I'm acting on your father's behalf and I'm simply telling you, I don't think he's right for you. He's a bad apple.'

'Is he?' she asked. 'Or is he just someone you can't bully? His father humiliated you, not once but twice. Alexander's clever and handsome and he's not afraid of you. That doesn't make him rotten.'

For a moment, all was silent, then he dropped her arm and turned away, scooping up his shirt and belongings from the bench. He walked out of the cottage without another word, heading for the burn. Mhairi stared through the open door, knowing she'd gone too far in her defence of Alexander. She'd implied things about Donald's marriage that she had no right to imply.

'He's a miserable beggar,' a voice said, intruding on her thoughts. McLennan senior was standing in the doorway in his nightshirt and thermals. 'Likes nothing better than an argument, that one. Y'll be well shot of him.'

'. . . Aye,' she murmured, turning quickly back to the pan and cracking the eggs, watching them sizzle on the heat. How much had he overheard?

Alexander was back, bathed and dressed, within ten minutes, but they were all sitting down to eat by the time they heard footsteps in the yard.

'What took you so long?' Hugh demanded, talking with his mouth full as Donald walked through.

For a moment, no one quite recognized him. Mhairi felt her jaw drop down and even Alexander dropped his knife as they took in the sight of him, beardless. It was so shocking, he might as well have been naked.

'Holy mother of Jesus, you'll have blocked up the burn shaving that lot off!' Hugh quipped.

Alexander laughed, but Mhairi could only stare. She had known this man her entire life – she must have seen him every single day – and yet it was as though she had never met him before. His face had been completely rebalanced – suddenly she saw the sharpness of his eyebrows, the cut of his jaw, the curve of his cheek. Only his eyes – those piercing, hard blue, fire-ringed eyes – remained unchanged, and for a moment, as they stared at one another, she had a sensation of time slowing, as if dragging through treacle . . .

'Someone's speechless!' Hugh chuckled, stabbing his fork into a tomato.

'I – I was just thinking Mary's going to dance a jig when she gets a look at you,' she managed to respond, getting to her feet and going over to get a better look at Donald's cut. 'Just let me have a quick look,' she said, seeing how he instinctively arched back as she reached up and examined it, for want of something to do.

He stood stiffly, as if it was gentleness that hurt him. Without the thicket of beard around it and with all the dried blood now gone, the cut didn't look as bad as she'd feared;

but he only tolerated her fussing for a moment before turning away from her probing fingers again.

'Enough. It's fine now,' he snapped, taking his seat at the table.

Mhairi sat again too, aware of Alexander's eyes on her. Then on Donald. Back on her again. She smiled at him but she was aware of a tension now humming in the small room, like a pot on simmer trying not to overflow.

After breakfast they all settled down to morning chores, the guests not needing to be asked. Donald went with Hugh McLennan to tether the haystacks; Alexander was taking the pony and trap to the whaling station to collect meat for the pigs. Mhairi was left to the house, and after cleaning the dishes, refilling the pails, boiling the sheets and pegging them to the line – her gaze constantly falling to the horizon – she set to scrubbing the congoleum floor with some carbolic soap found on the shelf.

The day was bright but an autumn chill frilled the breeze, the chickens chooking beyond the open door as she worked, solitary songbirds twittering mournful melodies as the summer skies emptied. Her ears strained for sounds of the men coming back. The old farmer had mentioned making the most of extra hands and catching the sheep before they left this evening. They had a flock of eighty-two Cross Cheviots that yielded a fine wool which she and her mother could doubtless card and spin into a grade-A yarn back home, but there was no spinning wheel here. Women's work was overlooked or outsourced on this all-male farm, and McLennan sold his wool wholesale at the Leverburgh roup.

An unfamiliar sound carried over the sound of her scrubbing

brush and she sat back on her heels to listen. It had a rumbling, guttural quality to it, like a hiccup of thunder tripping over itself, and she got up to see what it could be. She stepped outside and stood in the yard, chickens pecking around her ankles as she saw a shiny red high-sided vehicle shivering and rocking on wheels. It stopped with an abrupt wheeze and a moment later a man jumped out, carrying a satchel. There was no formal track between the road and the farm gate but he was halfway down the worn grass when he noticed Mhairi watching him. He stopped in surprise and the two of them stared at one another for a few moments before he tipped a hand to his cap and approached once more.

'Hallo there!' he called in a spry voice. 'Well now, you're not a McLennan, for they're none so pretty as you.' He stopped just before her, dark eyes pleated at the edges with deep laughter lines. 'I'm Jessie the Post.'

'Pleased to meet you, Jessie the Post,' she said shyly. 'My name's Mhairi MacKinnon. I'm visiting with a neighbour from St Kilda.'

'St Kilda, is it?' Jessie asked, pleasantly surprised. 'Then you must know Ian MacKinnon, their postmaster?'

She beamed. 'Aye. He's my father.'

'Get away,' he said, looking delighted. 'I don't envy him the number of sacks he has to sort through,' he tutted pityingly.

'No. It's a trouble.'

'And what's brought y' over the water?'

Mhairi's own smile faltered. 'Husband hunting' didn't sound very seemly. 'I'm assisting my neighbour with selling on some surplus produce.'

'Had a glut, did y'?'

A falling out with the factor more like, she thought to herself. 'Aye.'

'And they've got you working, have they?' He saw the scrubbing brush in her hand. 'Don't tell me y' scouring the floors?'

'I don't mind. It's better to stay busy. The devil finds work for idle hands.'

But it wasn't her hands that she needed to occupy. Alexander had taken root in her head and she couldn't shift him from her thoughts. After this morning's brief excitement before breakfast, she wanted . . . more. Their gazes had become entangled several times over the meal and her stomach had pitched in reply each time, but with Donald breathing down their necks and chores to be attended to, time together seemed pushed to the back burner. Was fetching whale meat for the pigs really more pressing than deciding whether to spend the rest of their lives together?

'Well, so your minister would have y' believe, anyway,' Jessie said with hitched eyebrows.

'Do you know Reverend Lyon?'

'By reputation only. An afeared man by all accounts.'

'He's devout, it's true. He takes the guarding of our souls seriously.'

'Well, you're certainly a more captive flock than ole McLennan's got – you can tell Hughie when y' see him that I just saw some of his sheep up by the bluffs. They've been scattered by the eagles again. Ted McCulloch's lost two lambs this week.'

'Oh.' She was taken aback. There had been no eagles back home and certainly nothing to worry the sheep. 'I'll pass that on. I know Hugh wants to round them up and get the shearing done while he's got us to help him.'

'How long are y' here for?'

'Heading back tonight, we think. We're waiting on the *Endurance*,' she shrugged.

Jessie made a thoughtful sound as he cast a look about the sky. 'Hmm, seems reasonable.'

He handed her the letter he was holding. 'Can y' also tell Hughie the *Heb* has left Glasgow and will be here in four days. That's the boat as brings us most supplies here,' he added for her benefit. 'Hugh's got a big order coming in, so he'll not have long to wait now. And as for young Xander' – he cleared his throat – 'I'm told the storm has passed in Stockinish.'

'The *Heb* has left Glasgow and will be here in four days. And the storm has passed in Stockinish,' she repeated.

'Aye,' he said, touching his cap. 'Well, I'll bid you a good day, Miss MacKinnon, and hope I see you back here again. You brighten this place up no end; from a distance back there, you looked like a poppy in a field.'

Mhairi smiled, taken aback by the compliment, as he made his way back over the worn grass towards the road where the motor vehicle sat. She watched as he started up the engine again, waving cheerily through the open window as the vehicle rolled down the hill, dipping in and out of sight around the bends until it was just a dot in the heathered hills. She had a feeling she had just made her first friend here.

Chapter Eight

'You need a dog!' Mhairi laughed, as the sheep shot straight past Alexander – again – and up onto a small bluff, staring back down at him triumphantly, its heavy coat quivering.

'Or a St Kildan,' Alexander retorted, his cheeks a port wine colour, as Donald strode up the slope yet again, barefooted and agile, taking a wide curve around the animal to come in above it, not even a puff out of breath. Alexander caught her with another look. He'd been throwing them at her all day, ever since he'd returned from his morning chores with the leather *crios-f heile*. She didn't know where he'd got it from, or from whom. 'Here,' he'd said, without warning putting the kilt band around her waist and then hitching up her skirt so that it caught on the lower looped strap. 'So you can walk the moors.'

Donald had looked like he might explode with fury but Alexander was treading a careful and wily path, getting close, closer, but never quite overstepping the line. He was finding opportunities to touch and be near her, she could tell, and she felt like a daisy opening in the sun. He made her feel beautiful and she felt giddy with anticipation. He would try to kiss her again, of that she was certain. Every look told her so. It was telling her as much now.

They had been herding for most of the afternoon, the sheep having been scattered far beyond their usual grazing pastures.

Something had spooked them, the McLennan men agreed, and she and Donald, with their surefootedness and peak fitness, had taken on the jobs of the island dogs, rounding them up. Mhairi could feel the ache in her bones now though and she stood with her hands on her thighs, watching as Donald harassed the sheep back down towards Alexander who, with one 'Ha!' and a swing of his arms, sent it running straight past him. She positioned herself too – arms and legs wide – scaring the creature straight into the enclosure, where Hugh was shearing them at pace.

She'd never seen sheep sheared with clippers before – back home, they'd moult, the fleece pulled painlessly from their coats – but the process was largely similar: the sheep wrested onto their backs, emerging minutes later several pounds lighter.

Positioned as they were some way up the slopes, she looked around at the open landscape. The grassy moors were dotted with boulders from higher rockfalls; below lay the machair, the belt of land comprised of sand and peat which ran to the sea and was surprisingly fertile. From this elevation she could see the growing plots were scattered about, according to wind and sun exposure. As back home, too, the harvest on the outer isles was always several months behind the mainland and strewn, golden parcels of heavy-headed barley seemed almost to laugh and shimmy in the sun as thick clouds scudded overhead, throwing down fat shadows. She could see the haystacks where Donald and Hugh had been toiling all morning, ready to be pitched tomorrow when a neighbour – several miles hence – came by with the loan of his hay wagon. The croft was just a distant speck from here – it was only the bedsheets on the line that caught the eye . . .

A curious sound behind her made her turn suddenly, and she noticed something small and bright tumbling down a small rocky outcrop. She ran over to find the animal was dead – broken neck, seemingly. She glanced up at the vast sky. Had it lost its footing?

'You've lost one here!' she called, straightening up just as a shadow fell across her face.

'Mhairi, look out!' someone yelled, but the warning was too late. Something suddenly shot at her – or rather, swooped – and she felt a sharpness drag against her skull.

She screamed, already falling to the ground. She curled into a ball on her side, clasping her head in her hands as she felt sharp slices of wind and the drumbeat of powerful wings right beside her, a staccato of angry, barking cries tearing through the sky.

Then silence. As quickly as it had come, it was gone again. She opened her eyes to find the lamb had been taken.

'Mhairi!' Hands were upon her shoulder, rolling her over. Alexander stared down at her. 'You're safe now. It's gone.'

'What . . . what happened?' she whispered as he reached a hand over and pulled her up to standing.

'Eagle. There's a mating pair up the rocks there.' He pointed to the granite bluffs above them. 'Father thinks one o' them may be injured and the other's having to do all the hunting. We must have disturbed them when we came up here. It didn't want y' stealing its dinner, I reckon.'

'Oh,' she murmured, noticing that he was still holding her arm, holding her so close she could feel his ribs expanding like bellows against her.

Donald bore up to them. 'Are you all right?' he panted.

Alexander stepped back, allowing an air gap between them.

'I'm fine. It just swiped at me,' she said, putting a hand to the top of her head to smooth her hair. Her fingers came back bloodied. '. . . Oh.'

'Let me see,' Donald said, roughly nodding her head down to take a closer look. 'Hmm. That's a bit more than a swipe,' he muttered. 'It'll need cleaning.'

'We've zinc ointment back at the croft. I'll take her,' Alexander said quickly.

Donald looked at him sharply. 'That won't be necessary. The sheep are in the pens now. You carry on shearing w' your father. I'll take her back.'

'But I've jobs down there anyway,' he argued. 'The cow will need her milking soon.'

'Mhairi can do that once she's cleaned up. You're needed here,' Donald argued back.

Several moments passed in silence as the men stared at one another. They both knew what was happening – Alexander was trying to get her alone and Donald, now firmly against him, was determined to deny them. It had become a battle of wills between the two men and almost nothing to do with Mhairi at all. She glanced at Alexander, seeing the frustration in his face as Donald led her by the elbow down the slope. The St Kildan had won this particular battle, but the minutes were ticking down. Their time together was running out.

'This is ridiculous, I'm perfectly well,' she huffed, even though her head was throbbing. The talon had gouged the very top of her scalp and she could feel the warm trickle of blood in her hair.

'I'm not taking any chances with infection setting in,' he muttered. 'We'll not miss the *Endurance*'s departure this evening for anything. We sail tonight or not at all.'

Mhairi didn't reply. Whatever fledgling emotions she felt for Alexander, whatever tacit acceptance she was coming to about the idea of making a life here with him, she wasn't ready for it to begin yet. They did need to get home. She needed time to ready herself properly for this new path, to ask things of her mother and to speak to her friends. She needed to tell Flora about the things he'd said, the way he'd looked at her . . . as if the telling of it was even better than the having of it.

Back at the farm, Donald cleaned the wound, pouring a jug of water over it as she tipped her head back, letting her hair flow down. The water ran red onto the ground and it took several refills before it was clear. He came back with the zinc found on the kitchen shelf and she looked up at him as he stood in front of her and applied it as lightly as he could; it stung badly and she gasped, but she could tell he was at least trying to be gentle.

She still couldn't adjust to his new face; it was a shock every time she looked at him. He looked ten years younger, and although he couldn't compete with Alexander's sculpted bones, he was nonetheless a far more handsome man than he had bothered to show before. She wondered what Mary would say when this upgraded version of her husband came home. Might the ice between them thaw?

'There. It's washed and sealed at least,' he muttered, stepping back and catching her staring. She smiled but he didn't smile back. 'Lorna can pick up the rest when we're back.'

She watched him head back inside, screwing the lid onto the pot of ointment. 'I'll milk the cow, then, shall I?' she said to his unfriendly back.

'Aye.'

'And you?'

'I'll finish on the haystacks before the light goes,' he said over his shoulder, not bothering to look back.

The cows were grazing in the small pasture behind the byre and the henhouse. Mhairi could tell from the way the brown one trotted over to her that she was ready for stripping. She took the three-legged stool and the pail from the byre and settled down by the beast but, unfamiliar with Mhairi, she kept moving about, desperate to be milked but resistant to the unfamiliar touch. Perhaps the McLennans only milked single-handed?

'Ach, come on then,' Mhairi said impatiently after several attempts, as the cow kicked the bucket for a fifth time and spilt what little milk she'd been able to come by. 'In with you! If y' can't stand out here, you'll have to go inside.'

Tugging the cow along by the length of rope around her neck, she brought her into the byre. It was dim and cool in there and she tethered her to the iron ring built into the stacked stone wall, then fastened the fetter strap that would keep her back legs from kicking out. She returned for the stool and pail, grabbing at some dock leaves as she passed.

'Come now, you're to let me strip you properly. It's for your own good,' she murmured, patting and rubbing the creature's neck a few times to settle her down. She passed over some of the dock leaves and, once she was sure the cow was relaxed, Mhairi settled down once more on the stool, with her cheek to her flank, and began to milk. She began to hum the tune her mother always sang when milking Rusty, their own cow. Now held in place and unable to walk away, the creature was able to sense her skill and dexterity, and she began to relax. The milk flowed, filling the bucket at a good rate.

'Good girl,' Mhairi said warmly a short while later when she was all done, patting her flank and moving the bucket quickly lest a leg should suddenly kick back, undoing her good work. She had two gallons there by her reckoning. The milk was pungent and thick, with a rich layer at the top that would make some good butter. She turned to carry it into the house . . .

Alexander smiled back at her from where he was leaning against the wall, his ankles crossed.

'Oh,' she gasped, with a small laugh. 'You surprised me . . . I never heard you come in. How long have you been standing there?'

'Long enough,' he replied. 'I was enjoying watching you. You're a fine milkmaid.'

Another test? 'Thank you. It's one of my chores back home. Our cow's called Rusty.'

'Don't tell me, she's black?' The smile gleamed in his eyes only, his face impassive, his body still as he watched her.

She laughed at his dry wit, but it quickly faded to silence as she realized this was the moment she'd been hoping for all day, the one they had both known was coming. Donald had tried to thwart them at every turn but love, like water, always finds a way through; that was what Flora said, anyway. She felt the butterflies take wing again in her stomach, as they always seemed to in his presence. From their first look yesterday morning, her nervous excitement around him had only grown, not dissipated, and she wasn't sure now whether to run to him or from him.

He made no move at all. 'Dotty likes you,' was all he said, as if reading her nerves.

'I like her.'

'She never stands as still for me. I think your hands must be gentler than mine.' He looked down at his hands query- ingly. It seemed to be an invitation to comment. She watched him for a moment, then she came closer, setting down the bucket, and studied them too. She turned them gently in her own, enjoying how it felt to have his skin against hers. His skin ran hot, the knuckles reddened, callouses on his fingers.

'I think you have fine hands,' she said finally.

He looked up, catching her gaze. 'You think so?'

'Aye,' she whispered.

He closed his fingers around hers then, clasping them and raising them to his mouth. Never breaking eye contact, he kissed them lightly, gently. Mhairi felt a rush gather inside her, as though her blood was fizzing. Her heart began to beat at triple time. Was this it, then? Was she falling in love? No wonder Flora had such a giddiness to her, she could understand it now. Wait till she told her . . .

He leant slowly towards her, his eyes on hers and sending every thought out of her head as he pressed his lips to her mouth. She looked back at him, eyeball to eyeball, knowing this was the moment she had been waiting for. Should she close her eyes? She closed them and felt the pressure increase on her lips.

After a few seconds of silent connection, he pulled back and Mhairi stared at him, feeling an instinct to laugh. Her first proper kiss! It hadn't felt quite as she had imagined it would; in fact, unlike last night's, it had felt a little awkward. More awkward without an audience, strangely.

'Must you really go tonight?' he asked in a low voice, his gaze still on her mouth as he raised a hand and pushed her hair back on one side, sweeping it off her shoulder. Before she could reply, he swooped down and kissed her in the curve of her neck. It caught her by surprise; she hadn't known a man might kiss her there, and the small gasp she gave seemed to talk to him on a new level.

'Aye,' she breathed, feeling him uncross his legs and stand taller.

'But it's not enough time together,' he murmured, pulling back and running his hands over the sides of her face this time, dazzling her with his dancing caresses. 'Is it fair on a man to have you dangled before him and snatched away again? You'll not be back till the spring, when we could be wed within weeks and having a bairn by then!'

She felt a blush stain her cheeks at his immodesty but his face was buried in her neck again in the next moment. Her eyes closed in bewilderment as she felt his tongue upon her skin, the graze of his . . . was that his teeth? Would he bite her?

'. . . My father needs to give his approval,' she said faintly as he kept up his repertoire, one moment stroking her cheek, the next tugging her hair, kissing her mouth, her neck . . . She felt like a mouse being toyed by a cat. And she wasn't sure she liked it.

'But he's not here.'

'Donald will report back to him.'

He pulled away then. 'Well if it's him I've to impress, then you'll never be back.' A note of bitterness rang through the words. 'He doesn't much like me.'

'Donald doesn't much like anyone. Not even his own wife.'

The comment pulled a wry smile from him. 'Aye, well, she made her choice, poor fool.' He kissed her lips again, spinning her round suddenly so that she was the one leaning against the wall now and he against her. 'And now you've to make yours. Is it me you want, Mhairi MacKinnon?'

She felt pinned up by his gaze, his body pressed against her and sending sensations swirling through her body that made it hard to think straight. She had a sense of the weight of him now, his strength. 'Aye,' she whispered.

He kissed her mouth again but his eyes bored into hers. 'How do I know you'll come back?'

'Because I say I will.'

'But how can I be sure?' he pressed.

This time she smiled. 'We'll write. Lots of letters.'

A shadow passed behind his eyes. '. . . I don't write so well. I read, but there's no call for writing here.'

She felt the moment constrict into a tight knot. 'I wouldn't mind any mistakes. There's no shame in it and it would be all the more precious to me.' This time she leant forward and kissed his lips; for a moment he didn't respond and she felt a quiver of alarm that she'd ruined things between them, humiliated him, but then his passion returned with even more vigour than before, his teeth grazing her lips, his tongue in her mouth.

She pushed him back a little by the shoulders but he was too strong to move.

'Give me something to remember you by,' he said urgently, his mouth falling instead to her neck again.

'Well,' she said uncertainly as she felt his hot breath against her skin. Flora had alluded many times to men's ardour, their raging passions, and she sensed it now; she was driving him crazy with desire, just as Flora always did to the men who chased her. This was what it was to be a seductress. Her hands were still pressed against his shoulders but achieving nothing as he nuzzled at her. 'I will.'

It would be so different this time, giving him a lock of her hair, compared to how it had been yesterday with the lonely old man. She went to move her arm up to free her hair and find a curl for him, but his hand caught her by the wrist.

'Here,' he said, bringing it towards his body, low down. She felt something hot and smooth as his hand closed tightly around hers, keeping it there as he began to move and thrust, his mouth still at her neck but no longer kissing her, his lips slack against her skin.

What . . . ?

'No!' she whispered, knowing and yet not knowing what was going on, instinctively understanding this was wrong. She tried to pull back but he was too strong, his body moving back and forth rhythmically, as unstoppable as a train upon tracks. 'Alexander, no!'

He didn't hear her. He had fallen inside of himself, sounds and utterances coming from him as he moved ever faster against her hand. She didn't understand what was happening and she did.

His breathing was ragged now in her ear. She could feel his body straining, his muscles shaking, his grip so tight around hers that her finger bones felt crushed. Her panic was rising with his excitement. She would be punished for this.

She felt him tense and he cried out her name suddenly, a deep guttural groan escaping him as his body bucked wildly, then suddenly slackened and eased. He slumped against her, seemingly exhausted, his breathing hard against the nub of her shoulder. She was aware of a warmth seeping over her hand but she didn't dare move. Shock had her in its grip as much as he did and they stood, still conjoined for several moments more.

Finally he pulled back, glancing at her as he rearranged his trousers. She didn't dare look down to see it. She could only stare at the back of the cow's head, the poor beast still tethered to the wall as their breathing settled back into regular patterns again. She couldn't comprehend what had just happened, her heart leaping like a startled hare.

'Well, I'll no' forget you now, that's for sure,' he mumbled with a smile. 'Who was it said hunger is the best appetizer?'

But his words sounded faint to her ear; she was a sinner

now. A Fallen Woman. Would the minister see it when she returned home? Would her father? Her mother? Flora?

'Mhairi!'

The shout, coming from outside, jolted her from her thoughts. Donald?

Alexander turned suddenly and picked up the pail, handing it to her. His eyes narrowed as he saw she was trembling. He watched her for a moment, as if only now seeing her sorrow. *'But if they cannot control themselves, they should marry, for it is better to marry than to burn with passion,'* he said in a low voice.

She looked at him. Corinthians 7, verse 9. It somehow made it worse that he knew his Bible. Could he see her crisis? Did he understand what his actions meant for her?

He was untying Dotty from her berth when Donald looked in a moment later. 'What's going on in here?' he asked with his customary scowl.

Alexander glanced back over his shoulder. 'What does it look like? Mhairi's just been doing the milking.'

Mhairi looked across at him sharply – was that a joke? – but Alexander wasn't looking her way for once, concentrating instead on releasing the fetter strap.

Donald's gaze fell to the full pail, though his eyes were narrowed with suspicion, as if he could feel the heat of their passion. '. . . Well, bring it through,' he said to her finally. 'We need to head off. The men are readying to leave.'

He stepped back outside and she hurried after him, not wanting to be alone with Alexander for another moment. He followed anyway and they walked together in an untidy, unhappy straggle.

'She should cover her hair,' Alexander said conversationally to Donald, hands in his pockets as they walked. 'The whalers won't like—'

'It's already arranged,' Donald snapped. 'Everyone's been warned she's coming. They'll not cross her path till she's on board.'

'Aye, very good,' Alexander muttered with an easy shrug. 'They're a superstitious bunch, that's all.'

Donald glanced at her as they all walked back towards the house. 'You're very quiet.' It sounded like an accusation.

'She was just saying she has a headache from the eagle attack earlier,' Alexander said for her.

'All the more reason to get you back and Lorna can take a look,' Donald said to her, as if it was she who had spoken and not Alexander.

Mhairi kept her gaze to the ground. It felt more than she was capable of to speak, converse, pretend that she was still the same person she'd been ten minutes ago.

'I'll get my things,' she said stiffly, setting down the pail by the door and going to fetch her tweed bundle. Hugh McLennan, puffing on his pipe, watched her with an expression that suggested he could read everything on her face.

The men were shaking hands when she returned. Her red plaid scarf was arranged over her hair, and she had mended the tear in her skirt last night, so she could stand before them with some last shred of dignity.

'We'll be in touch, then,' Donald was saying. 'Ian will write to you in due course.'

'Right enough,' Hugh McLennan nodded. 'But be sure to tell him we'd be pleased to welcome his fine young daughter to the family. She feels like one o' us already.'

The words felt pointed but still Mhairi kept her gaze down to the ground.

'I hope we'll be seeing y' anon, lass,' Hugh said to her, sensing her evasion.

She made no direct reply. 'Goodbye,' she said, turning to go without meeting Alexander's gaze.

Donald, frowning, led her over the worn grass. They had arrived by trap but, by seemingly silent mutual consent, it was agreed they would leave on foot.

'Mhairi!' Alexander called after her as they reached the gate. She flinched but her feet stopped all the same. Slowly she turned but she wouldn't – couldn't – meet his eyes. She could hear the smile in his words, though: 'I'll write.'

Chapter Nine

The sea was against them on the journey back, the ship ploughing through grey foaming furrows that pitched them forward in one instant and threw them back in the next. Mhairi went straight below deck and tethered herself in the bunk for the duration of the journey. She had said not a word on their walk to the whaling station and refused all food and water Donald brought down for her.

'You have to drink at least!' he frowned when he came to collect the tray, but she kept her back to him and pretended to sleep, staring out through the porthole where a whale wasn't yet lashed to the side. She remembered her companion on the outward passage – a bloody fate had awaited them both on Harris. She was free again now, but for how long? She was just as captured, just as tethered.

It took hours for the tremors to subside, her mind replaying what had happened in the byre over and over again. When had been the exact moment things had taken the wrong turn? What had she done to make Alexander think she had wanted that? Why hadn't he listened when she'd said no? Why hadn't he stopped? She'd been enjoying his affections, she wouldn't deny it. His kisses she'd welcomed, revelling in the feelings he brought out in her and feeling herself to be a woman now; but then it had changed in an instant, joy turning to horror, happiness to fear . . . She could still feel his hot breath on her neck, the juddering rhythms of his body that overtook him and overwhelmed her. He'd been at the mercy of his own lust, helpless and lost, no more than an animal. How could she marry someone like that?

And now, how could she not? She could still hear his voice: *But if they cannot control themselves, they should marry, for it is better to marry than to burn with passion.*

Donald knew there was something wrong. He had asked her several times as they'd walked along the road to the whaling station. 'Mhairi, what is it?' he'd said. 'Has something happened?' But how could she tell him of their sinful act? He would only crow that he had been right, Alexander McLennan was a bad apple – he'd seen it from the start! Not only that, if he was to tell her father what Alexander had made her do, the sky really would come falling down.

No. What they had done couldn't be undone, and redemption would come in only one form. She had to marry Alexander McLennan now, come what may.

The night was long and sleepless for all, Donald maintaining his silent vigil outside her door, unaware of her eye at the spyhole. She couldn't believe he would keep it up, but every time she looked out, he was there – limp as a rag doll, pale as the moon, as unlikely a defender against drunk marauders as she could imagine. And yet it was clear to her now how he had come by his injuries on the way out: he hadn't been drinking with the whalers – far from it – and in the spinning, plunging darkness, he didn't leave his post once. Only when the ship slipped into Village Bay, and the protective arm of Dun encircled them, did the sea finally settle and he was given respite. A lazy sun was rising and Mhairi watched, pale-faced from her bunk, as the familiar cliffs glided past the tiny window, the early birds diving for fish. Home again.

She was up on deck at the first rattle of the anchor chain, her shawl on her head as she saw the small crescent arc of cottages smiling against the rocks, chimneys puffing grey smoke, the men already heaving out the smack as the dogs barked on the shore. The whalers weren't intending to stay over but to make headway north, before conditions really shifted.

'Three nights away – and yet it feels longer,' Donald said, standing beside her, baggy-eyed too as they watched their neighbours row towards them in steady strokes. No mention had been made among the fishermen, it seemed, of the night's failed 'caper'. They moved about as if without seeing her, only Donald's bruised knuckles testifying to the truth of the whisky-induced chaos. Was this what men did, then? Was this their 'fun'?

Still Mhairi didn't reply to his comment and she felt him cast a quizzical gaze in response to her silence.

'Mhairi, what is it?' he asked again. 'Why are you angry with me? Tell me, before they get here.'

Tears sprang to her eyes and she looked away; she couldn't bring herself even to look at him, but he took her by the elbow and turned her to him.

'You want me to tell your father he's a good man, is that it? You really believe you'd have a good life with him?'

No.

'Aye,' she nodded firmly. 'I do.'

He stared back at her as if seeing the lie in her eyes. He looked so different from the man she had left with, bounding aboard with defiance and ambition – and bearded, of course.

Now he was returning clean-shaven, with cuts and bruises. He looked exhausted from his night spent sleeping upright and slamming into posts and rivets. She wanted to thank him and she didn't. He had protected her and he hadn't.

'Ahoy!' the men called up and a rope was thrown down, allowing the dinghy to position itself alongside. Mhairi could see her father with one of the oars. Quickly she disembarked, the two tweed bundles thrown over each shoulder, and sank onto the bench seat beside him with a small cry of relief. She nestled her head on his shoulder, feeling his chuckle as he draped an arm around her.

'It's good to have you back, lass,' he said, kissing her forehead. 'That was a bad parting. Your mother's not stopped fretting since y' left.'

'I'm fine. Donald was a keen guardian.'

Donald himself was following down the ladder in quick, sure strides, the tools strapped to his body with some short lengths of rope.

'God's truth!' her father spluttered at the sight of him as he turned and jumped into the boat. 'What happened to you, man? Your face is as bare as a baby's bottom!'

It wasn't quite true; Donald boasted an eleven o'clock shadow that belonged on no baby, but he grinned. 'Your daughter kept fussing I'd get gangrene from a cut.' He rolled his eyes, meeting hers only briefly as he took his seat in the boat. The tension between them lingered, his bafflement only sharpening her anger.

'Well, it looks like you did us proud, Donald,' Hamish said, eyeing the prized equipment.

'We've much here to soften the strife of winter,' Donald said, looking pleased. 'Though it was an inauspicious departure, we made the best of it.'

His gaze flickered towards her again, not quite landing.

'I'll be having words with Cap Ferg next time he thinks to drop his anchor here,' her father said ominously.

'He'll be in no rush,' Donald muttered. 'He knows he's burnt some bridges.'

'Hmm.' The sound came from her father's chest like a low growl.

'Till we see you anon!' Hamish called up to the whaler as he released the rope and pushed them away from the ship's hull with the oar.

'All's been well here?' Donald asked as they began to move.

'Aye, nae bother,' Hamish said, beginning to pull. 'Mary's been fine enough and we've been finishing repairing the ropes. David MacQueen thinks there's been another rock fall down Mullach Bi needs clearing.'

Donald made a sound of discontentment.

'I was sorry for you that things passed the way they did,' her father said to Donald. 'I hope it wasn't a burden t' you, having to chaperone in my absence? I'd no idea the skipper was in such a rush. We were just caught fussin' with that one sheep.'

'Ach, it was the drink talking. If it had been a fin or a sei that popped, I doubt he'd have cared half so much, but the sperms are that rare now . . . He kept saying at the very least we should have cut the head and baled the spermaceti.'

Hamish threw his head back and laughed. 'And how the devil were we to do that from a smack?'

'That's what I said to him,' Donald grumbled, looking to shore. Some of the women had come to the beach, but his wife appeared not to be one of them. Mhairi could see her mother, though, and Molly, Flora and Effie.

She saw Flora's black hair streaming in the wind – no modest red shawl on for her – and without knowing she was going to do it, Mhairi pulled her shawl back too, freeing her own hair. She tipped her face to the sky, feeling the breeze ripple over her, a sudden defiance settling in her bones. What good was modesty? It had been no better protector than Donald.

She looked back and found him watching her. Did he sense the shift in her? Could he see her fatal flaw now? Had he believed Alexander's lies in the byre or had he caught a trace of the scent of their sin, like ashes smouldering?

She narrowed her eyes at him, feeling the familiar red flash quickening her pulse. Wasn't this in fact his fault? Forcing her over there in the first place, introducing her to a man like that, making her trade parts of herself to strangers just so he could have his spades, leaving her with a temptation for which she hadn't been ready. 'Are you going to tell my father about the McLennans, then, Donald?' she asked in a challenging tone.

She saw him swallow, as if confused by her behaviour. 'I had been going to wait till we could speak privately.'

'But why should it be private? I want the whole village to know how happy I am!'

'. . . Y' mean y' liked the fellow?' her father asked with surprise.

'Father, he's wonderful! He's clever and hard-working and so fine-looking! If you could have grown him for me especially to your will, he couldn't be more suitable.'

'Is that right, Donald?' her father asked, pulling back on the oars. 'Do y' approve?'

Donald stared at her, sensing something of the tension humming beneath her too-bright words, the contrast with her earlier mood.

'How could he not?' Mhairi interjected bullishly. 'It was his introduction, after all. You've him to thank for all of it! He made such a good bargain with Farmer McLennan for himself and all of you – and an even better one for me and the son.'

There it was. A threat vibrated within the lie, for they both knew perfectly well his deal with McLennan had been scarce better than anything the factor had offered. Not only that, but he'd been short-changed too and then forced into an improper trade. Her position was clear: if he wanted to save face among his neighbours, he wouldn't voice any concerns that ran contrary to her wishes.

'He's fine, aye,' Donald muttered.

'Fine? Och well, high praise indeed,' Hamish chuckled as they neared the shore.

'What's his name, young McLennan?' her father asked.

'Alexander. And I went on his bicycle and they've a pony and trap. In the spring he says we'll go to the cattle sale in Stornoway and there's a fair at Scarista—'

'Hoa!' Hamish grinned. 'Don't run away w' him just yet! Sounds like y' did well bringing her back, Donald.'

Donald made a noncommittal sound as he caught her father's gaze, but nothing more was said and she had the impression that the men would talk again later, out of her earshot, in the way they often did.

But she had had first blood.

They rowed in silence for a few more minutes until the boat bumped against the shore. Hamish and Donald jumped out, pulling it aground. Donald held his hand out to help her down but she ignored it, hitching her skirt high – she was still wearing the kilt band – and jumping into the water with a splash. She felt his eyes questioning on her back at the snub as she waded towards her mother and friends, waiting with outstretched arms for her.

'You're returned!' her mother cried, clasping her close. Mhairi closed her eyes. She was returned, yes, but that didn't mean she was unchanged. She wished she could still be the girl who had left here, but a fault-line ran through her now.

She saw Flora catch sight of the kilt band, an amazed look on her face to see Mhairi's bare thighs. 'It's a *crios-f heile*,' she said proudly, showing them. 'For walking the moors without y' skirt restricting the legs. All the women wear them over there.'

'Well, don't let the minister see it!' Effie spluttered.

But there was no chance of the minister being around at a landing, for it was another superstition, considered to foretell loss of life or a disaster. They would have a few minutes' grace from his presence, at least.

'Cover y' legs now, Mhairi,' her mother said, tugging at her skirts.

Mhairi pulled down at the heavy fabric, seeing how they were all looking at her with slightly curious expressions. 'What?'

'You seem . . . different,' Flora said as they began to walk up the beach.

Mhairi felt her heart catch in her chest. Flora was an astute reader of character, plain-speaking and instinctive. It meant her observations were well regarded. 'I do? How?'

Flora shook her head. 'I can't quite say yet.'

Yet.

'What was it like over there?' Effie asked. 'Have they good cliffs?'

'Ha, you'd be sorely disappointed,' Mhairi tutted. 'And there's nowhere near the number of birds there as here.'

Effie looked appalled. 'So then what do they eat?'

'Chicken. Beef. Pork. Hogget. The food is better,' she conceded.

'I made a mutton stew, Ma, and the way they all fussed over it, you should have seen them.'

Her mother was watching her closely as if discerning a change too. 'And the young man? How's he?'

'He's clever and hard-working and fine-looking too!' she said excitedly, repeating what she'd said in the boat.

'Is he really fine-looking?' Molly asked, looking as amazed as she did thrilled.

'Aye.' Mhairi gave a little squeal and clapped her hands together with an excitement that encouraged Molly to do the same. Her mother laughed; Effie just scowled and rolled her eyes.

'But is he a good man?' her mother asked.

Mhairi swallowed, dropping her hands down. 'He's hard-working and so clever,' she repeated. 'He's as cunning as a fox, I'd say. No one would get the better of him.' She hoped her words were carrying back to Donald, walking just behind them. His own wife hadn't come to meet him on the beach. What did that say about him?

'I thought you were going to come back here desperate,' Flora laughed.

'I am! Who was it said hunger is the best appetizer?'

'Mhairi!' her mother gasped, shocked at the bawdy riposte.

She tossed her head in the air again, feeling the defiance rip through her. It made her feel strong. 'What, Mother? Am I not allowed to be excited to see again the man I'm to marry?'

'Well now, nothing has been decided yet,' her mother said quickly. 'Your father has to discuss things with Donald and take his view first.'

'Och, Donald thought he was a perfect match,' she said more loudly. 'He and Alexander's father were solid business partners.'

'Aye? Well, that's good to hear,' her mother said. 'The more we can extricate ourselves from the factor's grip, the better – or so your father says anyway.' She looped an arm through Mhairi's. 'I'm just glad you're back safe and sound, pet, but whatever may come to pass in the spring, we'll not think on it too much yet. You're here now and y' know I'm not one to look into the future. I was so frightened the sea would rise up and you'd ha' been stranded there.'

Mhairi clutched her mother's arm more tightly. 'Well, I'm home again, so don't fret. We've two seasons together before . . .' She felt a sudden constriction of her throat. 'We've two seasons.'

The girls waited till her parents were back in the cottage and her brothers and sisters had calmed down at her return before linking arms with her and walking up the Street, away from the rest of the village. Effie's dog, Poppit, trotted at their heels. They passed by Ma Peg and then Lorna's house, which sat right at the end, and clambered down the banks to the burn just beyond. It was getting too cold now to sit with their feet in the water, but the high banks provided a useful cover and they often escaped here, whether to avoid chores or simply swap some urgent news.

'Tell us truthfully, then,' Flora said, her eyes burning with intensity. 'Was he really fine?'

Mhairi nodded. Her courage was coming and going now like a flame in a draught. Away from her anger, away from Donald, it threatened to disappear altogether. She kept remembering moments in hot flashes – his grip, his breathing, his tremors – that made her both jump and freeze all at once.

'Tell us what happened when you first met,' Molly said,

146

sitting with her chin cradled in her cupped palm as she hugged her knees. 'The moment when you first set eyes on him.'

Mhairi closed her eyes, not wanting to remember it. None of it. '. . . I was pinning out the washing. There was a line up on the hill and when I turned back he was standing there, watching me.'

Molly gave a gasp that suggested she could envisage it perfectly. 'And he's handsome?'

She nodded.

'How? Describe him.'

Mhairi closed her eyes again, not wanting to conjure his face. Her heart felt shrivelled to a nut, her blood running cool. 'He has . . . it's his eyes, I think.'

'They're blue?'

Full of shadows. 'Aye, and well-shaped . . . But it's more that he seems to see more than most people, if that makes sense? He's . . . he's a bit like you, Flora – he's a watcher. He sees things others don't.'

'Am I a watcher?' Flora queried, and Mhairi knew her assumption was that she was the watched.

'And he's very still, he doesn't move unnecessarily.'

'Like a heron?' Effie queried.

'But when he does, he's . . . precise.'

'How old?'

'Twenty-six.'

'Is he big, tall, short, bow-legged, bog-eyed?' Effie asked, sounding slightly bored as she pulled on a stalk of yarrow and began sucking on it.

'Not tall, but not short. Taller than Donald.'

'And not bow-legged?'

'Not that I noticed.'

'What about his hands?' Flora asked. 'Mother always says you can tell a lot about a man from his hands.'

Mhairi stared into the water, remembering their grip, the callouses on the sides, swollen knuckles . . .

'Mhar?' Flora pressed.

'. . . His hands . . .' she whispered, but she couldn't say the words. It was his hands that she would see in her dreams now, his hands she would remember upon hers.

There grew a disappointed silence.

'Well, when you came off the boat, he sounded quite the prospect, I'll tell you,' Flora sighed, leaning back on her elbows. 'But you're not sounding so sweet on him now, Mhar. You're only back five minutes and already the passion's cooling?'

Mhairi felt a frisson of fear at Flora's waning interest. For as long as her story had echoes of her friend's, she could hope for an ally, a guide to navigate her through this shadowland. But if Flora was to give up on her . . . 'He said he'll write. He didn't want me to leave,' she said hurriedly. 'In fact, he was begging me to stay. He said if I stayed we could be wed within weeks and having a bairn by the spring.'

Flora's eyebrows shot up. 'He said that?'

Mhairi nodded.

There was a shocked silence, then Flora laughed. 'He sounds like a man desperate to get on w' the business of being married!' There was a note of innuendo in her laugh, her eyes dancing again. 'Well, I hope he wasn't handsy with you?'

'Handsy?'

Flora rolled her eyes. 'He didn't put his hands on you?'

Mhairi felt her cheeks burn. '. . . No,' she managed. It was no word of a lie; technically her hands had been on him.

'You're quite sure?' Flora asked, the laughter fading somewhat as she watched Mhairi with her keen eyes.

'F-Flora, how could anything ha' been possible? We had Donald McKinnon standing by us like a guard! Everywhere I turned he was there, scowling and tutting.'

'I thought you said he approved the match?' Effie queried.

'Aye, but you know Donald – can't bear to see anyone actually happy. He expects me to be as miserable in marriage as he is.'

Molly chuckled. 'It's true enough Mary was in a bonny mood the past few days,' Effie grinned. 'She even helped me with carding my wool.'

'She did not!' Flora said, incredulous.

'Aye, she did!'

Poppit, sitting by Effie's feet, lifted her head and a moment later, Lorna MacDonald appeared on the bank carrying some dressings that needed washing. She was momentarily startled to find them there, sitting in their huddle.

'What are you all doing hiding down here?' she asked suspiciously, recovering in an instant and stepping barefooted down the steep bank.

'Just catching up,' Flora sighed, leaning back on her elbows again.

'Gossiping, y'mean?' Lorna said in a knowing tone, bending down to soak the bandages in the running water. 'And I can guess about what.'

Mhairi bit her lip, feeling suddenly uncomfortable. Lorna was much closer in age to Alexander McLennan than she was. Should it not have been she who had had the introduction made with him? She talked – joked even – about herself as the isle's resident old maid, but she was a handsome woman, still very much in her prime. Was it right that Mhairi should be matched before her?

Then again, Lorna was also a woman of independence who

149

had come over from the mainland of her own free will. A registered nurse from Stornoway, she had chosen this life and all its relative privations of foodstuffs, creature comforts and men. Far from being a burden on anyone, she earnt her own keep as well as assisting the village in ways no one else could – as its resident medic, and assisting Mhairi's father too. She didn't seem to be in much rush to find a husband.

Mhairi could offer nothing so distinctive or special. She was trained only to survive this landscape and make a home within it, that was all. The fact that the McLennans were impressed she could write and speak English – skills they lacked – had come as an utter surprise to her. She had never been able to do more than anyone else before.

'What's Donald saying about him?' Flora asked her, knowing there was a high chance Lorna had already been privy to his thoughts. Lorna and Crabbit Mary were as close friends as the four girls were, always to be found in each other's company whenever chores allowed.

Lorna glanced up and gave her a knowing look as she scrubbed at a blood stain, for she was as discreet as she was accomplished. 'Nothing, right now. I suspect he wants to speak to your father first, Mhairi, which would be only right.' She was also a stickler for etiquette.

Flora gave a dramatic groan. 'Ugh! The only opinion that should count is Mhairi's, surely?'

Lorna picked up the next dressing and began scouring it too. The water ran off it, rust-coloured, and Mhairi was reminded of Donald washing her hair in the yard. '. . . Aye, but we all know that's not how the world works. We can't necessarily have someone just because we want them.'

The four girls swapped looks. It was the closest Lorna had ever come to betraying a personal opinion on the topic of love. Flora was convinced – and accordingly had convinced them all – that it was a failed romance and a broken heart that had driven Lorna over the water to their lonesome isle.

'Have you ever wanted someone but not been able to have them, then, Lorna?' Flora asked with her usual precociousness.

Lorna smiled, as if she knew their various theories about her. 'Life is complicated, and nowhere more so than here. What matters is kinship and fortitude.'

'But natural attraction to one another must carry weight too? If Mhairi would have been expected to marry a man she didn't want, just because of need, surely the fact that she did want him should carry added weight in the alliance's favour?'

Lorna chuckled. 'Are you asking for Mhairi or yourself, Flora?' She wrung out the dressings and straightened up, seeming to hear something. '. . . Oh, your father's calling for you, Eff,' was all she said as she made her way back up the bank. She reached the top and stopped, bringing her hand up to shield her eyes as she looked towards the water.

'What is it?' Effie asked, seeing her frown.

'Lorna?' Mhairi said after a moment, when she didn't immediately respond.

'. . . The dogs are barking on the beach,' Lorna said in a puzzled voice.

The dogs? Poppit was standing too, her ears erect, body stiff, though she remained silent.

Alexander McLennan and Lorna's opaque romantic past were immediately forgotten as the girls scrambled to their feet and rushed up the bank after her, their gazes set towards the shore.

The dogs barking on the beach meant only one thing. A ship was coming. But friend or foe? The whaling ship had been the only vessel scheduled to pass by them. It was the sixth day of September and winter would already be on the wing. On St Kilda the third season wasn't the time of heady fruitfulness enjoyed in the wider world's imagination, but a sharp intake of breath before the winter breach. Their treeless palette wasn't one of golds and red and russets, but steel greys and icy blues where the landscape didn't so much fade as wither. Autumn was but a wink on a cold face that would soon set and freeze. The seas were already rising, heavy and restless, and Hirta's drawbridge had been pulled up in readiness for the winter attacks.

But someone wasn't listening. They either didn't know or didn't care, but whichever one, it marked them out as a fool. Mhairi stood beside her friends, trembling that even here, even now, they could still be reached. Against the odds, the world wasn't quite done with them for this year. Not yet.

Chapter Ten

Like the scoop of a spoon, the yacht sat low in the water, her navy hull sluicing sharp angles and the billowing sails wrapping tightly against the masts as she curled around the headland. Cries of surprise were forced from the islanders, for the like was rarely seen here; crude, heavy and stocky whaling ships, fishing vessels and steamships were usually the only stock in trade in this bay. And while it was true that during the early summer months, rich tourists occasionally dropped anchor from neat cruise boats – with many portholes indicating luxurious berths below deck, gleaming bow rails and long passageways suggestive of leisurely walks and cocktails at sunset – this was a different beast entirely, built for speed and finesse.

How did the giant waves of the fearsome Atlantic swell not wash over the sides and swamp the yacht, pulling her down into the depths? How many men did it take to rig and man those two towering masts? None of the islanders could quite believe what their eyes were showing them.

The women stood at the doors to their cottages, the men now on the shore with the dogs and pulling back into the water the smack that they had only an hour before brought in.

Mhairi, Molly, Flora and Effie stood together on the Street

outside Lorna's house. Even Lorna, who affected a weariness of the riches from the Other Side, was transfixed. 'I believe they call it a J class. It's a racing yacht.'

'Perhaps it's your sweetheart McLennan chasing after you, Mhairi,' Effie teased.

'He owns a bicycle, not a boat,' she murmured, glancing at Flora.

Flora was standing rigid, silent for once, her gaze un-wavering on the yacht. There was something in her posture that suggested anticipation – the slight tip down of her chin, the shallowness of her breath, the way her arms – always animated, always engaged – hung limp by her sides. Mhairi felt a bubble of shocked laughter, of fear, rising up through her torso. Surely she didn't think . . . ?

Mhairi looked back at the water, seeing how a crew of men ran and crawled over the vessel like black ants, all working in perfect symphony and bringing the flying yacht to an elegant, gliding halt.

'*Shamrock . . . Shamrock V*,' Lorna said, just able to read the lettering along the hull.

The island men were rowing out now, as synchronized as the yachtsmen, albeit in cloth caps and tweeds. Silently, the four women began to walk along the Street, their eyes upon the action at all times. Poppit trotted along the stone wall beside them so as not to be deprived of a vantage point.

'Who is it, do we know?' Lorna asked Ma Peg and Mad Annie, who were sitting on their stools together, knitting socks. Even with their attention diverted, their hands never stopped their industry.

'An eejit,' Mad Annie said dismissively.

Outside Effie's cottage, her father, lame and in need of his stick, was smoking his pipe as he sat on the wall, watching, tutting, puffing. Effie stopped with him, Poppit sitting upright on the wall beside them both.

Mhairi and Flora stopped again outside the MacKinnons' cottage. 'Do y' know, Father?' Mhairi asked him. Like the others, he simply shook his head.

'None is scheduled to come by,' he muttered, looking concerned.

The two young women moved on to the MacQueens' cottage, but Flora didn't peel away to stand with her mother and brothers and sisters. Without saying a word, she stayed by Mhairi's side, wanting to come further down the Street, nearer to the jetty.

At the McKinnons' croft, Lorna went and stood with Mary; Donald was already away in the smack with the other men. 'Do we know who it is?' she asked, but Mary only shook her head, still holding the long-dead salted fulmar she had been retrieving from the cleit when the first cries had echoed around the glen.

The visitors were in the smack now and being rowed back to shore. There were two men that they could see, silhouetted from this distance, but their homburg hats picked them out from afar. Not whalers then. The village seemed to be holding its breath as the dinghy was brought along to the jetty – there would be no wading through the shallows for these guests – and they came ashore.

Mhairi looked at Flora again. She had never seen her friend so still. She looked poised, as if she was about to jump off Connachair and dive into the sea fathoms below.

Gradually, the guests were greeted as they began to make their way up the Street. The younger children burst free from their mothers' skirts and ran down, overtaken by curiosity to see the faces of those who had stepped from the yacht. The minister, Reverend Lyon, and his wife came out from the manse to issue a formal welcome, the quartet standing together for several minutes as they talked.

Mhairi felt her agitation grow, her fingers twitching against her skirt in a counterpoint to Flora, who grew ever more still. Who was it? Who was it?

Then a name carried. *Lipton! Lipton!*

It was as though a spell had been broken, the villagers breaking free from their positions on their doorsteps and hurrying down with cries of happiness. Even Mad Annie. Even Ma Peg.

Mhairi looked at Flora with a burst of relief. Sir Thomas Lipton had been the St Kildans' saviour almost twenty years earlier – before Mhairi, Molly, Flora and Effie were even born – when, after the savage winter of 1911 when the islanders had almost starved and frozen to death, the famous tea merchant had delivered a lifesaving cargo of flour, potatoes, meat, sugar and, of course, tea. To this day, Lipton's was the only tea brewed on the isle.

Flora seemed to sag; though outwardly her posture remained upright, Mhairi detected her deflation and she felt a stab of shame – yet more shame – that she should have felt pleasure that her friend's wild dreams were still just that, dreams. When had her benign envy of her beautiful friend – always there – overflowed into a jealousy that was so ugly and so alive? How could she want to see her dearest friend unhappy?

'Shall we meet him, then, Flossie?' Mhairi said, looping an arm through Flora's and reverting to the nickname, the sweetness, of her childhood. They had grown up on tales of the millionaire's benediction.

Flora nodded and together they walked as their neighbours and relatives bustled past in unbridled excitement. A gaggle had formed around the distinguished guests by the time they arrived at the spot outside Old Fin's cottage, and for several minutes they could see nothing but the tops of the visitors' hats and occasionally the sharp angle of a well-tailored shoulder.

Then there was a clearing and a white-moustachioed man with twinkling eyes emerged. He was stooped and certainly as aged, if not more so, than Ma Peg, the oldest inhabitant on the isle. But he had a vigour, a . . . what was that word she had heard one of the rich tourists say in the summer . . . ? A *vim* about him. Whatever his physical age, his spiritual one was twenty years younger.

'Ah, yes. Miss MacQueen, Miss MacQueen,' he said, stepping forward and taking Flora's hand. 'I was told I would recognize you on sight.' He pressed her hand lightly to his lips.

'Sir Thomas, sir . . .' Flora stammered, looking – for once – taken aback by the attention from this stranger.

'I have with me someone who wanted very much to see you.' He stepped aside and Mhairi gasped, along with the other women, as James Callaghan – whose face had been obscured by his hat till now – looked up at her friend.

Flora gave a cry of happiness, all her poise and arch manners forgotten as their eyes met. Her hands flew to her mouth. 'James! What are y' doing here?'

'I have something for you. Something you said you would like.' He reached into his pocket and brought out a small golden barrel.

Everyone's eyes widened at the foreign object.

'Is it . . . ?' she whispered, her hands reaching for it but not daring to touch. 'Is it . . . ?'

'Yes. I wanted you to have it before the winter comes in.' He held it out for her, a smile growing across his lips as he saw her shock. '. . . Take it.' Mhairi saw how their fingers brushed against one another, bright eyes flitting at the brief touch, and she remembered again her last touch with Alexander. It had had nothing of this chivalry, this honour, this bewitching glamour and romance. Rather it had been crude, hurried, rough, hidden. Everything opposite. Everything wrong.

'Y' came all this way, to bring me a lipstick?' Flora asked him, her voice whickering with disbelief.

'My dear, he all but hijacked us in his determination to bring it to you,' Sir Thomas smiled. '*Shamrock* had just been sailed up to me in Glasgow from Pendennis, that I might give her a run before she's sailed over to Newport for the next Americas Cup. Mr Callaghan, however, knowing of my long-held attachment to your people, convinced me a quick dilly over here would satisfy us both.'

Mhairi watched on, her heart feeling like it was on fire, as he showed Flora how to lift off the lid, revealing inside a vivid, waxy vermilion bullet.

Mhairi heard a reproving intake of breath and saw the minister looking on with a frown.

'It is a fashion from the mainland, Reverend,' James said quickly. 'But I appreciate it may not be suitable for island life. It is simply intended as an aide-memoire – something to remember me by,' he said, looking back again to Flora, wholly unabashed that their encounter was being observed by the entire village.

An aide-memoire? Mhairi looked on, feeling sick, sickened. He'd written a letter, hadn't he? How many men like him did he think came to St Kilda? How could he honestly fear that even Flora – beautiful though she was – could forget a man like him?

She saw the look that was held between her friend and the gentleman. The lipstick was already forgotten.

'Did y' bring us some more brew, Sir T?' Ma Peg asked, interrupting the private moment playing out before them all.

'Naturally, Ma Peg,' he smiled. 'Along with some other provisions I thought you might enjoy. I hope you don't mind the presumption?'

'Och, no, we'll indulge you!' Peg chuckled. 'Shall we boil the pot, then? Tea and a piece?' She beckoned him towards her cottage with a tilt of her head.

'That would be splendid, though I'm afraid we can dedicate no more than an hour ashore. My crew are on a strict timetable for the Atlantic crossing. My captain was quite displeased when I asked him to push back for a day to oblige our little outing.'

'How long did it take y' to cross?' Mhairi heard Old Fin ask as the elder villagers – those who had known Sir Thomas during his first intervention – made their way up the Street.

James Callaghan didn't make to follow after him. He and Flora seemed locked into a silent parallel universe, where everything and nothing was said. Mhairi felt tears gather at her eyes, a constriction at her chest and her own feet unwilling to move. She loved her friend but it was more than she could bear, Flora's wildest dreams coming true on the very heels of her own worst nightmare.

'Mr MacQueen, I wondered if we might talk together, you and I?' James asked Flora's father, making Flora's eyes dance again. Her mouth parted in silent exclamation as her father slowly nodded.

'I'll boil the pot too, then,' her mother said warily. 'Flora, y' can help me,' she added, drawing her daughter away by the elbow.

Mhairi watched as the four players departed the scene,

feeling herself tremble, her knees unlock, her heart wobbly in its frame.

'You know what that means?' Effie murmured, beside her suddenly like a small dark storm cloud.

Mhairi could only nod. There was only one thing it could mean.

They were at the beginning of an ending.

Chapter Eleven

The betrothal was celebrated without the groom. In spite of his wide smile and dancing eyes, James Callaghan, along with his accommodating friend Sir Thomas Lipton, was back on board the *Shamrock* forty-five minutes after Archie MacQueen agreed to give him his daughter's hand. Flora's cries of delight could be heard all the way down at Lorna's croft, where the old maid had tutted to herself as she pegged the washed dressings to the line.

Mhairi sat on her bed, trying to calm down. Her body felt unlike itself, as if too small suddenly – her spirit, or something else vast and uncontainable, struggling to get out. Her hands rubbed restlessly up and down her arms and thighs, the rough drugget leaving long red streaks upon her pale skin as she rocked on her sit-bones. She wanted to scream, but also to cry. She wanted to be happy but all she could feel was rage. She was both full and empty all at once.

Through the window, she could see the women fussing as they planned for the unexpected feast: salted hogget, their greatest culinary treat – but she had no appetite. She got up with a whimper and began to pace, wringing her hands. How could she pretend to be happy for her friend? How could she force a smile when her body wouldn't obey her, when it did things she didn't want it to do?

She stopped at the window and looked out. Flora's mother, Christina, was standing talking with Jayne Ferguson, Molly and Big Mary. Christina's eyes were shining and she was nodding vigorously as Big Mary clasped her hands, saying something in earnest. Was she lamenting losing her daughter? For no one entertained the notion, not even for a single moment, that a man like James Callaghan would be moving here. No, Hirta was being robbed of one of its most vital young women – but who could protest it? It was a match beyond anyone's wildest dreams. Well, anyone but Flora's. Possibly she had envisaged it many times. Possibly she had felt the tremors of her own destiny flickering at the very edges of her life here, knowing, even as she scrubbed the floor and milked the cow and plucked the fulmars, that one day she would be moving on to better, far better, than this.

She could see Flora walking along the shore with Effie, Poppit as always trotting on just ahead or just behind, her nose to the ground. The small pails they were carrying suggested they were out to scrape some crotal from the rocks, but they were making a poor show of pretending to work, their heads bent together in deep conversation, arms tightly linked. Mhairi knew Effie was no happier with the news of the engagement than she was, but she was able to rejoice. To be a friend.

She felt her bitterness rise sharply again, bile hitting the back of her throat. Where was the celebration for her match? She had been sent away among strangers for three nights, she had crossed the sea without the protection of her family, she had made the best of her lot and tried to do the right thing. And it had cost her. It had cost her more than they would ever know. And yet, no announcement or proclamation had been made as to her fate – the men needed to discuss it. She had been completely forgotten in the face of Flora's momentous news; a rich man had hijacked a racing yacht just to bring her a red lipstick to remember him by, just to ask her father for her hand . . . Who cared that Alexander McLennan had pigs and a bicycle, and would take Mhairi to the cattle market in Stornoway next spring?

'Mhairi, what are y' doing through there?' her mother called from the next room. 'You'll wear the floor down.'

Mhairi went through to where her mother was chopping vegetables.

'Has father spoken to Donald yet, Mother?' she asked quietly, her hands pulled into fists, hidden in the folds of her skirt.

'I don't believe so. He's busy in the post room at the minute.'

Mhairi was quiet for a moment. 'Is he not interested, then, in what is to become of me?'

'Become of y'?' Her mother gave a bemused smile, glancing up. 'Mhairi, what's got into you? You're only just returned. What's the rush?'

'The rush was me being sent away to strangers with a few hours' notice. Am I not within my rights to know what'll happen to me?'

'Within your rights?' Her mother's hands fell still, the knife inert against an open palm. 'Mhar, the only hurry was for catching the ships before the weather turned. Now you're back, the rest can wait. Besides, Flora's got her news now. It wouldn't be right to overshadow that. This isn't the right time for making big decisions.'

Mhairi couldn't suppress a bitter laugh. As if she, or anyone, could ever overshadow Flora! The crease in her mother's brow deepened as she read something of the storm in the back of her eyes. 'Or it could be a double celebration,' Mhairi said quietly, taking another calming breath, refusing to drop it. She felt the struggle to keep her voice level. 'I came back with a match first. I told you I want to marry him.'

'Aye. But as we said before, having not met the man, it's important Donald discusses it with him first.'

'But why should Donald have any say in the matter?'

'Because he's a man, pet—'

'So?' Mhairi cried. 'I'm the one who'd be married to him!'

'Mhairi, Mhairi,' her mother sighed. 'I don't understand what's got into you. You're not yourself at the moment. Why is it all so urgent?' Her expression changed. 'Something's not happened, has it?'

Mhairi stared at her, feeling herself shake. She knew she could never shape those words. 'Of course not.'

Her mother gripped the knife again and went back to the chopping. 'So then be patient. All will be settled soon enough,' she said, clearly feeling the discussion was over. 'In the meantime, you can earn your penny and pick up on turning those slops for the factor. I've been doing it the past few days and it's a thankless task. That stench rightly turns m' stomach—'

Mhairi felt her own stomach drop, and not just at the dismissal of the conversation. She'd completely forgotten about her extra arrangement with the factor.

'—and then after that, go to Big Mary's and see if she needs any help with deboning the meat. It's all well and good flying in on a racing yacht to ask for her hand, but we're on the back foot now with no notice.'

Mhairi stared at the stone floor. Not congoleum, like the McLennans'. There was no bicycle propped against the wall here, either, no hens pecking around outside, no Modern Mistress, no indoor tap. If she did marry Alexander, she'd be getting more than her own mother had ever had; and yet it would still be a life of poverty, of making do and mending. And she was having to beg for it. If she was ultimately granted these meagre pickings, she must consider herself lucky. This was her lot and all she deserved.

'Aye,' she muttered, walking out disconsolately, her mother's eyes on her back.

Little had changed in her brief absence. Her whole world might have collapsed but the whale guts were still black and slimy viscera, throwing out an odour that made her eyes water. Listlessly, she carried the pail down to the shore and carefully emptied it of water, before refilling it with a fresh load, her eyes all the while on her friends walking away from her further along the beach. She knew that if they saw her, they would call her over excitedly, run to her delightedly, that sooner or later Flora would be standing before her, radiant with love, and Mhairi would have to smile and feign a happiness that was opposite to all the emotions coursing through her. She would have to somehow escape herself in those few moments because none of this was Flora's fault, she knew that. She loved her friend and somewhere in her soul, she was happy for her. But why – why, for once – couldn't Mhairi have had the happy ending, the big love affair, the moment in the sun? Why should it have been that what had started with such promise had ended in horror?

She walked back to the factor's house and set the pail in the sunniest spot, stirring the slops with the metal fire poker the factor had left out for her specifically. They turned, spun and twisted in a loose heap, looking a very long way off from being something he could shave. Would he really feed these to his own mother?

A sudden distant laugh made her look up. Effie was twirling Flora, the two of them dancing girlishly on the sand,

Flora holding her skirt delicately with one hand as if prac-tising for the lady she was soon to become. Mhairi looked back down at the gelatinous black slops, and the chasm between their respective fates had never seemed so wide. It seemed to embody the difference in their coming stations. A hint of musk rose from the bucket, catching her unawares, and another memory assailed her. She fell to her knees, retching, but her stomach was empty and she could only bring up bile. She heaved and heaved until she thought she would be pulled inside out, eventually rolling onto her side, knees pulled up, her eyes streaming and exhausted. She lay in the grass, hidden behind the stone wall, as Flora laughed and danced on the beach; two old friends divided by a common fate.

The fire had been built on the large outdoor hearth reserved for boiling the wool and Mhairi watched as the flames leapt into the dark sky. The days were already short, light fading by late afternoon so that the double-wick oil lamps glowed warmly from the windows, the cows stripped of their day's milk, nodding and lowing softly in their byres. The villagers had feasted on the hoggets with some turnips and potatoes, the barrel of rum which had washed ashore following a storm and some distant wrecking ten months past had finally been drunk, and now Old Fin had brought out his accordion so that they might dance. In generations past, the islanders had regularly danced and played music, with fiddles and tin whis-tles and bagpipes, but successive ministers preaching the severe asceticism of Presbyterianism had driven it out till only the sheep danced in the wind.

Everyone knew of Old Fin's accordion. It sat in a corner of his cottage, propped on its very own stool to keep from the damp and dust. It was his most treasured possession, given by one of the navy men stationed on the isle during the Great War. Rarely was it played, lest he draw opprobrium from the minister; mostly he just polished it. Reverend Lyon tended to disapprove of displays of gaiety. His was a sterner god that required appeasement through ritual prayer, abstinence and chores, but even he was prepared to concede that one of his flock had been granted an exceptional grace which should be honoured. Mhairi, still burdened by a blackened soul, also suspected he was probably hoping to be remembered by the soon-to-be-influential Mrs Callaghan, for he wouldn't stay on Hirta forever, and it was no secret that the minister was always particularly fulsome and hearty in his welcomes to the richer visitors. Certainly the whaling men wouldn't recognize him as the same man who had greeted Sir Thomas earlier.

Mhairi watched her parents in the flickering firelight. They were dancing a reel with the Big Gillies, the MacQueens and Fergusons. Donald and Crabbit Mary were in a set with the reverend and Lorna and some of the older Gillies and MacQueen children; while Effie and Flora, and Molly Ferguson, were dancing with Mhairi's own elder brothers Angus and Fin, and Flora's brother David. Their bodies whirled, silhouetted, past the burning peats, creating a spectacle rarely seen so that even the little children had stopped their tagging games to watch as the couples moved largely in unison, sometimes skipping in circles, other times linking arms or twirling. It didn't matter that Old Fin knew only three jigs; Ma Peg and Mad Annie tapped their feet in time as they continued to knit, never stopping talking.

Mhairi remained where she was, sitting on the wall, quiet and still, pleading motion sickness from the crossing. Her mother had seemed almost relieved by the plea; it was true that she had come back pale and waxy from stirring the slops, her skin covered with a sheen of sweat. Lorna had been called down, but despite there being no fever, she had been allowed to pass the rest of the day resting on her bed.

She had spent it waiting for a sound of Donald McKinnon's voice or her father's to come to her ear. The excitement of the *Shamrock*'s landing and Flora's betrothal had skewered the village's routine but the men must and would speak – if not sooner, then later. She had only to wait and let everything come to pass. When Effie and Flora had looked in on their way past she had closed her eyes and feigned sleep, unable, still, to rouse herself to tell lies of happiness; but perhaps she had fallen asleep after all, for the sun had set and neither her father nor her neighbour had stepped into the house.

She seemed to become quieter, smaller, as the village's celebrations grew bigger and louder. For the most part she had been allowed to sit and watch, without too much interference from anyone. No one doubted her cover story – especially as Lorna would wander over every now and then to press a hand to her forehead – though she had caught Donald McKinnon staring at her several times with such a watchful expression, she wondered again whether he suspected the lies told in the byre. Was that why his verdict was suspended? She tried to catch him in her gaze, to stare him down and hold threats between her blinks, but he appeared unmoved, looking away again in the next moments.

She watched as the firelight cast an amber glow upon the laughing, smiling faces of her family, friends and neighbours; but if there was festivity and joy, it was also cut through with the bittersweetness of losing Hirta's fairest face, and she sensed an edginess to the celebrations. There had always been a cachet, a reflected glory, to being in Flora's orbit, and the villagers had become aware – as the number of visitors ever increased – that to count her as a friend or a sister, or even a daughter, conferred upon them a special status too. They would be diminished by her absence. For sure, they would scarcely notice the pair less of hands about the place, for Flora had never been skilful with the sheep nor diligent with the harvests, nor even enthusiastic about carding the wool; but they knew all the same it would be like the sun slipping behind a cloud when she boarded the boat to the mainland, and they would fall into a shadow.

Everyone cheered as Old Fin finished playing 'Bratach Bàna' with a flourish that seemed to have switched keys. It seemed to Mhairi the world had gone mad, as though it was spinning a little faster on its axis. Everyone was talking more loudly, laughing more; shrieks punctuated the night sky, but for once it wasn't the birds.

'Now "Mairi's Wedding"!' Mad Annie cried, her pipe dangling from her lower lip and no hint of irony – for once – lacing the words. Mhairi jerked her head up and stared at her. 'Mairi's Wedding' was a favourite Hebridean reel, but even if the name was only a coincidence, it provoked no remembrance among her neighbours of her excitement as she had disembarked this morning. The entire purpose of her trip was now completely forgotten. The spades had received a more rapturous welcome than she had. She looked over at her own parents, oblivious to the words spoken; they were sipping rum from their cups as if to quench their thirst between dances, a hot blush on both their cheeks from the unusual exertions and clearly not a thought in either of their heads for their own daughter's wedding.

Mhairi stared down at the finger's width of amber liqueur in her cup, then threw her head back and swallowed it down in one.

'Y'll dance this one at least, Mhairi?' she heard someone say, and she turned to see David MacQueen, Flora's brother, holding his hand out to her.

She stared at it in bewilderment for a moment, feeling the rum burn the inside of her throat, all the way down to her stomach. She shook her head quickly, looking up at him and seeing the easy friendship in his blue eyes. It was a pity they had never been able to look at one another with more heat – the way she had looked at John Gillies before he went over the top; the way he always looked at Molly Ferguson even though she had eighteen months on him.

Over his shoulder, a rapid movement caught her eye and she saw Crabbit Mary turn away from her husband with an angry look. Hamish had come over and was talking with their group, Lorna and the minister sipping on rum. Mhairi watched as Donald stared at his wife for a moment, but she had her gaze to the ground, refusing to meet his eye, their squabble played out in silence before everyone.

After a moment, Donald moved away, stepping out of the firelight and into the shadows. If he was in a sulk, he was forgotten in the next instant as Old Fin played a few introductory chords for the next dance. Mhairi remained unmoving but her neighbours took their places in several circles, David and Molly clasping hands with bright-eyed looks, Flora laughing delightedly and raising spirits further. Everyone began moving like rolling wheels, but Mhairi, forgotten too, sensed an opportunity. She cut a line towards Donald.

He was leaning on the wall, his legs outstretched and crossed at the ankles, head low as he stared into a full cup of rum. He glanced up as he saw her feet stop beside him.

'Oh. It's you,' he sighed, sounding displeased. 'What do you want?'

She squared her shoulders, trying to look imposing, but the wind was playing imp with her hair, tossing it around like the flames behind her. 'Why haven't you spoken to my father yet?'

He regarded her blankly, his denuded face still a shock. 'You know why.'

'But you have no right to stand in the way of what I want. It's my life.'

'And your father's good name. His honour. There's more to marriage than just having your head turned by a fair face.'

She made a scoffing sound, her arm swinging out towards Mary, dancing without him in the reel. 'Who are you to say what makes a happy marri—?'

'Stop right there,' he snapped, his blue eyes flashing and his finger pointed in warning. '. . . Remember yourself.'

She swallowed, knowing he was right, but the indignation still coursed in her veins. She had to make him see things her way, whatever it took.

'Well, I've decided on him, Donald, and that's all there is to it.' She stared at him levelly, determined not to look away – she would not be treated like a child – but his blue eyes seemed to pull her in and for a moment she remembered kissing him in front of the fire, her lips planted upon his in shocked paralysis.

She averted her gaze.

'And I've decided he's not good enough.'

So he had decided, then? 'My father needs me married quickly.'

'Not at any price. He'd not want that for you.'

'And if I'd not liked the look of him, but you thought he was worthy, what then? Would I still have to marry him? Would that price be worth paying?'

He didn't reply.

'You're just sore they beat you down in business,' she taunted, trying to provoke a rise.

'Aye, they're swindlers and cheats. And if your father was to learn of it, he'd agree he's no good.'

'Then who would be?'

He watched her, in no rush to reply. '. . . We'll know when we find him, I expect.'

'We? We! It's nothing to do with you!'

He took a sip of his rum and nodded, growing calmer in the face of her temper. 'No, you're right enough about that. It's your father's duty. He'll decide. But I'll do the right thing by him and give him my honest opinion about McLennan, you can be sure of that.'

'Then I'll tell him how he and his father ran circles around you.'

His jaw pulsed once. '. . . You do that.'

She felt her heart rate accelerate as the threat slithered to the ground. She could feel her solution, her only answer to her catastrophe, slipping away from her. 'I will. I'll do it, you know.'

'So be it, then.'

Another silence pulsed. '. . . And . . . and I'll say what you made me do . . . for the store owner.'

His eyes flashed and this time there was a long hesitation; she saw the shame on his face. '. . . A decision was made for the greater good, Mhairi. The tools we bought will benefit the entire village. You weren't harmed by what he asked.'

'But it was improper,' she hissed. 'You know it was.'

He didn't reply but he looked away, and she could tell he did know it.

'Just tell my father you approve of the match, that's all I'm asking,' she breathed, stepping closer, imploring now. 'Donald, please – I beg of you.'

Something in her tone seemed to startle him and as he regarded her, she saw that look come upon his face again, the one she'd seen in the store when he had followed the store-keeper's gaze – as if he'd never seen her before. Was it the same way she had looked at him as he'd come in for breakfast, freshly shaved, seeing him anew? It made her feel strange, these moments, as though the dynamic between them shape-shifted into something else: not her chaperone, not her father's representative, not her neighbour – but what?

He turned away, draining his cup of rum, wincing as it burnt his throat. 'You deserve better, Mhairi, and that's all I've to say on the matter. I'm sorry if you can't see it yet, but you'll thank me one day.'

She shook her head, feeling the tears shine in her eyes. He had no idea what his decision meant for her. Yet again, he was torpedoing her entire destiny. 'Then I'll tell everyone! I will – I swear I will.'

He nodded. 'You can do that. I'll not try to stop you.'

She felt a bolt of panic, the mortal sin like a weight in her heart. Nothing worked with him! Not threats, not beseeching, imploring, outright begging. The man who had first made this happen was now blocking it from happening.

'I hate you, Donald McKinnon!' she whispered, feeling the tears shine in her eyes as behind her, the village danced. 'I hate you!'

'I know you do—'

The words stopped her. Or rather, the tone of them did. He believed her. For the past twenty-four hours she had punished him without explanation, frozen him out, threatened and ridiculed him.

'—but I won't change my mind. I've told you plainly, Alexander McLennan is a bad apple. He's not good enough for you and that's the truth of it.'

'But why not? What makes him so bad? He and his father were hospitable, kind. He gave up his bed for me, gave me a ride on his bicycle. The farm is a good size, the croft is fair—'

'It's not about that.'

'What, then?'

He stared into the fire and her eyes travelled over his face, still not used to the sight of him beardless. Had it pleased Mary, she wondered, to be reminded of how handsome her husband was? She saw the bruises still on his face, earnt as he had guarded her door, sleeping upright on a ship in a storm.

She realized he was watching her watching him. She blinked back into focus.

'A man can tell another's . . . character,' he said quietly.

'What does that mean – character?'

He sighed, shaking his head in frustration. 'Mhairi, believe it or not, I am trying to act in your best interests. I need you to just accept there are certain things I can't explain to you—'

'Why not?'

'Because it would be improper.'

'Improper?' A scoffing sound escaped her.

'You're a child, Mhairi,' he hissed.

'I'm eighteen years old! My mother was married a year by now.'

'No, I know that. What I meant was, you're . . . you're . . . innocent.'

The word tore into her like a bullet. She felt the full weight of the sin bear down on her again, sounds and sensations pressing in her mind. She felt an overwhelming urge to laugh. To cry. '. . . And you're sure of that, are you?'

She watched the puzzlement climb into his eyes. '. . . What?'

She let her comment take root, a blood supply beginning to flow through the words. 'Tell my father you approve the match.'

He stood up, his body tense again. 'Mhairi, tell me what you meant by that.'

'Tell my father Alexander McLennan's a good man.'

He stared down at her. 'No. I'm not doing anything till you tell me what you meant.'

She stared back defiantly, feeling the power of her silence and knowing it would torment him to realize he had failed twice over – in business, but also in his self-appointed duty as chaperone.

'Did he . . . ?' His gaze roamed over her, looking for signs of physical harm. 'Did he . . . ?' He swallowed and she watched the minute agonies spasm across his face. He would have to tell her father he had let him – her – down. '. . . Did he touch you?'

'You mean, besides my leg?'

He withdrew as though she'd scalded him, his eyes boring into her and trying to read the horrors she had kept from him. She knew he had sensed something amiss – her silence in the cowshed, the way she'd turned her back on the crossing, her refusal to eat, her erratic mood in the smack. 'The byre . . .' he whispered, his eyes narrowing as instinct asserted itself.

She didn't stir. She wouldn't give him the satisfaction of knowing anything. Let him suffer in his ignorance.

'Something happened in there. I know it did. I knew it the second I walked in.'

Silence.

He grabbed her angrily by the arm. 'What did he do to you, Mhairi?'

She grew icy against his heat, letting him shake her, waiting for it to pass.

'Did he force himself upon you? Y' have to tell me!'

The words alone made her tremble and she knew he could feel it beneath his hands. She took a steadying breath. 'You have to tell my father he's a good match. That I couldn't do better. That he couldn't hope for more for me.'

'. . . But it's not true.' His voice was hoarse.

She let several moments beat in silence. 'It's all that can be done. It's what has to be done.' It was the closest she would give him to an agreement and she saw the way his breath caught at it. He dropped his hands from her and rubbed his face in them. He turned away. She knew he was seeing, finally, what his doggedness had cost her. He had taken her there, put her in that place, and he had failed her there. She saw it all in the slope of his shoulders, the weight of his head. 'Mhairi . . .'

He turned back to face her, but she had already gone.

Chapter Twelve

She was carding the wool, her mother beside her on the spinning wheel, when her father came through the next afternoon. Mhairi could tell from the soft light in his eyes that it had been done. She nodded and smiled and agreed as her father proudly recounted Donald's testimony – a fine man, fair in business, a good farmer, hard-working, God-fearing . . .

Donald had outdone himself, every word a lie, but she watched as her father comforted her mother, reassuring her that their daughter was going to a better life – one where she would be provided for; where if she wanted an egg she had only to walk into the yard to get it. She would travel by pony and trap, cook on a Modern Mistress, benefit from a running tap. They had sheep – more sheep! – but also chickens and pigs and two cows. By the time he'd finished, Mhairi had almost been convinced herself that she was going on to somewhere better. Marrying a good man.

The news spread quickly, as it always did in the village. Flora was the first to drop her duties and tear down the Street to hug her hard – Effie was less effusive, for it meant she was another friend down – and Mhairi found she was able to laugh and smile on cue. She was able to pass herself off as another excited young bride-to-be when Old Fin hummed 'Mairi's Wedding' as she walked down the Street. No matter her personal dismay at the situation in which she now found herself, a patch was better than a hole.

It was the second betrothal in twenty-four hours to be celebrated without the groom even being on the isle, but unlike James Callaghan, who had left with assurances, she was nervous. Until Alexander knew their union was happening, she couldn't shift a nibbling fear that he might yet find and choose someone else. She didn't trust him, and for as long as there was no formal agreement between the two families, absolution for their sin might still hang in the balance.

Mhairi convinced her father to write to Hugh McLennan that very afternoon, even though no further landings were scheduled and delivery of the letter was impossible. She was on edge, irritable and distant with everyone, but in the end she only had to wait nine days. The first of the autumn tempests blew in, raising force eight gales upon the steely sea and sending a Norwegian ship into the harbour in urgent need of shelter. The sailors didn't disembark immediately – even in the bay, the swell was fierce – and they dropped anchor for only seven hours, but at the first sign of the storm dying down, the islanders sent out the smack, Donald McKinnon himself handing over the paltry mail bag.

After the excitement of the double engagements, life soon settled back into its normal rhythm. With the days shortening fast, the familiar clack of the looms could be heard up and down the Street every evening as the tweeds were woven. Very often the men and women worked till after midnight when the moon cradled high above them, keeping watch. During the days, the potatoes were dug up, the barley scythed (what there was of it) and the wools dyed. The peats that had been cut and stored to air dry in the upper cleits, on the Oiseval and Ruival slopes, were brought down to the village and stacked in the cleits behind the cottages. Everyone lauded the new tools that made the chores easier and quicker, and their brief autumn window seemed to glow golden for once.

Mhairi continued to turn the slops every day, though it seemed a pointless task to her. Then again, many things now seemed pointless; very little made her smile or rejoice. She had managed to avoid being alone with Donald since the engagement had been agreed, though she often caught him watching her when the villagers convened, or looking her way if she was passing on the Street. She could see he was suffering, imagining but not quite knowing what had happened to her in the byre; sometimes she saw his gaze fall to her stomach and she knew he assumed something even worse than what had actually happened. He was waiting for her belly to swell, fearing that a baby would reveal what his lies had been intended to conceal.

Good. Let him suffer. For all his tortured imaginings, she was the one who had lived it. She was the one condemned to live with the consequences. Her mother was worrying already about the dowry. It was custom, over the water, for the bride's parents to give a cow in calf on the marriage day, but that seemed logistically difficult in this instance. The custom here was to present a rope, but equally that seemed unnecessary for a farm set upon rolling moors. Several times Mhairi had overheard her parents trying to think of alternatives – a short cut of a specially woven tweed? A sack of salted puffins?

But she knew it didn't matter. She knew exactly what Alexander McLennan wanted from her – and come the spring, he would get it.

Chapter Thirteen

The isle was steadily closing up for winter. The potatoes had been lifted from the ground, the peats carried down from the higher slopes, the smack weighted down with rocks to keep it from being blown back into the water as the winds began to tear and chase through the glen, gannets and fulmars darting like white arrows through cloud-tossed skies. The sea shifted restlessly all the time now, relentlessly churning brown and grey, and not a ship had been seen passing by for weeks. The children wore their boots to the schoolhouse, each taking it in turns to bring a peat for the day's fire. The animals had been herded to the village side of the dyke and now grazed the crofting pastures that sloped down to the shore.

Everything was closing in on itself, like a flower folding in its petals waiting for the sun, life here becoming concentrated, distilled to its very essence. The sun only cast a light from eight in the morning till mid-afternoon and the pervasive darkness increasingly confined everyone to their homes. Some cottages were quieter than others. Lorna's, at the far end, sat in solitary silence; occasionally, cackles of laughter would erupt from Mad Annie's as she played cards with Ma Peg and Old Fin, in spite of the minister's frequent exhortations that the devil was 'in every pack'. But the MacKinnons', with eleven to accommodate, seemed to bulge at the walls, as parents and children occupied every stool, bench and bed, all clustering like moths around the oil lamps. Like the MacQueens' and Big Gillies', it reverberated to a riot of shouts, cries and a continual buzz of chatter.

Mhairi looked up from under her lashes at her friends gathered on the bales. They were sitting in Effie's byre, the two cows already in for the night and sitting down, their heads nodding towards the ground as the young women knitted in their private refuge. The lipstick lay on a cotton handkerchief between them, there for anyone to pick up and handle should the urge take them.

Effie was sitting cross-legged in her trews, fiddling with her needles like they were fighting back. Molly had her keen eyes cast dutifully upon her neat rows of knitting, her loose auburn curls tumbling over her shoulders, a shawl tucked round her. Flora had her ball of yarn and a half-turned sock in her lap but was making no pretence of knitting this evening. She had brought James's letter with her and was rereading it by the soft light of the lamp that hung from a nail.

'He has such an elegant hand,' she sighed, holding up the sheet. 'Don't y' think? See his f's, and his j's?'

Effie rolled her eyes. All the recent talk about engagements and love affairs was beginning to get her down.

Flora caught the movement and her arm dropped. 'We shall have to find a husband for you too, you do know that, Eff?'

Her friend gave a scornful laugh. 'I'll never marry. My father needs me.'

'He needs a son-in-law,' Flora remarked.

It was the wrong thing to have said. Effie stabbed her lightly in the thigh with a needle. 'Don't! Don't even joke about it.'

'I'm not joking.'

'This matrimony business is a fool's errand, if you ask me. I'm already mistress of my own house. I'll not have some man telling me how to live and what I can and can't do.' She was quiet for a moment. 'Not to mention, there's none here as would have me, or me them.'

'Oh, I don't know,' Flora murmured. 'I catch Angus with his eyes on you enough.'

'He calls me a strip of wind!'

Flora laughed. 'And Fin looks at you, too . . . You should take Fin. He's much nicer.'

Mhairi arched an eyebrow, somewhat displeased that one of her brothers should be insulted. On the other hand, she couldn't help but agree.

'Maybe they could battle it out for your hand at the old trials?' Molly smiled impishly. 'May the best man win.'

Effie relied on a retching motion to make her point.

'How about you and David?' Mhairi asked quietly. She'd said barely a word all evening; she rarely did these days – conversation didn't delight her as it once had, she felt wrapped in a cloud, muffled from her friends. 'Has he said anything more about getting wed? He was talking about it before me and Flora even knew our fates.'

Molly shook her head, a faint blush colouring her cheeks. 'No. He says it's not the right time now.'

'But why not?'

Molly looked evasive. 'He thinks Norman will block it.'

'Why would he do that?' Mhairi frowned.

Molly's hands fell still. 'You know what my brother's like, always so . . . ambitious. Now Flora's marrying up, he thinks I'll meet someone like that too when the spring comes.' She tutted. 'I said to him I don't care about marrying a rich man, but he won't be told.'

Flora, to her credit, looked aghast that her happiness had torpedoed Molly and her own brother's plans. 'Oh Moll, why didn't y' say anything?' She reached over to touch her hand.

Molly squeezed it affectionately. 'Because it's all a nonsense. Norman gets carried away, you know how he is, but there's not some rich man going to come here and steal m' heart!' she scoffed. 'I'm for David and he's for me – we can afford to wait till he sees sense.'

'But why don't you just tell him?' Effie asked hotly.

'Say no to Norman?' Molly raised an eyebrow and gave a bemused smile. 'It would only make him dig in his heels even deeper. No, we'll just bide our time. What's six months when we'll have our whole lives together?'

'You'd think he'd be pleased that you marrying my brother would mean one less of us leaving the isle,' Flora tutted.

'Well, that's true. We canna all leave the isle in search of husbands or there'll be no lasses left!'

'Me!' Effie piped up.

'You don't count,' Flora said, prodding her with a stock-inged foot as Molly's laugh slid into a coughing fit so that she had to pat her chest a few times.

Mhairi watched, feeling dislocated from their jokes. Though they were all sitting here together, as they so often did on the dark nights – though they had grown up on this two-and-a-half-mile stretch of rock, in this shared space – their lives were not all the same, and now their futures were diverging. Effie wanted nothing to change at all, for life to continue like this as it always had, but the dies were already cast: Flora's dream was coming true, Molly's was on hold and Mhairi was walking into her own nightmare. Only last night she had awoken with a gasp, her mind still caught between worlds, stuck in that moment of the heinous sin – but to her horror it hadn't been Alexander's groan in her ear, but Donald's. Not Alexander's hand over hers, but Donald's. In her tormented mind, their different roles in the sin had become one, the three of them inextricably connected.

If he cannot control himself, let him marry. It is better to marry than burn. It was a mantra she repeated every time she felt her courage fail. Every time she thought she couldn't go through with it and marry a man who was none of the things promised to her father, she intoned those words and reminded herself it was her only hope of absolution.

'What's going on with Mary and Donald, do you think?' Flora asked, eyes narrowing thoughtfully.

Mhairi stiffened, as though it could be seen that Donald lived in her thoughts. 'Hmm?' she frowned absently, picking up her knitting again.

'He's grown thinner.'

'I'd not noticed.'

'He looks so fine without his beard!' Molly chimed in.

A devilish look scampered across Flora's face. 'Maybe Mary's "working" him too hard. You know well how much she wants that baby.'

The others laughed at the bawdy joke but Mhairi found she couldn't.

Beside her, Effie leant in, her breath caught as if she was thinking through her words before speaking them.

'What is it, Eff?' she asked.

'. . . He was fair reckless on the ropes the other day. Usually he's the one telling me to beware and spoiling all my fun, but Hamish had to stop him from grabbing a bird that would have sent him over the top, for sure.'

Mhairi frowned. They all did. Cragging was no joke, and

though the men were supremely confident in their abilities, no one took the task lightly. Accidents happened.

'Has Mary said anything?' Molly asked with a light frown.

Flora shrugged. 'Not to me, but Ma Peg thinks he's got the black dog.'

Mhairi listened in, feeling as if her ears were burning. It was true Donald had cut a forlorn figure recently, walking with his head down, but she had been so fixed on avoiding him, so determined to make him suffer; punishing him had made her feel better, it had given her somewhere to direct her rage . . .

'But why should he be down in the mouth?' Molly asked. 'He's the village saviour. We've not heard the end of it from Norman now there's a peat spade. It's saved his back threefold already.' She looked directly across at Mhairi. 'Nothing happened when you went over the other side the other week, did it?'

Mhairi couldn't blink as all eyes swivelled towards her. '. . . Like what?'

'I don't know – he didn't hurt himself? He wasn't sick?'

Mhairi shook her head dumbly, not wanting to lie to her friends. 'Not that I saw.'

Did they notice she was ashen? Wooden-limbed? She tried to keep knitting through her friends' idle conjectures but she'd dropped several stitches and her fingers fumbled with the fine yarn.

Effie looked back at Flora. 'Perhaps Lorna should have a look at him. There's no cause for losing weight in October.'

'Or maybe we should leave well enough alone,' Molly said cautiously. 'It might be something private.'

They all knew what that meant and a respectful silence descended, lasting all of a few moments before one of the cows passed wind in a long and leisurely fashion.

'Och!' Flora cried, sitting the closest to the animal's rump and fanning the air wildly. Everyone laughed – everyone but Mhairi, and she sat still as the conversation moved on to Euan Gillies's fledgling beard.

'I should get on,' she said, rising suddenly just as Flora was getting into full flow.

'But why so early?' Molly asked, disappointed. 'I've another sock to finish.'

'Mam's asked me to fetch some more oil from the top. We're out down here.'

'The top? Well then, shall I come with you?' Effie asked, going to set aside her knitting. She never needed to be asked twice. 'There's a testy wind tonight.'

'I'll be fine. It'll be good to clear my head. I hate being in so much this time of year. It makes me feel woolly.'

'Aye,' Effie agreed sadly. She was in her element outdoors, scrabbling over the rocks, tearing over the grass like she was still a little girl . . .

'I'll see you tomorrow.'

'Tomorrow,' they replied, socks on their laps and lapsing back into bubbly chatter.

Mhairi shut the door behind her and stood outside for a moment, watching the moon sketch a wobbly path over the water. It looked how she felt. Was this how it would be for the next six months? Would her heart always beat this hard, would her stomach feel so tight as she waited for the day to come when she must leave here? Was she doomed to become a stranger around her friends? She wanted to tell them what had happened, to reveal the horror in the hope that sharing it made it lose its power, but it was an impossible wish.

She walked past the cottage windows, glimpsing golden vignettes of the scenes within: Effie's father weaving a tweed on his loom in the firelight; Old Fin puffing on his pipe in his rocking chair and reading the newspaper that Sir Thomas had brought over on the *Shamrock* those several weeks back, which was being gradually passed around the villagers; Big Mary patching a shirt; and her own mother standing at the stove, Wee Al holding onto her skirt, while her father was working at the table, his head bowed, a pencil in his hand . . . She stood there for a few moments, watching her own family as they quietly, unremarkably went about their evening.

She passed the factor's house, which sat dark and lonely, a white ghost on the isle, the slops in their bucket stinking through the night. Lights glowed in the manse – the minister often worked late into the night – but the featherstore stood like a shadow too.

She was at the periphery of the village now and the gradient sharpened as she headed up the steep slope on the western flank of Oiseval. The mountain had two distinct personalities – the village side rose up as a smooth, heathered moor but the eastern face was dark granite cliffs stippled with tors and gorges, dropping vertically in deep pleats from an unannounced ridge. The slightest sea mist could, and in the past, had, betrayed even well-accustomed villagers and seen them dashed upon the rocks.

It was too cold for any such mist tonight, the night sky dazzlingly clear and studded with diamond galaxies. The cleit where her family stored their barrelled oil sat just down from the ridge. During the fulmar harvest – usually a ten-day hunt in which the entire village was involved – the men would scale the cliffs, catching the birds by their lower wings to prevent them from defensively disgorging the oil in their stomachs, before skilfully breaking their necks with a single twist. They would strap the dead birds to the rope harnesses, dozens at a time, bringing them up to the women on the top only when they had so many as were cumbersome for climbing. The women would pluck the birds where they sat on the hilltop, so that white feathers snowed upon the grass and the water and danced on the wind in dizzying torrents. Once they were plucked, the oil would be drained from the birds' stomachs and the carcasses taken lower down the slopes to be stored in salted barrels, ready for feeding the villagers through the winter, when most of the pelagic birds were back in the open sea. It would be the men's job, any day now, to bring down the barrels to the oil cleits nearer the crofts, but the MacKinnons often ran short early on account of her father's long hours working into the night, in the post office.

The wind was squally, making a nuisance of itself as it played with her hair. She walked steadily uphill, without Effie's speed or Flora's grace or Molly's goodwill. She felt trudging and heavy in her body, moving through the motions with a deadened spirit. Deadened feet, too, for her winter boots still felt unfamiliar and unwieldy, the leather sole smudging out the myriad tiny undulations underfoot. She slowed down as she approached the ridge. Even on a clear night – a clear day – it didn't do to be overly confident. The cleits were scattered in a seemingly haphazard order that made sense to none but the islanders. Their storage system had been in use throughout the isle for centuries and the knowledge of what was where, and whose, was passed down from family to family.

She stooped low and ducked in, grateful to get out of the wind. It was pitch dark inside and the briny, acrid smell hit her; she had to breathe for a moment to let her eyes and stomach adjust. She squatted on her haunches, feeling for the tap on the nearest barrel and filling the glass bottle – washed ashore from a wreck years ago – that was kept for this purpose.

She stowed it in her sack bag with her knitting and stepped out into the night again. The wind slapped her, as if in punishment for hiding. She immediately turned to head back to the village, when something – a dark shape further along – caught in the corner of her eye.

'Hello?' she asked, but the wind swallowed the word whole. She walked closer. Someone was standing there, looking out to sea, their clothes flapping like flags. 'Hello?'

This time the figure turned.

'Oh, it's you,' she said in surprise.

'Aye,' Donald replied, startling too at the sight of her. He had supposed himself quite alone. 'What're you doing up here at this hour?'

'I was about to ask you the same thing.'

'I asked first,' he said stubbornly.

She fished out the bottle of oil.

'Oh,' he nodded.

'And you?'

'. . . Just getting some air,' he said after a moment.

'Quite a lot of air,' she gasped as another squall harried them.

'Aye,' he agreed with the ghost of a smile.

She glanced at him, seeing how his eyes remained fixed on the horizon, as if escape lay that way. It vaguely occurred to her that she didn't like the thought of him 'escaping'.

'How long have you been up here?'

'A while.'

'Mary sick of the sight of y', is she?' she teased, but his sharp glance told her it was no laughing matter. She swallowed. '. . . How did she take the lack of beard?'

'She's not said. I'm not sure she's even noticed.'

She gave a laugh, as if he was joking, but another glance silenced her again. 'You're not serious?'

He shrugged. 'I'm not not serious.'

'But –' she spluttered. 'You look so well without it. Everyone says so.'

'Who says so?'

'Just now the girls were sayin' . . . Effie, Flora, Molly—'

'You?'

She hesitated as his eyes tangled with hers; it always seemed to trip her up the moment when that happened, she noticed. 'I'm taking full responsibility for it, actually,' she joked.

'I'm your pet now, am I?' He looked ever so faintly bemused.

'Perhaps. Effie has Poppit and I can have you.'

'You can have me,' he echoed; but the words were ambiguous, not quite a question, almost a statement. She watched as he stared back out to sea, standing in his shirtsleeves, hands stuffed in his trouser pockets and oblivious to the cold. For all the half smiles and attempts at levity, something heavy lay within him.

'Why are y' really up here, Donald?'

He didn't reply for a long time.

'Because I want to kill him,' he said eventually.

She didn't need to ask who; he was staring towards Harris. She knew there was no chance of glimpsing any of the outer isles at night, when it was barely possible on the brightest of days, but she wondered for a moment whether the lights might carry – the McLennans' lights? But of course the farmhouse was nestled in the dip behind the hillock.

They looked across the water together and it made her feel better to know Alexander was snatched from her sight here.

Or rather, she was snatched from his. She was still free for as long as she was here. She wasn't trapped yet.

'He's not worth killing,' she mumbled.

'Yes, he is. If he's hurt you . . . I keep asking myself how it can be that the one thing I tried to stop is the one thing I made happen,' he said in a low voice, so low it was almost a rumble.

She watched him, seeing his disbelief, his pain.

He looked across at her. 'Can you forgive me, Mhairi? I canna sleep thinking on what I've done to you.'

'You didn't do it, Donald,' she said quietly, regretting now her severity towards him. She had needed someone to blame, yes, but it was Alexander, and Alexander alone, who had forced her hands onto him in the byre.

'I didn't . . .' He hesitated, looking conflicted. 'And I did. In my mind I did.'

'No, you did your best to protect me. It wasn't your fault.'

'You don't understand!' he said, as if suddenly angry. 'I was jealous of him! I was covetous . . .' His voice broke. 'He put his hands on you and I didn't – but I wanted to, don't you see that? I wanted to.'

He looked back at her but Mhairi couldn't reply as she saw the storm in his eyes. What was happening to them? He wanted to but didn't? She hated him but didn't. She blamed him but didn't. He walked in her dreams, he was everywhere she looked; and now he was right here, saying things that only confused her more. She stared at his new face, at the full lips that her own had touched, and she realized she wanted to end not just his misery, but also her own—

'There you are! At last! I've been searching for you!' a voice called.

Mhairi whirled round to find Fin heading up the steep slope.

191

'Ma sent me,' he panted, seeing her surprise as he crossed the ground in long-legged strides. 'Flora looked in and was surprised you weren't back. She said you'd left way back to come up for more oil.' He frowned at the sight of them standing there, planting his hands on his hips as he tried to get his breath back. '. . . What's taken you so long? We were getting worried.'

'I just ran into Donald,' she said lightly. 'We were chatting, is all.' She showed him the oil bottle in her hand and started walking over to him, Donald's eyes on her back.

'Right. Well, are you coming back down, Donald?' Fin asked, jerking his head towards the village below.

Donald's gaze grazed over her slowly. 'No. I think I'll stay up here a bit longer.'

'You're sure?' Fin persisted. 'It's perishing and you're in your shirtsleeves.'

'Don't worry about me, I don't feel much,' he said, looking back out to sea and into the darkness, bristling with anger and something else she didn't dare name.

Chapter Fourteen

'Mhairi . . . ? Hello? Are you daydreaming?'

Mhairi jumped, and looked over to see her mother holding up the bolt of tweed.

'What on earth has got into you today, girl?' she tutted as Mhairi brought her attention back to the job in hand. All the women of the village would be waulking the tweeds today, a demanding job at the best of times; and this really didn't feel like the best of times. They were all dressed in their oldest clothes, sleeves rolled up and hair held in place by their shawls. Even Effie was bare-legged and in a skirt.

The men would be making repairs to the cottages – Old Fin's leaking roof needed patching, the Big Gillies' front wall needed re-liming and Mad Annie was in dire need of a new window, having simply stuffed her old broken one with cuts of peat. She was adamant she'd never slept so well as in the new darkness it brought her, but the menfolk were insistent it needed replacing, for reasons of adequate ventilation if not for the light. Lorna had been at her sternest, warning Annie that come the winter and the heavy rains, the damp from the sodden sods would 'go to her chest'.

There was a feeling of industry in the air, everyone moving with purpose as the equipment was set into place: the long wooden tray that would serve as a table-top had been carried up from the coffin cleit behind the manse and set upon two barrels; the piss pot was simmering on the fire; and the ells of tweed were carried down from the lofts of each cottage, where they had been stored since they'd come off the loom.

The children were up by the head dyke playing games, having been granted a day's grace from lessons. Waulking the tweed was a community affair and even the minister's wife would be sitting and working with them today. Benches were carried out from the kitchens until they had enough to seat all the women in two rows, facing opposite one another. Mhairi sat with Molly on her right and Lorna on her left. Opposite were Effie, Flora and Flora's mother, Christina. Ma Peg sat at the head of the table, Mad Annie beside her, with Jayne Ferguson, Big Mary, Crabbit Mary, Mhairi's mother and Mrs Lyon arranged around and between them.

The first bolt of cloth had been laid out lengthways on the table, loosely rolled and looped in a horseshoe. Mhairi met Effie's eyes and beamed as Mad Annie got up and carefully poured the urine from the kettle onto the fabric. It steamed and settled immediately within the fibres, swelling them up and beginning its work.

Waulking the tweed, or fulling as it was sometimes known in other parts of the Hebrides, was a job with many functions – to raise the nap and soften the tweed, to preshrink it and to make it weatherfast. 'Hot piss sets the dye fast,' Mad Annie said with a gleam in her eye as she caught the minister's wife's look of suppressed distaste.

She refilled the kettle and set it back on the tripod, before sitting down again and looking expectantly at Ma Peg. Mhairi felt the hairs raise on her arms. She still remembered her joy at the first time she had been allowed to take part. Ma Peg began to sing. For a woman in her late eighties – no one knew exactly how old she was, Ma Peg included – she retained a youthful singing voice. The others began to move in unison, to the tempo of the song.

Mhairi knew all the words. She didn't recall ever having sat down and learnt them but they were in her somehow, already known. She swayed forward and then back, sometimes side to side to side, with her mother and friends and neighbours as the cloth was slowly pummelled between them in a rhythmic movement – hit with the side of a fist, squeezed in crab-like pincers – so that it was roughed up and urine-soaked, the dirt and lanolin lifting off the fibres.

The men did their own work around them, but they worked in near silence, looking over frequently as the women's songs broke past even the birds. They sat astride the roof ridges and leant on the windowsills, watching. This was the women's day, the one time when the feminine spirit won out. There would be no killing or climbing or twisting of necks today.

The song broke into sections, everyone having their own couplet to sing, and as they swayed and pummelled, Mhairi closed her eyes. She felt the feminine energy around her like the pull of a tide, the connection with her own heritage rooting her here like she was part of the bedrock. Soon it was her turn to sing and she sang her lines with the knowledge that this would be the last time she would sit on this bench, with these women, doing this. She sang with all her heart, the pain and confusion of the past few weeks overwritten by love for her home.

Flora was watching her with a teary look that said she understood; this tradition would be continuing without either one of them next year. They swayed as one, pounding the cloth in time, but over Flora's shoulder her gaze snagged on something conspicuous by its very stillness. Donald

McKinnon was leaning against a door-post, having stopped his work to listen to her. She had told herself, as she had lain awake in her bed last night, that his words had been the ravings of a man filled with guilt for what had happened to her – *I wanted to* – but that in the cold light of day they would fall back into the shadows, never to be referenced again. Wouldn't they?

She swallowed and tried to look away but she was caught firm again, and this time there was no cover of darkness to hide under, no wind to carry the words and looks away, no one to interrupt what had been an inevitable conclusion. It was all still there. They had done nothing wrong, she told herself, but the way he was staring at her, so openly, told her the door that had opened between them last night remained ajar. They hadn't walked through it – but she knew the light from the other side was shining on both their faces.

The day was a long one. Every household's entire tweed harvest had to be waulked, and by the time the light was fading their forearms throbbed and their voices were growing thin. But if the arms were tired, the legs were fresh, and it was tradition to finish the day with a ceilidh. The MacQueens' byre always served as the ceilidh house, and the men were ready for the women when they came through. Old Fin had his accordion ready and the villagers, young and old, arranged themselves in sets of four and eight. It was a terrific squeeze but they danced the reels as night came in, whooping and cheering, embracing life against the odds and a strengthening wind.

Mhairi felt herself twirled and flung about like a spinning top. She laughed and yelped as the music sped up in 'Strip the Willow', as David MacQueen spun her ever faster in the eightsome and Fin trod on her toes. But her attention was fractured; all the while she danced, her eyes searched for the one not dancing, and then later, for the one not even there.

Where was he? She waited for him as she danced, her eyes watchful for the silhouette she could instinctively discern now from all others. She felt agitation growing inside her. Was this a game? Why would he say those things and look upon her the way he had and then – when there was an opportunity to touch palms and link arms, to stand close and make their hearts race – just disappear?

The entire village was here. Would he not come too? Not that Mary was concerned. She was dancing and laughing with her neighbours like she'd never heard of a Donald McKinnon, much less married him.

'Ach, Mhairi, I'll be stiff as a corpse after this,' Effie puffed during the break, coming to stand beside her at the table where refreshments were being served. Several of the younger children were sitting huddled beneath it, watching the show, but everyone pretended not to see them. Getting them into bed meant putting them into bed, and they weren't ready to break up the party yet. High days and holidays were too rare on the isle to be squandered on account of bedtimes.

'Aye.' She saw Molly and David standing talking in the corner together, eyes locked, openly in love. Mhairi looked for Norman and saw him in conversation with Angus and Hamish Gillies, oblivious to what was playing out behind his back. Why did it all have to be so complicated? Why did people always seem to end up marrying the wrong partners?

Effie shot her a quizzical look. 'What's with you?'

'Nothing.'

'You're distracted.'

'I'm tired.'

Old Fin gave his accordion a wheeze and Effie was off again like a zephyr, blowing to another corner of the byre. 'Come on!' she called back.

Mhairi demurred. 'No, I've just remembered something.'

'What?'

Yes, what? 'I've not turned the slops.'

Effie pulled a face. 'Well, now's not the time! You can do it tomorrow. Come and dance.'

'No, I can't. I promised the factor I'd turn them every day.'

'But one day won't matter.'

'He's paying me extra to do it. Would you skip a day feeding Tiny?'

'It's not the same thing,' Effie laughed. 'Tiny's a bull! Those are slops in a bucket.'

'It's the principle of the thing,' Mhairi argued. 'I've my conscience to live with. I'll not sleep tonight if I don't get it done.'

Effie rolled her eyes, giving up on her. 'Ugh. If that's your idea of wickedness, it's a wonder Flora even talks to you!'

Mhairi stepped outside, pulling her shawl around her and walking quickly down the Street. She kept her head down as she passed the McKinnon croft window, though the lamp was lit and she knew he was in there. She walked but her ears were tuned to a higher frequency, listening out for the things her eyes could not see – footsteps, a whisper, her name . . .

Ahead she could see a figure on the grass. Her heart raced as she wished it was him again – what would she do with her chance a second time? – but it was a woman standing, staring into the distance, her arms dropped to her sides so that her shawl fluttered and threatened to fly off her shoulders. Mhairi frowned and slowed down; she had thought everyone, bar Donald, was still at the ceilidh.

'Jayne?' she asked as she drew closer.

There was no response. Nothing to indicate Jayne had heard her. She was as still as a statue, looking not out to sea but seemingly a fixed point a third of the way up Ruival, the mountain opposite. Mhairi followed her gaze, looking for a dog or sheep, Norman even, though Mhairi had seen him dancing just now.

'Jayne?' She put a hand to her neighbour's arm. It was a good ten or twelve seconds before she seemed to register, and when she did, she startled alarmingly, her knees almost buckling as she sprang back. Her pallor was ashen, as if she'd been exsanguinated, and she stared back with wide eyes. Mhairi felt herself frightened by her friend's alarm. '. . . Are you ill?'

Jayne swallowed, looking overcome. She could only shake her head as she clutched at her slipping shawl and gathered it tightly about her neck, standing there, trembling and pale. Had she had another fight with Norman, Mhairi wondered? Or rather, had he had a fight with her? Jayne wouldn't say boo to a goose; her husband, on the other hand, would pick a fight with the sun.

'You looked like you were under a spell,' Mhairi said lightly, but she barely got the words out.

'—Good night, Mhairi,' Jayne said suddenly, turning on her heel.

Surprised, Mhairi watched her go, slipping through the narrow gap in the low stone wall like a shadow. It was unlike her to be so abrupt but she was a curious woman, somehow there and not there at the same time. Mhairi often felt she didn't belong here, where big personalities jostled and joked and quarrelled on an hourly basis, yet it was hard to imagine where she might fit. A big city, a small town, a hut all alone on the hills – none seemed to fit. It was almost as if the world itself wasn't right for her.

With a perplexed sigh, Mhairi went on her way again. She felt disjointed from everyone at the moment, as if out of step. She took the bucket from the factor's garden and walked down to the beach, carefully emptying it and making sure none of the muck escaped. She had been turning it for a couple of months now and it had started to pale in colour – only a little but there was a discernible fade from black to a deep grey, and the loose strands of viscera had become conjoined so that it was slowly, seemingly, forming a ball. She wasn't sure if this was supposed to happen or whether she was doing something wrong; there was no way of asking. She could only continue in good faith.

The waves pounded on the shore and the sound was so encompassing it was as if the edge of the ocean was trying to lift itself up like the skirts of a grand Victorian lady climbing the stairs. Back in the garden, she stirred with the stick, doing her duty like the good daughter she was, and within minutes she was heading up the Street again, past the crofts.

She felt her heart beating faster again, though she didn't know why. She felt a sensation of undertow, as if she was being moved by forces greater than her own will. And yet, her will was at work – she tried to think of a reason to stop in at the McKinnons' croft, to speak to Donald, to see him. Perhaps when they were alone again, and he was brusque and she resentful, she would realize this strange yearning that had tickled inside her all day had been just a windswept delirium that had confused them both.

But there were no reasons she could think of to stop in and enquire after him, and as she drew closer to the door, her courage failed her. Her heart pounded like it wanted to be set free but she kept her feet moving. She walked past the window again with her head bowed, wondering why she wanted to cry, when suddenly she found herself being whirled again, her arm caught, spinning back into the narrow side path between croft and byre.

Donald pressed her against his chest and they stared at one another in silence. Words were superfluous. What needed to be said had already been said and this, here in the shadows, was simply a question.

Distantly, she knew what her answer should be. She should step away, protest this intrusion, tell him no – but she didn't want to cry out; she didn't want to be saved. He wasn't free to marry and she wasn't free not to marry. They could never be.

That was precisely the point.

He bent his head to kiss her and she closed her eyes, sinking into it, because she knew it would only ever be this. And it would only ever be now.

Chapter Fifteen

'Do you think it hurts?' Flora wondered aloud as they sat on the bed in Effie's box room, knitting. It was snowing outside, the first fall of winter, and for several days it had been coming in hard as if in a statement of intent for the season. The villagers had been largely confined to their crofts, unable even to enjoy their walks down the street after tea and take the evening news of the day's events, though the school remained open, its chimney frantically puffing to keep the bundled children warm.

Effie particularly was never happy to be housebound, but there was a comfort that came from the high, crackling fire, the click of their needles and the clack of the loom from the other room as her father wove an ell of dogtooth check.

'Does what hurt?' Molly frowned.

'It.' Flora shared a scandalous look that left them in no doubts.

Everyone was quiet, as though even to discuss it was sinful. Mhairi concentrated hard on her purl stitch, her stitch rate picking up to hide her shaking hands. She longed for Flora to provide the answer; for once she wouldn't be jealous, she would be happy to follow in her footsteps.

It had been several weeks now since her kiss with Donald, and every day since had crackled with anticipation, like a question in need of an answer. Her sleep was fitful, her dreams bewildering, her body permanently on high alert even as she went about the most mundane tasks – turning the slops, milking the cow, fetching the peat, carrying the butter churn . . . anything that took her outside and presented the chance of seeing him. When their eyes met now, it was as though thunderbolts were shot between them; sometimes when they passed one another his hand would graze hers, but nothing was ever said. The kiss burnt like a holy prayer, sacred, pure and definitive.

She wished he would follow her to the burn, where they could kiss again between the high banks, or follow her into a cleit – but he never did. She saw the longing in his eyes, she had heard it in his groans as she'd kissed his neck, felt the way he had trembled as he held himself back. But unlike Alexander, he had resisted.

He continued to resist.

'Quick! You're needed!' a voice called through, rapping hard on the kitchen window but not stopping. Effie's father struggled up from the loom and limped to the door as the girls ran through.

'What's happening?' Effie asked as they joined him at the doorway, fat flakes skidding past. She gasped in surprise. They had been sitting together in the windowless box room for a couple of hours and the weather hadn't so much closed in as the sky had fallen; clouds enveloping them in a white haze, the bay completely pulled from view. They could make out Archie and David MacQueen struggling up the Street, knee-deep in snow, buttoning their jackets against a driving wind. Further along, Hamish Gillies was staggering up the path, raising the alarm at all the cottages.

'An Lag's buried!'

'An Lag?' Effie echoed, reaching for her jacket and cap. They all knew what that meant – the sheep were herded in the fanks there. They'd be suffocating in the drifts. Without another word, they ran back to their homes.

'An Lag's buried,' Mhairi said, running through and shaking off the snow that had settled upon her in those few moments outside. But they already knew. Her father, Angus and Fin were readying to leave.

'Aye. We'll need all hands up there to dig them out.'

'Ian, I canna leave the bairns,' her mother fretted. 'If they were to waken and go outside . . .'

Her father nodded. One sniff of adventure and Wee Murran would be out on the moor in his bedclothes. 'Of course not. You must stay here. Mhairi, come.'

'Aye, Father.' She began tying her shawl on her head. The cottage was warm and womblike even in the face of this weatherbomb that had drifted over the sea, peered over the mountaintops and silently detonated. It was an omen of a harsh winter – there had been several fierce storms already and it was only November, but there had been none of the usual precursors warning them. No one had been prepared for the flurries to become a deluge.

'And wear this,' her mother said, wrapping her own shawl around Mhairi's torso too, then her jacket. 'It's perishing out there.'

Within moments, Mhairi was stepping outside, taking a sharp breath as the wind snapped at her in warning. She tried to keep up with her brothers but they were long-legged and soon left her in their wake – or rather, footsteps. It was difficult to see and impossible to hear, the wind a rabid wolf that howled and snapped as she walked through the gap in the dyke and up the sharp slope towards the An Lag plateau. Norman Ferguson was up ahead with Jayne and Molly, almost at the top with Euan Gillies and David MacQueen; Archie limped at a distance behind them. Their strong movements were impeded by bodies made bulky with layers upon layers.

She was panting hard when she got to level ground but she still caught her breath at the sight. The plateau sat halfway up the gap between the Connachair and Oiseval mountains, a flat plain with several large drystone enclosures they used for capturing the sheep during plucking season or early lambing. Being high-sided at the back and sides, but open at the front, made for some challenging consequences during extreme weather. When it rained in torrents, particularly on hard ground in the summer, the water would come skinning down the slopes and pool briefly in the plateau before brimming over and flooding the village. Snow, though, depending on the wind direction, could do the opposite, being driven back against the high sides and piling up into deep drifts, turning the enclosures from places of safety to death-traps.

So it was now, the stone walls lost from sight and the men wading through with arms aloft, trying to find the sheep with their feet. She saw Effie, a head shorter than the men, already pitching in with her usual determination, Poppit's tail poking up above the surface like a feather on a stick. What had been knee-deep in the village up here came almost to their chests.

'Here!' A shout went up and she looked over to see Donald a short way off, already digging with his bare hands and throwing back plumes of snow to reveal a sheep's head. 'Another one. Alive!'

The men seemed to instinctively separate, fanning out to cover more ground, but Mhairi made her way over to where Donald was digging out the rest of the animal's body. Lorna, digging with a spade near to him, threw it down and reached her arms out as he tugged it free, lifting it up and shoving the sheep towards her; great chunks of ice clung to its thick coat, its legs buckling beneath the uncommon weight, but it appeared well enough and no more dazed than sheep usually looked. Lorna grabbed it by the horns and pulled it down towards what, Mhairi could see now, was a narrow pit dug out against one of the walls.

'Mhairi, help me here!' she said, throwing another spade towards her and resuming digging.

At the sound of her name, Donald's head jerked up and their eyes met for an electric moment; he looked exhausted and wired, but she saw still his yearning for her. Then he was back to it, feeling with his feet and sticking a piece of drift-wood they used as a shepherd's crook deep into the snow, probing for resistance.

Mhairi helped Lorna with digging out the rest of the narrow channel until it fed into the opening of the large buried fank. The animals needed to be freed but then put somewhere safe, where they could stand and breathe as the others were rescued; the sheep that had been found so far stood huddled together in the tight space that had been cleared, but the channel was nowhere near big enough to hold the entire flock.

'We've got to clear this fank,' Lorna said, wading a path into the submerged enclosure. 'I'll start working in the middle, you start at that end.'

It was a race against time and their breath was coming fast, cheeks pinked. Mhairi felt her back ache as she bent double, digging down through the compacted depths. Every now and then another shout of 'Here!' went up, causing a commotion. The sheep tended to cluster in groups, so finding one often meant finding several more immediately nearby. Once they were freed, Effie made it her job to half-drag, half-carry them over.

It was punishing work in brutal conditions. The wind wouldn't let up, nor the snow clouds that continued to throw down flakes, filling up where they had cleared. It seemed an impossible task. Mhairi felt sure she must have dug out the whole plateau but when she looked up, it was only a small clearance zone around her – several feet deep but only a few feet wide. Her gaze roamed the plateau. The once pristine blanket of snow had been carved and ploughed, great chasms of sheep-shaped furrows running like scars.

Everyone was tiring; even Norman Ferguson was leaning on a spade and looking spent. They'd been going for a couple of hours now and sunset wouldn't be far off. Visibility was limited with a flat light that made it hard to distinguish mountain from sky; the villagers, dressed in their sodden brown tweeds, were the only dots on the landscape. Too many of their flock were still missing. Trying not to be dispirited, Mhairi hunched over and went to dig again, feeling something move – or rather, give – as the tip of the shovel pressed into the snow. She gasped, crouching down and catching sight of a single narrow hoof.

'Oh!' she breathed, putting down the tool and, getting on her hands and knees, beginning to use her hands instead. She scrabbled against the snow, soon uncovering the animal's whole leg. It was a wonder it could support itself on such skinny limbs, especially beneath this colossal weight – the snow was so icy, it clung to the sheep's fleeces in heavy wet chunks, adding to their bulk.

'The women should go back,' she heard Hamish declare. 'We'll likely find the stragglers all together in the next spot. It shouldn't be long now.'

'No!' Effie cried vehemently.

'There's no point in all o' us staying out up here now on account of dumb beasts!' Hamish shouted. 'The weather's getting worse. The women must head back down.'

'I'm fine!' Effie argued.

'Back down! Y're father needs y' alive or there'll be none to get his eggs.'

Mhairi listened from her prone position on the ground as she continued to dig out the sheep. She didn't understand her friend's objections. The prospect of getting out of this squall was dizzyingly welcome. She had scooped and cleared the snow around the back end of the sheep and could get her hands on its haunches now. 'Come . . . on,' she panted, kneeling and pulling on it with what strength remained to her. 'Out with you! . . . Get . . . out!'

The animal came unstuck suddenly and she fell back under its full weight as its legs kicked desperately at the air. 'Oof!' she panted, shoving it off its back, onto its stomach and onto the ground; ungainly beneath the extra weight locked into its fleece, it was several moments before it could bring itself up to standing again.

Mhairi wished she could do the same. Instead, she peered into the dark, narrow cavity from which the animal had been freed. More legs.

'Curses,' she muttered under her breath as she reached an arm in. 'Come on, walk it back,' she cajoled, her hand grasping for a hunk of wool. She found it and, moving her hand down to the leg, began to pull. 'Come on!' she coaxed. 'Come to me, come to me.'

The animal's leg lifted instinctively away from her touch, finding the surprise of sudden space; it put its leg back slightly, finding more.

'Yes, that's it!' she encouraged. 'Step back! This way!'

But – whether spooked or stupid – the animal stayed still in its icy prison.

'Ugh,' she groaned, frustrated. 'I said this way.' She reached in further. She would need to get two hands to its legs, as with the other one, but her frozen fingers were losing sensation fast in the snow, her hands becoming clubby.

She grasped, getting a hand to bone and sinew, but in the next moment she heard a rush of sound and contact was lost. The sheep was gone. Light was gone. And air.

She couldn't move, her body compressed beneath a colossal weight and held in its curious outstretched position so that she couldn't pull her arms back in to protect her head, to scrape the biting ice away from her cheeks; she was so firmly encased, there wasn't even room for a teardrop to slide from her eye. Somewhere, millimetres from her fingers, was a sheep. And somewhere, several feet above, was her family. Her friends. Donald.

She felt her heart break into a gallop as panic began to override the shock, her brain rapidly understanding what had happened.

Oh God! Would anyone even know she was here? Was she completely buried? She'd been kneeling down, hidden from view, as her neighbours talked. Who would realize she was missing? The women were leaving to go back to the village – they would assume she was with the men. And the men would think the opposite, that she was back home. By the time anyone noticed . . .

She felt her lungs draw, trying to drag the oxygen from the minute, crystalline air pockets, but nothing came. Her lungs grabbed again, as her hand had done only moments before, trying to grasp something just out of reach.

Nothing.

She would have only minutes.

Not even that.

* * *

'Mhairi?'

The word was distant. Coddled. Wrapped in a snow cloud. Or perhaps a woollen fleece. She felt blanketed, even warm, in the silent pitch of darkness. Time had become elastic. She was so far away now . . .

She felt movement against her skin, her clothes roughly disturbed as the world moved against her – and then the sudden slap of air. Freezing, fully oxygenated air that inflated her lungs and reddened her blood.

'Mhairi!?' The word was closer now. Right there, by her ear. She could hear in it all the textures of horror, of fear – a ragged, hoarse, sharp bark, tremulous and demanding all at once – but there was no sound to come out of her; she had been emptied, crushed, and only the battering wind screamed as if in laughter. '. . . Please God, don't leave us. Don't leave.' The voice came closer. 'Don't leave me.'

Something warm and wet prodded against her cheek, a low whine breaking through the horrified silence, a sweep of fur against her skin. She felt her eyelids flicker in response, her body waking up now that it was no longer protected in its icy cocoon.

Brown and white fur. A patch over one eye.

'Oh sweet Jesus! She's alive!' someone shouted, and a chorus of cries went up.

Dully she looked up to find a crescent of faces staring down upon her as she felt herself moved again, her head and shoulders lifted off the ground. Her head lolled back heavily. She had never felt so weak.

'Donald?' she whispered, as his arm gripped her tightly and he shrugged off his jacket with his other one.

'We need to get you into the warmth,' he said, laying his jacket over her and tucking it in around her like she was a doll in a crib.

'Let me through!' someone cried.

Lorna was beside her in the next moment, two fingers at her neck as she began to count.

'Her lips are blue!' someone worried.

'Don't worry, I've got you, Mhairi,' Donald whispered down to her. 'I've got you. You're safe.'

Yes. She looked into his eyes, feeling his arms around her. She had never felt safer.

'She's hypoxic and hypothermic. We need to get her back down and warmed up as fast as possible,' Lorna said sternly, but Donald was already moving. In one movement, he had her off the ground and cradled in his arms.

'Let the others help you!' Lorna instructed. 'It's too far for just one man to carry.'

'I've got her!' Donald said, almost snatching her away from Lorna's hands. 'I'll take her.'

Mhairi blankly watched everyone step back as he carried her, his knees stepping high as he moved through the deep trenches they had made. She saw how everyone's teeth were chattering, the weight of their sodden clothes pressed against their bodies. Strange that she should feel so warm.

Donald switched direction with an adjoining furrow and for several strides, she was able to see back the way they had come from her snowy coffin. Everyone was watching, but . . . she felt another kind of stare upon her too, the way the lamb senses the eagle. It had a different quality to it, or perhaps a weight. Her gaze slid blankly over the crowd of faces, stopping on one that slow-blinked. Saw more.

Lorna was watching them.

Lorna knew.

Chapter Sixteen

The sheep drama, as it came to be called, shook the whole village. The last sixteen sheep were lost in the end, forfeited in the wake of her accident, which was considered an omen to get back. Donald had carried her all the way down, his voice rumbling against her ear and telling her to hold on, that she mustn't sleep, couldn't leave him . . . She would have gripped him back if she could, but she'd been so weak; she would never forget the sound of her mother's cry as he brought her into the cottage.

A bath had been filled for her, the neighbours running and staggering through with their pots of boiled water, and when Lorna had deemed her suitably warmed up she was put into her bed, which had been warmed with three clay bottles. There she had lain through two nosebleeds and a headache that wouldn't let up for three days. She had suffered a 'trauma', Lorna told her as she came in to check on her, in between nursing those who had also come down with heavy colds; working for hours, waist- and chest-deep in the snow, had been bound to have consequences, and in the days after-wards, her brother Fin, Flora's father, Effie, Molly Ferguson and even the indomitable Hamish Gillies were all laid low with heavy chests and confined to their beds. Lorna was moving between almost all the crofts, taking temperatures, administering fluids and cod liver oil, while Jayne Ferguson, her mother told her, was taking it upon herself to pray for their souls, tirelessly trekking a path to and from the kirk every morning and every night.

Mhairi felt guilty to be 'resting' as she watched her parents work tirelessly, not one but two vital pairs of hands down, with Fin laid low too. The fires needed to be kept burning day and night, keeping the croft – and, more importantly, her – warm. But as well as the guilt she was restless, her spirit in a state of perpetual agitation. It was almost more than she could stand being confined to her bed or, if she was lucky, a fireside chair. She yearned to get outside and see other faces – his face – but they were all trapped, the snow continuing to fall and keeping everyone sequestered inside. Only those chores which could not be avoided, such as milking the cows, justified a quick dash out into the elements. Patience was wearing thin and tempers were at breaking point as they all jostled in the small crofts like kittens in a bag.

But on the fourth day after the drama there dawned a bright, cold November morning, the sort where the sun blistered listlessly in a pale sky, nature held in a frigid silence. Only the sea spoke up, long grey waves falling heavily upon the beach in lolloping lazy sighs before retreating with a sizzle and a hiss. Most of the birds were far out at sea now, or else had emigrated to their winter roosts, unwilling to joust with winds that were no longer playful but bullying and sharp.

Mhairi insisted on getting up from the chair where she had sat swaddled by the fire, rereading the tattered copy of *Howard's End*, their only book in the house besides the Bible. She brewed a pot of tea, stirred the stew and knitted a pair of socks.

'I feel perfectly fine,' she told her mother as she moved about on coltish legs, but the headache still buzzed faintly. 'No, let me,' she said, pulling her shawl around her shoulders as her mother asked Christina to fetch in a peat. 'The fresh air will clear my head.'

She stepped out into the albino landscape, feeling her body's automatic recoil against the sub-zero temperatures, and for a moment, just one, she was under the snow again – blind, buried, burnt by the ice and thinking it was over . . .

'Mhairi! You're up then?'

She turned and saw Big Mary walking back from the burn with Mabel, her eldest daughter, both carrying pails of water.

'Aye. It's taken long enough.'

'Nonsense. It was a terrible thing. You were lucky is what you were.'

Mhairi smiled. 'Hamish recovering well?'

'Och, don't give him a thought!' His wife rolled her eyes. 'He's enjoying the fuss far too much! Lorna says he's her worst patient.'

Mary passed her with a wink and Mhairi turned off the Street onto the narrow path between the croft and byre. She retrieved the peat from the cleit around the back and was walking back when she heard more footsteps crunching on the snow.

She looked up just in time to see Donald passing by on the Street. She caught his profile – strong nose, heavy brow, his jaw still clean-shaven. He was out of sight in two strides but a moment later he filled the frame again between the two stone structures, looking up the path at her like she was a celestial vision. A moment of shock, followed by elation, contracted between them. It was her first time seeing him since the accident, though he'd passed by her window on countless occasions –

yesterday, three times that she had seen, though there could have been more. Had he been hoping she would glimpse him? She had yearned for the sound of his voice at the door, willing an excuse to be found for him to come over their threshold and check on her.

'Mhairi.' The word was a whisper but his voice still cracked on it. She remembered how fast his heart had beaten as he'd carried her down the slope, his words almost an incantation, and now, standing here, she could see what she was to him. It was all there in his face. Hers too? Ever since their kiss, that solitary lapse, they had been at pains to stay apart and do the right thing, but to have almost been lost to one another when they had never been each other's to lose . . .

He stepped onto the side path and she saw him go to move towards her – a reflexive action, as necessary as breathing – but she swivelled widened eyes in the direction of the byre beside them. Her brothers were within and any whisper, pause or indiscretion out here would be overheard.

Immediately he understood, his arm dropping away from her. 'Are you feeling recovered now then, Mhairi?' he asked in a bland voice, eyes burning.

'Aye. Lorna's been a watchful nurse.'

'Well, that's good. I overheard her telling Mary you were strong.'

Mhairi nodded. What else had Lorna told Mary? The two women were best friends, after all. Why wouldn't she share the secret she had stumbled upon? In the heat of crisis, Mhairi and Donald had betrayed themselves. Didn't Mary have a right to know that her husband was looking at another woman with private eyes?

And yet, these past few days, as Lorna had sat upon her bed, taking her temperature, Mhairi had braced for the stern look or the 'quiet word' that would shine a light on the terrible shame she carried – she had kissed a married man; she had wanted him then and she wanted him still – but Lorna had treated her with her usual brisk but pleasant manner. There were no contemptuous or enquiring glances, no questioning stares. She was preoccupied, of course, with her many patients – 'run off her feet', her father had said – but slowly, by degrees, Mhairi was beginning to wonder whether she might not betray them after all.

'Still, you gave us all a big scare. We were worried. We've scarce been able to think of anything else. How close it all came, just on account of some sheep. We wanted to help but weren't sure how.'

We. She knew what he meant.

'Truly, there was no need to fret. I'd have been up and out the same day if Mother would have allowed it. I've not enjoyed being stuck in,' she said, looking at him meaningfully and seeing him understand her code in return.

'Well, I'm glad you're fit and strong again; though I . . . I wish the same could be said of the others. It's been four days now that they're laid up.'

'Aye,' she sighed. 'I just saw Big Mary; it's not like Hamish to be knocked off his feet.'

'No. And Lorna says Molly's temperature is back up again,' he said sombrely. 'I saw Fin earlier, though, he looks better.'

'Aye.' Although her brother had only got out of his bed after she climbed out of hers – as if a cold could compare to almost being suffocated to death.

'Is Effie recovered?'

She had to smile. 'She's a tyrant, apparently. Christina went and sat with her earlier. She thought Effie might like it if she read to her, but she spent the whole time trying to persuade

Christina to take her place in the bed and pretend to be sleeping, so she could escape through the back window and fetch some birds.'

'The back window?' Donald chuckled. 'She's a cunning one. Especially when Robert's perfectly capable of getting to the cleit, even with his hip.'

'I know. She worries about him. Poor thing, Christina said she's like a caged bird with her father guarding the door, forcing her to rest.'

'Another gatekeeper? Perhaps Lorna's been issuing instructions.'

Their laughter faded as Lorna herself suddenly rushed past them on the Street. She seemed not to see them talking on the side path, nor to have heard her own name, but Mhairi felt a spike of fear lest she should double back – as Donald had – and catch them alone here, her worst suspicions confirmed. She hoisted the cut of peat higher in her arms, holding it across her body like a baby and creating a greater physical barrier between them, just in case the nurse did return – anything to dispel a suggestion of intimacy, or even familiarity, between them.

She saw him read her actions, walling herself away, that familiar frown puckering his brow. She wished she could just walk up to him and put her head upon his chest. Why did something so simple have to be forbidden? But of course they both knew why. What lay between them had its own heartbeat, its own pulse.

'Well . . . I should get on,' she said reluctantly. She couldn't think of what more to say; speaking for an audience was stultifying.

He winced, his jaw balling twice as he stepped aside for her to pass. 'Aye . . . Good afternoon, Mhairi.'

She dropped her head. 'Good afternoon, Donald.' She went to walk past him but he clasped her arm and in a moment of daring, of sheer utter madness and desperation, he kissed her, spinning them both back to the night of the ceilidh when they'd last succumbed to this desperate need.

She stared back at him, breathless with longing but stunned by his recklessness. It was an action that couldn't possibly be misinterpreted should anyone have come round the corner. It would be around the village within minutes. He was risking everything.

'Meet me tonight, during the evening news,' he whispered, his voice buried in her hair. 'Mary's helping Lorna.'

'But—'

'I have to see you. I'll be waiting in the coffin cleit.'

The coffin cleit was the largest of the stone stores: tall and long, it was where the driftwood was stored, as well as the planks the factor brought over for the making of coffins as required. It was also set behind the kirk and schoolhouse further down the Street; no one would be down there at that time of the evening.

'But Donald,' she whispered. She needed to tell him about Lorna's look, even though it hadn't led to any of Lorna's words. He didn't know how close they were to being exposed; they had to be so much more careful than he realized.

'Please – I thought I'd lost you. I can't go another day apart.' His voice cracked again and instinctively she reached for him, but he turned and left, leaving her alone on the path.

She stared into the void, shaking. She hadn't given him her reply.

But they both knew her answer.

* * *

218

Her parents ventured out after tea. After almost a week of being confined to their crofts, everyone spilt onto the Street, eager to come together again.

'Are you coming out to take some air, Mhairi?' Angus asked her as he pulled on his jacket and cap. He was off to see David MacQueen and Euan Gillies; Fin was under firm instructions by her mother to 'stay in the warm', his earlier stalling tactics to fall back into chores now working against him.

'Aye, I'll just finish turning this heel,' she said, trying to sound absorbed in her work, even though her hands automatically did the job without requiring a single conscious thought. Which was just as well; she'd scarcely been able to keep a thought in her head since coming back inside. She felt jittery and febrile, distractible. She was finally going to get what she'd longed for as she'd lain in her bed, craving a sound or sight of him. Now they would be together, and they'd be alone. Would he kiss her again?

'Suit y'self.'

The door closed behind him and for a while the cottage thrummed with the sounds of contented domesticity – the rustle of the newspaper as Fin sat in their father's chair and impatiently turned the pages; her little sisters playing with their cloth dolls; her little brothers stacking towers with flat pebbles. Silhouettes slid past the window, voices carrying through the lilac sky.

Every minute felt like an hour. She could no longer see the sock in her hands. Her mind was already out there, with Donald, and yet she was still sitting on her stool, unable to move. She could feel a force against her back, urging her on, but she also knew that if she stirred – if she left here tonight – she would not come back as the same girl. Their determination to do the right thing had fallen away in the wake of the crisis and they no longer had the power, nor the will, to resist this. There would be a fundamental splitting of her life into two parts: before tonight, and after it.

Outside the windows she could hear the conversations bedding in, the excitable high chatter of the villagers' initial greetings settling into something more engrossing. They would talk for as long as the weather would allow, but if the snow had stopped falling, the temperatures remained stubbornly arctic, and they would be driven back indoors soon. It was now or never. Donald was waiting for her and she had to decide.

With great care, she set down her knitting. 'I'm off to turn the slops.'

'Lucky you,' Fin muttered, not looking up from his pages, and she couldn't quite tell whether he was being sarcastic or not.

She wrapped herself in her shawls, fingers trembling as she tied the knots. Would anyone be able to see the heat coming from her? She was sure she was burning up, but Fin took no notice of her and she stepped outside, unmissed. She looked around. Her mother was in conversation further up the Street with Big Mary and Christina MacQueen, but from the frowns on their brows and the way they were shaking their heads, it was a sombre reunion. Hamish and Archie had been afflicted with this heavy chest of course; she supposed the past days would have been hard for the wives, doing everything themselves. Down the Street, Mad Annie was carefully walking arm in arm with Old Fin, the two of them heading up to Ma Peg's; others were clustered in pairs, but the body language of all was muted. The sheep drama would take some more getting over, it seemed, and she couldn't help but see the irony that she, as the principal victim in it, was feeling very much alive. In fact, never more so.

She slipped up the side path before anyone could see her, and round the back of the croft. Squares of golden light still pooled on the ground from the back windows, but there were fewer there and she was able to dart between the houses, unseen.

She passed behind Donald's own house, the Big Gillies' and Mad Annie's, crouching low as she came to the brief but open expanse that lay between the factor's house and the kirk and manse. In the darkness she was just another shadow among many, but still she darted from cleit to cleit, taking cover, her heart hammering.

Ahead she could see a glimmer of pale light just winking through the gaps of the coffin cleit. It lay parallel to the buildings, just uphill, and was set into a wall that formed a grassy enclosure behind the kirk and manse, where the schoolchildren often played during their breaks.

She crept silently towards the door and pushed on it. Donald, inside, leaning against the stone wall, looked up.

'You came,' he said, almost as if in disbelief.

Was this a mistake? Had he expected her to resist, to bow to her better judgement?

'I shouldn't have,' she said, feeling a spark of panic as she saw wax candles had been set upon stones and some wool fleeces laid out along the ground, a warm bed in the shelter.

He followed her eyeline. 'That's not . . . it's not what you think . . . I didn't want you to be cold out here, is all,' he explained, approaching her and guiding her in. 'But we need to keep the door closed or they'll see the light.' He shut it behind them.

'Oh.' He was standing right by her and she felt his solidity just in proximity. She could smell his smell; she was beginning to recognize it now – somehow mossy, salty, tobacco-y, which perhaps might be said of a lot of the men, and yet somehow his was different, stood apart.

She felt suddenly shy and unable to meet his eyes, and an awkward moment passed between them. Strangers again. But then he tipped her chin with the crook of his finger until she was staring back at him, and a volt of attraction shot between them, connecting them with an invisible charge.

'I won't touch you. I only wanted to look at you,' he whispered. 'I've missed just being able to look on you.'

'I've missed looking on you too.'

'Did you see me passing the windows?'

'Sometimes.'

A small smile curved the edge of his mouth. 'I looked for every excuse to go past.'

'I kept looking for you.'

The smile grew, a sense of relief in his face. 'You did?'

She nodded.

'And now you're here.' He stroked her cheek and she instinctively leant into the movement; she heard him exhale in turn, their nervous tension beginning to bleed away from them. He set his hand upon her waist. 'It was almost more than I could bear earlier, seeing you but not being able to talk freely.'

'I know.'

'Do you? Ever since I saw you under the snow . . . I haven't been able to get it from my mind . . . I've had nightmares, Mhairi, dreamt I couldn't get to you in time, that I couldn't find you at all. Mary says I've been shouting in my sleep.'

She gripped his hand. 'But I'm fine, Donald. You did find me and you did get me out in time. You saved me.'

'The thought of losing you . . .' He shook his head, looking down and away. 'When you're not even mine to lose.'

She watched him, seeing the spasms of pain cross his face. 'Yes, I am,' she whispered.

'No. Alexander—'

'He'll never be to me what you are. He'll be my husband, nothing more.'

'But it's already too much! What he'll do to you, Mhairi . . .' His voice tailed off and he winced, as if in pain. 'I can't even bear to think on it.'

'Then don't,' she urged, desperately not wanting to face it either. 'That life doesn't exist yet. Only this one here, with you and me.'

'But it's coming and nothing can stop it. Nothing I can think of can stop it! The thought of his hands on you . . . God, just let me kill him.' He shook his head as if trying to throw out the thoughts.

She put her hands to his face. 'Look at me, Donald. Feel me. This is what's real.' She placed her hands over his own, positioning them on her waist and – she could scarcely believe it of herself – gliding them upwards. A small sound escaped him as he cupped her breasts. 'I belong to you and no other,' she whispered. 'You will always be the man who touched me first.'

'But . . . ?' He looked at her questioningly. 'I thought—'

'No, he forced my hands on him,' she said, seeing him wince. 'It was different. This is different. He can't take this from us.' And she squeezed her hands over his so that her breasts swelled against his palms.

He looked back at her as if she was shining, a vision he couldn't trust himself to believe – but in the next instant she was in his arms, his mouth upon hers, their bodies pressed together with an urgency she had never experienced, and she knew this was the only real thing in the world. They sank down upon the fleeces and she felt his hands fumbling at the knots in her shawl, struggling with the buttons on her blouse as he repeated her name like it was a blessing. She untucked his shirt and he pulled it over his head in a single movement.

She swept her hands over his skin, marvelling at his solidity as he unfastened her skirt.

'Are you sure this is safe?' she gasped as he kissed her neck. 'What if someone comes in?'

He pulled back and stared down at her. 'Well then we're damned to hell. Mary's gone to help Lorna but if anyone finds us, there's no explaining this other than what it is. We either take this moment as ours or we let it slip away . . . You decide.'

She stared back at him, her heart thundering against his chest. 'Take it,' she whispered, and with one hand, he lifted her hips and pushed her skirt down to their feet. A moment later, his trousers and her chemise lay in a puddle with it, creased, crumpled, forgotten. She didn't notice the cold. In the flickering candlelight and trapped between the soft fleeces and the heat of his body, she felt warmer and more alive than at any other point in her life.

His mouth slackened at the sight of her. '. . . You're even more beautiful than I dreamt.'

She hadn't yet had the conversation with her mother about what came next – no doubt, her mother was waiting for the eve of her wedding night – but somehow she knew exactly what to do. Her body responded to his instinctively, greedily, her back arching as his hands dipped down over her hips and between her legs. He groaned as he found she was ready for him and without another word he positioned himself between her legs, gently pushing into her with a relief that made them both cry out. She clung to him as he moved, slowly at first but then faster. It was as if her soul itself was stirring, for she felt herself steadily climb, rise and then dissolve, wholly lost.

Her surrender seemed to trigger his and she heard his breath quicken. Overjoyed and triumphal, she felt herself come back into her own body – only something was different. A cooling upon her skin, she had that sense again, of the eagle and the lamb. She opened her eyes and froze, just as she felt him begin to pull away from her, his body straining.

'Mary!' she uttered, the sound a half-whisper, half-cry.

The word stopped him in his tracks but everything else was unstoppable – she knew it from Alexander – and she felt him groan, his body out of his own control as Mhairi stared back in horror at Mary standing in the doorway, a cold wind blowing over them now.

For several long moments, there was silence. Mhairi felt as if she was made from ice and that with one single movement, a tap from one of Mary's nails, she would shatter into a thousand pieces. The horror of the scene, this frozen vignette, was more than she could bear. To have been discovered at all was terrifying, but like this, in that most private of moments . . . it was unconscionable. Mary's eyes were almost swollen shut, tear tracks like snail trails winding down her cheeks as she waited for them to uncouple. How . . . how long had she been standing there?

Donald pulled away from her, pulling a fleece over her nakedness before pulling on his trousers. He handed back her chemise and skirt in silence and Mhairi began to dress herself as quickly as she could, aware of the other woman's curious gaze upon her body. She wished her hands weren't shaking. Everything seemed to take twice as long.

By the time she was clothed again, it had been at least two

minutes since Mary had discovered them and not a single word had yet been uttered.

Finally, Donald looked at his wife from his seated position on the floor, his elbows on his knees. He swallowed but there was nothing repentant in his gaze. 'You're back early.'

Mhairi looked at him, shocked. It certainly wasn't what she'd have called an apology. If Mary was to start screaming and wailing, the whole village would be here in moments.

But his wife's mouth simply flattened into a set line. 'Aye.'

Husband and wife stared at one another coldly.

'You suspected us then, was that it? You set a trap and this was what you hoped to see?'

She didn't reply immediately. 'No, Donald. I never hoped to see that.' Disgust curled the words like two-day-old bread.

'And yet you don't seem surprised.' He stood up now.

'I am,' she said, looking at Mhairi. 'And I'm not.' She stared back at him.

Mhairi felt a growing sense of foreboding, an instinct beginning to twitch that something else was at play here, something even worse than what she could see. Mary was a strong, fearsome and quarrelsome woman. This wasn't how she should be reacting. She shouted if the eggs were old, if the shirts were stained, if the water bucket was empty. To walk in on her husband with another woman and respond with this level of calm wasn't just unexpected. It was . . . wrong. Everything was off.

She looked again at Mary's tears – her eyes were reddened and puffy, grotesquely swollen in the way eyes only get after prolonged crying, not what could have only been a few moments' worth of silent weeping.

'What, then? Why are you back so soon?'

Donald had told her she'd been helping with Lorna.

Lorna, who knew about them.

Lorna, who she'd seen rushing past on the Street earlier, blind and deaf to their presence as she headed . . . where? To whom had she been racing?

Mhairi felt a small shiver trickle down her spine as she remembered the sombre reunions in the Street on her way over here, as news finally fed down properly for the first time in days, trickling from house to house . . . She'd been so desperate to get over here, so stuck in her own head, she hadn't given any thought to anyone but Donald. Had something happened? To whom?

'Mary, what's happened?' she asked, her voice quavering with fear.

Fin was fine. Hamish, fine. Effie . . . ? Christina had said fine.

She remembered her mother telling her Jayne had been going to the kirk, morning and night . . . Jayne, whom she'd startled on the night of the ceilidh. Mhairi had assumed she'd argued with Norman, but what if it had been something worse? The poor woman was cursed with second sight. She had terrible premonitions. Had she . . . had she seen something? Jayne knew better than anyone that nothing could be done for a fated soul. But for someone she loved, someone close . . . she would try anything, surely? She would pray anyway . . .

'Oh God,' Mhairi cried, pressing her hand to her mouth as she remembered – *temperature is back up again* . . . 'No! . . . Please don't . . .'

'Poor Molly Ferguson just died.'

The words fell to the ground like broken glass and Mhairi doubled over.

'I came back because I thought you'd want to know,' Mary said dully.

Mhairi couldn't bear it. Her friend had been dying, and she had been in wicked ecstasies? What had she done? What had she done?

She sobbed, feeling broken in half, but Donald was silent and very still, and Mhairi looked up at him. Tears were shining in his eyes, but she could see they would not fall – as if his pain might be taken as a weakness or vulnerability, something for Mary to exploit.

Mhairi stared between the two of them, horrified by their impasse; husband and wife were suspended in a mutual anti-pathy that would brook no weakness, even in the face of tragedy. Her breath juddered as she saw Mary resuming her usual self now, her eyes scornful and hard-hearted, a sneer on her lips now that her message had been delivered and a secret revealed.

'Well, I'll leave you to say your goodbyes then,' she said flatly. 'Remember, Donald, to bring in a peat.'

Chapter Seventeen

Six months later – May 1930

Glen Bay

St Kilda was awake once more, twitching beneath a sultry sky. As Mhairi sat on the rock looking out to sea she could almost feel the daisies and pink thrift opening at her feet, hear the butterflies on the wing. All around her the sheep grazed on lush, sappy grasses, their lambs beginning to skip and prance, their fleeces still a bright white so that from a distance the glen looked speckled with cottongrass. The skies were full again too; the birds had been returning from their distant overwintering spots since mid-March, colonizing the great scarred granite cliffs and sea stacks. They were now almost entirely white and the villagers would be preparing for the next of the spring harvests; the night hunt for the gannets that had 'opened' the new season a few weeks ago would be followed by the adult puffin catches, along with the shearwaters and fulmars.

Right now, the men were on Boreray catching eggs and counting the sheep. Though it was over five miles distant from here, she and Flora had seen the boat going over a few days ago. It had been strange to know it was their own fathers and brothers – and her lover – rowing the waves as they stood here, out of sight and out of mind in the distant bay. Mhairi and Flora had come over Am Blaid with the sheep and lambs a couple of weeks earlier, twelve hundred in all (minus the sixteen lost in the drama in November), setting themselves up in the souterrain referred to by visitors as the Amazon's House.

The St Kildans themselves weren't much preoccupied with names. All that mattered to them was that the ancient underground structure provided a necessary shelter, for the standard cleits weren't big enough for any long-term use. But the Amazon's House was unlike any other structure on the isle on account of its size. A narrow opening led down to a small ovoid space that fed off on the right to a large central chamber, with smaller cells lying off that at the back. The girls were using each of those as their sleeping spaces. They couldn't light a fire inside as there was no hole in the roof for the smoke to escape, so occasionally, particularly with any mists, it could be dank and musty; dark too, though their eyes adjusted quickly. But it was deep enough that they could stand and it provided solid shelter from the wind and rain. For two young women who had grown up living in shared rooms, the space and solitude they enjoyed here was a pleasing novelty.

It wasn't usual for the villagers to spend an entire season over here in Glen Bay; ordinarily the women would walk over every few days to milk the sheep themselves, but Donald, at one of the parliaments, had had an idea for trying a 'more efficient system'. Instead of the women walking to and from the summer pastures, carrying heavy churns and losing valuable time, he argued it made more sense to split the distance by having two shepherds stationed in Glen Bay all summer who could work exclusively on separating the cream, making the cheese and churning the butter. It could be stored over there till the summer's end and brought back in one village expedition. The smaller daily amounts required for the village could be brought up and left in the cleits on the Am Blaid ridge halfway between both bays, to be collected as required.

If the system was more streamlined for the village as a whole, it was hard work for the shepherds, requiring countless trips up and down the glen with the filled churns – but Mhairi would do whatever it took. Staying in the village was untenable now. The fragile truce that had followed Molly's death, as the entire community mourned, could only hold for so long. Mary had been wronged – she would not bite her tongue forever – and as the weeks had passed into months, their situation worsened.

The showdown, when it eventually came, had been mercifully private – the three of them meeting at the storm cleit one evening in March as accusations were thrown and compromises sought. Mary needed her gone, as far away from her as this tiny isle could accommodate, and she had left Mhairi in no doubt about the shame, humiliation and scorn that would be poured upon her should the liaison be revealed. She would be rejected by her community, disowned by her family. It would be a disaster of her own making. There was no other way but this.

Mhairi had been prepared to spend her exile here alone, but the chores were too much for just one and, to her surprise, Flora had readily agreed to join her on this side when Donald had asked. Possibly sentimentality was getting the better of her and she was wanting, in anticipation of her departure from here, to spend her final weeks on every last bit of the isle. Or perhaps she saw it as an opportunity to slowly disengage herself from village life, for she occupied a highly visible role and would be greatly missed when she came to leave.

Mhairi didn't fool herself that she would leave behind such a gaping hole when her own time arrived, but it didn't concern her. She had long since left behind her adolescent envy of her old friend. Life had moved onto another plane; this was the adult world, and her problems were far bigger than red lipsticks and love letters. She had confided the full story to Flora during their first night here together, and it had been sobering to see her friend's shock over the unlikely love affair. It didn't bode well for the reaction she might expect from anyone else learning the truth.

Donald was protecting her as best he could – from Mary, from everyone. He had convinced her father to delay the marriage to Alexander and keep her on the isle until the summer, when the bulk of the bird harvests and crop seeding needed as many hands at work as possible. Her father had duly written to Hugh explaining the short delay, prompting a terse reply that had upset her mother.

Donald's intervention had worked, but it still only bought them a few months' grace. She couldn't remain here forever, they both knew that – perhaps it was what cast their stolen hours in such golden light. Often, he would steal away at sundown, after a day of catching the puffins or fetching some eggs, and all the isolation and sadness would fall away. She would laugh, he would smile, his hands in her bright flaming hair . . . These moments were too fleeting but they were the pockets of perfection that sustained her.

All of which was why it mattered so greatly that what Mhairi could see now – those cuts in the grass across the water – shouldn't concern him. The semaphore alarm was rarely deployed. Huge slabs of turf, each one the length of three men, would be carved up and turned over, making a dark scar show up against the grass: a simple but foolproof way for the men over on Boreray to communicate with the villagers. One cut meant they were ready to return; two meant there'd been an accident or sickness; three, a death. Each morning and evening, some of the older children would run up to the gap and check there wasn't anything to see, never expecting there would be.

This morning, though, there had been two turned over. The sight had drawn a cry from Mhairi as she glanced across from Cambir Point. Flora hadn't needed to be asked twice, setting off for Village Bay immediately, but she'd been gone now almost all day. Where was she? What could be taking so long? Was it bad news? It had to be – why else would she linger?

A sound came to her ear and she turned and looked back up the slope, seeing finally her friend's distinctive figure coming over the grass, black hair streaming, her red shawl tied at her waist. It was too hot to run, the heat building to a crescendo that was going to have to topple; the horizon was already smudged with haze, a new weather front on the march.

'Oh, thank God!' Mhairi cried, hastening towards her to breach the gap and hear her news all the sooner. Every minute counted, every second . . . Flora's hands were outstretched in a calming motion, but Mhairi noticed that she didn't say, 'It's not him.'

She felt her heart gripped by a cold hand. 'Donald?'

'Aye,' Flora nodded as Mhairi gave another cry. '. . . But he's going to be fine. Lorna's looking after him. She's staying with Mary for the next few nights, just to see him through the worst.'

Through the worst? 'Wh-what happened?'

'He slipped and knocked his head on some rocks. There was a lot of blood and he was unconscious a while, but Lorna is certain he's going to be well in a few days.'

'I should go over there!' Mhairi gasped, her eyes wide.

'That wouldn't be wise,' Flora countered with a knowing look.

'But he needs me!'

Flora squeezed her hands. 'Yes, but that's not possible right now. You have to trust Lorna; you saw how she was after Molly died. She'll not let anything happen to him if she can help it.'

'But she may not be able to help it! Molly needed a hospital and we couldn't get her there. The pneumonia would have been treatable on the other side. What if Donald needs the same – help there that we've not got here?'

'If she thought he needed to go over the other side, she'd have sent him, you can be sure of that.'

Mhairi's hands escaped her grip, needing to flutter and shake. 'How? We've nothing here!'

'Actually, we do,' Flora sighed. 'It's why I've taken so long to get back. There's a sloop in the bay that just came the other day. If Lorna needed it to take Donald to the mainland, do y' think there's anyone brave enough to stop her?'

Mhairi blinked. Their island nurse was fearsome. 'No.'

'Exactly. He'll be fine, stop worrying.'

Mhairi exhaled, shaking her hands out and trying to calm herself as they began walking back down towards the Amazon's House together.

'But why were you over there so long?' she asked, still worrying.

'Well, it's quite the story,' Flora said in a confiding tone. 'You won't believe your ears.'

Mhairi shrugged an eyebrow, her curiosity piqued. 'Tell me.'

'It belongs to the Earl of Dumfries. He's one of MacLeod's friends – sailed over with his son and they brought over the factor too.'

'Ugh, no.' Frank Mathieson's reappearance would be guaranteed to put Donald in a bad mood when he woke up.

'I know, and he's as odious as ever.' Flora rolled her eyes. 'The visitors, however . . .' Her voice changed, becoming lower. 'They're spending a week here, bird-spotting and catching eggs – and Effie's being paid to guide them.'

'That'll make her happy!'

'Aye. Especially as the son, Lord Sholto, is as handsome a man as you've ever seen.'

Mhairi was surprised. 'As handsome as James?'

Flora hesitated. 'Different. He's . . . golden. Like a sun god.'

'Really?' Mhairi breathed. She couldn't imagine a man like a sun god. Donald was a man of the earth – craggy, dense, dark, his skin stained by the soil. Alexander was a finer-looking man for sure, but he still wasn't approaching what she would call god status.

'So don't tell me – now he's in love with you, and you're going to throw James over and marry him instead?'

Flora made of sound of indignation. 'How dare you!' But she laughed too. 'No. No, I'm not, but not because of that.' She turned and looked at Mhairi with enormous, dancing eyes. 'He's wildly in love with Effie. A blind man could see it!'

'What?' Mhairi screeched.

'Aye! And she's in love with him!'

'No!' Mhairi gasped in disbelief. 'Effie's in love?' They had scarcely seen her since coming over to the far glen. She was with the men on the ropes most days at the moment and couldn't spare the three or so hours it took to get here and back.

'Aye!'

'Effie's in love?' she repeated in a whisper, saying it over and over, as if the words needed time to fit. No one could have imagined it happening. Their friend rebuffed every tender word, look or gesture that came her way. She met the men as their equal, dressing in their clothes, sharing their chores, utterly oblivious to her own wild, gamine charm and the effect it could have. Mhairi well knew her own brothers both watched her when they thought she wasn't looking; and David MacQueen, though fiercely mourning Molly, would have to one day in the future look to rebuild his future prospects. To lose her, of all the island girls, to an outsider . . . St Kilda simply couldn't support any more of the next generation 'marrying out'.

'. . . But he's a laird, you said? An earl's son.' She frowned. A man like that could have anyone, take his pick from the Mayfair debutantes. Why would he choose Effie? Why couldn't everyone just fall in love with the people they were supposed to? Effie with Fin, Flora with Angus, her with Euan . . . But she had liked John Gillies, and he'd died. And David had loved Molly and she'd died. Either death snatched them with one hand or life tormented them with the other. Mhairi had fallen in love with an island man, but he was married. Wrong. Forbidden. The path could seemingly never just be straight.

Flora's smile faded. 'I know. And I had to tell her it can never be.' She bit her lip. 'The way she looked at me, Mhairi, I think I broke her heart. I told her she can't stay in the village, not till he leaves again. She's going to come over here in the morning.'

Mhairi's gaze rose to the sky, looking towards the distant storm. If the laird had any sense, he'd go tonight and get ahead of it; outsiders could rarely cope with the conditions here when the weather turned. And yet, if it was as Flora said – if this really was love – he would stay until the last possible moment. Mhairi was on a countdown of her own, but it was ticking out over months, not minutes . . . She wondered which was worse.

'It's just all so quick!'

'But it is, isn't it, when it's right? You just know.'

The comment made Mhairi uncomfortable. It hadn't been like that with Donald. For eighteen years she'd scarcely noticed him. When he'd shaved his beard off it had helped her to see him anew, but she'd had to completely recast him in her mind's eye to see him as a man and not just a neighbour.

'. . . I wish I could have let her have her happiness, but you should have seen the way he was looking at her. And her at him,' Flora was saying. 'They're not fooling anyone, it's plain as day what's happening between them. She's an innocent. Eff's not like us, she doesn't have a mother to guide her through this; she might not realize the consequences . . .'

'No.' Effie's mother had died when she was only ten, and although John had died three years ago, hers had always been a male household – the word *love* had probably not been mentioned in two generations.

'But it's for her own good. She'll never see him again once he leaves here. She has to be realistic.'

As Mhairi knew she had to be. '. . . Aye.'

'I warned her. I reminded her what happened to Kitty.' The fate of Flora's cousin had long been used by the minister as a warning for fallen girls. She had succumbed to a love affair with a naval officer who was stationed on the isle during the Great War; he'd left for home when his posting ended and she, her belly already swelling, had jumped from the rocks. Her family, devastated and disgraced, had emigrated to Australia shortly afterwards and the entire community had been weakened by the affair.

Flora reached around her waist and unknotted the red shawl. 'Here, thanks for this,' she said, holding out her hand.

Mhairi took it back, along with the brooch she had used to fasten it. Donald had given it to her, and she stared at it, still thinking about fallen women. It should belong to his wife, of course; all the married women wore them. But this wasn't the first – or worst – thing Mhairi had taken from Mary. And besides, in time Mary would take from Mhairi too.

Only Mary – when her turn came – she would take everything.

Chapter Eighteen

'Where is she?' Mhairi asked over the low wall. They were herding the sheep into the folds, separating the ewes from their lambs for the last of the morning milking, but it was slow going, yesterday's heat now simmering just off the boil. They had both abandoned their clothes and were wearing just their slips; there was no one here to see, after all, they had the entire glen to themselves. 'I thought you said she'd be over this morning?' Mhairi asked, glancing up the glen for the hundredth time.

'Aye, I did. She promised she'd be over at first light.'

'So then her da' must have stopped her.'

'Mmm.' Flora wrestled with a particularly resistant ewe. 'Or else someone promised her a run on the ropes.'

'Well, just so long as she's not with her sun god.' Mhairi had had a fretful night, worrying about all the things she could not see – Donald, lying so injured in his bed that Lorna had to provide through-the-night care; Effie, wholly unaware of the consequences of a dazzling attraction . . .

'She won't. I could see I frightened her off him.'

And yet she still wasn't here. Mhairi said nothing. The humidity was oppressive now; even if Flora had failed in her mission to get Effie over to this side of the isle, the brewing storm would chase her dashing lord off before time. Effie would be heartbroken, however it happened.

They moved through the last of the herd slowly – milking could never be rushed – filling the churns as the sun slid drowsily through the sky. Mhairi could feel her hairline was damp, beads of sweat at her brow as she sat with her cheek pressed to those hot woollen flanks. Her arms were sunburnt and aching when she caught sight of a dark dot, travelling downhill. She straightened up, squinting into the distance. 'Who's that?'

'At last! Better late than never,' Flora declared triumphantly.

'No . . . I don't think that's Eff,' Mhairi murmured, failing to spot Poppit, Effie's brown shadow, at the figure's heels.

They watched and waited, both growing tense.

'Oh no,' Flora groaned. 'It's Mathieson . . . What's he doing over here?'

Mhairi could guess. She felt the panic course through her.

'Quick, we'd best make ourselves decent,' Flora muttered, picking up the pails and walking back towards the souterrain to fetch their clothes. 'It would hardly do presenting ourselves like this to him now, would it?' she asked archly.

Flora was fastening her own shawl when she came out into the communal space a few minutes later and saw Mhairi was sitting on her sleeping platform, still in her slip. 'Why aren't you dressed?' She frowned.

'. . . I can't. I can't do it. He mustn't see me.' Mhairi's voice was quiet.

'Of course you can, it'll be fine.'

'I can't, Flora. I can't lie to a man like him. He's too clever for me.'

Flora stared at her for a moment, not denying it.

'Please – he's come down to check on the slops, it must be that he's here for. Won't you just show him yourself? Tell him I'm poorly.'

'But you know how he despises me. I won't flatter him, and it only ever makes things worse.'

'No. He'll not do that now you're engaged. James is a powerful man, he knows that. Please . . .'

Flora gave a reluctant groan. 'Fine. But y' owe me.'

'Anything.' Mhairi handed back over the brooch without needing to be asked.

With a final tug, tightening her shawl at her waist, Flora went back outside again and walked a short distance over the grass to wait for the factor. Mhairi stood by the entrance, just out of sight and listening hard. She could see the bottom edge of Flora's skirt blowing into her frame of vision every few moments.

'Mr Mathieson, to what do we owe the honour?' she heard Flora ask brightly, but there was a discernible wry note in her voice. 'This is quite a stroll, coming all the way over here.'

'Fetch Mhairi. I need to speak to her.' His voice was abrupt, harsh even.

There was a short pause as Flora registered that the factor was not in the mood to play social niceties. 'I'm afraid she's resting. She's poorly.'

He made a sound of annoyance. 'God's truth,' he muttered. 'Effie said the same.'

'She did?' Flora asked, sounding surprised. 'When?'

'This morning.'

'Oh? We were hoping to see her today.'

'Aye, she said that too, but she's ditched coming to help you for learning to swim with his lordship instead. She's completely forgotten herself; her father's in a rage.'

Mhairi frowned. She could see Flora shifting her weight uncertainly. 'Well, I'm . . . sorry to hear that.'

'Why? It's nothing to do with you.'

'I just meant, it's not nice to think of people being upset.'

There followed a short pause and Mhairi could well imagine the scowl on the factor's face. He could be irritable at the best of times, but something had got his goat today. 'Well, where are the slops? Fin MacKinnon told me Mhairi brought them over here with her,' he said, finally getting to the point of his visit.

'Aye. They're over there,' Flora said, pointing to the pail carefully nestled in the crook of a fank to protect it from frolicking sheep. 'Mhairi's been diligent in turning them and keeping them in the sun. She goes down to the cove every morning and evening and refreshes the water. She's not missed a single day since you left last summer.'

'The cove?' He sounded scandalized. 'But the water's rough there! If they were to fall in, she couldn't recover them. They'd be lost to the sea and what would my father do then?'

'Well, there's nowhere else over here where she can do it, is there? But she's very careful. She lies on the low rocks as she does it and takes great care with them.'

Her voice had grown more distant and Mhairi could see she was following behind the factor as he bent over the bucket and inspected the contents. Mhairi dared to peek her head around the entrance and saw him crouched on his haunches, seemingly unperturbed by the stink. The slops had, over the course of the seasons, hardened into a solid form and now were turning ever paler, a far cry from their original visceral state.

She watched him nod his head a few times, then rise. Miraculously, he seemed pleased. 'Very well. You can tell her I can see she's keeping to her side of the bargain. A few more months and I'll be able to take them back with me on the smack.'

'As you wish,' Flora replied noncommittally.

The factor gave her a quizzical look.

'What?'

'There's something different about you.'

Flora lapsed into one of her dazzling smiles. 'Really? Perhaps it's the glow of love? Have you heard I'm engaged? I'm to be Mrs James Callaghan in—'

'Yes, I heard.' He cut her off. 'It's not that.'

'My suntan, then? We're working outside here from dawn to dusk. Effie thinks we're lying about in the sun, but twelve hundred sheep to look after is a mighty number for just two of us.'

The factor made a derisory sound. 'Yes, McKinnon told me about his new scheme. It sounds a ridiculous undertaking to me. You'll be half dead by the end of it.'

He was absolutely right. They had thought the lambing season had finished before coming over this side, but only the other day, Mhairi had discovered that a few of the ewes were still carrying and would for a few weeks yet; one of the tups must have escaped and mated them later, unseen. It was a complication she and Flora could do without when they were already stretched past their limits.

'Still, what do I care? So long as the rents come in on time, it's no business of mine how you divvy up the labour.'

His intimation that it was irrelevant to him if they were half dead or not made Mhairi flinch – she could only imagine the look on Flora's face right now. She watched him turn to head back up the slope, satisfied his precious remedy was in good hands.

'Oh, Mr Mathieson,' Flora called after him, and Mhairi ducked her head back in as she saw the factor turn back. 'Could I possibly prevail upon you to carry two of the churns up to the cleit on Am Blaid? It would save us an extra loop there and back.' Mhairi could hear in her voice that her friend was smiling her most dazzling smile.

The factor gave a sudden laugh; it was the most spontaneous, genuine response Mhairi had ever heard from him. No one could resist Flora, after all, not even him, the most disagreeable man on—

'Does a man keep a dog and bark himself?' she heard him ask.

'. . . Excuse me?'

'Beauty won't boil the pot, Miss MacQueen, now will it?'

There followed an astounded silence. Had he really been so rude? Mhairi dared to look back out again, but the factor was already marching uphill, his strong arms swinging freely. She watched him go, hating him for his bare-faced disdain and contempt for every one of them. He liked to believe he was so much better than them, so much cleverer . . .

She squinted as he grew smaller, but as she watched him go, she had a sense of something catching deep inside her mind, a small pull in the silk folds of her memory. Something was off, or somehow . . . wrong. If she could just think . . . think back . . . But it eluded her, a white smoke she couldn't catch, drifting among the clouds.

The light was dying as Mhairi brought the last of the filled churns up to the cleit on Am Blaid and set it down, staring at what was and wasn't there: no empty churns from the village, the filled ones still stacked in a pile. Nothing had been collected and nothing had been left all day.

Had something happened? She walked over to the brow of the slope and looked down upon Village Bay – it made her heart ache to see the curve of lights in the cottages, life continuing on without her. She saw the silhouette of the sloop, too: a fine craft, different to the Lipton yacht but still elegant, a token of another world.

'Mhairi!'

She was startled to hear her own name called and immediately recoiled as she saw a figure striding up to the ridge. He had been hidden from view by a cleit.

'David?' she asked, recognizing his gait, panicking that she had been caught up here. She tried to reassure herself that the light was fading but one look at his face and she knew he barely even saw her; grief still had him in a firm grip. He was a man moving through the motions, that was all.

'Good, you're here,' he panted. 'I've something to tell you.'

She felt herself go cold. Donald? Had something happened? ' . . . What is it? What's wrong?' She waited impatiently for him to get his breath back. 'Just say it, David.'

'We've had a letter back.'

She stared at him blankly. Her brain had been primed to hear Donald's name. What . . . letter? Was it from James? Or, God forbid, Alexander?

'It's happening. We're doing it. We're being evacuated at the end of the summer.'

If every word had been a punch, she couldn't have been more surprised. 'What?' she whispered. *That* letter?

'Aye. Word came this afternoon. We thought you and Flora should know. It might change the timing of things for you both . . . you know, for leaving here. We'll need all the help we can get to get this place loaded up.'

Mhairi blinked, trying to take in the enormity of his words. 'Evacuated?' she repeated.

'Everyone's in shock. There's upset. The older ones are taking it bad, like,' he said. 'Some are pleased – your brothers, and Lorna, of course.'

Of course. Lorna had been the architect of it all. Devastated by what she had called Molly's 'needless' death, she had sat with the minister in the days and weeks that followed, talking

245

long into the night. They had finally called a village meeting in March. The pitch had been a simple one, the facts stark: this was their second severe winter on the bounce when the harvest had failed and animals had been lost, when the villagers had been confined to their crofts for up to a week at a time. Coupled with the fact that Molly's death would have been preventable on the mainland, as well as the coming loss of another of their two young women to marriage, their numbers were now too few to make continuing here possible. Generations past might have managed to repopulate with willing Harris men and women, but times had changed. The old ways were dying and the world was moving fast, industrializing and becoming more comfortable. Why would anyone move to St Kilda and risk his life cragging for his dinner, when he could live on Skye and travel on a bus and see a talking picture? They wouldn't. Being born to the life here was one thing, choosing it quite another. It wasn't lost on any of the islanders that they were being told this by a woman who had once chosen it herself.

But it was too hard. Too hopeless. In this age, it wasn't acceptable for a healthy young woman to die of pneumonia, or for men to fall from cliffs catching eggs when they could just keep chickens.

Even so, resistance had been fierce. Ma Peg, Mad Annie, Old Fin and Robert Gillies wanted – expected – to live out their days here, to be buried in the cemetery beside their families: parents, lost husbands, wives and far too many children. But the younger ones were enticed. They had heard many of the whalers' and trawlermen's reports of the comforts of life on the other side, the opportunities and choices they would have. In the end, agreement had been reached on one abiding principle – they would request evacuation but the outcome must be total. They would either all go, or all stay.

Most of them didn't think the request to the British govern-ment stood a chance. Nothing else they had asked for had ever been granted – not a wireless transmitter, a regular mail service, nor even a bigger boat or fishing nets. Uprooting an entire community of thirty-six villagers, their livestock and all worldly possessions, and relocating them to the mainland, finding them homes and jobs . . . and all in a matter of months? It didn't seem possible.

And yet . . .

Mhairi felt her heart beat faster, harder, as the initial shock settled and the next wave of questions came: What did this mean for her engagement? She was only being married off to Alexander because her father couldn't afford to support her here. If all her family was being moved . . . But of course, it was no longer that simple. The minister's teachings had told her that the salvation of her soul depended upon marriage to the man she had sinned with. Her fate was sealed, wherever her fellow St Kildans ended up.

'How have my parents taken it, do you know?' she asked him.

'Bewildered. Conflicted. It was a big shock.'

'Aye.' Mhairi bit her lip, well able to imagine their dismay. Her mother loved their life here, hard though it was, their large family always within arm's reach. And her father, with his exalted position as the postmaster: what would become of him on the mainland? Just another man? Where would they go? Harris? Glasgow? London?

'. . . And you, David? How do y' feel about it?' she asked, seeing how he stared into the distance, a look of utter deso-lation upon his handsome face. He had none of the intensity of his sister's look, nor her dark gypsy colouring either. His countenance was open and ruddy-cheeked, but he shared her

247

generous lips, strong brows and long dark lashes. His jaw slid forward like a brake, holding back emotion.

'. . . I can't . . . I can't imagine leaving her here.' He shook his head and Mhairi knew he was staring down at the burial ground. He had loved Molly deeply and had been patient for the future he had believed would be his, but nothing at all would remain of their dreams, it seemed. 'I don't want to leave her behind.'

'No,' Mhairi whispered, touching his arm. 'I know you don't.'

The wind gusted suddenly, sending the sloop rocking wildly on its anchor chains in the bay, a continuous clink of cleats knocking against the mast. She could see a train of crew moving up and down the jetty, carrying things.

'They're going, then? The earl and his son?'

'Aye. And the factor too.'

Poor Effie, Mhairi thought, thinking of her friend down there, watching, waiting, her heart breaking piece by piece. She must be desperate. Even today's shocking news couldn't bring her any relief, for it wasn't just distance that would keep her apart from the man she loved. Class was just a concept here, but on the other side of the water, it was a prison.

'I should get back down there,' he said, turning to leave again. 'You don't need anything?'

'No. We're fine.'

He went to leave.

'David . . .'

'Aye?'

She swallowed, hoping her voice wouldn't betray her. 'How's Donald? Flora said he hit his head?'

'Aye. He's in bed still, but sitting up now. Lorna's keeping a close eye.'

'That's good. Tell him I . . . I said hello, will you?'

'Aye, will do.'

She watched him disappear into the night, biting her lip anxiously. If Donald was sitting up, then he must have heard the news, surely? What did he think about it? Where would he go? It had been one thing to know he would be over here while she was in Harris; she thought she could have borne that. But for him to slip into the vastness of the mainland . . .

A scattering sound suddenly ripped towards her and she froze and braced just as something tore past. 'Poppit?' she called, recognizing the distinctive brown flash. Her eyes narrowed as the dog disappeared into the distance, racing up the hill. She was at full pelt, chasing after something – but there was no sign of Effie. Mhairi frowned; that dog was devoted to her mistress, never not at her side.

She didn't hesitate. Something was wrong with Effie, she knew it. She ran after the dog as best she could, following the ridge along the top towards Ruival. The wind was buffeting the first fingers of the storm harassing the isle, but she stumbled along in the darkness, calling for Poppit. Wherever she found the dog, she would find Effie, she knew that much. Far below to her left, the lights shone in the crescent village, like a smile of golden nuggets on the ground. To her right, a short distance off, where the coastline folded inwards in a small inlet, she could hear the crash of waves thundering against the black cliffs.

'Poppit!' she called, just as a scream tore through the sky. She froze.

'Poppit!' someone else called back. Or rather, screamed too. 'Poppit!'

Effie? Mhairi heard the terror in her friend's voice. She ran past the storm cleit, pulling up short at the sight of a man lying on the ground, clutching his calf in agony.

'Hai!' she exclaimed in fright, panting heavily. '. . . W-what's going on up here?'

Effie wheeled round to face her, looking wilder and more feral than Mhairi had ever seen her; one cheek was a vivid scarlet. Poppit, her jowls bloodied and her hackles up, was standing guard over the man, who Mhairi could see now was Frank Mathieson, their factor.

She looked back up at Effie in disbelief. 'What . . . ? What has he done?' She ran to her friend, holding her, scanning her for injuries.

'I'm all right. I'm not hurt,' Effie said in a shaky voice. 'Really.'

Mhairi didn't believe her. What on earth was her friend doing up here with Mathieson? And why had Poppit attacked him? She looked between the two of them again, trying to make it all make sense. There was no reason for them to be up here, in such an isolated spot, after dark, during a coming storm. He was due to leave at any moment, surely? 'Effie? What's going on?'

For a moment Effie couldn't seem to find her voice. Terror was running through her wide eyes. '. . . There was a misunderstanding, that's all. I was just about to head back.'

Head back? And pretend the factor wasn't lying injured on the ground? Mhairi frowned. None of this made sense. 'But why are you all the way up here?'

'Why are you? I thought you were over the side?' Effie's voice was strained but she was clearly making a tremendous effort to appear normal, relaxed.

Mhairi tipped her head to the side, knowing something was terribly wrong. Why was Effie protecting Mathieson? She stepped between her friend and the man on the ground, needing Effie's attention to be on her and not him. 'Aye, I was,' she said warily. 'But David MacQueen just came over to tell us the big news and I thought I should check how Ma and Da were taking it. Then Poppit tore past me at Am Blaid and shot up here like a rocket. It got me worried. She never leaves your side, but she looked like she was just going to race off the cliffs.'

Effie dropped her head suddenly, as if Mhairi's words had undone her. She began to cry. Effie never cried!

'Effie, just tell me what happened,' Mhairi whispered desperately, placing her hands upon her friend's shoulders. 'Let me help.'

Effie looked up again. Their gazes connected, but then Effie's eyes slid away from Mhairi, over her shoulder, and as if in slow motion her face contorted into a look of horror. The world crumbled then. Mhairi saw nothing, she understood nothing.

'No!' Effie screamed as Mhairi felt her head jerked violently back, hair torn from her scalp as she was thrown through the air, before hitting the ground hard. She felt the breath knocked from her, her body heavy and gasping for air.

'*Poppit!*' Effie's scream was the worst yet and from the corner of her eye, she saw the silky brown dog hit a rock with sickening force.

'One word about any of this and I'll see to it that your father doesn't see the sun rise. Do you understand me?' The words were a hiss, vicious and venomous. Mhairi, winded on the ground, was stunned it could be the factor saying them. Saying them to Effie. What had she done to provoke such violence?

'You should be thanking me. I've thrown you a lifeline. You'll never survive the mainland. You're already saddled with debt and you've no skills of use over there. If you want a future for him, you'll accept the way things are and not try to fight me, do you hear?'

What . . . what did he mean? Mhairi tried to lift her head but her body was still caught in a state of abeyance, unable to inhale or exhale, gasping for breath.

'I'll be back soon enough. Now I have an evacuation to organize, I'll need to come back here multiple times this summer . . . You'd better be ready for me. We've jumped the broom and that makes you my wife now—'

What?

'—I'll be back for what is mine! Lawfully *mine*, do you hear? I will take what is owed to me – if it's the last thing I do!'

There was a sudden sharp slapping sound, followed again by a sickening thud. And then silence. Only the wind stirred, rustling the grasses, flapping their clothes.

Mhairi felt her diaphragm release at last and she took a full breath. She moved fractionally. 'Eff . . . ?' she groaned, but only silence came back at first. She tried to lift her head.

'It's fine. I'm here,' Effie whispered haltingly from the ground. '. . . He's gone.'

Mhairi let her head drop again.

'Poppit?' Effie whispered, straining as she reached for her pet. '. . . Pops?'

Nothing. Then a low whimper provided reassurance and brought a sob from her friend. 'Oh, thank God!' Effie sobbed, getting onto her hands and knees and crawling over to the animal.

Mhairi wanted to feel relief too. She wanted to feel like the danger had passed and that she was safe. Everything would be all right. Only, she had a low, dull ache in her abdomen.

And nausea.

And a wet stickiness between her legs, that was starting as a trickle. And becoming a tide.

Chapter Nineteen

Mhairi lay on her side, staring into the gloom. The voices coming from the main space were low, occasional words drifting through like stray cats looking for somewhere to sit. Lorna's tone was unmistakable, though. This was *serious*. She was *concerned*. It was *imperative* that she rest.

She closed her eyes again, as if that would block out the sounds. Try as she might to reach for happiness, life kept falling apart upon her. If only she had hidden from David. If only she hadn't followed a racing dog into the dark. If only she hadn't run into a scenario that even now made no sense to her. That had led to this. Each tiny decision had led her away from the future she was trying to reach.

She heard the sound of feet on the ground, and then Flora was kneeling in front of her.

'She's gone. She'll be back in the morning,' Flora said, looking anxious as she clasped Mhairi's forearm and squeezed it gently. '. . . How are you feeling?'

Mhairi closed her eyes as if the words themselves hurt her. 'Better.' She felt Flora's hand gently push back her hair.

'Lorna says it's imperative that you rest. Completely. No getting up at all.'

'No.'

'The bleeding's still stopped?'

Mhairi flinched, but nodded. Lying on the ground, feeling the dampness spreading as Effie had torn down the hill to fetch the nurse, had felt like the longest wait of her life. She had been certain it was all over.

'Well, as long as there's no more, she thinks the baby will be safe.' Flora squeezed her arm in reassurance.

'. . . Really?' Mhairi whispered, still not daring to hope.

'Aye. But no getting up,' Flora reiterated.

Mhairi felt the tears pool. Could it . . . would it all be fine? She must lie there, bedbound in the dark. Stricken.

Donald, stricken.

Their baby, stricken.

She felt the first tear fall as she was reminded how close she'd come to losing everything, as if Fate itself was against them. Was this God's will? Retribution for her sins?

'What . . . what happened up there?' Flora whispered.

Mhairi caught her breath. Effie had pleaded with her – whispering into her ear just before Lorna had helped her down the slope – *Don't tell Lorna! Don't mention him!* It was an accident in the dark, that was all.

Effie's caution was well placed. Lorna wouldn't hesitate to act if she knew what had really happened, but Mhairi had heard what Mathieson had hissed to Effie as she lay on the ground clearly – his threat to Effie's father's life. Effie was terrified he would act on it, and after his violence against both of them, Mhairi didn't doubt it either. Frank Mathieson had never inconvenienced himself with being a pleasant or charming man, yet before tonight, she wouldn't have thought him a monster. But he had been a man possessed; he had been capable of anything.

'I think . . .' she said haltingly. 'I think I walked in on Effie jumping the broom.'

'. . . What?'

Flora, of course, understood what a broomstick marriage was. They had all grown up to stories of the old custom of 'jumping the broom' when there was no minister in residence on the isle.

'She married Lord Sholto?'

Mhairi looked at her. 'No . . . The factor.'

Flora fell back on her heels as if she'd been pushed, her eyes and mouth wide open. 'The f . . . ?' It was almost impossible for her to say the words. 'Effie jumped the broom with Frank Mathieson?'

'He forced her to do it. He was wild, Flora,' Mhairi whispered. 'Deranged! A madman! I never could have imagined he could be like that. He was attacking her.'

Flora's hands flew to her mouth. '. . . You mean . . . ?'

'They had been fighting, I think. Poppit had bitten him.'

She closed her eyes as if in pain again, remembering how she had dragged herself to lie against the injured animal and try to comfort her too as they waited for Effie to return with help. Had it not been for the dog's broken leg, and possibly ribs, Effie would have come down here with the nurse as well; but Lorna had had to insist that she take the dog back down to the village and get her warm until she could return and examine her properly. Although she was no vet, a bone was a bone, she had said. 'He almost killed Poppit.'

It had all so happened so fast, in the dark, everything a blur, the wind howling and dizzying them all.

'. . . Effie and Mathieson?' Flora repeated, aghast. 'It makes no sense. He's twice her age! He's never . . . I mean . . . !'

'I know. She was horrified, Flora. Terrified. I don't think she had any idea he . . . thought of her like that.'

'My God. My God. And where is he now? Is Effie back

home? Is she safe from him? We need to get over there and tell everyone what he did!'

'No. No.' Mhairi spoke softly, calming her friend. 'He's gone again. He left with the earl and his son. He came with them and he's set sail with them.'

'Oh.' Flora's face changed again as she realized what else that meant for Effie; a different kind of heartbreak. 'Poor Eff,' Flora whispered. 'All that in one night.'

'I know. Although right now, I don't think she can think on anything beyond Poppit being all right.'

'Of course.' Flora frowned, looking upset. '. . . It just makes no sense, coming out of nowhere like that. Why? Why now?'

Mhairi blinked, realizing her friend still didn't know their big news. In all the chaos, it had been overlooked. 'I think it might have been because he knows he's going to lose her. Or rather, lose control over her.'

'. . . Huh?'

'I met David on the ridge when I was bringing up the churns. There's been some news.' She took a deep breath. 'They've granted the request. We're going to be evacuated at the end of the summer.'

Mhairi watched as Flora's face paled again. 'What . . . ? They actually said yes?'

'They did.' For Flora – for both of them – it was academic, their futures off the isle already arranged. But the shock was still immense. Everything would change. 'But it means Mathieson is going to come back here again soon. The evacuation will mean things need sorting.'

Flora's jaw clenched as she understood the threat to their friend. 'So then we have to tell people what he did. He canna just come back and—'

'No. Effie doesn't want that. At least, not yet. We need to

talk to her first. She begged me not to tell Lorna that Mathieson had even been up there; he made all sorts of threats against her father. She's terrified he'll act on it. We have to do as she asks. She made me say we'd just been walking and fell down in the dark.'

Flora took a deep inhale, looking unconvinced. '. . . And Lorna believed that?'

'Seemed to.'

Flora shook her head in her hands. 'Everything's such a mess!' she despaired.

'I know.' Mhairi's hand went to her belly, stroking the gentle swell; it had only just begun to protrude. She was six months gone now. Six months since that evening in the coffin cleit when Mary had walked in at precisely the wrong moment. There had only been that one time, but once had been all it took.

Flora looked back at her, all her fire and spirit quenched for once. 'How did we get here, Mhairi?' she asked, her eyes shining with tears.

Mhairi could only shrug. '. . . Love.'

She had been underground for four days now. Lying in the dark. Lying in the damp. Clutching her belly and willing her baby to stay alive. Lorna came down each morning to check on her and was satisfied the danger had passed – there had been no further bleeding since that night – but Mhairi was afraid to stir. How could she trust her body again? Could she trust anyone?

There was safety in a hole in the ground – no prying eyes, no harsh elements, no violent men. The sunlight couldn't penetrate the souterrain as deeply as her sleeping chamber but the very tips of the sunbeams alleviated the pervasive gloom in the central chamber and she would watch them flicker with the shadows of passing sheep. Flora's shadow too.

Flora was out there looking after the flock, almost entirely on her own. Lorna would milk as many as she could manage when she came over the ridge each morning, and Effie – although she was needed on the other side through the days – would come over at sunset to help too. Poppit's leg was broken, but Lorna had somehow splinted it with some stored driftwood and she was beginning to hobble around with it quite well. She was recovering.

Which was more than could be said of her mistress. Pale-faced and red-eyed, Effie looked broken by what had happened during the storm. Each time she left to head back to Village Bay, Flora would duck back into the souterrain to fret over her. She couldn't tell whether it was the trauma of the factor's madness or the loss of Sholto that had winged their friend, but Effie was almost silent in her duties now and even avoiding the ropes, her spiritual playground. No one could fail to see the change in her; she was terrified of Mathieson's return.

A shadow rippled past the beams in the doorway, gradually filling it until Mhairi heard footsteps. She blinked, waiting for Flora's distinctive silhouette, but the one that came was the one she had dreamt of.

'Donald?' she whispered, seeing how his bulk filled the narrow space as he squeezed through to her chamber. She went to throw the blanket off her, to reach him, but he held her down with a hand.

'Shhh,' he hushed her, looking down with a pale face, his eyes glassy as he took in her prostrate form – her rounded tummy still held their baby within it. She watched as he laid a hand reverentially upon her, as if in holy communion. 'Mhairi,' he winced. 'I knew nothing of what had passed till this morning.'

'We're fine. Lorna's been checking in every day. I've scarce moved.' Her eyes roamed over him and she realized his injuries had been worse than Flora had led her to believe. His eyes were sunken, his skin sallow and there was a balded patch of scalp where the dark hair had been crudely cut away, a thick crusted scar crossing the pale flesh. She reached up, tracing it lightly with a finger, the site of his only vulnerability. 'But what happened to you?'

'It was a misunderstanding, that's all,' he said, shaking his head dismissively.

'Misunderstanding?' she frowned. 'But I thought you slipped?'

His eyes darkened. 'Is that what he said?'

He? 'You mean Mathieson?' she frowned.

'Never mind—'

'Donald, no, tell me the truth . . . Flora said Mathieson came back saying you slipped on rocks chasing sheep. Are you saying you didn't?'

He swallowed. 'You mustn't worry about it. It's not important. All that matters is that you're well.'

She stared at him. '. . . And what if I didn't slip either?'

His eyes narrowed, his body pulling back slightly as he looked down at her. 'What? Lorna said—'

'I know. Because Effie wanted it that way.'

'Effie?' He straightened up, openly alarmed now. 'Mhairi – what in God's name happened?'

But she shook her head. 'Tell me your news first. What really went on over there, Donald?'

He sighed, but he knew her stubborn streak now; she would not be deterred. 'We had a disagreement – another one – over the prices he'll give us this year. It's getting worse, not better. Tweed's falling through the floor. He says things are bad out there and no one will pay; there's weavers on the mainland with whole houses full of bolts they can't shift. He's wanting us to provide almost half as much again, for a third less – and what options do we have? There's no diversification here! What we get from the birds and the sheep, that's all we can harvest, he knows that. I told him I'd had enough and wouldn't accept it. I'd go to MacLeod myself if I had to.'

'And so, what? He hit you?'

'It got physical, aye. He was a boxer in his younger years.' He looked down. 'Knows how to throw a right hook for sure. I went down, struck a rock.'

'You could have been killed!'

'But I wasn't. Things just got heated, that's all, and I came out on the wrong side of it.' His hand rose to the scar on his scalp. 'I don't like the man but it wasn't any more than a disagreement.'

Mhairi stared at him. She wanted to believe him – but if it was so innocent, why had Mathieson lied?

'Now your turn. What happened?'

She closed her eyes, hating having to relive it. 'The night of the storm, I came upon him struggling with Effie.' She saw a frown pucker his brow. 'He had forced her to jump the broom and he was trying to . . . consummate the marriage.'

Donald pulled back. 'What?'

'I know. We can't believe it.'

'We . . . ?'

'Me and Flora. Effie, of course. She's in shock.'

'But Lorna doesn't know?'

She shook her head. 'When I came across them, Poppit had just bitten him and Frank was . . . he was wild with rage. Effie was trying to make little of it to me, I could see; she was terrified. But then he grabbed me and threw me . . .'

Her voice failed as she saw his expression change. It was like watching thunder roll across a sky.

'I couldn't get up. I knew I'd started bleeding. I thought I was losing the baby . . . When he'd gone, Effie ran down to the village to get Lorna while I stayed with Poppit. She told Lorna we'd just slipped in the dark. She doesn't want anyone knowing what Mathieson did.'

There was a long silence, Donald's breathing heavy and slow in the dark. 'I'll kill him,' he breathed, an expression in his eyes she had never seen before.

'Donald, no.' She clutched his arm. 'He was trying to get Effie – I was just in the way. And he didn't know about the baby.'

'He hurt you! He almost killed our child! You're making excuses for him?'

'But he didn't. The baby's well. And I am too. It's Effie I'm worried about.'

He was shaking his head and she could feel from his forearms that his hands were pulled into his fists.

'Please listen to me, Donald,' she begged. 'I'm fine and we're safe. Mathieson's not interested in us. It's Effie he wants. And he's going to come back again soon; the evacuation means he needs to make another trip this summer. He's said he's going to "claim what is his". She's the one you need to protect, Donald. No one else knows what he's done. She's not safe over there.' She clutched his arm tighter. 'You have to watch over her; make sure when he comes back that he can never be alone with her.'

He stared back at her, eyes gleaming darkly. Was he hearing a word she said?

'Donald, please,' she urged. 'For me.'

He sighed, looking away and giving only the faintest of nods.

'Thank you,' she whispered, clutching his arm. 'It's behind us. He won't hurt us again.' She took his hand and kissed the back of it, trying to calm him down. 'Besides, I've already thought of the perfect revenge. I've had four days to think on it.'

'Oh?'

'I'm going to throw his precious slops in the sea. I'm going to tell him a wave caught me as I was changing the water and there'll be nothing he can do; it was just an accident.' She shrugged. 'I know it's not much, but seeing as it's the only thing he seems to care about, curing his father.'

He seemed underwhelmed by her method of vengeance. 'His mother, you mean,' he muttered sourly.

'Huh?'

'It's his mother with the gout, not his father.'

Mhairi thought back. 'No, he definitely said the other day that it was for his father.'

Donald frowned at her as they stared at one another and she felt that itch in her brain again, the one she'd felt as she'd eavesdropped on the conversation. She tried to remember the fuss that day on the shore last September – Donald's bad mood, Effie's fierce sulk as she had vied for every last opportunity to earn a coin and support her father.

'But he *did* say his mother that first time, didn't he?' she whispered. '*And my poor mother is much afflicted by it.*'

'Aye. He did.' Donald's eyes narrowed as he sat back again thoughtfully. '. . . What's that bastard up to now?'

Neither of them spoke for a few moments. What could be so special about those slops that the factor needed to lie about them?

'Where are they now?'

'In a bucket by the wall outside. He came all the way over here just to see them. I kept well out of the way, but he insulted Flora every opportunity he got. I thought he might be angry when he saw them; they're nothing like they were. But he seemed pleased.'

'How have they changed? What's happened to them?'

'Well, they've hardened into a big lump, and gone pale.'

She shrugged as he looked past her into space, concentrating hard. His eyes had narrowed and his mouth was parted. It was another moment before he looked back at her. 'Don't throw them away, not yet . . . I might have a better revenge.'

'What is it?' She watched him carefully, seeing how his eyes darted, his brain firing hard.

'I'll not raise your hopes till I know for sure. I'll need to take another trip first and make some enquiries.'

'What? But where?'

'Back to Harris,' he murmured, looking back at her with eyes that were starting to gleam. 'If those slops are what I think they might be, there could be a deal to be made.'

A deal? 'You mean with old McLennan?'

'No, not him,' he demurred, a smile growing on his lips. 'This time I'm going straight to the top.'

Chapter Twenty

Summer rolled out, heavy and listless. Though the birds were caught from the cliffs, though the children went to school and the villagers to the kirk, there was a feeling of drift. The knowledge that they were leaving before another harsh winter could strike them down meant summer could be enjoyed with a freedom not previously known. The women began to lie in the grass and watch the clouds; everyone stopped when a pod of orcas came to play in the bay one afternoon; the men fished off the rocks most evenings without fretting whether they caught anything, just enjoying the sunsets; and the whalers and trawlermen found their hosts more inclined to long conversation on the Street. The number of visitors had trebled, as those who could turned their yachts north-wards to glimpse the last days of an island nation. Over two thousand years of continuous human settlement was drawing to a close and people wanted to see the final act. Even those who couldn't visit in person still wanted their piece of the isle: the post bags were doubling, tripling in volume, as people from afar vied for St Kildan stamped postcards. Lorna was having to help Mhairi's father almost full time in the post office now, confiding to Mhairi and Flora – on her discreet twice-weekly visits – that Effie stood by the post office every time a ship came in, waiting for a letter that never came.

Mhairi couldn't bear the forlorn image. Effie was like a butterfly, compelled to perpetual motion. The thought of her waiting on the wall for a letter with her name on it . . . Her eyes flickered to where Effie sat now. The three of them were together again, plucking the fulmars Effie had come over to catch on their behalf for this week's meals. They were sitting cross-legged in the grass, the sun dropping softly from its high arch. All around them the sheep were dozing on the slopes, tails flicking at the flies as they sought pale shelter against the stone dykes, waiting for a breeze. It was summer's longest day and the sky was holding its breath, the dry heat suspended above their heads like a tethered veil. Their fingers worked in unison as they pulled feathers from the bird carcasses, plumes of white down speckling the meadow like daisies.

'I'll not miss this,' Flora sighed, pressing the back of her hand to her brow.

'Of course you won't. You won't even remember it,' Effie said. 'You'll be a grand lady in your house with stairs and you'll have lipstick and a wireless and you simply won't believe that you ever had to pluck the fulmars.' She said it without any jealousy or bitterness, her broken heart a private sadness, and Flora looked delighted by the image that she had conjured.

'You must come to visit. James says there'll be a bedroom for each of you and we'll get you a new dress every time you come to stay, and we'll go to shows and we'll dine in restaurants . . .'

'Real-life restaurants?' Mhairi asked. She had heard about them from one of the ship captains – places where food was simply brought to you on a plate, already caught, already cooked.

She realized she must have sounded simple, for even Effie laughed. 'Yes! Actual places where they pluck and cook the birds for you.'

'Oh . . . That must be nice,' she said, feeling chastened. There would be nothing like that awaiting her in Harris.

'James says in Glasgow you could go out every night for a month and not eat in the same place twice.' Flora tossed her hair back, looking thrilled by this too. Not just convenience, but variety too!

'So long as m' belly's full, I'll not much care what's in it,' Effie shrugged.

Mhairi's gaze fell to her friend's flat stomach. It was everything's Mhairi's now wasn't – she had grown a lot in the past month, in spite of the very near miss caused by the factor's violence. But in a few weeks, this baby would be born and her body would return to its girlish form. Her secret would be safe, her good family name intact. As Mary had told her, she would have 'got away with it'. She would be a mother and no one over the ridge would ever know.

And she didn't think she could bear it.

'Hush now, Mhairi,' Flora said quickly, seeing how she had fallen still and was desperately biting back the tears; they came regularly now, often unbidden. 'You'll be fine.'

'How can you say that?' she cried. 'It's not the same for me as it is for you. When we cross over, you'll get everything you ever wanted. But I'm going to *lose* everything. And nothing can stop it.'

'A wave will rise on quiet water, Mhairi,' Flora replied, smoothing Mhairi's hair and reaching for her hand. She had spent much of her time in the past few weeks calming her friend down. 'You have to just trust your happiness lies in another place.'

Mhairi snatched her hands away, for she knew full well there was no happiness awaiting her in Harris. 'You keep saying that, but what's being asked of me . . . it's too much!' Her heart pounded with panic. Every night she woke up in a sweat, crying. And when she did sleep, Alexander invaded her dreams again, the old memories coming back as she counted down not just the days till the birth, but till evacuation. The last day in August was when they would leave here, two months from now . . . Everyone she loved, she would lose in one day. How was it to be borne? She felt herself falling apart.

'I know. And I'd be raging too. I'd be mad with grief if it was me who had to do it,' Flora said. 'But you're a better person than me. You're good all the way through. I'm not even good skin deep.'

'You're not that bad,' Effie tutted, rolling her eyes.

'Aren't I? I lose my temper if the wind messes my hair! I curse if I bang my knee in kirk. If it wasn't for this . . .' Flora framed her beautiful face with cupped hands. 'They'd have thrown me over the top years ago.' She gave an impish smile.

Even Mhairi had to smile. Flora always knew how to bring her down, draw her back out of herself. She hiccupped softly. 'They would not,' she chided, lightly slapping Flora's knee. 'You have lots of good qualities.'

'I'm a beautiful monster,' Flora argued, refusing the compliment for once. 'And Effie's a tow-haired wildling . . .'

'Oi!' Effie protested, as if she wasn't sitting there in a pair of her brother's trousers, covered in cuts and bruises, her hair a knotted mess.

Flora smiled at Mhairi lovingly. 'You're the best of us, Mhairi. There's no way you're not going to get your reward. It is coming . . . Even if you can't see it yet. You have to believe it's coming.'

Mhairi wished she could see it. She wished she could have Flora's confidence. Determination. Beauty. Luck. She smiled but said nothing more as she shook her head sadly. She knew exactly what was coming her way. The path was not just set, but fully paved. If Flora knew what her life was going to look like three months from now, so did Mhairi. That was the problem.

'The same goes for you,' Flora said, turning her attention to Effie. Heartbreak was gnawing her from the inside out; she had always been thin, but now she was fading before their very eyes. She moved through the motions, doing what needed to be done, but something in her spirit had been broken. '. . . You'll be free there.'

Effie paled but nodded too. She was terrified of the factor's return, her ears always pricked for the sound of the dogs barking on the beach, heralding the imminent arrival of a new boat. Would he be on this one? What about that one? As much as anything, it was the not knowing when he would arrive that had her living on her nerves.

'There's only a few weeks to go now, but you must be ready just in case,' Flora said with her usual authority. 'You must dig your bait while the tide is out.'

Together, the three of them had come up with a contingency plan should Mathieson ever apprehend her again.

'I know. And I'm almost there, if Captain McGregor will help me.'

Her request for the captain to bring over a bottle of whisky on his next trip had been a highly unusual one, given their notoriously ascetic minister, but Mhairi didn't doubt he would oblige. Effie had the money she had earnt guiding the earl and Lord Sholto last month, and Captain McGregor was, after all, one of the islanders' closest friends.

'When is he hauling anchor?' she asked. Donald had told her the ship had come in last night.

'Soon. I should be heading back.' Effie tucked her legs in to stand but Flora reached for her hand first.

'Before you go . . .'

They sat joined together in their small circle, the crash of the sea and the chatter of wrens a symphony around them.

'I know it's hard. Hardest of all on the two of you. In a couple of months, our lives are going to change forever. We'll leave here and everything we know will be different. Every single thing. Some will be better, some will be worse. But I also know a day will come when we'll look back on this moment – on the three of us sitting in the grass, with feathers in our hair and dead birds by our feet – and there'll be something of it that still remains.'

'What?' Mhairi blinked. All she could see ahead was total loss. Total destruction.

'Us. *This*.' Flora squeezed their hands tighter. 'We'll always be Kilda girls, no matter where we end up. Ma's forever saying there's no secret if three know it, but she's wrong in our case. What we three do, only we three will ever know.' She pressed her finger to her lips. 'We're sisters. Yes?'

Mhairi hesitated, then nodded. Maybe Flora was right. No one else in her life could ever know or understand what she had gone through over here.

'. . . I'll be back over when I can,' Effie said finally, getting up stiffly, looking as if she might break.

Mhairi watched her friend walk away: already heartbroken, already living in fear. For now, at least, Mhairi still had Donald by her side and she still had their baby in her belly. But her turn at heartbreak was fast approaching.

Her soul seemed to fold down on itself, a little smaller, with each passing day – even though the arrangement made perfect sense. It was 'the only solution', Mary had argued when Donald had broken to her the news of the pregnancy – for how could he not? This way they would avoid disgrace, shame and humiliation. She, the wronged wife, would have to walk through fire, holding her tongue and maintaining a tricky deception to all her friends and neighbours – but it wouldn't be for nothing. She would get her reward at the end of it.

The arrangement had even improved things between husband and wife. From the moment it was agreed, Mary no longer scolded and harangued Donald when he came in late for his tea, though she knew perfectly well where he'd been; she had begun patching his clothes again, where previously she had left them to fray; and she would sing in the kitchen while she cooked or knitted or worked at the wheel. Effie had overheard Mad Annie commenting that she was looking 'bonny' one morning, and Big Mary had asked what she was putting in her tea to make her smile so much these days. Within a week, the word in the village had been that Crabbit Mary was finally in the family way.

And not a single doubt wrinkled the lie, for everyone knew there's no smoke in a lark's house.

The heat made her drowsy. She had to take a short nap in the afternoons most days. It didn't matter where she was, she could just lie on the ground, curl up like a shell and fall asleep within moments, the grass warm against her cheek. She would sleep to the sounds of the birds and the sheep, the wind and the waves playing as a backdrop to her dreams.

Flora was carrying the churns to the ridge. Mhairi had had to all but stop that now, at Lorna's insistence – 'Too much strain for the baby,' she had said. To make it up to Flora,

Mhairi was taking on the lion's share of the milking instead and found herself over on the Cambir headland that afternoon. Most of the flock had steadily drifted that way, enjoying the stronger breezes they caught there, the promontory exposed to the sea on a three-hundred-degree span. It was the northernmost point of the isle – diametrically opposite Village Bay – with Soay, the fourth isle in the archipelago, a mere hop, skip and jump away and Boreray looking magnificent in the east, even five miles distant.

A fly buzzed around her hair and she stirred from her foetal position, one hand absently swatting at it. She felt herself roused from oblivion, sounds coming back to her ear, her skin stroked by the breeze. She was wearing just her chemise again, her freckles speckling her pale skin like kittiwake eggs. Her skin would never darken to the tawny colour of Flora's summer complexion, but nonetheless, she was sunswept by her long days working outside; Donald said she had never looked more beautiful.

Mhairi opened her eyes and stared into the distance, into the endless blue of a softly pulsing summer sky. She could see the white sails of a yacht, far out to sea; when she focused, she saw a ladybird was climbing a stalk of grass just inches from her nose; and between the two, a lamb was just yonder, chasing after its mother for another feed, its tail flicking wildly, delightedly, as it began to suckle.

Mhairi lifted her head and pushed herself up to sitting, blinking slowly as she came to. Her hand automatically went to her stomach in a silent plea for contact with her unborn child. What had started as flutters several weeks back had now graduated to full-blown kicks and sometimes they took her breath away; sometimes they made her gasp so that Flora looked upon her in concern, but she always smiled in the next moment. She loved every one of those tiny blows. If she could, she would keep the baby inside her for always.

She stood up and looked around at the flock. The lambs were strong now and enjoying playing together, frolicking and bleating loudly around grassy knolls. All the sheep moved as a herd.

Except one.

She and Flora had been watching it for several days, after they had noticed a change in its behaviour. It was one of the late-tupped ewes; she was heavily pregnant now and due any day. She had reduced her grazing as the lamb took up more space and her teats had filled with colostrum in antici-pation. But Mhairi was bothered by the way she had taken to holding herself apart from the others, standing dully, her head hanging. The ewes always put on a significant amount of growth in the final stage of pregnancy but this one had been looking increasingly thin, and now she seemed to be in distress.

Even from this distance, Mhairi could see the animal was straining, bleating pitifully, trying to get down but then standing again, as if she didn't know what to do with herself. She looked back up to the ridge – Flora was still making her ascent with the churn, having to stop every so often to put it down and rest. Mhairi called up but the distance between them was far too great, Flora oblivious to the drama unfolding at her back.

Mhairi hurried over to the ewe and examined her from a short distance. Though she was standing, the animal was in labour and, it appeared, had been for several hours; Mhairi could see the cervical seal had been passed and that the first waterbag was in the fully dilated cervix. Wait, no . . . she could see the lamb through the membranes. That meant it was the second waterbag; the first must have already burst and passed through.

Mhairi frowned as she looked harder and saw more. She should be seeing the lamb's nose between its two forelegs, but . . . it was difficult to tell exactly, but she thought she could only see its rump. She stepped back in dismay. The birth position couldn't be changed now and a hind-leg presentation would need assistance.

She looked back up the slope once more. Flora was still heading to the ridge, her head down as she trudged. She would reach the cleit in another eight, ten minutes. It would only take her forty minutes back down to the Amazon's House, but beyond and over here to Cambir, another fifteen? An hour then, give or take. An hour.

Mhairi gripped her chin, her arm balanced atop her stomach as she waited anxiously, the minutes slowly ticking past. An hour was manageable. The sheep usually laboured for five hours but even if this ewe was already approaching that, she could go for longer. Mhairi was observing her now. She'd be safe. She'd—

The animal buckled forward, her head striking the ground as she fell heavily.

'Oh!' Mhairi yelped, running forward.

The ewe had fallen onto her side, her legs sticking out as the contractions continued.

'No, no, no, no,' Mhairi cried, getting down beside her and trying to see as the animal began to bleat in distress. The lamb was still stuck inside the cervix and there was no way the dam could push it out without assistance. Mhairi could see the strain on her body; her change in behaviour during the past few days had already told them she was weak in nutrients, but now her heart might simply give out if the toll wasn't lessened.

This sheep couldn't die. They had lost too many in the winter – despite the evacuation, they still had to pay this year's rents to MacLeod, after which every surplus animal would be sold at market on the mainland and the money used to set the villagers up in their new lives across the water. This sheep had never been more valuable to them. It couldn't die. She simply wouldn't let it.

Reaching in, she got her hands to the waterbag. She could feel the lamb's rump through it as she began to pull. She knew she had to pull straight back until the legs were out, else the pelvis would become wedged in the birth canal and then both mother and baby would be done for.

The ewe resisted her interventions, panicking in its pain and kicking its legs, but she pulled and pulled. At first there was only resistance, but after a while she felt something 'give' and the lamb's hind legs came free, tearing through the waterbag. Mhairi fell onto her back with a cry, her thin chemise soaked by the umbilical fluids, but there was no time to protest. Any delay now and both animals would be lost.

'Come on! Come on!' Mhairi urged the dam as she got back onto her knees and grabbed the lamb again. She knew she had to pull downwards now to release the head and forelegs, but it was difficult when the ewe was lying on its side. Mhairi scrambled downhill of the animal and tried again.

Within four pulls, the lamb was out, slithering to the ground in a greasy mass. Mhairi gave a cry of relief, quickly checking its nose was clear of membranes as the mother wriggled herself around and began licking it clean.

Mhairi went to drop her head in her hands, only to catch sight of the state of them. They were bloodied and soiled, and the nearest burn was ten minutes from here, by the old lazybeds.

She got to her feet and went to take herself off to get clean. Over on the ridge, Flora was making her descent; there had been no chance of her getting back in time, Mhairi realized now. But she had travelled only ten paces when she heard that strangled cry again – and realized there was another one.

'What happened?' Flora asked in surprise as she set down the empty churns. Mhairi was sitting on the grass outside the souterrain, hair wet and draped in her blanket, still shivering. It didn't matter how hot the air temperature was, St Kildan water always ran ice cold.

'One of the late-tups went into labour. I had to wash in the burn after the fluids went all over me.'

Flora looked at her oddly. 'But . . . you shouldn't have done that.'

'I had no choice. She was breech, the first one was stuck.'

'You mean it was twins?'

'Triplets, but the last one died.' Mhairi shrugged sadly. It wasn't something anyone – not her, not her father, not Old Fin or Mad Annie – could ever get used to: that awful stillness after the struggle, that whistling silence, the mother's cries as she realized . . . 'I've been lambing almost the whole time it's taken you to come back down. It was as well I was over that way. We'd have lost the mother for sure if she'd gone into labour overnight. Another sheep down.'

Flora smiled and nodded. But gave no reply.

Chapter Twenty-One

'Well, well, guess who's back!' Flora said with a smile as she sat on the rock, paddling the butter between the wooden pats.

Mhairi looked up from the butter churn, her heart somersaulting at the sight of Donald running down the slope towards her. At just over eight months, she wasn't capable of running anywhere now, but she stood awaiting him, feeling her soul dance.

He ran to her and she shivered as he ran a hand around the back of her head to pull her towards him for a kiss. The world softened again and became good. Safe.

'Y' came back to me,' she smiled, basking in his gaze.

He stared down at her, eyes shining. 'Always.' She watched as he ran a hand over her tummy, waiting for a kick. '. . . Sleeping?'

She grinned. 'Aye, must be.' She saw his gaze flutter towards Flora and knew what it meant. He wanted to be alone. Time was always short. 'How long have y' got?'

'Not long. Hamish is pushing on a night trip to Stac Lee for the gannets.'

'Tonight? But you're only just back!'

'Aye, but he's not. It's not his concern if I've spent the day at sea. The water's flat and that's all that matters.'

Mhairi felt herself sag. They were permanently racing the clock, chasing the sun, never quite getting enough of one another. Their time together was bracketed and misery was coming for them. If happiness for most was fleeting, for them it was finite. They knew their ending was imminent; it was already on the wind.

'Go have your walk,' Flora murmured, not even looking up. 'I'll finish up here.'

Mhairi placed a hand gratefully on her shoulder as she passed.

Donald held her hand as they walked to what had become their nook. It wasn't so far from the Amazon's House – just a hundred yards above it, in fact – but further east round the headland, so they couldn't be seen by anyone approaching from the ridge. It gave them both privacy and a view out to sea during their precious time together.

He had brought over a blanket one time, which they kept here now, stuffed inside an abandoned cleit; she watched now as he threw it out over the ground, smoothing the wrinkles and helping her down. She lay on her side as he stroked her cheek, marvelling at her extraordinary shape. The miracle of her, their baby. Slowly he unbuttoned her blouse, revealing her sunswept, freckled skin.

'I missed you,' he whispered, kissing her neck.

'I always miss you,' she replied. 'All the time.' She would never comprehend why life was so cruel. They loved each other. And yet his own wife didn't even like him. How could it be that he and Mary were 'right', and yet they were wrong?

'. . . How was the trip?' she asked, trying to be happy. Dwelling on the future only robbed them of their joy now.

'Successful,' he murmured, his eyes flitting up to her and off again, a tremor of excitement in the move, and she knew he had something to tell her. 'I saw the man I told you about.'

'The one at the top?'

'Aye . . . I saw Mr Salvesen himself.'

She blinked as she looked back at him. 'You mean, like . . . Salvesen ships?'

'He's the whaling company owner. Captain MacGregor had said he'd be over in Harris from Norway this week and I figured if my hunch was right, he'd be the man to approach. That's why I delayed going till he was here.'

'You met Mr Salvesen?' she repeated.

He smiled openly now, revelling in her amazement.

'Just what are you up to, Donald?'

'Mathieson wants you to believe you're just stirring slops for him,' he said carefully. 'But I've fought that man; I've stood toe to toe with him and I've seen his black heart – well, we both have. He would no sooner care to remedy his mother's, or father's, gout, than eat his own leg.' He traced a whorl on her swollen belly. 'No, his . . . agitation on the beach that day, his fuss about it – it had me suspicious at the time, but then I forgot about it and I shouldn't have. There's nothing accidental in what he does, ever. So when he tripped up in his own lie, I knew there had to be something more about it we didn't know.'

'And is there?'

His eyes shone. 'Have you ever heard of ambergris?'

'No.'

'It's treasure, Mhairi. Real treasure.'

'The slops?' she grinned. 'But they're just a lump of stink!'

'Aye, they're unsavoury when fresh. But most ambergris is passed naturally from the sperm whale and floats in the ocean for years, decades even. Usually by the time it's found, it's been turned by the saltwater and cured by the sun, slowly hardening and growing paler until it becomes something the rich will pay a lot of money for. And I mean – a *lot* of money! They use it in their perfumes, Mhairi. It's a . . . "musk", I think he called it.'

278

Perfumes?

'Of course, Salvesen gave me a hard time. He put two and two together. He had obviously heard about Cap Ferg's popped sperm whale last year and he said anything taken from the whale was his property.'

'And is it?'

Donald shrugged. 'Maybe. But he can't prove it. I said it just washed ashore, and how can he show otherwise? It's that valuable and rare, he can't risk me selling it to someone else.'

'But isn't that stealing?'

'Mhairi, who said that because he caught the whale, he owned it? It was one of God's creatures. Free, till his men killed it; but it popped in our bay.' He traced her cheek with the crook of his finger. 'Besides, Mathieson didn't think twice about defrauding him or us. And the man that divides the pudding will always have the thick end to himself – we need to remember that. This is a new world we're going into. We need to think differently. Survival will be another beast over there.'

'But . . .' She looked back at him; she didn't want him to be like Mathieson. That man was an unscrupulous monster who had almost cost them the most valuable thing of all. 'So you're going to sell it to him?'

'No, *we're* going to sell it to him. You're the one who's been working on it all these months, so I wanted to talk to you about it first. I'll take it to him on the next boat that's crossing back, before Mathieson returns. We'll be . . . not rich, I don't think, but we'll have money. Enough to buy a croft, a plot.'

She looked at him, beginning to understand now the reason for the brightness in his eyes. '. . . We?'

'You and me, Mhairi. We could set ourselves up in a new life together, go somewhere no one knows us.'

She put a hand on his arm, knowing she had to stop him. 'But Mary . . .'

His eyes deadened. 'What about her?'

'You can't just leave her. She's your wife.'

'She's not been a wife to me for over a year. It's all a lie, you know it is. And it might be one thing having to pretend when we're living here, but the evacuation changes everything. The future doesn't have to be more of our past. We married for convenience, to bear children that would repopulate the village, but what use is it when she will not lie with me and I have no appetite for her?'

'But you made vows, Donald. Before God.'

He stared at her. 'There's nothing godly about a woman who wants to take another woman's child.'

She winced at the baldness of the words. 'You're the baby's father,' she stammered, trying to hold on to reason. 'So long as you're there—'

He pulled himself up onto his elbow, staring down at her. 'The baby needs its mother. And I need you. I'll face the consequences of what we've done, Mhairi: let them pour on the shame, the humiliation, the ostracization – everything she said would rain down upon us! The minister can damn us to hell and back, I don't care. We won't be here by then. It's different over there. Marriages do end and divorces are . . . they're possible! We could be wed, you and me. This could be a chance to start over right from the very beginning.' He clutched her hand and held it to his chest, looking at her with such urgency, pleading with her to agree. 'Mhairi, we could go somewhere no one knows us and they would never know. We'd have each other! We'd be a family!'

'But—'

He pressed a finger to her lips, looking down at her with

burning eyes. 'No, *listen* to me. This could be real. This could be our life, together. You, me and our wee baby. It's not a dream. I know we talked on it before and it seemed impossible, but we'll have the means to make it happen now.'

She blinked, wanting so desperately to believe him, to allow herself to dream of a future like that. Every part of her wanted to let go and say yes, to sink into the fantasy of a happy ending with him. But her sins couldn't be absolved with money. 'No, I can't,' she whispered, shaking her head, her eyes squeezed shut. 'I've accepted how it has to be. I know it's the right thing even . . . even though it destroys me.'

'Mhairi, you are not damned for what that man made you do.'

'I am though.'

'No. He forced himself upon you. The shame of the sin is not yours.'

'But I can't allow myself to think of another way now. It would be too painful, too devastating if something went wrong.'

'But what could go wrong?' he argued. 'You're safe over here, no one knows about the baby. It's grown so big already – and Lorna is helping you. She's a nurse.' He cupped her cheek. 'We're so close to reaching our dreams, Mhairi, we're so close now . . . Look at me, look at me . . . I know you're scared but I'll keep you both safe. I'll protect you. I'll build us a life together if you'll just trust me.'

Tears slid silently down her cheeks as her mind played out images of them with their baby in their arms, walking on a beach, kissing openly, no more hiding, no more shame . . . How many times had he tried to convince her of this? But too much had stood in the way. Now, though, they had means as well as will and she could feel her heart instinctively open up, petals unfurling, hope rising in her like a spring sap.

'I'll speak to Mary and we'll work something out,' he continued, drawing hope from her silence. 'I'd not abandon her – we'll give her some of the money so she can be independent. I do believe, once she's had time to think on it, she'll welcome a fresh start too. We're both dying over here. I know it. You know it. She knows it . . .' He kissed her lightly on the lips. 'Trust me, Mhairi, we can make this work . . . Just say yes.'

She looked at him, seeing the love in his eyes and his refusal to give up. She did trust him; she did believe in him. He made her feel protected. Safe. Adored. He was the man she would choose, not the one with the pretty face and cold heart . . . 'Okay. Yes,' she nodded slowly.

'Yes? Really?' he whispered, disbelief and delight shining in his eyes. 'We can be a family?'

'Aye,' she smiled as he began excitedly kissing her face and neck, tickling her and making her laugh. 'So long as nothing goes wrong.'

'It won't. I won't let it.' He pressed his hand against her stomach again, waiting for the kick. '. . . Still sleeping?' he whispered.

'Aye,' she sighed contentedly. 'Still sleeping.'

It was dark when she awoke, the silence so heavy it almost buzzed in her head. There were no shadows flickering at this hour; Flora was fast asleep in her chamber next door.

Mhairi blinked several times, wondering what it was that had roused her. A stray bird screeching as it escaped the hunt on Stac Lee? She tried not to think of Donald out there, clinging to wet rock, the sea an ominous black far below his bare feet. He would be tired, possibly distracted too by their conversation earlier.

She sat up and swung her legs out, planting them on the

bare earth. It felt good to ground herself. She felt peculiar, agitated, her legs restless . . .

She rose and walked through to the central chamber, just able to hear the heavy modulated breaths of her friend. Outside, she looked up at the sky, taking in a lungful of air and seeing the galaxies of stars that hung in tight twists and languid swoops. The moon was on the wane and cast little light upon the slack water. It was a perfect night for the hunt: the birds would never see the men approaching.

Pulling her shawl around her shoulders, she walked a little way around their encampment. The sheep were huddled in small herds, making no sound. It felt as if the entire world belonged to her alone—

She stopped, her back hunching over as she felt an abrupt pain. It came from the very centre of her, a tightening that stopped her breath for ten, fifteen seconds, before she felt herself released again. She panted lightly as the intensity eased, her muscles softening with the loosening grip.

She knew exactly what it was. Lorna had described to her what would happen when the baby was coming, but this was too early. Too soon. If the dates had been calculated correctly, there should be another seventeen days.

'Please no, little one,' she hushed, leaning against a wall and trying to make her body relax. 'Not yet . . . It's not time . . . Sleep. Keep sleeping.'

She began to hum the lullaby her mother always sang as she fed her babies. '*Oh hush thee, my dove, oh hush thee my sweet love; oh hush thee my lapwing, my dear little bir—*'

It came again, the tightening, stopping her breath as her body ratcheted around an invisible point. It was stronger this time, longer too, and as she felt it ease once more, there was a sudden wetness down her legs.

She panted, staring down at the puddle. 'No, please . . .' she whispered, feeling a tear slide from her eye. But the fear arrowed through her veins. Instinct told her this couldn't be delayed or stopped.

She looked up at the distant ridge. It would be hours before Flora could get Lorna back over here. Hours in which she would be alone, in the dark: Donald was on a rock in the sea. Her mother, oblivious; Effie, asleep . . .

Her body was shaking as she took one step, then another, knowing she had to get to Flora before the next wave hit her. Every minute counted now. The end of her old life had already begun. There was no turning back.

Chapter Twenty-Two

Three weeks later – 29 August 1930

Mhairi held Red Annie and Wee Murran's hands as they walked the Street for the last time. No one could quite believe it was really happening; all week bright, slightly glazed eyes had been tearing up without notice, brisk footsteps halting suddenly mid-step . . . before moving on again. They had been cleaning, clearing and packing up for days, but as incessant activity was normal here, they had been able to tell themselves that these were just more chores. Tables, chairs, beds, looms and spinning wheels had been strapped to backs and carried down to the jetty, but everyone was used to cumbersome and heavy lifting – it might easily have been peat creels or feather sacks or looms being lifted down from the lofts, or sheep being rescued from crags.

It was only when the crofts finally stood empty that the consequences of their actions laid bare the reality that they were actually leaving.

Her mother had stood by the fire and wept, the ashes still glowing in the hearth, the chimney wall retaining a gentle warmth. 'What are we doing, lass?' she had asked, looking back at Mhairi, as pale as the moon.

Mhairi hadn't been able to answer immediately. She

urgently wanted to leave and desperately wanted to stay. She felt like a captured tornado, spinning on the ground.

'. . . It'll be better over there.' But her voice had lilted, phrasing it as a question back and revealing that she thought no such thing. This was their home – stark, harsh, brutal at times, yes; but also, as on a day like this where the sky flowered a forget-me-not blue and the turquoise sea lay at rest, dizzyingly beautiful. It was almost as if Mother Nature herself was trying to persuade them to stay. Perhaps if they had been leaving in a storm it would have been easier to turn their backs, but instead they must leave when she was at her best – dazzling, majestic and serene.

She walked slowly, limping a little over the rough ground, and Murran took advantage of her weak grip to slide his hand free of hers and tear ahead. Mhairi didn't stop him; he wouldn't get anywhere. The jetty was just ahead, the navy men that had been sent over standing smartly in their white ducks. She passed by Mad Annie and Old Fin's windows but she didn't need to look in to know they weren't there. They were gathered in the burial ground with Ma Peg, saying goodbye to the loved ones they had expected their whole long lives to join, but were now leaving behind.

She felt another sob escape her, though she was trying her best to remain strong, and she stopped where she was, trying to gather her composure. This was the day she had known was coming. Somehow she needed to get through it; they all did. She pressed her hands against the rough stone wall of Mad Annie's house as if trying to imprint it into her skin and take it with her, a cast she could carry.

But her feet wouldn't move. She felt leaden. Everything in her body was telling her to resist, to pull back.

'Effie Gillies!'

Robert's angry voice boomed around the glen again. He had been calling and calling for his errant daughter as the village's life here entered its death throes. She looked back. David MacQueen was throwing a bucket of dirty water into the run-off, a clean floor the final closing up of their home.

Mhairi's father, along with Lorna, was still in the post office, the two of them stamping the last of the eight hundred post-cards that had been brought over with the ship yesterday. He had been working through the night, stopping only for their final service in the kirk. Almost everyone had been there, even Mad Annie – her first time in years – and it had been a form of torture for Mhairi to stare upon Donald's back, to see the curl of his hair at the nape of his neck which she liked to twist with her finger. His knuckles had blanched white as he had prayed, their haunted gazes tangling and making time slip off its cradle as he had passed her pew. He was her world in private, a mere neighbour in public.

'Effie Gillies!' Robert thundered again. His legs might be weak but there was nothing wrong with his chest.

'Mhairi, come,' her mother said, placing a hand on her shoulder as she passed. 'Don't worry the bairns.'

Mhairi let her hand fall, walking on and glancing in as she passed by the factor's house. The windows glinted back darkly, no signs of movement within there either. She looked quickly away again with a shiver.

They walked onto the jetty, where Jayne Ferguson was standing. She was staring back at the village, at the burial ground where Molly, her husband's dear sister and her closest friend, now lay. Often solitary, she looked as alone as Mhairi had ever seen her; Norman was nowhere to be seen, of course.

'Jayne,' she heard her mother say, embracing her loosely with the baby in her arms. 'Are y' ready?'

'No,' Jayne said softly, her eyes shining with tears. 'But I think I never will be.'

'Aye,' her mother agreed, a small sob escaping her, and she pressed her shawl to her lips. The children gathered around them, clutching her skirts, as if understanding, at last, the solemnity of the occasion. This was it. They were leaving their home. Even Murran stood obediently, meekly, as the important-looking men in their smart uniforms began to bring them aboard the dinghies. Jayne and Mhairi's mother climbed in first, Rachel handing the baby to Mhairi to hold while she steadied herself on the bench seat. Mhairi watched as one of the sailors began lifting over her young siblings – Wee Alasdair, then Murran, his legs kicking in the air dramatically; Red Annie squealing excitedly; Euphemia and Christina, dainty and girlish . . .

'Sit quietly!' her mother scolded them as the boat rocked. 'Are we to drown in our own bay?'

At last, Mhairi went to hand over her baby brother – he was swaddled and drowsy from all the rush and bother, his body heavy now in her arms . . .

'. . . Mhairi?'

Memories rushed at her, cold hands pulling at her skin, a dread fear settling in her bones—

'. . . Mhairi!'

She blinked. Her mother was staring at her with a look of horror. The sailor was straddling the side of the boat and the jetty, Wee Rory held between her and him, a strip of deep water below.

'Sorry,' she gasped, relinquishing her grip. In the next instant, she was aboard too.

'What's wrong wi' you?' her mother demanded, slapping her thigh crossly as she sat down. 'Y're away with the fairies!'

'Sorry,' she whispered again, looking back to the village as the sailors unwound the ropes and set them adrift, jumping down with ease and taking the oars. Mhairi could see Lorna now, standing at the foot of the scree slope on Ruival, opposite the crofts. Mhairi followed the nurse's line of sight upwards and saw, finally, the pale scrap on the bluffs – Effie, clutching Poppit. Their voices didn't carry but Effie's body language did; she was hunched and agitated, as though getting ready to flee. Mhairi could see Hamish Gillies and her brother Angus striding across the grass to where Lorna was standing. In the next moment Effie was scrambling to her feet and scaling the cliffs again, the dog roped to her back.

Mhairi watched her as they were rowed across the bay, but too soon, HMS *Harebell*, the steamship sent by His Majesty's Government, towered above them, steady on its chains. Ropes were thrown and the dinghy secured, and Mhairi felt the past claw at her again – memories of the night she had climbed aboard the *Endurance*, and all that that had led to, resurfacing. She was being taken back to Alexander again. Everything was happening as planned, all her nightmares coming true: her spirit crushed, her soul saved.

They climbed the ladder onboard, the MacQueens and Big Gillies clustering around the bow rails as if counting them on and making sure none stayed behind. There had been an excitement earlier when the *Times* reporter from London, a Mr Bonner, had been found hiding out in one of the cleits – intending to be left behind! Norman Ferguson, who had found him, had removed him roughly, demanding to know with what he had expected to survive? The crops had been lifted, the sheep removed to the mainland; MacLeod's own flock had been moved over from Boreray but if the reporter had fancied himself catching and eating those, he would have found a bill for his dinners on his return. No one could understand it. The SS *Dunara* was scheduled to drop anchor with its tourists in a few days' time but there would have been no guarantee of being picked up; the captain would sail only when and if conditions allowed, and the weather would be turning any day now. He had been risking his life.

Big Mary was singing a lament, which sent Mhairi's mother off again. Christina MacQueen put an arm around her as, together with Jayne, they stood looking back to shore, awaiting their men. The elders were making their way slowly towards the jetty, Mad Annie and Ma Peg holding on to each of Old Fin's arms, the gate to the burial ground closed behind them for the final time.

Mhairi looked around the deck for Donald and Mary; her heart felt like it was pounding too hard. Where were they? Where were they?

'Where's Flora?' she asked Neil, Flora's younger brother, who was swinging on the rails restlessly. He shrugged.

She walked down the deck towards a sailor hauling on a rope. 'Where's Flora MacQueen?' she asked him.

He looked back at her blankly.

'The pretty one?'

'Ah.' He nodded. 'Gone below, Miss. Said she was feeling sick.'

'Can I go dow—'

'Mhairi!'

She turned to find her mother waving at her with a harassed look. 'Get back here! Keep an eye on the wee 'uns, they could slip through these bars and we'd be none the wiser.'

Dutifully, she turned back to help. Now that the novelty of being on a ship was beginning to wear off – for the other families had been boarded for almost forty minutes now –

nerves were beginning to tell. It felt to Mhairi like those moments in a storm between the lightning flash and thunder; she was waiting for the roll, the reverberations in her chest. Tension was seeping from everyone's seams and setting the children on edge: the babies were crying, the mothers weeping. Mhairi caught the tail end of a squabble between Murran and Red Annie, seeing Murran pull hard on Annie's hair, swiftly followed by Annie kicking him on the shins. She saw Murran go rigid, ready to scream, but she quickly tore them apart as his mouth opened wide.

'Behave! Or I'll box your ears!' she hissed, shocking her brother into silence. 'It's not the time, can't you see that?'

Her siblings blinked at her in surprise, taken aback by her uncharacteristic roughness. She realized her wagging finger was an inch from their noses, her eyes ablaze with a rage that had nothing to do with them. They were innocent. Innocents. It wasn't their fault her entire world had imploded. She dropped her hand, trying to regain control of herself, but she felt pushed past her breaking point and unsure of her reserves, as if she couldn't trust her own body.

Knowing she couldn't.

Her intake of breath was shaky and jagged as she pulled them over to the bulkhead and sat them down upon it. 'Now just sit there, and no fighting,' she said in a low voice. 'Or I'll tell Father you've been causing a ruckus and he'll put you over his knee!' The threat of their father's punishment was always worse than the reality of it, but they blinked back meekly.

The dinghy went to and from the ship, collecting the last of the islanders. The children and mothers were now boarded, the elders, Lorna and most of the fathers too, including Robert Gillies. Only Effie, Norman and Mhairi's own father remained.

The protected bay had never seen so many criss-crossings in one period. It had taken days and countless trips to load up the sheep – Hamish Gillies was sporting a magnificent shiner from being headbutted by one of them on the water – while the cows were towed by their horns behind the rowing boat.

'Mhairi.'

She looked up as a hand was placed on her shoulder. 'Flora . . . I was coming down to see you,' she said as her friend came to sit carefully beside her. Her beauty had withered in these final days; she was pale and drawn, with dark circles below her eyes. Mhairi knew she must look the same too, for they had both endured the worst night of their lives. 'Are you all right?'

Flora shook her head, staring back to shore; she was trembling still. Mhairi knew from experience that it would take hours to subside. Trauma was a restless spirit trapped in the body. '. . . No.'

'No.' Mhairi squeezed her hand harder still. 'Of course not,' she said quietly. 'But . . . it's . . . the worst is done now. A few more hours and it'll be behind us . . . behind you.'

Flora looked at her, a question in her bleak eyes.

'Chin up, girls,' Mrs Lyon, the minister's wife, said as she passed. 'This is the start of your new lives. It's a happy occasion, mark my words.'

They watched her go, both of them ghosts.

'Donald asked if you were on board so I said I'd check,' Flora said under her breath. 'I needed some air anyway . . .' She tossed her head back as she took some deep breaths, the wind playing with her hair.

Mhairi watched her friend with concern. 'You shouldn't be up here.'

But Flora glanced around them, taking in who was on

deck. 'I need to show my face . . .' She glanced at Mhairi pityingly. 'You should go down while it's quiet. It might be your last chance.'

'But I'm worried about you,' Mhairi whispered desperately.

It was a moment before Flora responded. 'I'll survive it, like you.'

Mhairi nodded. She looked back towards her home. The dinghy was making the last crossing now with Effie, Norman and Mhairi's father, who was holding the last of the bulging mail sacks. Big Mary was still singing, wringing her hands as the sailors began to move more quickly on deck. The captain was eager to get underway, she knew. If she went below deck to see Donald now, she might not get back up in time for a final look at her home; but once they set off, she might not get a chance to stay down there with him. She had to choose.

'So, the day has come,' Flora murmured, looking out blankly. It was the one they had waited for all summer, the one they had thought they were prepared for, even just a few weeks ago. But now it was here and it wasn't what they had feared – it was worse. Their fates had become completely intertwined. The days when all that had mattered was a letter and a lipstick were long gone.

They pressed their heads together as they took a final look. The crofts seemed, to Mhairi's eye, not just empty now but hollowed out, disembowelled. Like her – where before there had been life, now there was nothing at all. No trace. Her body had shrunk back within days, although she felt scarred by her experience, as though it had left a mark on her skin, as well as her soul. She had thought, the first time she went back over the ridge, that her mother might see the fundamental change in her and instinctively know what had passed. But there seemingly wasn't a trace upon her. Lorna had marvelled that it was almost as if it had never been at all.

Flora inhaled sharply and pulled away. 'Go down and speak to him,' she said firmly. 'While you still can. I'll look after the wee 'uns.'

Mhairi nodded gratefully, getting up. She made her way past the sailors and down the stairs, feeling the memories crowd her again: the whale lashed to the side, blood on the slipway, a swooping eagle, a tethered cow in the byre, Alexander by the door . . . But she was no longer that girl. No longer a girl.

She stepped down into the narrow gloom. Donald, who was pacing in the corridor, wild-eyed and gaunt, stopped short as he saw her at the bottom of the steps.

'Where have you been?' he whispered, rushing over and taking her in his arms. She felt his desperation through his fingertips, pressing on her skin. They were down to the last few grains of sand and every touch now might be their last. He kissed her, urgent and wretched, his hands clasping her cheeks. 'Flora said she'd send y' down.'

'The last boat's coming now,' she said, realizing she was crying, her tears spilling over his fingers as he squeezed and crushed and kissed her. It was as if he didn't know what to do with himself, how to get enough of her in the time remaining to them.

'I can't do it, Mhairi,' he whispered urgently. 'I can't . . . I know you said it was for the best but . . .' He swallowed. 'Please. Reconsider. I beg of you.'

She stared at him through her tears, wishing it could be that easy; wishing that their future had unfurled the way he had said it would and not twisted like a ribbon into a new shape with a single flick of destiny's wrist. It wasn't to be, couldn't he see that? For every wish they made, fate struck them down. They weren't supposed to be together.

From behind a closed door, there came the sound of the baby crying, and she froze. Her body went rigid, her breathing shallow. Every cry was a hammer to her crystal heart as she heard the low murmur of Mary's voice vibrate through to them. Mary had never sounded so soft – it was as if the hard crust that edged her all these years had finally flaked off, revealing her as someone vulnerable and tender.

Mhairi began to cry harder, shaking her head. It was too much to bear . . . Donald reached for her again, pained, his forehead pressed to hers, his eyes red-rimmed.

'There's still time for it to be different,' he whispered, the desperation bracing in his voice, his hands upon her hips. 'We could be happy.'

'We were happy. We were perfect,' she wept. 'Every moment we shared, I'll remember forever.'

'No. Don't remember it. Live it! Just be brave, I beg of you. Nothing they throw at us would be worse than being apart. I've got the money now – more than we ever dreamt! Come with me!'

The baby mewled again and she felt that familiar trickle up her spine – the eagle upon the lamb. The baby's cries were distinctly louder.

Closer.

She looked over and saw the door was open now; that Mary was watching them, carrying her son tightly against her breast.

'Touching,' she said coldly as her husband dropped his arms from Mhairi's waist and they stepped apart. '. . . But the baby needs feeding.'

Chapter Twenty-Three

Mhairi stared down at the waving crowds, a sea of faces turned towards her and her neighbours as the captain gave a valedictory toot of the horn that only made them cheer harder. She could see a bank of pressmen with cameras forming a wall, flashbulbs popping as the ship moored with surprising grace. Had . . . had all these people come out to see them?

She looked at her mother, jigging the baby in her arms but her eyes darting this way and that, trying to understand the spectacle too. Her father was gripping the top of the mail sack as though it contained the Crown Jewels. Her little brothers and sisters were perfectly silent and utterly still for once. Further along, she could see Hamish Gillies clenching his jaw uncertainly, standing like a sailor himself, his back straight and Mary a half step hidden behind him, as he tried to fathom what would be required of him here. Effie had her back turned to where Mhairi stood with her family, but she was birdlike and nervous, glancing constantly to her father, whose hand was shaking on his stick. Old Fin and Mad Annie had linked arms, Lorna supporting Ma Peg with a firm arm.

Flora was standing at the back of her family group, looking like an alabaster statue of Diana. She looked over as if sensing Mhairi's stare and for a moment their gazes held, but there could be no further comfort here. They must step into their futures apart, although they would not be fully separated just yet. Of the thirty-six islanders, only nine would go on from here to Oban: the Big Gillies, Donald and Mary – and of course the baby, which, strictly speaking, now made it ten. The rest of them would stay in Lochaline, where homes and jobs had been found for them. There was apprehension, of course – were the houses close to one another, or scattered? Having spent their lives living cheek by jowl on a single street, living in the same town would prove notional if they were still miles apart.

The gangplank was down now, the crowd pushing forward slightly as if intending to board the ship. Mhairi caught her breath, feeling a growing sense of otherness as her gaze attuned and she began to take in their differences in hair and dress. It was quite a feat that the St Kildans were in their boots this time of year – there would usually be another six weeks before the ground was too cold and wet for bare feet – but here the women wore shoes that were low on the foot, with shaped heels and decorative cut-outs; some were in colours other than brown, too. As for their clothes, not a single woman wore a plaid shawl on her head or shoulders. Many wore their hair short or fashioned, somehow, into neat rows of curls. Their skirts were narrow and shorter than the St Kildans' heavy navy worsted wool types, the blouses printed and fine. Everything about the women here seemed . . . lighter, as if air-spun. Mhairi looked around for some red-painted lips but, to her disappointment, saw none.

She watched Lorna give her arm to Ma Peg, helping her slowly down the gangplank to where some other men in dark suits and shiny shoes were waiting. One of the officials asked them some questions and although he seemed friendly enough, Mhairi immediately noticed that he addressed them not in Gaelic, their native language, but English. Her father, she saw, noted it too, looking at her mother with alarm. His English was passable, her mother's was more limited. The minister's wife had taught English to the children in the school but for those islanders of an age greater than Mrs Lyon's residency there, they communicated in the ancient tongue. The first difficulty here had presented itself and they hadn't yet stepped on firm land.

Effie and her father went next, following the same procedure – a slow walk, questions, then they were led away from the crowd. Mhairi felt her heart rate begin to climb as her friend began to disappear into the press of bodies – she was tall, so her bright hair was visible for a few moments more . . .

Effie was going. It was really happening.

No.

Mhairi felt herself tremble as she looked out at the sea of faces. Strangers. Looking back at them like curiosities. Oddities.

No.

'I canna,' she whispered, looking around her community, at the cragged, weather-worn brown faces she had known all her life. They didn't belong here, none of them did. This was all a mistake, a terrible mistake.

She looked for Donald, finding him at the far end of the deck, standing slightly apart from their neighbours, with Mary and the baby. Had Mary kept him further away on purpose? A final act of spite? He was in profile to her, immobile and dignified, but she could see from the set of his jaw, from the quickened rise and fall of his chest, that he was scarcely held together.

He was already lost to her, their baby too. Sequestered in the narrow embrace of Glen Bay, lying in his arms in their nook, dreaming impossible dreams, it had been easy to think this day would never come. Fate had conspired to buy them extra time, after all; tomorrow was always a day away . . . It had been easy to think the world a small place when living on a two-mile-long rock, but now they were here and she could see the land rolling back endlessly . . . In just five miles he would be swallowed up and gone for good.

She wanted to run to him, but her legs wouldn't work and she heard a mournful sound that she didn't at first recognize as coming from her. Nor had she realized she had slipped to the ground, her hands holding the bow rail in a death grip. 'I canna! I canna!' She reached out for someone, anyone, to help her. If they knew what she had endured, they wouldn't ask this of her.

'Mhairi,' her mother hissed below her breath. 'What are y' doing? Get up!'

'Don't make me! Please don't make me!'

'You're making a scene! Get up!' Her mother shot a look to her father and he let go of Red Annie's hand to pull Mhairi up by the arm instead.

She looked back at Donald and their eyes locked. A spasm of pain crossed his face and he instinctively made a move towards her but Mary's arm shot out, holding him in place. She said something to him that kept him there.

'Father! Leave me be!' Mhairi cried, pleading desperately, her feet scrabbling as she tried to pull back, to get to where he stood, but her father's strength was fuelled by an anger rarely seen back home. Blankly, she saw Red Annie and Murran, themselves threatened with this very punishment, watching in horror as she was revealed as the one to misbehave and lose control. 'No! No! No!' she wept, her knees buckling as she staggered and was dragged towards the titillated crowd.

Flashbulbs popped, blinding her, blinding them all. One of the men with the shiny shoes talked politely to her father, making no outward sign he had even noticed that Ian MacKinnon was holding up the half-limp body of his nineteen-year-old daughter.

She felt her strength leave her then. Her feet were on Scottish soil and the transition was effected. She was now officially in Lochaline, and Donald – and Mary and the baby – were still on the ship, bound for Oban.

'Boys! Get back here!' she heard her mother cry as Alasdair and Murran, emboldened by her display, ran ahead to where a fleet of cars was parked in a line. They had never seen a car before. To them, this was a brave new world. To her it was the end of the world.

She twisted back to get a final glimpse of Donald but it was Flora she saw, pale-faced, coming down the gangplank. Unlike Mhairi, she kept her composure and her dignity, even as the sky turned white with the popping of flashbulbs when her uncommon beauty was registered.

Norman and Jayne Ferguson followed almost immediately, Norman looking a heroic figure as he gripped his shy wife's hand, though he was nothing of the sort – Effie had told Flora he had flung her beloved Poppit from the cliffs before they left. The poor girl had been mute for the entire journey.

'Ahoy!' Hamish Gillies called suddenly from behind them. 'Where's Mathieson?' he asked one of the dockers who were sorting the cargo. 'MacLeod's factor?'

Flora's head jerked up as if she had been pulled from a trance, her eyes somehow finding Mhairi's in the crowd, her gaze shot through with horror.

'Not here,' the man shrugged.

'He's got my money!'

'Not here.'

There was a heavy silence, as the question began to bounce through people's minds: come to think of it – where was the factor?

'The smack left after the *Dunara Castle* yesterday!' Flora called up to him, her voice as assured as ever. The cargo vessel had left with their livestock and furniture late the previous evening.

'Oban, then!' someone shouted.

'Aye.' Hamish nodded briskly as he pulled back, but he looked displeased.

Flora looked back to Mhairi. They had only a moment before the crowd closed again, but a memory spanned like a rainbow between them – a summer's day in Glen Bay, Effie, Flora and she plucking birds together, and the echoes of a promise ringing in her ears:

What we three do, only we three will ever know.

Chapter Twenty-Four

The bus pulled up, the glossy pea-green shell shaking on its wheels, the engine wheezing rheumatically. Mhairi glanced across at her father, who was holding the small bag of her belongings. He was looking anxiously at the vehicle as if debating whether it could be trusted to transport his eldest daughter.

'It'll be all right,' she said quietly, putting a hand on his arm. 'People travel in these all the time.'

Still he regarded it suspiciously. Everything over here needed to be digested, it seemed: the buses and cars that still made them jump every time they passed; running taps that were piped inside the houses; indoor bathrooms; carpets; stairs; bank notes; shops that had food just there, on shelves.

Her mother switched the baby to the other hip, jigging up and down. 'And you'll write? Every week?' She pinned her eldest daughter with a stern look, wanting a promise.

'Aye. Every week,' she said tonelessly. 'And please write back. I want to hear everyone's news.'

There was already so much to tell. They'd been here a week and a half and her little sisters and Murran had already started at school; Angus and Fin were enjoying their new jobs as lumberjacks at the Forestry Commission. Her father worked there as well, but Mhairi knew he was pained by the loss of status now that his postmaster duties had gone and he was 'just another' worker. Even her mother worked – their new home was at the end of a short block of pretty white houses with front gardens and gabled roofs. It had three bedrooms upstairs and a water closet. Mad Annie lived next to them with Ma Peg, and the MacQueens were on their other side. It had been agreed that the two older women would look after baby Rory and Alasdair while their mothers worked the looms at a tweed factory; they all needed to earn a wage now.

Only Mhairi had faltered during this new chapter. Her body, or perhaps her spirit, had failed her, seemingly just giving up. Even Flora was able to carry on, though she was noticeably diminished; but the sense of duty that had always propelled Mhairi had suddenly stuttered to a complete stop. For the best part of this first week, she had slept all day and lain awake all night, scarcely eating or talking; barely even existing. Her careworn mother had called out the local doctor, who had diagnosed nervous exhaustion. Trauma from leaving their home, he surmised. 'Bed rest,' he had advised. So many times she had wanted to tell her mother the truth – that she was a mother too, or at least had been, for a short while. But where could she begin?

Her mother hugged her tightly and Mhairi could feel the pressure in her fingertips, wanting to grip her more tightly and never let her go. It reminded her of Donald's desperation on the boat and she felt that slackening within her again, everything falling loose and out of shape, as if her body was collapsing. It had been eleven days now since she had seen him and the baby and every new day felt like a fresh death. How could she survive this? How could she wake up each morning and go through it all again?

'Remember to write to Effie, too,' her mother said, finally releasing her. 'You've the address?'

'Aye. Dumfries House,' Mhairi nodded.

'That's it. She's all alone there. She needs her friends.'

Mhairi nodded. She had been sleeping when Effie had stopped by to tell her she had been offered a position working for the Earl of Dumfries, organizing his bird egg collection at his seat in Ayrshire. It had been only their second day here and her mother had relayed to her that it was the most lively she had seen Effie for months. She was moving back into Sholto's orbit. Was her friend destined for her happy ending after all?

Mhairi wasn't so lucky. Alexander had written, notifying her that the first of the banns had already been read in church that first Sunday. Three banns had to be read on three consecutive Sundays before they could marry, and it was expected that she would be in the district for the final two. The clock was still ticking down . . . The worst hadn't happened to her yet.

The bus doors opened and the driver looked down at her questioningly. Was she getting on?

She blinked at him blankly as her father handed her the bag, planting a kiss on her forehead. 'We'll be with y' for the wedding,' he said ruefully; their new jobs made it impossible for her parents to travel to Harris with her and back in time. She knew it troubled them that they hadn't yet met their future son-in-law, but the seventy-mile journey was arduous and long. This bus would take her north through Strontian and Acharacle to Mallaig; from there she would catch the ferry to Skye, take another bus to the north of the isle, and then hop on a final boat to Leverburgh on Harris. From there she was under instruction to catch the Stornoway bus, get off at Ardhasaig – the site of the general store – and walk the rest of the way to the lodging house, where a Mrs Buchanan was expecting her. It would be her home for the next three and a half weeks, until the wedding.

Robotically, she stepped aboard, bought her ticket with the coin she had been given, and took her seat. Her parents waved from the pavement on the other side of the glass as the doors closed and the bus engine rumbled again. She smiled as best she could until they were out of sight, waving as if this was a happy beginning. But it was just another ending.

She felt the boat slow and looked up. She had been travelling now for ten hours and dusk was shimmying down over the Minch like a grey veil. The undulating mountainscape was gentler here than the dramatic Highland crenellations through which she'd travelled, as if the earth was easing itself into the North Atlantic sea like a timid swimmer. A pod of bottlenose dolphins had played in their wake for much of this short crossing from Skye, dipping and rising with stunning synchronicity, tiny isles scattered through the Sound like sleeping seals. Leverburgh Harbour was just ahead, a dense cluster of crofts and handsome white houses speckling the green slopes that surrounded the bay; some fishing boats were already docked, the sounds of industry a low drone across the water.

Mhairi was relieved to see there was no welcoming committee this time: no pressmen or ladies in their Sunday best. It was just an ordinary Wednesday evening in September, people going about their business and paying no mind to her. She walked along the pier towards the road where she had been told the bus would stop, not noticing at first the pony and trap that clipped into motion as she passed.

It drew alongside her and she looked up.

'Good evening, Miss MacKinnon,' Alexander said, with that small smile on his lips as he doffed his cap to her. Still fine-looking. Still terrifying.

She felt her insides collapse again, her body drawing down at the sight of him. 'What are you doing here?' she breathed. She wasn't due to see him till tomorrow.

'I thought you might appreciate the lift,' he said, reaching over to take her bag. She hesitated, then handed it to him. What else could she do?

He pulled her up too and she sat down on the bench beside him, flinching as she felt his leg against hers. She went to move away but he stopped her with a hand on her thigh – proprietorial; familiar, picking up where he'd left off. 'I've missed you,' he said, looking deep into her eyes. She felt her heart rate rocket at his touch, his proximity, the casual way he handled her body, as though it was really his – or already his. She felt a metallic tang of fear in her mouth as she stared back. Would he read her secrets?

A silence pulsed between them as he registered her evident lack of excitement to see him, a tension sitting between them now where there had been flirtation. Before, Donald had kept them apart, but now their own past barked like an attack dog and she saw a quizzical look dart through his eyes like a shadow.

Then he smiled.

'Hmm. You need some feeding up, I think,' he murmured, as with a flick of his wrist he shook the reins and got the horse moving again.

'You didn't need to do this,' she said quietly. 'I was very happy to make my own way to the lodging house.'

He glanced at her, seeming bemused by her display of independence. 'Ah, but as I said – I missed you, Mhairi,' he murmured as the wheels began to roll through the street. 'You've kept me waiting far too long.' And he squeezed her thigh, slowly and hard, as if in a statement of intent. Starting as he meant to go on.

Chapter Twenty-Five

'Brose, Miss MacKinnon,' the landlady said, setting down the bowl of oats.

'Thank you,' Mhairi smiled weakly, pulling her gaze back from the view and trying to summon an appetite. She was sitting by the window watching the cattle graze on the machair, their long toffee-coloured coats ruffled in the breeze, white horses racing on the sea.

The front room had been set up as a dining room, with several small tables draped with linens and a mirror hanging on a gold chain on the wall. There was a gentleman in a brown suit at one table, reading a newspaper; a young woman just a few years older than Mhairi sat at another. She had her hair pinned and rolled at the sides and was wearing nylons, rather than the heavy stockings Mhairi knew.

Mhairi felt aware that her clothes marked her out as different, somehow 'foreign'. They were heavy and ill-fitting, monochromatic. Back home, clothing was simply a matter of protection from the elements – as well as modesty, clearly. But here she sensed they were a matter of individual taste, as well as fashion. Clothes could be used to 'present' someone. They spoke a silent language unknown to her.

She wondered how Donald was faring in Oban and what he was finding new. Was the baby feeding well? Sleeping?

Was he exhausted . . . ? They were now half the length of the country away from her, already setting down roots in their new life—

'Tea.' Mrs Buchanan was back again, setting down a small green teapot. She was a tallish, thin woman with spectacles and her hair worn back in a bun. She didn't seem prone to unnecessary smiling, but she was stern rather than hard. Mhairi wondered what she sounded like when she laughed. If she laughed.

'Is it Lipton's?' Mhairi asked quietly. There had been nuanced differences here on Harris too, as on the mainland. Since leaving St Kilda, she'd not had a brew that tasted like those back home; it was such a little detail and yet it was another tiny reminder that she was away, adrift, from the place of her birth.

'Sun-Ray Tips,' Mrs Buchanan replied. 'It's brewed especially for the Harris water. You'll no' find any but this on the isle.'

'Ah.' She stared sadly at the pot. There was to be no comfort even in her tea.

The landlady hovered, seeming reluctant to go. 'And so young McLennan picked you up last night, did he?'

Mhairi looked up in surprise. Had Mrs Buchanan seen them as he had dropped her off? Had she seen how Alexander had gone to kiss her and she had looked away, presenting him with her cheek? He had stared at her for several full seconds before putting his hand to her chin and forcibly turning her to him, kissing her hard with an inscrutable expression in his eyes. '. . . Aye, it was kind of him. I'd been expecting to get the bus over. I was happy to.'

'Well, he was keen to see you, I expect. He was bitterly disappointed when the news came of the evacuation and your delay.'

'Aye. It was very . . . unexpected,' she faltered. 'We had a lot to do.' She felt the older lady's scrutiny upon her.

'It must be strange for you, being here.'

Mhairi nodded. 'My family are settling in Lochaline, which feels just as far away from here as St Kilda.'

''Tis distant, aye. And you've none else here but McLennan?'

Mhairi looked up at her again. How could she tell the landlady that she knew this man only a little better than she knew her? That they were, in effect, strangers? 'No.'

Mrs Buchanan opened her mouth to say something, then appeared to think better of it. She looked sad, for a moment, but the look was gone with a blink. 'Eat up before it's cold. You look like you could do with a hot meal.'

Mhairi forced a smile and looked down at the bowl of brose. She had no appetite but she picked up her spoon and ate some anyway. Dutifully.

Father and son were nowhere to be found when she arrived at Hollow Farm. She hadn't seen them in the fields as she'd passed, and they weren't in the yard or any of the outbuildings. The cottage was unlocked, though, and the state of the kitchen told her she was expected – the dishes needed doing, the windows cleaning, the cloths boiling and the floor washing. Jobs had been left for her, ready to do. In fact, she wasn't sure they'd been done since her last visit.

'Hello?' she called again, standing in the yard, hearing the chickens clucking in their pen round the back, her hands by her sides. This was no welcome. All that fuss and pressure to get her here, and they couldn't even be bothered to be in when she arrived?

She saw the bicycle propped against the stone wall and slowly scuffed her way over to it. This time a year ago, it had excited her; she had thought it emblematic of the dynamic new way of life over here. But then James Callaghan had sailed in on the *Shamrock V* and she had known this was but a single rung above the St Kildan ladder. She stared at the silver skeleton shining in the morning sun; she pulled it by the handlebars and swung her leg over, sitting back disconsolately on the seat so that she was on her tiptoes – it no longer brought her any joy. Her fingers pulled on the brakes. She deliberated, then lifted her feet off the ground, balancing for only a few seconds before she had to put a foot down again. How was it possible to balance and move at once? She tried to see herself riding it alone; she tried to see herself as a modern young woman, free, but she was none of those things.

She set to work, slowly but diligently, scrubbing and polishing everything to a shine; when she hung the washing on the line again she looked out to sea for the St Kildan-shaped smudge on the horizon, but the clouds were too thick, snubbing her. It made her heart ache to think of it, just over there, abandoned. A ghost isle now, with no one left to tell its secrets; especially not its last.

She was cooking when she heard voices come into the yard, old McLennan kicking off his boots and walking in like he'd seen her only this morning.

'What are we eating, lass?' he asked, sniffing the air as he walked over to the range and peered into the pot.

'Um . . . I found some leftover beef and dripping so I pulled some tatties and thought I'd make some stovies,' she said quietly, stunned by the lack of formal greeting.

Hugh smiled, looking back to where his son filled the doorway, hands in his pockets, his chin down, his signature watchful pose. 'Hear that? Stovies. Something from nothing!' He chuckled. 'She was worth the wait after all!'

Mhairi watched as he wandered through to the bedroom, pulling his suspenders off his shoulders. She swallowed, waiting for Alexander to approach next, knowing he would.

'You've been busy,' he said in a low voice, tossing his cap onto the table and coming into the room. She felt her body tense as he too leant over the pot and inhaled the aroma. 'Mmm, that does smell good,' he murmured. 'You're giving me an appetite.'

Innuendo skirted the words like a black lace frill beneath calico hems.

'I wasn't sure when you'd be back,' she said, turning away, unable to bear his proximity, that penetrating stare that seemed to mock her. She could still hear the sounds he had made in her ear; her body remembered the strain of him.

'We were seeing a man about a ram,' he said, his voice still too close to her, his gaze heavy upon her back. She froze as she felt his hand sweep her hair across her shoulders, his hand warm and firm around the back of her neck. Could he sense her distress? See the shallow sips she took for breath? Like the hand on her thigh, the kiss on her mouth, he was showing her he could touch her if he so chose, that her body was his. Donald wasn't here to protect her now. 'It's good to have you here at last, Mhairi. My father's right – you are worth the wait.'

He dropped his hand and moved away, walking to the tap and running himself a glass of water. She watched as he, like his father, shrugged off his suspenders, his trousers dropping an inch on his hips. He sat down at the square table, his legs stretched along the settle where Donald had slept. His ghost lingered there still. She could easily conjure the memory of him – stiff and bad-tempered after his bad night's sleep, irritated by her flirtations with the cocky young farmer.

She realized Alexander had said something and was awaiting an answer. 'I'm sorry, what?' she asked, dragging herself back into the moment and reluctantly letting Donald's ghost fade.

His eyes narrowed as if he could tell what she'd been thinking. '. . . I asked what you made of the news.'

She blinked. 'What news?'

'Surely you've heard? It's one of your own, after all,' he drawled.

'I've been on the road. I've not heard any news.'

He pulled a tobacco paper from his shirt pocket and began rolling a cigarette. 'They found the factor that was missing.'

'Mr Mathieson?' She swallowed. 'I . . . I wasn't aware that he was missing,' she said unconvincingly, Flora's instructions echoing in her head.

At that he laughed. 'Dear God, where have you been hiding yourself? You're not living on a rock any more, y' know! How could you have missed it? It's been all over the newspapers. MacLeod's worked himself into a frenzy trying to locate his man.'

'Oh.'

'Oh?' he echoed, mockingly.

She tried to recover herself. 'Well, I'm glad he's got him back.'

At that, Alexander snorted. 'Oh aye, he's back. But not in any state that you'd wish on your worst enemy.'

She stared at him, feeling her heart tremble. Was she hot? Pale? Should she run, or would she collapse? She felt herself tethered again, pivoting nowhere, a tornado grounded.

'He's dead, Mhairi. Murdered, by all accounts.'

'Murdered?'

'Well, his death was "suspicious", it said,' he shrugged. 'But it means the same thing. They're just waiting on the proof. Hard evidence.'

She stared at him. 'And will they get that?'

'Scotland Yard's on the case. MacLeod wants answers,' he tutted, licking the cigarette paper, his eyes lifting towards her. 'It wasn't you, was it, Mhairi?'

'Me?' The tornado drove harder against the ground.

'Well, Donald said you had a touch of the red flash.'

'I don't know how Donald would know that,' she said quietly. 'He scarcely knows me.'

The tornado had turned – away from the factor, towards Donald, his old foe – but as his eyes narrowed, it felt just as dangerous. 'Strictly speaking, I think he was relaying your father's words.' His tone was light, almost playful.

'Right.' She looked away.

'How is dear Donald, anyway?' Sarcasm hovered like a heat haze above the words.

'He's fine.'

'Only fine? I'd have thought he'd be delighted by the evacuation. He fancies himself quite the businessman, as I recall! Maybe now he's in the real world he'll make his fortune.'

Mhairi fell still. 'Aye. Maybe.' It was easier to agree with him.

He lit his cigarette. '. . . Or maybe he already has.' He took a drag so that the tip glowed, his eyes never lifting off her.

'How . . . how would that be possible? We've been gone only a couple of weeks.'

'You never know, he might have made his small fortune before y' ever left the isle.'

Mhairi didn't stir, but she knew in that moment that he knew about the ambergris. Alexander was too precise a man, too direct, for this to be conjecture or bluff. Had Salvesen talked, was that it? One of his men?

'Well if he did, he never mentioned it to any of us,' she said, forcing a shrug. 'But I don't see how it would have been possible. We had no money over there. Nothing of value. Fulmar oil's not wanted now there's electricity, and tweed prices are plummeting—'

'Not tweed,' he said with a shake of his head. 'He had something much more valuable than that.'

'Then what?' She kept her tone light. Ignorant.

He didn't reply straight away, but she saw the scrutiny in his eyes. '. . . Where is he now, anyway?'

She felt a stab of alarm. Why did he want to know? Then again, Donald's whereabouts were no secret. Their evacuation had made the newspapers not just in this country but across the globe, being reported in Canada, America and even Australia. It was written in black ink that the islanders had been rehomed in only two locations.

'Oban, I believe,' she swallowed. 'He and his wife . . . had a baby.' Did he hear the slight break in her voice? 'But I don't know if they've stayed there or moved on.'

'He's a father now?' He raised an eyebrow. 'Eeesht, poor child.'

She continued chopping the vegetables.

'Then I suppose we shall have to play catch-up,' he said behind her, dragging on the cigarette again and hearing the knife stop against the wooden board once more. 'I'll have you pregnant by this time next month, what do you say?'

'What are y' two discussing in here?' Hugh asked, walking through from the bedroom in his long johns, a towel over his shoulder indicating he was going out for a bath.

'How many children we shall have,' Alexander replied, not missing a beat. 'I'm saying as many as she'll bear me. One a year, with plenty of practice in between.'

The older man laughed. 'Ha! You say that now but mark my words – marriage takes the heat out of love.'

'Never,' Alexander grinned. 'I will always burn for my future wife. Look at her! How could I resist such beauty? Such modesty?'

'But will she burn for you, lad?' his father said, shooting her a sly glance, seeing how she stood half turned away. 'That's the real question. Will she for you? You know what they say – the night is long for the husband of a bad wife.'

The sky was the colour of a plum by the time she stepped up into the trap, the pony twitching its tail against the evening midges. She settled herself beside Alexander in silence, pulling her red shawl over her shoulders. She had to managed to keep her distance for most of the afternoon, fussing over a spot of grease or mending holes, demurring against his suggestions to come outside, but a sense of threat lingered in their every interaction.

'Ha!' Alexander cried, shaking the reins and moving the pony onwards, the trap lurching slightly as the wheels began to turn. For several minutes, neither one of them spoke. She looked away, out towards the stony hills, and wondered how many secrets they kept. What scenes had been played out in these glens? Nothing as fearsome as on St Kilda, surely.

'You seem changed, Mhairi,' he said finally.

She didn't respond immediately. 'Do I?'

'Mm. You're no longer a girl.'

Her head whipped around to him and she saw him register her knee-jerk response. She stared at him, breathing hard. 'Well, perhaps I'm not,' she said in a steady voice, the hint of steel drawing his gaze towards her. 'Perhaps I stopped being a girl when you trapped me in the byre.'

His head angled slightly, his brows pointing to a steeple. 'So then you really were a child, before?'

How could he say such a thing to her, as if it should be a surprise that she had been innocent? 'I'm a Christian. I live by the commandments.'

'Aye, well, your minister is well known for his puritanical stance.'

'Puritanical?'

'You'll be glad to hear that such a literal translation of the scripture isn't much adhered to over here, in the modern world.'

'Oh. This is the modern world here, is it?' she asked, sweeping a hand over the pony and trap.

For the first time she saw a look of annoyance cross his face. 'Remember yourself, Mhairi. That tone is unattractive.'

She stared at him with contempt. He had sullied her with his sin but her sarcasm was unattractive? She was the one who had to remember herself?

She looked away again, feeling tears bud. This man was a stranger to her. She had despised his memory over the course of this past year – he was everything that Donald was not – but that hadn't been the worst of it, for he was even more abhorrent now that she saw he was unrepentant.

The horse trotted with bored rhythm, passing the general store where she had given up a small piece of herself. She wondered if it was there still, a tiny flame flickering in the dark.

Soon enough, the electric lights of the small town shone. They had a different quality to the lights of home: brighter, whiter, stronger, harsher. It was another nuance to add to her list – the tea, the clothes, the lighting . . . Mrs Buchanan's lodging house sat at the edge of the town's main street, over-looking the small isles in the bay. It was a two-storeyed, white-rendered building much like the factor's house, only bigger. There were attic rooms in the roof and Mrs Buchanan had A Girl who helped her with the laundry and cooking.

Mhairi felt a rush of relief to know they were almost there and that, for a few hours overnight, she would have refuge here. Her father had allowed her to join the McLennans before the wedding only on the condition that they put her up in this accommodation. 'He's waited an extra three months, lass,' her father had said as she had pleaded to spend the final few weeks with them. 'It's not unreasonable. And it'll give y' a chance to meet your new neighbours. There's no point in putting down roots here now, is there?'

Alexander pulled on the reins and the horse came to a languid halt, jerking its head downwards as if looking for dandelions in the road. He turned to her. 'You did well today. Father's pleased with you.'

She didn't reply and she felt his scrutiny deepen, as if he was trying to read her in the darkness.

'Well, g'night then,' he said, leaning over to her. Instinctively she drew back but this time his hand clasped the back of her head. 'No.' She struggled but he held her in a firm grip. 'No, you don't. We'll start as we mean to go on.'

'We'll no' start anything till we've made our holy vows before God,' she whispered, feeling his fingertips press against her scalp, his face only inches from hers.

'You'll not be damned on account of a kiss,' he said evenly and before she could respond, he closed the gap between them, kissing her hard on the mouth again.

'There. That wasn't so bad, now, was it?' he asked when he finally released her. She touched her mouth, her lips feeling bruised, but he just smirked. 'It's hardly a scandal. No one resents a man kissing his sweetheart.'

'You have no honour!' she whispered, feeling the sob in her throat.

'No honour?' he echoed, grabbing her chin with one hand and holding her there, his eyes locked upon her. 'Would a dishonourable man have protected your virtue the way I did that day?'

Her eyes widened in disbelief. He couldn't be serious? He couldn't honestly believe his actions had saved her in any way?

He tutted. 'Don't rewrite history. Whatever you choose to believe now, in that moment you wanted me as much as I wanted you.'

'A kiss!' she cried. 'That was all I—'

He shook his head, tightening his grip. 'But I held back and I waited. I've waited a year for you. I'll not feel bad for wanting some favours in return.'

'Favours?'

'Aye. Favours,' he murmured, placing his other hand on her breast and squeezing it.

She tried to shake her head free, to pull herself back, but he had her in a vice-like grip and he released her only when he was ready. She turned away with a barely suppressed sob, clambering down from the trap and pulling her shawl tighter around her. 'No!' she cried, now she was at a distance from him.

But he only laughed and shook the reins again, pulling the trap round in a wide arc and heading back from whence they'd come. She ran up the path and into the house, closing the door behind her and leaning against it, feeling the sobs high in her chest. She rested her head against it and stared at the ceiling, tears sliding from the corners of her eyes. How could this be endured? It had been only one day. How could she endure a lifetime of—

A rattle startled her and she looked up to see Mrs Buchanan walking through from the dining room with a tray of glasses.

'Good evening, Miss MacKinnon,' she said, looking not at all surprised to find Mhairi propping up the door.

'Good evening, Mrs Buchanan,' she said quietly, quickly wiping her eyes dry as she made a movement to push her hair back from her face. Her heart was still pounding. Had her landlady seen them from the window, as she had last night?

'I trust you've had a pleasant first day?'

Mhairi nodded.

'. . . Xander must be pleased to have y' here after waiting so long.'

This time she couldn't even nod, and the landlady stared at her as the comment went unaffirmed. Her eyes narrowed a little, as if seeing Mhairi's distress. Mhairi swallowed, but it was more than she was capable of to make small talk right now. '. . . Good night, Mrs Buchanan.'

She walked across the narrow hall and up the stairs in neat steps. She closed her bedroom door and let the tears stream now that there was no one to see. She collapsed onto the bed, not even bothering to undress, her gaze unfocused on the tiny room. The metal bed creaked with her every move, springs stuck in her back; come the morning, the yellow floral curtains would do nothing to keep out the light, and yet this was sanctuary. This was refuge. In just a few short weeks she would be married to that man and she would remember these as her final days of comfort. This wasn't yet rock bottom; there was seemingly always further to fall.

Chapter Twenty-Six

Mhairi stood on the road and looked across at the grey stone hut. Sunlight was glinting off the windows, some tools propped against the walls, purple heather bristling on the moors behind. She had been standing there for several minutes now, ever since a sudden idea had stopped her feet on the road to Bunavoneader. She was staring at it, trying to find the courage to go in, but she didn't know what to say; what to offer.

An unfamiliar sound suddenly came to her ear and she stepped back with a gasp as the bus appeared over the brow of the hill and came thundering past. Faces flashed past at the windows – pale and glassy-eyed – and were gone again in the next moment. It would take some getting used to, the notion of traffic.

Heart thudding, she crossed over and climbed the steps to the door. She peered in, finding the old man standing behind the counter as before. He had his back to her, stacking the shelves, and she watched for a moment before clearing her throat.

He turned, a small frown puckering his brow at the sight of her. She knew her clothes marked her out – the heavy dark skirt, the woollen blouse, the red shawl – and she kept her gaze averted as she stepped in. Did he recognize her? Her gaze fell to the fob watch in his jacket pocket. How could it be that a part of her lay nestled against his chest?

'Good day, sir,' she said, unable to meet his gaze.

There was a slight pause. 'Good day, miss. How can I help y'?'

'I'm in need of a . . . tool.'

She saw him place his hands flat on the counter. 'What sort of tool?'

'Something small, and sharp.'

'How small?'

'Small enough that I can carry with it me.'

'Well, what's it for?'

She took a shallow breath and swallowed hard. She couldn't think how to reply. 'I'm not sure . . .' Her voice faded out.

'Is it a chisel you need?' he asked, reaching under the counter and placing it on the counter for her to see.

'No. It needs to be sharper.'

He replaced the chisel with another tool. 'A gimlet, then?'

She stared at the T-shaped weapon; it would never fit in her pocket. 'Smaller than that.'

There was a pause. Then he reached under the counter and brought up a wooden box, filled with myriad tools. 'Then why don't you have a look yourself?'

She stared down at it, a cornucopia of cast-iron and wooden implements. Raising an arm, she rifled carefully past forks, calipers, axe heads, bevels and sickles until she came across a small hook. It was perfectly curved with a sharp point, a turned wooden handle that would fit inside her palm, and a leather loop. She picked it up, feeling a burst of relief – it looked small enough that she might even be able to keep the strap looped over her wrist and the hook hidden in her sleeve, ready at all times.

'That's the one?' he asked, watching her as she handled it, feeling the weight, pricking the tip against the soft pad of her finger.

She nodded.

'It's for digging the potatoes,' he said.

She hesitated, then nodded again. 'Aye. For digging the potatoes,' she agreed.

There was a pause. 'It's nine shillings eight pence.'

For several moments, she could not find her voice. Her heart began thudding again as she set the hook back on the countertop. '. . . I have no money, sir.'

'No . . . ?' She saw the hands splay upon the counter again as her words settled, his fingers reaching for the tool. She knew what he was going to say – this was a store; there would be no sale if she couldn't pay.

The silence lengthened but she didn't dare look up; she could feel the weight of his stare, his open suspicion.

'You're McLennan's new bride,' he said finally. 'From St Kilda.'

It wasn't a question. She knew he could identify her by her clothes alone. 'Yes, sir.'

She startled as he reached forward suddenly and pulled down her shawl, revealing her bright red hair. 'And you came here before.'

'Yes, sir.' She kept her eyes down, but she knew her cheeks were burning as the intimacy she had permitted was recalled between them.

'. . . Where's the man that was with you then?'

'Oban, sir. With his f-family.' She could scarcely get the word out. 'He was my neighbour and chaperone.'

'So you're here alone?'

She swallowed, knowing her vulnerability was exposed now. 'Aye, sir.'

There was a long silence as the man handled the small hook, rolling it in his palm and all the while regarding her keenly. '. . . So then we'll trade.'

She swallowed and dropped her head, dreading his next words. What would he demand of her? Another lock of hair? Or something more?

'In exchange for this, you'll go to the golf course in Scarista every day for a week and collect for me the stray balls in the long grass.'

She looked up in surprise. 'What?'

'My knees,' he shrugged. 'I canna be bending down like that, but the tourists often ask for them on their way down . . . You'll need to go at dusk each day, after the playing's finished.'

She nodded. 'I can do that.'

'I'll give you a basket or some way of carrying them back. They get heavy when there's a many of them.' He reached under the counter and passed to her a woven basket.

'Yes,' she said, taking it.

'And you mustn't miss a night. The summer walkers will get here soon and then they'll have the spoils to themselves for as long as they stay.'

'The who?' she asked, perplexed.

'Summer walkers. The tinkers. They're on their way down from Balallan and they'll strip the grounds of every last ball to sell for themselves. We'll not be robbed by the likes o' them.'

'No, sir.'

There was another pause, the old man still watching her keenly. 'My name's Murdo MacAskill, but you can call me Murdo. What is your name, lass?'

'Mhairi. Mhairi MacKinnon, sir. I'm lodging with Mrs Buchanan till the wedding but I'll be passing by here each morning to the farm. I can drop the balls off on my way.'

He nodded, seeming satisfied with the arrangement. 'Then I'll see you on the morrow, Mhairi.'

'Aye, thank you . . . Murdo.' Her eyes flitted down towards the hook, now back on the counter, but she turned to leave with just the basket.

'No. Take it,' Murdo said, pushing it towards her.

'Oh, but . . .' she began to demur.

'You showed me a kindness once, now I can repay the debt. I trust y', Mhairi.'

She glanced at him gratefully. 'Thank you.'

He watched her again, before clearing his throat. '. . . He's a decent enough man, Xander.'

Her gaze dropped again. 'Aye.'

'But . . . impatient.'

She fell still, sensing weight in the word as he pushed the hook towards her.

'You'll be needing it. For the potatoes,' he said carefully.

She went to reach it for it but he placed a hand upon hers.

'Just be careful, it's very sharp. We wouldn't want any accidents.'

She bit her lip. 'Thank you,' she whispered, slipping it into her pocket. 'I'll see you tomorrow morning, then.'

'Aye,' he murmured, watching her closely. 'Tomorrow.'

The two men walked slowly back up the green, wholly unaware they were being followed. They were only at the seventh hole, but light was fading too quickly for the game to be completed and after the last swing had sent the turf flying further than the ball, they had shaken hands and retired.

Mhairi lay on her stomach in the long grass, watching them go. If they'd had any wild instincts left about them at all, they would have felt her stare, but in their patterned socks and belted tweeds, they struck her as being far removed from any wildness; she doubted they had ever even walked barefoot over grass, much less dangled on a rope above an angry sea. They seemed to look around without seeing, to talk without really saying anything, laughing like honking geese.

As they grew smaller in her frame of vision, she got to her knees, staying in a low crouch, her eyes flitting back to them every few seconds as she scanned 'the green' and 'the rough' – as Murdo had called it – for stray balls; should they glance behind them, she would be completely exposed, her red hair not easily camouflaged in this all-green landscape. She was taking a risk picking up so early in the evening, without the cover of darkness and not a single tree to hide behind. The course had been set in dazzling countryside, with the bright white sands of Scarista Beach smiling at its back and the humped hills of the north on the horizon like breaching whales, but the ground beneath her feet pitched and swooped in smooth, undulating waves with only occasional shallow bunkers or low bushes providing any degree of cover.

There was nothing else for it, though. Her previous two excursions here had taught her that this was a race, not against the tinkers – or summer walkers, as Murdo had called them – but the local bloods who had their own racket going, selling balls to the pub landlord. He in turn offered them on the side to tourists who came in for dinner. There seemed to be a few of these other ball-gatherers, coming just after dusk. The first evening, she had arrived too late and found only six balls across the nine-hole course. Murdo had been disappointed with her spoils, so the next day she had come earlier and picked up eighteen; still not a boon, but she had at least chanced upon the bloods finishing up on the same mission this time and understood it was a job for the early bird.

And her gamble was paying off: the basket Murdo had loaned her was creaking under the weight now, the balls surprisingly heavy en masse. She wasn't entirely sure how she would get them into the boarding house unseen and past her landlady's watchful gaze, for the woman seemed to have eyes in the back of her head. It certainly hadn't escaped Mrs Buchanan's notice that Alexander hadn't brought her back for the last few evenings, for example, and Mhairi had been compelled to explain that he had gone to the livestock sale in Stornoway and would be away for much of the week. That was more than Alexander himself had bothered to tell her – she had arrived at the farm on her second morning braced for the next affray, only to find him gone. The relief had made her knees buckle. If he had intended it as a slight, she had taken it as a reprieve.

Hugh was easy enough to look after on his own and they had immediately fallen into an easy pattern. As long as his stomach was full, he was out in the fields for the day, leaving her in peace; she would cook, clean, launder, feed the chickens, milk the cows, churn the butter, make some crowdie, patch, mend, sew and knit. Jessie the Post would stop at the gate and talk with her, sharing some gossip from the village and no doubt trying to collect some from her. She was even teaching herself to ride the bicycle; she still wobbled wildly but she could now go a full revolution of the wheels with both feet off the ground.

She would make dinner for noon, then – to get down here in good time – prepare and leave covered his tea for when he returned at dusk; and she would put oats simmering in the range overnight for his breakfast the next morning, so that he wasn't waiting on her arrival either. Which was just as well, for Murdo would have a pot brewing when she dropped by in the morning, and the talk between them flowed easily. He reminded her of Old Fin, a grandfather figure dispensing quiet wisdom over strong tea.

If only Alexander could stay away forever, she thought she might be able to live here contentedly after all. This could be enough for her – a quiet life of domesticity, routine and solitude. She had had her big love, and Donald and the baby lived in her mind's eye like an inner sun, the memories they had made together a playbook on loop as she worked by day and sat at her boarding house bedroom window by night.

She scooped up another seven balls at the seventh hole; they glowed in the gloaming and it wasn't so very different from catching eggs, just with less precipitous cliffs and angry birds – a job she could do almost in her sleep. She had no idea if she was retrieving enough to cover the cost of the hook, but she felt Murdo would be pleased with this haul at last. She turned to head back; the bloods could help themselves to whatever was left at the last two holes but even with that, they'd be in for a nasty shock tonight.

She stayed well back behind the men, slowing her long stride to match their more leisurely dawdle. She had never walked at this pace before and it felt odd, unnatural, but should they turn back and see her, she would need to look indistinct from a distance.

The golfers were almost at the clubhouse now, their shadows long and dark as they walked through the golden pools thrown down onto the lawn. It was a long, low grey stone building with large windows; Mhairi hadn't been this close to it before, and as she approached in the shadows she could see a shiny brass chandelier hanging from the ceiling, polished wood panelling on walls groaning with silver trophies, a stag's head mounted above a fireplace.

There were men standing around inside, all wearing the peculiar outfits she'd seen on the golfers just now, holding tumblers of whisky and talking with bright-pink cheeks. The golfers she'd followed up the fairway walked into the room as she watched, greeting the others like old friends. Were they? It was a foreign image to her – monied, grand, elitist – and yet there was something in the atmosphere of their revelry that reminded her of the evenings back home when everyone would walk the Street, gossiping and sharing news. Community, she supposed, came in different forms.

She turned away to skirt past the front of the building but as she approached the corner, a woman's voice carried over. Even if she hadn't been carrying a basket laden with stolen golf balls, there was something in its tone that made Mhairi stop.

'—It's a scandal!'

'Well, quite!' another woman replied. 'That's exactly what I said!'

'Lady Dunmore, your coat,' a man said in a local accent.

Lady Dunmore? The name rang a bell for Mhairi; Murdo had mentioned the lady when they were discussing the tweed crisis that morning. The Bad Times on the mainland and in the wider world were beginning to bite here too, and a Lady Dunmore had had the idea of forming a company name under which all the locally spun weaves could be sold. Harris Tweed, she was calling it, or some such.

Mhairi set the basket down and peered around the corner to see two women talking by the front porch. Lady Dunmore was being helped into her coat by a man in a uniform while she smoked a cigarette from a long-handled holder, the likes of which Flora had once shown her in a magazine; they were fashionable, apparently. The other woman was much shorter, with a fox stole around her neck and her face obscured by a felt hat.

'So what shall you do?' Lady Dunmore enquired, her voice drifting around the corner like a steamy stew.

'Well, what *can* one do?' the other lady replied. 'We believed Weir to have been a loyal steward to our family all these years and we supported him, of course we did; but now he's been arrested and charged with handling stolen goods, can you believe it—?'

With a sigh, Mhairi drew back, wondering what to do now. There was no way she could pass by the two women without being seen, but she didn't want to walk several hundred yards in the wrong direction around the building carrying this basket either; it was as unwieldy as it was heavy.

'—We certainly didn't believe it, not until the police showed us a rare book he had stolen. Do you know, it's exactly like a copy we have at Dumfries House . . .'

Mhairi froze. Wasn't that where Effie was working? She peered around the corner again and looked more closely at the shorter woman. They were talking as equals, clearly friends. *Loyal steward . . . Our family . . . Dumfries House . . .*

'. . . only his came from Dunvegan. Apparently he was in cahoots with MacLeod's factor.'

'The dead fellow?'

'Yes, my dear, exactly so. It seems they were working together, stealing valuables and works of art to order for private buyers. They took the view that no one would notice if some silver plates went missing, or a few paintings, or a priceless pair of books.'

'No,' Lady Dunmore breathed, sounding scandalized and delighted all at once.

'I'm afraid so. Of course, as steward, Weir was able to

exploit his position shamelessly and cover up any losses in the ledgers – so who really knows how long they had been racketeering for? What else has gone missing that we haven't noticed? We've got no idea.'

'How beastly!'

'Isn't it?'

Both were quiet for a moment as Lady Dunmore took a particularly deep drag of her cigarette. It was hard to see their faces clearly but the lighted tip glowed in the darkness, dancing as the two women talked.

'. . . What's really deplorable is that he's shown no honour at all. I'm afraid we're only just seeing his true colours now. He's been trying to implicate this young woman the earl's got working on his egg collection, just to save his own skin. She's one of those St Kildans that's come over.'

'That's where Sir John's man was found.'

'Exactly. My husband thinks Weir's tactic is to couple the crimes together – you know, if one of them was capable of killing a man, they'd certainly be capable of thieving too.' She tutted. 'He's trying to make out that he found the Dunvegan book under this poor girl's bed at Dumfries.'

There was a short pause.

'Ridiculous! . . . How exactly could anyone explain a feral girl from St Kilda having got hold of MacLeod's book? They were on a rock in the middle of the sea!' Lady Dunmore's cigarette tip drew circles in the air. 'It makes no sense.'

But Mhairi felt her blood run cold. It made perfect sense to her. Effie might never have been to Dunvegan, but Frank Mathieson had – and he'd been obsessed with her. Mhairi knew it better than anyone; she had seen him that night in the storm, when he'd lost control and gone wild with jealousy. If Frank had given Effie a book as some sort of love token, it could prove his obsession with her and his unnatural lust. And if the police were to discover the forced broomstick marriage, it would give Effie the perfect motive for murder.

Mhairi's heart gathered into a gallop as she thought back to that night at the storm cleit. Who knew the truth besides herself and Effie? Donald . . . Flora. She would trust them both with her life; Effie's secret would be safe with them. But there was a small breach in their wall – Lorna had been involved too, even though the full story had been kept from her. They'd tripped in the dark, that was what they had agreed to say; but did Lorna really believe it? If the police were to ask her the right question, might it trigger a doubt in her mind?

'Despicable, isn't it? To think he'd stoop so low. I mean, the girl in question is wild, there's no doubt about it – she walks about in men's clothes and she threw a rope over the roof and climbed up the back of the house to rescue Miss Petunia last week! But she's no thief.' She drew breath. 'She joined us for dinner the other week – in a borrowed dress – but do you know, at first glance you really couldn't have told that she grew up . . . as she did.'

'Well, the world seems to be moving that way – the old boundaries breaking down, Labour in government. I suppose we must get used to shepherdesses at the dinner table,' Lady Dunmore drawled.

'Mmm.'

A sweep of headlights over the drive was accompanied this time by the crunch of wheels on gravel and a gleaming car pulled up slowly to the front of the clubhouse. Mhairi watched as a man in a coat and peaked cap stepped out and went round to open one of its rear doors.

'Thank you, Wilson,' Lady Dunmore said, sliding in. Her companion did the same.

Mhairi watched as the heavy door was slammed shut. The driver walked around to the front and after a moment, the car pulled away with a throaty purr. She leant back against the wall, out of the sweep of the lights, feeling a new worry in her heart. She would need to write to her friend. If Effie was in trouble, then they all were.

She turned back for the basket to hurry back to the boarding house.

. . . Where was it?

She squinted at the patch on the ground where the basket no longer sat, giving a gasp as she heard the snapping of a twig and caught sight of dark shapes tearing down the ninth green. Feeling the red flash zip through her like a devil, she gave chase. There were three bloods sprinting off that she could see; the one carrying the basket was running awkwardly but he was tall and long-legged, with too great a head start for her to catch up. She could only gain on the smallest one, grabbing onto his shirt-tail.

'Hey!' she cried, yanking him back. 'You give me back my basket!'

'I've not got it, lady!' the boy retorted cheekily, holding up his empty hands and sticking his tongue out at her.

She grabbed his ear between her finger and thumb and pinched it hard. 'But you know the boy who does! Tell him to get back here!'

'Or what?'

She twisted his ear.

He yelled but was unrepentant. 'You've no right coming in and stealing like that!'

'I've every bit as much right as you!'

'No! We live here.'

'As do I now! I'm marrying Alexander McLennan and if I

tell him what you've done, he'll come after you and scalp the lot of y'.'

Alexander had a good ten years on this boy but he simply laughed, not fazed in the least. 'That old soak? He couldn't hit his own reflection.'

She gasped. 'He's not a drunk!'

He laughed harder still. 'You should run while y've still got the chance, miss! What are y' doing getting shackled to the likes o' him!'

'He's a good man,' she said grimly, her tone utterly lacking in conviction.

'Oh, aye? Well, don't try telling that to the misses in Stockinish! The weather's always hella stormy over there!'

'What? What are y' talking about?' she frowned, releasing her grip slightly as a memory surfaced, opaque and distant. *As for young Xander, the storm has passed in Stockinish.*

In an instant the boy had wriggled free, still laughing as he broke into a fresh sprint.

'Hey! Tell me what you mean!' she yelled. But her words disappeared with him, into the darkness.

Chapter Twenty-Seven

Mhairi sat on the hard, narrow seat, her feet on tiptoes as she tried to balance the bicycle. She could travel the width of the yard now – stop, go, turn. It had become her reward, a private solace, to practise during the long, lonely afternoons. It was the only good thing about life over here, the one advantage over St Kilda.

She had her feet on the pedals, beginning to turn them, when she heard the now familiar rumble of the red van and saw Jessie the Post climbing out.

'Hallo there, Mhairi!' he hailed with an arm aloft, opening the back of the van and disappearing from sight for a few moments. By the time he reappeared she was already at the gate, the bike propped in its usual position against the wall. 'Teaching y'self to ride, are you?'

'I'll no' get far,' she smiled, embarrassed to have been caught out. 'I'm like a drunken sailor on that thing!'

'So's Xander!'

They laughed easily together, but she remembered the young blood's insult last night – *That old soak?* – and her smile faded.

'Hughie out again?' he asked, casting a look over her shoulder.

'Aye. He's rebuilding a section of wall over by the bridge.'

'Och, aye. That'll keep him busy awhile. He doesna want the sheep getting past to that gorge; he lost a fair few in the fog some years back. Damned sheep, they're so stupid—'

'They'd die twice!' Mhairi finished for him. 'M' father always used to say that too.'

Jessie chuckled. 'And is Xander not back yet?'

'Still droving,' she shrugged. 'Hugh thinks he'll be back tomorrow.' She tried to keep her voice neutral at these words. No doubt Jessie would expect her to be happy at Alexander's return; she could see the pity in his eyes at the sight of her alone here, teaching herself to ride a bicycle with no one but the chickens for company. He probably couldn't imagine how much better she liked it this way. She would take the chickens' company over that of the men any day. 'So what have you there today?' she asked, as brightly as she could.

He reached into his sack and pulled out the newspaper and a letter for Hugh. 'And one for you too, Miss Mhairi . . .'

A letter for her? Her first ever. She smiled, feeling her heart skip at the thought of her father's confident handwriting – he had promised to send her all the family's news – but as she looked at the envelope Jessie handed over, she saw the hand was unfamiliar. She frowned.

'. . . As well as an important message from Mrs Sinclair.'

'Mrs Sinclair?' she echoed after a beat, dragging her mind back to the moment and looking up at him. She had never met the woman, nor even heard of her.

'Of number six Braeside,' he said solemnly, as if that explained it. 'She says your rèiteach will be Friday after next, in the church hall.'

Mhairi blinked. She would have a rèiteach here? Flora's engagement had been celebrated back home, of course, but Mhairi had pleaded with her father and mother not to celebrate hers. She had argued it was too much, too soon after Flora's: no one had the spare mutton now and the keg had been drunk dry. But the truth had been that she could not bear to watch her family, friends and neighbours toasting a union that would rest on rotten foundations. The idea of observing the custom now – with people she might one day know but as of yet, did not – was not an appealing one either.

'Can I politely decline?'

At that, Jessie laughed. 'Can I politely watch if y' try?' he asked. 'Mrs Sinclair is something of a dragon, you might say. The village matriarch. Poor Dougie Sinclair walks with a stoop from trying to escape her tongue-lashings.'

'I see.'

'Fret not, lass. Folk are friendly enough around here – and keen to meet y'. I know it's not easy at the moment, being tucked away down here, but everyone on the round asks me what y're like. Do you have two heads? That kind of thing.'

She had to smile.

'Of course, word gets round anyway, you should know that. Mrs Buchanan's never far from a secret and the bloods are parched for adventure. Their word is you've been robbing them right under their own noses.' He chuckled again, but his eyes glinted with curiosity. She knew she was distinctive – her hair, her dress – how many redheaded, strangely dressed women were there in these parts? Still, it would be their word against hers, even if she had foolishly betrayed her own identity by revealing herself as Alexander McLennan's Fiancée.

'Me?' she scoffed, arching an eyebrow. 'A likely thief I'd be!'

'Well now, that's just what I told them. You're a God-fearing Christian soul, I said.' He winked. 'We all will be, now the tinkers are just a day away.'

'They're that close?'

'They move fast when it suits them and drag their feet the same too.' His expression changed. 'You do know you wouldn't want to chance upon them, lassie? You're not from here, you won't have had their sort back on the Wild Isle, but they can have black hearts – some of them, not all, but take no chances. Don't trust their words and don't venture near their camp – especially at night when they've been drinking. The devil gets inside them then.'

'I'm sure I won't even see them.'

He arched a thick, wiry eyebrow. 'They'll come knocking.'

'They will?'

'Aye. To fix your pots and pans and anything else like that needs mending. Y' might choose to get them sorted and ready now so you can be rid of them all the sooner. It doesn't do to give them time standing at your door and having a look around. Things tend to disappear when they're about.'

'But how will I pay them?' She felt a stab of fear at the prospect of another debt. How did anyone keep up here? The constant need for coins was a tyranny.

'Fret not. Hughie will have something kept aside. Even he won't cross them, and Hughie McLennan's not afeared of many.'

'All right then,' she murmured. 'I'll ask him when he comes back for his dinner.'

'You do that. And remember to pass on to him about the rèiteach, too. He'll be expected, but it's bad luck for the groom t' attend. Xander won't be happy about it, mind – he thinks there's no party without him in it – but tell him Mrs Sinclair will be having none of it. She's almost as terrifying as the tinkers.'

She cracked a half-smile. 'I'll tell him.'

'He'll need telling more than once, I should wager. Always does, that one.' His smile faded on the words, as though he'd said something he shouldn't, and he puffed his chest up. He went to give one of his comical salutes. 'Well, I'll be seeing y—'

'Jessie, wait! Before you go . . .' She reached into her waistband, pulling out a letter of her own. 'Could I prevail upon y' to see this gets sent?'

He looked at it, then back at her. 'It'll need a stamp, lass.'

She bit her lip, then reached into the basket she had set by the gate earlier. '. . . I have this,' she said, hopefully holding out half a cake. She had baked it that morning, having found a recipe in a Mrs Beeton's book on the shelf. It hadn't risen as well as she might have liked – she didn't have enough flour and had had to substitute with some cooked potato instead – but it was all she could offer. She saw Jessie notice how her hands were trembling as she held it up. 'I thought you must get awful hungry on the road all day,' she added.

'Well now it's true, I do,' he said after a pause, taking it from her. 'That was thoughtful of you.' He glanced again at the letter. 'Dumfries House, eh?'

'A good friend of mine from home is working there,' she shrugged. 'I miss her.' She made no mention of arrests, or dead factors, or thieving stewards, though there was plenty about them in the newspapers he delivered. 'And if y' like the cake, then I shall make y' another one next week too,' she added with a smile. What price was a stamp? How much for a cake? These were all things she didn't yet know; she had yet to feel the weight of coins in her pocket as she went about her days. She was walking through this new world, both a part of it and yet apart. 'To say thank y' again.'

Jessie dropped the letter into his sack with a wink and gave her his salute. 'Tomorrow, then, Mhairi.'

'Aye, tomorrow, Jessie,' she said with relief as she watched him go, gripping the gate in one hand and the letter in the other.

Mhairi wrapped the thin towel around her as she climbed out of the small tin tub, her ears pricked for the slightest sound outside. Although she was alone for almost all of the day, it was still impossible to relax when she couldn't absolutely guarantee that Hugh wouldn't return to the farmhouse unexpectedly, and she dressed quickly, her skin still damp so that the chemise clung to her body, the wool skirt itchy against her legs. She began scooping bucketloads of her bathwater into the pail and crossed the room to toss it out the window; the tub would be too heavy to lift till it was almost entirely empty but she was eager to be rid of the evidence of her private indulgence. Her afternoon had taken a most unexpected turn and for the first time in weeks, she had felt a glow of happiness within her.

She was tossing the bucket for the fourth time, the water flying through the air in scattered droplets, when her worst fear came true: someone suddenly walked right past the window. Mhairi gasped in horror as she saw Alexander stop dead in shock, arms held away from his dripping clothes, his hair thrown back by the force of the jet.

'Oh!' she cried, her hands flying to her mouth as they stared at one another through the open window.

'Wha—? What—?' he spluttered, so stunned by the onslaught that she could see he couldn't quite register what had just happened.

'What are you doing here?' she asked from within the bedroom, feeling her knees buckle in fear.

'What am I doing here?' he repeated. 'I live here! The question is, what are you doing?'

'I was throwing out the bathwater,' she replied in a small voice, seeing how his eyes hardened.

'Oh, were you, indeed?'

She watched in mute horror as he shook his arms out, droplets flying off him, and stalked into the house. Within a moment he was standing at the door to his bedroom, staring in as if he half expected to find another man lying in the bed.

There was a short pause as he looked around the quiet room. 'Why are y' having a bath in the middle of the afternoon?' he demanded suspiciously.

'Well?' he asked again as she stood in a trembling silence. 'Do you fancy y'self a lady of leisure, is that it? M' father and I will work ourselves to the bone while you lie about taking baths in the middle of the day?'

She bridled.

'Does it look like I've been lying about?' she asked quietly, sweeping a hand around the room to indicate the small pale blue patch now in the upper left quadrant of his bedsheet, which she had mended before washing; the knitted blanket now extended with a border to cover the whole bed; the small jug of heather on the table by the window, which gleamed from its fresh polish. Probably this place hadn't been so well kept for years, ten or more at her guess, and she was already moving about the farmhouse and yard with familiarity. She knew where the carbolic soap was kept, the mop, the extra salt; she was working her way through father and son's jumpers and socks, darning up the holes; she knew how long the milk had been sitting in the saucers, and which was for butter and which for cream.

Her list of chores was endless. She still had the sills to scrub and the cobwebs to pull down from the roof; the fireside rug needed to be soaked and Hugh had asked her to look for some stones – 'yea size' – that could be used to hold down the nets on the thatch; but to accuse her of indolence . . . She felt her mother's pride bristle within her, for the day had been productive and, till now, peaceful, with Hugh only popping in for his dinner and disappearing within the hour. His breakfast oats were already on a low simmer in the range, the cows were milked, and she had prepared some sliced ham and potatoes for his tea. She had carded the wool he had brought back the previous evening and ordinarily she would have made a start on spinning it now, but instead she'd planned to head over to the golf club and make good her promise with Murdo once and for all. He had been kind when she'd recalled the bloods' theft the previous night, telling her that 'it mattered not', but it mattered to her; her debt was still outstanding and she must pay it. The tinkers would be here any hour, any minute . . . she couldn't delay. Jessie had told her, with a shaking head and a bleak expression, that no one ever knew how long they would stay when they set up their camp.

'I thought . . . I thought you weren't due back till tomorrow?' She changed the subject, trying to recover her voice and sound stronger than she felt. Being alone with him anywhere, but especially in his bedroom, made her weak with fear, and her fingers reached for the strap on her wrist. Only . . . the hook wasn't there. It was in her skirt pocket. She had thought she had another day.

He shrugged off his jacket, a small puddle of water collecting at his feet. She went to take it from him. 'There's never any telling with sheep,' he said, regarding her almost suspiciously. 'They'll go when they go and we get here when we get here.' He pulled his shirt off in one fell swoop and let it drop to the ground, bare-chested, muscled, stinking; he had spent six days and nights droving sheep over the hills, after all.

She reached for it timidly, trying not to get too close to him. He was pulling off his boots now and she knew what would be coming off next. She needed to get out of this room but he was blocking the door. 'Are . . . are you pleased with them, the ones you got?' she asked.

She thought she saw his eyebrow arch slightly at her attempt to make conversation. Did it surprise him to think they might talk? 'They'll do well enough,' he muttered. 'I've bought from the fellow before. His quality is reliable; he knows what he's doing.'

'Good. That's good.' She tried to think of something to say next. 'You must be hungry.'

'Not really.'

'Still, I'll get a meal going for you. If I'd known you'd be back today, I'd have had something prepared—' She went to walk past him but he caught her lightly, easily, at the elbow, and she felt that kick of panic through her body again.

'Don't I at least get an apology for having a bucket of water thrown over me?'

'I'm sorry I threw water over you,' she said quietly. Obediently. 'It wasn't intentional. I'll get your clothes drying by the fire for you.' And before he could stop her again, she slipped past like a blade.

The kitchen felt safer – an open space, public – and she moved with greater confidence in there, pulling together a hot meal with the few fresh ingredients available to her. She chopped a turnip, then began on the carrot and potato. Her gaze flickered up to the window, to the fast-dying light, and she knew her cause today was lost. There was no way she could leave early now and the bloods would already be making their way to the course for today's pickings, if they weren't there already. They might have come earlier today, wanting to make sure she didn't steal a march on them again. How would she explain it to Murdo this time?

She heard the sounds of Alexander moving about in the bedroom – the creak of the wardrobe door, the slide of the window shutting – and they blended with the chop of the knife in the kitchen, the crackle of the low fire. The murmurings of a false domestic harmony. She could imagine them here at night, sitting by the fire, he and his father taking it in turns to read the paper and letting the flames do the entertaining. She tried to imagine herself in the corner, knitting, spinning, darning . . . The all-pervading quiet. The utter dread of retiring to bed.

'What is this?'

Something in the timbre of his voice made the hair on her arms stand on end. Slowly, she looked up to find him holding the photograph between his forefinger and thumb: her most treasured possession.

She tried to give her best approximation of puzzlement but inwardly her heart contracted at the sight of Donald's image, fragile in his grasp. She leant forward, squinting for good measure, as her mind raced and her hand surreptitiously slid to her pocket for a touch of the letter within which it had come. The photograph must have slipped from the pocket as she got dressed.

'Oh, that,' she said finally. 'It's a photograph.'

A look of confoundment crossed his face. 'I'm well aware it's a photograph, Mhairi!' he exploded. 'My question is, why do y' have a photograph of *him*?'

Alarms were ringing through her entire body. Her head felt heavy on her neck. The room was spinning. 'It's a bookmark.'

'. . . What?'

She swallowed, knowing she had to keep her voice level. 'Yes. It was inside a book his wife loaned to my mother.'

She tried to resume chopping, to look relaxed, but her hand was trembling; if he should come any closer, he would see. 'She only realized she still had it after the evacuation and she gave it to me to read on the journey over here. I'm not sure if she even knows there's a photograph in there.' She gave a shrug. 'But I've been using it as a bookmark anyway. It's very useful.'

He gave a laugh of disbelief. 'You actually want me to believe the reason you have a photograph of the man you and I both know tried to stop this marriage, is because you're using it as a bookmark?'

She nodded. 'Donald didn't try to stop us. I know you had your disagreements but I'm here, aren't I? It was he who told my father to go ahead. He said you were a fine man and a good farmer. None of this would have happened without his say-so.'

Alexander's eyes narrowed as he shook his head slowly, in part because he didn't like hearing that his own destiny had rested upon another man's words. 'No. I saw the way he looked at you, Mhairi.'

She stopped chopping again and looked back at him. 'And I saw the way he looked at you. I don't think what went on between you was anything to do with me. You just didn't like each other.'

'So you want me to believe there was nothing between you?'

She tried to look insulted. 'Of course! What are you suggesting? He's married with a child!'

He stared at her unblinking, scrutinizing her face for every micro-expression. She could see him looking for ways in, other angles to try, chinks in her armour. 'Then if he means nothing to you, you'll not care if I rip it up into pieces.' He held the photograph higher.

She felt her heart startle again, an injured bird on the ground suddenly flapping its wings in a burst of adrenaline. 'Fine, but I'd rather you didn't. As I said, it was useful. Not to mention, I was intending on giving it back to my mother with the book when she comes to visit for the wedding and I believe they're expensive to procure. Mary must be sorry to have mislaid it. Back home, a photograph was a rare luxury indeed.'

Slowly, Alexander's hand dropped down. 'If it's a book-mark, where's the book?'

Oh God.

'I finished it last night. I put the photograph in my pocket hoping I might use it to read a book here, but . . .' She looked around her; there were no books to be seen on the shelves. 'It must have slipped out of my pocket when I got undressed to have the bath.' Another shrug.

Where did the lies come from, she wondered? She could scarcely believe how smoothly they tripped off her tongue, even though her body was buzzing with panic. A long silence followed as he watched her, waiting for a fatal slip-up. After several seconds, he threw the photograph into the room.

'Hmm,' he snorted as it spun through the air, falling just short of the table.

Mhairi didn't immediately retrieve it, prioritizing the chopped potato over her lover's handsome face, showing him that it meant nothing; that it wasn't her whole world lying there on the floor, contained within a few square inches. She just kept slicing and dicing into ever smaller cubes as she heard him turn on his heel and go back into the bedroom to finish changing. Only once she heard the creak of the bed as he sat to pull off his socks did she walk over, wipe the photo-graph clean and slip it safely back in her pocket, beside the letter she had already memorized word for word.

345

It burnt in her pocket like a hot coal, its message tattooed on her heart.

You told me to forget you but I know now it's impossible when another week has gone and there's not been an hour when I've not thought on you. I have become the old man in the store with only a red curl to sustain me. I looked on him with pity that day, never knowing he was my own future.

I work every hour that I can in a printworks. It's filthy and loud. I don't see the sky all day except for walking there and back, but pennies do not go very far here and no matter how hard I work, we are still short by the sabbath.

Baby Struan is growing well. Mary is a competent mother though the lack of sleep has done nothing for her moods; it is no bad thing to be so much out of the house. We are getting by but no more than that.

I hope your new life is happier though I am afeared for you, for I saw that man's true nature from the first. I rue the day I ever uttered the McLennan name. How different things would be now if I had only stayed quiet. It sticks in my craw that I am the architect of my own despair but I pray your life there is a pleasant surprise. I want only for you to be happy. I hope you have forgotten me. I hope you never will.

How many times had she read it in the bath, her fingers tracing over the indentations in the paper of where his pen had pushed, as if he might be found there? She heard Alexander moving about in the next room but even though Donald was a hundred miles away and lost to her, he had managed to make her feel protected, safe and adored. He was the man she would always choose, if only she could. She had wished once for a love letter from the mainland and she had got it at last. She smiled as she moved about the kitchen in silence. It was something to know that at least one dream had come true.

The church was twice the size of the one back home, but that wasn't saying much. It was a plain white building, with small windows and a wooden cross on the altar. Mhairi had come over with the two men on the trap, sitting between them like a bag of flour as the large wheels jolted over potholes and ruts.

They had passed the tinkers' camp on the road a mile back. It was far larger than she had expected, with half-barrel hooped tents arranged in a semicircle around a fire. Dark eyes had watched them as they passed, father and son raising their caps in friendly greeting as the horse trotted along slowly; the summer walkers had nodded back, a few had even waved, but there had been a very distinct watchful tension. They would be knocking on the door any day now, most likely when Mhairi was home alone. Alexander had made no offer to hang around and do jobs in the yard to protect her, but Hughie had already set out the pans and the bucket that needed patching and shown her where he'd left a couple of shillings on the windowsill under the eggs. Jessie the Post had been right when he'd said no one wanted the summer walkers lingering for any longer than was necessary.

The cart rolled to a stop and Alexander jumped down, turning back to offer her a hand. He'd offered no such courtesy on the way up and she understood that this was a show for the many pairs of eyes beginning to swivel in their direction. There was no mistaking her, of course; her bright hair marked her out in every crowd and in all weathers, and a hum of conversation rose up around them as word spread that Alexander McLennan's future bride was finally making her debut to the community.

'Hughie.' It was the minister, no less, walking up the short path to meet them. He was tall but walked with a rocking gait, as if his hip troubled him. A pair of spectacles was balanced on the end of his nose and he had thick, tufty eyebrows, sprouting in all directions, that gave him an air of gentle dishevelment and good humour. The two men shook hands, then Alexander too.

'Rev, this is my fiancée, Miss Mhairi MacKinnon. Mhairi, Reverend Boyle will be marrying us.'

Her executioner, then? The man to seal her living-death warrant? He shouldn't have such a warm smile.

'It's a pleasure to meet you, Reverend,' she said shyly. Could he see the stain upon her soul? Was she marked out as a sinner before this man of God?

'And you, Miss MacKinnon. We've been keen to welcome you into the community. We're glad to see y' here today.'

'Thank you. I'm sorry it's taken so long to make your acquaintance but the journey here was a long one and my family needed help settling into their new homes before I left them.'

She felt Alexander's eyes boring into her. Did he believe a word of it?

'Of course. Your world has changed greatly in a short space of time. Everything must feel very new.'

'G' morning, Rev!' a jaunty voice said, and she turned to see Jessie striding down the path in a brown tweed suit. He looked particularly avuncular out of his uniform and Mhairi could see the form of a hip flask pressing against his jacket pocket.

'G' morning, Jessie.' The minister smiled knowingly as Jessie caught them up and, without asking or being asked, joined their small party.

'Are y' advising this lass to make a clean break for it while she still can?' he joked.

'Hey!' Alexander protested, but his expression was relaxed; there was none of the tension he wore in private. He thrived with an audience.

Hughie chuckled too, but there was a quickness in the way he had looked over at her that betrayed nervousness as well. Did he believe she might bolt? He had no idea, of course, that both her mortal soul and Father's honour were at stake. But did it not occur to him that she had nowhere to go anyway, and no way to get there?

She watched the congregation file past them as the minister and Hughie talked; she was acutely aware of curious glances being cast in her direction, the quick up-down of eyes telling her that her clothes marked her out as different. The villagers, by contrast, wore Sunday best dresses of all different colours and patterns, tweed skirts with a pink or blue thread running through them, fancy hats, coats with brooches, nylon stockings that wrinkled at the ankles. They weren't rich – not like the ladies she had seen at the golf club – but they still had more. Would Alexander provide her with any new clothes, or was she to wear her old costume till it fell off her?

Her landlady, Mrs Buchanan, walked past arm in arm with a man Mhairi had to assume was Mr Buchanan, though she had had no sight of him at the boarding house. Did he hide away in the kitchen?

'Mrs Buchanan,' Mhairi greeted her quietly.

'Miss MacKinnon,' she smiled, looking elegant in a navy blue dotted dress and a black felted hat, her gaze washing

349

over the sight of Mhairi and Alexander together as if they were puzzle pieces that needed to be made to fit. Her smile faltered a little as she passed, as if she glimpsed something troubling, but her feet kept moving.

Mhairi felt something at her side and had to stop herself from leaping away as Alexander looped her arm through his. So they were copying everyone else now? He met her gaze briefly, with that same fleeting look of his father's, and she could tell he was nervous that she might not play along. She felt a flash of power. He couldn't scare her here – quite the opposite. What would the minister say if she was to tell him of what Alexander had done, and made her do, in the byre last year? Or the way he prowled around her like a hungry tiger as she worked, the threat to pounce upon her ever present. What would anyone say if they were to know she kept a potato hook in one pocket, and the image of the man she loved in the other? She overheard someone call them a 'handsome couple', but looks were deceiving. She knew now no one was as they seemed, that secrets swarmed below the surface of every person here.

They followed the minister inside and Alexander stood back to allow her to file into the pew after his father; it was no display of chivalry, though it might look that way, as she was hemmed in again. She looked around the small, plain space – wooden pews with no cushions, no organ, no stained-glass windows, no gilded Bible. But for all its starkness there was a warmth there, too, filled with the babble of hushed conversation and people clearing their throats. She looked around at the faces that would soon become familiar. There were plenty of children of school age at one end of the scale and those with false teeth at the other, but precious few around her own age. Those she did see had a good decade on her, if not more.

Murdo was in a pew at the front, his body looking hunched as if he was already in prayer. Jessie, just behind him, poked him in the back and said something that made him turn in Mhairi's direction and smile. She smiled back, wishing she could sit with them instead and escape the suffocating presence of the McLennan men, whose shoulders sat against hers and wedged her in.

She watched as Reverend Boyle walked to the pulpit and waited for the chatter to die down. He didn't have the same awe-inspiring presence of his counterpart back home. Silence would always rain down as soon as Reverend Lyon stepped into the kirk – he had cultivated a certain dramatic flair as he spoke of hellfire and warned against eternal damnation – but Reverend Boyle's approach seemed altogether more homely.

He lifted his register and reset the tone with a small pause. 'Welcome, parishioners and flock of the holy Tarbert Church, on this fine Sunday. We shall begin with the parish notices.' He glanced up at the congregation but his eyes seemed to find hers, as if giving her warning of what was to come. '. . . I, Reverend William Boyle, minister of Tarbert and placed in charge of the benefice of Tarbert and Ardagh, hereby publish the banns of marriage between Alexander Mungo McLennan, of Ardagh parish; and Mhairi Christabel MacKinnon, of St Kilda. If any of you know cause or just impediment why these two persons should not be joined together in holy matrimony, declare it now. This is the third and final time of asking.'

Eyes swivelled in their direction, a heavy silence punctuated by yet more low coughs and a solitary sneeze. Murdo was discreetly looking back at her over his shoulder again and she sensed – if only she would give the nod – that he would raise an objection; but even over the course of their morning cups of tea, she had given him no evidence, nothing with which to move. How could she? Where would she go? Mhairi crossed her hands in her lap, her sightline fixed upon the join between the ceiling and the wall, wishing someone would speak and knowing they must not. She wanted someone to save her, even though this marriage itself was meant to be her saviour. She wanted things to be what they were not, everything opposite.

Beside her, Alexander's leg jigged frantically but as the silence lengthened, it steadily slowed down, coming to a gradual halt as the minister smiled. 'Very well then, y' can't say y' weren't warned.'

A ripple of chuckles swept through the parishioners and Mhairi forced herself to smile too. Her soul would be saved even if her heart was lost.

'Then let us sing. Page seventeen in your hymn books.'

She opened to the page but the words were a blur, swimming before her as the first voices rose. It mattered not. As in this, so in the rest of life – and she opened her mouth and mimed.

'Well, you must be pleased that's the formalities done. That went as successfully as you could have hoped,' Hughie said to her as Alexander went ahead and opened the farm gate. The sunlight caught on his skin so that it glowed golden as the cart rolled past. Her future husband was a beautiful man on the outside.

'Aye. It's good,' she said in a low voice, keeping her gaze down.

He glanced at her. 'And what's for our dinner today?'

'Roast chicken. You were right about that kerfuffle you heard round the back last night. When I went to get the eggs, one had a bad leg injury – I think a fox had tried for it – so I wrung its neck.'

'A treat for us, then!' Hugh said with relish, jumping down. 'And Mr Fox can go hungry.'

'Aye,' she murmured, seeing how Alexander made no effort to help her down now there was no one to see it. She clambered down awkwardly, aware of her future fiancé striding towards the croft with an agitated march, as if the morning's forced pleasantries had depleted all his good humour.

He stopped suddenly and turned back on himself, a distracted look on his beautiful face.

'What is it?' she asked, feeling dread.

His head angled to the side as he walked back a few paces and looked around the yard.

Had she done something wrong? Left something out that she shouldn't have done? The chickens were all in their coop, the washing brought in from the line . . .

'Where's the bicycle?'

'The bi–?' She looked around her, Hughie too, their frowns deepening as they checked behind bushes and in the small storerooms, the byre . . .

Mhairi was puzzled. She was sure she had seen it earlier in its usual spot, propped against the wall. But the McLennans seemed to know exactly what had happened; Hughie grabbed his head in his hands as Alexander dashed his cap into the dirt. Both gave yells of frustration: 'Those bloody tinkers!'

Chapter Twenty-Eight

'This is for you, dear,' the woman said, holding up a dress by the shoulders. It had a busy green and violet floral pattern across it and a belt at the waist. The sleeves came to the elbow and there was a pretty, pointed violet lace collar too. The fabric was light and silky and as Mhairi reached to touch it a small 'oooh' escaped her, for she'd never felt such fine cloth before.

'Evabelle made it for you,' Mrs Sinclair said proudly. 'She had some fabric spare from another project, didn't you, Evabelle?'

'I did,' the woman replied, smiling back at Mhairi kindly. 'We noticed in church the other day that you didn't have any Sunday best, and when we asked Jessie he said you're always wearing . . . that.' She gestured vaguely towards Mhairi's striped, patched drugget skirt and woollen shirt.

Mhairi looked down at her clothes with a blush. They were clean and had been considered good enough for the Lord back home, but there were different standards here.

'We thought y' might like to wear something special for the rèiteach tonight, too,' Mrs Buchanan added. They were all sitting in her living room at the boarding house, enjoying morning tea and a piece; the other lodgers were now out till teatime. Notice of this 'treat' had been sprung upon her at breakfast that morning and she had discovered, as she protested

354

about her daily plans, that Murdo, Jessie the Post and Hugh had all been apprised of it. She was the last to know.

'It's so kind of you,' she said, looking back at the crowd of unfamiliar faces. Names had been thrown at her as the introductions were made – Pearl, Alice, Evabelle, Mabel, Mrs Sinclair – but she wasn't yet certain which face went with which name.

'I thought the colours would suit your hair,' Evabelle added. 'Although I had to rely on Jessie the Post for your measurements. When I asked how tall y' were, he put his hand up and said "Yea high," and when I asked how big, he squashed them in and said "Yea big"!' The woman laughed and clapped her hands. 'He might as well have been measuring a pig! Heaven knows whether it'll fit or not but I got a good look at y' m'self on Sunday too, so that helped, and of course the belt can bring it in if it's too big.'

Mhairi smiled. 'You've gone to so much trouble. I don't know what to say.'

'You can start by telling us how you've been getting on at Hollow Farm. Heaven only knows it's been needing a woman about the place,' Alice said.

'Mmm. It's a disgrace the way Hughie's let it fall to rack and ruin since Chrissie died,' another added.

'Aye, there's been a lot to do,' Mhairi said. 'I'm not sure the floor had been scrubbed in years.'

Mrs Sinclair sat back with a loud tut and eye roll as if that was exactly as she had suspected.

'But it's really not taken so long to put right,' Mhairi said quickly. She didn't want it to get back to the men that she had been decrying her future home. 'If you were to come down now, I think you'd be pleasantly surprised.'

'And so we shall, we shall,' Evabelle said delightedly, as if this invitation was the very reason for the women's gathering.

355

'Now that we've met y' and broken the ice, we'll be sure to make our way over and bring you some company. It's not always easy on the womenfolk around here, especially them as are scattered in the crofts.'

'Aye, poor Sheila at the whaling station only ever sees men from morning till night. Cooking for them, washing for them, putting up with that stench and their rough talk.' Another tut from Mrs Buchanan this time. 'It's no life.'

'I expect you'll be wanting to start on a family o' your own soon enough, won't you?' Alice asked.

Memories of that night in Glen Bay rushed at Mhairi – Flora gripping her hand, her screams through the valley, the awful whistling silence . . . Somehow she managed to smile. 'Well, I'm one of nine, so I've always dreamt of a big family.' How could her voice sound so normal?

'Ah, nine, that's nice. Which number were you?'

'Three. I've two older brothers.'

'Are they married?' Mabel asked hopefully.

'Not yet.' For the first time in a long time she wondered how Angus and Fin were getting on. They had new jobs at the Forestry Commission but, more exciting than that, a new pool of prospective sweethearts to swim in. Were their prospects better than hers?

'Well, then, it's a shame they didna' come here with you,' Mabel sighed. 'We need fresh blood. All the young ones are moving to the cities.' She brightened suddenly. 'Will they come for the wedding?'

'I don't think so,' Mhairi winced. 'It takes a long time to get here and they canna afford the time off work. But my parents will be coming.'

'Well, then, it'll be a pleasure to make their acquaintance,' Mrs Buchanan said. 'What do they do?'

Mhairi was faintly bemused by her barely restrained curiosity; it was almost as though her landlady had been hoarding questions for this ladies' gathering. This was the most they had spoken during her residency here.

'My father was the postmaster back home. Jessie has put a word in for him at Lochaline actually.'

'That's good of him.'

'Aye, he's been very kind to me.'

'He says you've a beautiful singing voice,' Pearl said, sipping her tea.

She was surprised. 'He does?'

'He's heard y' a couple of times when you've thought you were on your own. Says you're like the lark.'

Mhairi blushed. 'Och, I'm not, I just like singing.'

'See? She's modest as well as pretty,' Mrs Sinclair said to Mrs Buchanan approvingly, jogging her with her elbow. 'No wonder Alexander's smitten.'

Smitten wasn't the word Mhairi would have used for it. Every time she caught him looking at her, there was a look in his eyes that made her stomach pitch. He had kept his distance since his return, but the threat remained, always there. She felt like a fraud to be sitting here, accepting cake and dresses and the kindness of strangers, when there was a hook in her pocket.

'We did wonder if he would ever settle down,' Evabelle said. 'He was such a beautiful boy. His mother called him Alexandra for the first five years of his life.'

'Really?' Mhairi spluttered.

The women laughed at her reaction, as if they'd been waiting for it; another story to tell. There'd been so many already – the time the bloods sheared the legs of Farmer Murray's sheep, right before the roup; the schoolmistress's unrequited love for the widowed harbourmaster, resulting in overzealous fish-buying and subsequent mass food poisoning of the village's children; the butcher's wife's new motorbike . . .

'Aye. Chrissie badly wanted a girl and when he came out so bonny, she indulged herself, dressing him in smocks for as long as she could.'

'Until Hughie put his foot down,' Mrs Sinclair interjected in a firm tone.

'Aye, he was always saying she spoilt him rotten. He was the apple of her eye, that one. He took it badly when she died.'

'What happened to her?'

'Tuberculosis. When he was thirteen or so.'

'Oh.'

'It fair broke his heart losing her,' Mabel sighed. 'But Hughie had no interest in remarrying. I think he was determined to keep women off the farm after that and make a man of his son.'

Mhairi squinted, not quite sure what that meant. 'Make a man out of him, how?'

'Well . . . y'know . . .' Mabel looked flustered suddenly.

There was a short, tense silence, glances skating between the women awkwardly. 'Let's just say Hughie encouraged him to play the field,' Mrs Sinclair said primly.

'And looking as he did, he had no shortage of takers. He got a bit of a reputation,' Alice added. 'The lasses always liked at him.'

'At first,' Pearl muttered as she took a sip of tea.

But Mhairi heard her. 'At first?'

Panic bloomed in the women's eyes at the indiscretion. 'Well, he could take it too far sometimes . . . he did take it too far on occasion,' Mrs Sinclair said quickly.

'But really, what man hasn't?' Mabel interjected. 'And these, these . . .' She floundered, looking for the right word.

'Storms?' Mhairi supplied.

'Aye, storms – they always pass.' Mabel gave a relieved smile, glad to be understood. 'Really he's just been waiting on the right girl to come and look after him. And now he's found her!' She clapped her hands together towards Mhairi as though she was Alexander's princess on a white steed.

Mrs Buchanan lifted the teapot and refilled empty cups. 'I agree. I do believe he's ready to settle down now. He was like a cat on a hot tin roof the night you came over on the ferry; it was really very sweet. I watched him pacing up and down the street waiting on you.'

Mhairi could imagine why he'd been so expectant, and it certainly was nothing 'sweet'. The way things had finished between them last year, he'd thought he'd got himself an easy prospect – compliant, submissive, weak. But she was no longer that girl. She was a woman now: a mother bereft of her child and parted from the man she loved. She had suffered in ways he couldn't possibly imagine. None of them could. For all their kindness and hospitality, to them she was just the girl settling the local troublesome bachelor, in need of a new dress and a home to keep.

'It'll be the first wedding in the village for six years, so you can see why there's an excitement,' Pearl said, nudging the conversation back into safer territory. 'Murdo's got out his fiddle and Mr Sinclair is going to make his famous rum punch. Miss Stewart has had the children making paper chains to decorate the hall and she's said the children can miss afternoon lessons so we can all get on with preparations.'

'Aye, there's a lot of chicken's necks needing wringing this afternoon,' Mrs Sinclair said matter-of-factly. 'It'll be all hands to the deck.'

Mabel looked over at her. 'Are y' excited, Mhairi?'

Mhairi smiled back at their kind faces. If she had been marrying any other man, she would have been giddied by their plans: chicken sacrifices, skipped school lessons, new dresses, paper chains, rum punch and fiddles. 'Yes, I am. Very,' she assured them, dead inside.

'Well, look what the cat's dragged in,' Alexander drawled from his spot at the table as she walked into the kitchen in her new dress. He put down yesterday's newspaper and looked her up and down.

She averted her gaze, not wanting his approval, even though she had stood in front of the mirror in her bedroom at the boarding house, marvelling at her own reflection. In all her life, she had never seen herself in anything other than a cream blouse and lumpy navy skirt, so to be presented with an image of violets and greens that set off her hair, a silky fabric that skimmed her figure rather than shrouded it, pretty lace and covered buttons, deep pockets . . . She had cried, wishing Donald could see her and yet glad he couldn't, for the young woman staring back at her in the mirror didn't look like the woman he had fallen in love with. She was modern, a new version of herself, spinning away from him and everything they had been. Was he changed, too?

'Evabelle made it for me,' she said quietly.

'Well, just so long as she isn't counting on getting paid for it.'

Mhairi looked at him in alarm. Was she? Was that how it worked here? 'I . . . I'm sure it was intended as a gift. For Sunday best, she said. She thought I should wear it for the rèiteach tonight.'

'And the wedding too?'

She hadn't thought of that. She did her best not to think of it. 'Possibly. Aye.'

'Well, isn't it considered bad luck for the groom to see the bride in her dress before the marriage?'

Was it?

He gave an irritable sigh, as if she had already doomed them, and she turned away, not wanting him to see her upset.

She'd had a fright on her way over here – the tinker camp had been quiet as she'd passed, with only a few of the women and small children sitting between the tents, but on the next bend she'd run into some of the men, black-eyed and stocky, on their way back from 'working' further up the road. There had been only four of them but they had split into two pairs on sight, moving to either side of her and forcing her to walk between them. Jessie and Murdo's warnings had sounded like klaxons in her head as she greeted them quietly with her head down, their stares burning into her. She had heard them stop walking to watch her as she went, and her heart had felt like it would leap straight from her chest as she braced for them to suddenly give chase. The moment she had crested the next hill and dropped from their sight, she had run the rest of the way here.

'I've only come by to get your dinner sorted,' she said, fastening on her apron and beginning to fill the pot. She had decided on a stew; once she got it to a boil, she could leave it to simmer and be away again. That way the men could choose when they wanted to eat and she didn't need to be here to serve it. 'They're expecting me at the village hall at five.'

Following their 'tea and piece' this morning, the women had swung into action with a vigour and zeal she recognized from home. She would have liked to help with the preparations herself but had been told in no uncertain terms that it was bad luck for the bride to get involved.

From outside came the squeak of the gate and the sound of footsteps, and Mhairi felt her spirits rise.

'Halloo?' Jessie cried with his signature jolly tone.

Mhairi set down the pot and went to greet him – she needed to see a friendly face – but Alexander, setting down the paper, shot her a look that stopped her as he got up from the table.

'I'll go,' he muttered, leaving her standing rigid in the middle of the kitchen as he went outside, crossing the yard quickly to greet the postman.

'Ah, good day to y', Jessie,' he cried, a different man and beginning to chat.

Out of sight, Mhairi picked up a few stray words – her own name . . . *excitement* . . . *punch* . . . and could guess what they were talking about. The rèiteach was all anyone could talk about, it seemed. Was Alexander so angry about it because he couldn't attend? Did he believe traditions shouldn't extend to him?

She was tenderizing the meat when he came back through a few minutes later, carrying the post. The newspaper was rolled under his arm and he was shuffling through some letters. Mhairi caught her breath, waiting, hoping, dreading – what if Donald wrote again? – but he pointedly turned away, making it clear there was nothing there for her.

Mhairi bit her lip, concerned on another count too. A reply from Effie was now feeling overdue. Surely her friend had something to say in response to the fears and warnings she had outlined in her letter? Did she understand the threat posed to her by the Dumfries steward's accusations?

'Hmm,' he breathed, the sound rolling from him like a low thunder as he read and began to pace. Mhairi reached for the carrots, muddied and with a small beetle crawling in the green tops. She took them to the tap and washed them, still absorbed enough by the novelty of indoor plumbing not to notice that his feet had stopped tracking across the floor. Only as she turned back to the counter did she look up and sense a shift in the atmosphere. The letter was still in his hand but he was looking at her with a confoundment that had rooted him to the spot.

'What is it?' she whispered, aware of a gathering doom.

Still he stared.

She looked at the letter in his hand. '. . . Is that for me?' she asked, scarcely able to believe he would have dared to open her own post in front of her.

He seemed unable to reply and in her indignation and panic, she stepped forward, snatching it from his fingers, her eyes quickly scanning the sketchy script:

Donald arrested.
All yours.
Have him.
Good riddance.
A new life. Don't try to find us.

She gasped. Mary was giving him up? Giving him away? She was taking the baby?

No!

She felt the room spin, the floor drop beneath her feet as she staggered back a step. This couldn't be happening – Mary wouldn't . . . she wouldn't do this . . .

'A bookmark, you said,' he growled, like a dog getting ready to bite. His words reminded her of his presence. For a moment, as Mary's news had detonated, he had ceased to exist – but he was very much here, not Donald, and this was her reality right now. She was not safe, nor protected, nor adored.

Her blood stopped flowing through her veins, her heart forgetting to beat as she stared back at him and faced her fate at last. It had been a long time coming, she realized, ever since they had all had breakfast at that very table, the tension thrumming between the three of them. Each man's instinct had been right about the other. This moment had been fated from the first.

She tried to consider her options – bolt for the door? He'd catch her before she got there. Threaten him with the hook? It was deep in her pocket and she'd lose the element of surprise at the pivotal moment.

She swallowed, knowing he could see her trembling and hating that it made her look weak.

He made a strange guttural sound, spasms of disbelief and rage flickering across his face as the reality of her deception hit him over and over. His eyes were wide, wild, and she was reminded of another man who had been maddened by jealousy. She knew what such men were capable of, now. 'You think me a fool.'

She shook her head. 'No. You're more dangerous than that,' she murmured.

His eyes burnt with a dark flame as he nodded in agreement. 'Donald McKinnon . . . that thieving bastard,' he breathed. 'Acting so superior, when all the while he was plotting to have you for himself.'

'It wasn't like that.'

'Stop your lies!' he suddenly thundered, making her quake. 'I saw the way he looked at you! How he couldn't bear me flirting with you! He kept trying to keep us apart.'

'He just didn't trust you,' she said quietly, but there was a quiver in her voice. 'He didn't like you.'

'Because he liked *you*! He was guarding what was his. You

had an affair with a married man and thought you could come here and trick me into taking soiled goods. You thought I'd never be any the wiser.' His lips were drawn back, his teeth clamped together as his jaw clenched with scarcely suppressed rage. Her fingers pressed against the hook in her dress pocket as she watched him watching her. That probing gaze of his was reaching deep inside her, scouring for further clues of what he knew to be true.

'I underestimated you, Mhairi. I thought you a simpleton but you've played me for a cuckold!' He took a step forward suddenly, grabbing her roughly by the arm, his fingers closing around the bicep. 'And there's only one answer to that,' he spat, dragging her in the direction of the bedroom.

'No!' she screamed, desperately pulling back, reaching for a chair, anything to hold onto as her feet almost left the floor. She lunged for, and missed, the doorframe and he slammed the door shut with one hand as he threw her across the room with the other. She landed heavily against the wooden bed, unbalanced as she scrabbled in her pocket. He crossed the room in three strides, his suspenders already off his shoulders as he grabbed her by the hair and yanked her onto the mattress. She fell back with a cry, seeing him ready to fall upon her, his face contorted with rage, just as her fingers found the turned handle and she pulled the tool free in one huge sweeping arc.

Alexander swung back just in time, the glinting tip of the sharp hook missing his neck by less than an inch. For a moment time ceased its march, both of them stunned and paralysed by shock as the stakes suddenly changed. In an instant, she had the power. A silence pulsed, heavy and ominous, as they both absorbed what had almost come to pass, but she knew it would only be an instant in her favour. He was cunning and manipulative; she needed to act while he was still confused.

365

'Keep away from me,' she cried, her voice scaling the octaves as adrenaline took hold. She felt erratic, out of control, capable of anything. 'I'll use it, I swear! I'll gut you like a fish.'

She scrabbled her arms and legs to get off the bed, holding the hook towards him with a violently shaking hand.

'I believe you,' he replied quietly. Slowly. 'I believe you're capable of anything, Mhairi – seduce a man; deceive a man; kill him. I don't think there's much you wouldn't do.' His words were defiant, even with his hands up in surrender.

Slowly, he took a step back as she took one forward. He moved sidewards, opening up her path to the door and allowing her out. He always had been a lover, not a fighter.

She stared at him with contempt. It was finally over; her soul be damned. If she stayed, she'd only end up killing him eventually, or he her, a far greater sin. She edged towards the door, her knuckles white on the handle, not trusting him for a moment. She opened the bedroom door and stepped into the kitchen, but although Alexander watched her, he made no move to follow. He had a strong instinct for self-preservation. Instead, sensing the mortal peril had passed, he dropped his arms and stuffed his hands into his trouser pockets in his signature lackadaisical way, as if proving he was no threat. He looked exactly as he had the first time she had ever seen him: brooding, beautiful, mutinous.

Without taking her eyes off him, she picked up Mary's letter from the floor and turned to leave for the last time.

'You're a dangerous woman, Mhairi MacKinnon,' he said to her back, always having to get the last word. 'But hats off to you – you hide it well.'

* * *

She ran. Through the yard and onto the grass, past the gate and into the road, leaping over every rut, bump and pothole she had come to know in these last few weeks, the view beyond each bend and over every hillock now familiar to her eye. She ran without thinking, knowing only that she had to get away from him, and here. Somehow, she had to get to Donald, across the water and a hundred miles away.

Would he follow her? Saddle up the horse and give chase? She covered a mile at a sprint, maybe almost two—

'Hai!'

She tore around a tight turn and found herself swung around, a pair of arms upon hers, as she collided with someone coming in the opposite direction. Fingers gripped her hard again as she looked into the face of one of the men she had seen on the road earlier. Jessie and Murdo's warnings rang in her ears: *black hearts. Thieving hands. Rough mouths.* Oh God.

She had run straight from Alexander to the tinkers.

From the frying pan into the fire.

Chapter Twenty-Nine

She heard the sound of music from far off, a bow drawn long across the strings as voices raised up in delight and laughter. Carefully, not wanting to be seen, she approached the building and peered in through the windows.

Along the opposite wall she could see a long table laid out with food – several roasted chickens, some cold cuts of gammon, boiled potatoes, radishes, carrots, turnips, and a large fruit cake that looked like it could sink a whaling boat. Brightly coloured paper chains looped in swags from the opposite corners of the ceiling; children playing games as the adults talked in huddled groups and sipped on a suspiciously pink drink. She could see that they were all in their best clothes, the women's faces painted with make-up and their hair set in tight waves. Murdo was sitting on a three-legged stool in the corner, playing the fiddle, his eyes closed as the music took him to some place – or time – other than here.

She watched as the women who had feted her this morning fussed over the children, their husbands, the food, all of them looking over to the door every so often. Looking for her? It made her feel sick to think that they had gone to all this effort for nothing, when there would be no wedding now. The dress she was standing in had been made by a stranger, using the measuring techniques for a pig, and it was the most beautiful thing she owned. She watched the children chase around their parents' legs and had a flashback to her own family – Red Annie and Wee Murran playing chase on the grass, hopping between ancient stones as the dogs trotted past and the birds wheeled overhead . . .

'Well, now, I appreciate you probably did things differently back home – but you realize we hold the party *inside* the building over here?'

She looked back to find Jessie watching her from his perch on the wall, his pipe dangling on his lip as he tamped down his tobacco.

Mhairi smiled at the joke but it faded quickly – she couldn't go in there, and she saw understanding dawn across his features as she looked down and scuffed the ground with her foot. He gave a small nod. '. . . Ah, I see.'

'I'm sorry,' she said quietly.

'Nup,' he said, holding his breath for a moment before slowly exhaling. 'I can't say as anyone will be surprised.' He looked back up at her with bright eyes. 'They might even be pleased. I know I am.'

'You are?' she asked, amazed.

'Aye. It's not that he's a . . . bad man, exactly. He's just not a wholly good one.' He looked back at her. 'I'm sorry, lass. I thought several times of warning y', but I thought it might be different this time and that he might have changed. I thought you might change him.'

'I'm not sure that's possible.'

'No. Perhaps not.' He sighed and lit the pipe. 'Will y' stay here?'

She shook her head quickly. 'I have to leave tonight for the mainland. A friend from home is in trouble. I have to be with them.'

He watched her thoughtfully, seeing the desperation in her eyes. 'Aye, y' do, I can see that. How will y' manage?'

'I've got independent means to get to the port,' she said, jerking her chin towards the grass bank. She saw Jessie's eyes light up at the sight of the silver bicycle propped there. The whole community knew it had been pinched; the McLennans hadn't held back in their bitter complaints about the theft as Jessie had done his round the next day. 'The tinkers gave it to me.'

'Really?' He looked astonished.

'They were actually very kind to me.'

Jessie was quiet for a moment. 'Because they knew y' weren't from here, I imagine, like them.'

'Aye, maybe it was that,' she conceded. 'We're all outsiders, I suppose. But they were kind all the same, when they didn't need to be.'

Jessie nodded, taking her point. Every dog sets upon the stranger dog.

She looked in at the window again, at the party waiting to happen. She hadn't been able to cycle past without taking a last look.

'Y' know, you could come in for a wee dram and say your goodbyes. You might be surprised how many would want to wish y' well.'

'No, their party,' she protested. 'After all the effort they've gone to. How could I . . . ?'

He shrugged. 'Ach. They've got the food ready, the music, their glad rags on . . . there's nothing to stop them having one now anyway.' He gave her a cheeky wink, confirming her suspicion that all they had ever really wanted was an excuse.

'And Hughie's not here yet – before you say it. He's got a

cow stuck in a bog, according to David Sinclair. He'll be another hour at least.'

'Oh.'

'Come on,' he beseeched, holding out his arm for her to take. 'You know Murdo will want to say his goodbyes to you. Don't leave it to me to do it for you.'

She hesitated; there actually was something she needed to do. 'But what will I say to everyone?'

He winked at her. 'Don't you worry about that. I'll have a word with Mrs Buchanan. She'll handle it, just you watch.'

He waggled his looped arm again and she took it gratefully. They walked around the building together and she braced as a cheer went up when they entered the old hall. Murdo drew the bow across the strings again, a wide smile on his face, before sliding into a folk song.

Someone – Mr Sinclair? – put a glass of rum punch in her hand. 'It's no health if the glass is not emptied,' he smiled.

Mhairi drank it down, watching as Jessie made a beeline for her landlady, as promised. She knew time was short. 'Excuse me, please,' she said quickly, heading straight for Murdo before the local ladies could swarm her. She could see them admiring the dress upon her figure, and once the news got out that this was no longer a rèiteach . . .

'You play very well,' she said, crouching beside Murdo as he dipped and swayed with the bow, his foot tapping to the tune.

'Well, I've no one to talk to in the evenings,' he said without a trace of self-pity. 'I may as well make some noise the best I can.'

She grinned as she reached into her dress and pulled out the potato hook, discreetly slipping it into his jacket pocket. He registered the new weight of it as he played, a small frown puckering his brow.

'Now what's that?' he asked, continuing to play.

'I'm giving it back,' she said, not needing to elaborate.

'No—' he protested.

'Yes. I didn't repay the debt, Murdo, it's only right.' She saw his mouth open to protest further. 'And besides . . .' she went on quickly, 'there was almost an accident tonight.'

He didn't speak for several moments after that, but she saw his eyes water and his lips draw into a thin line. 'He's a brute,' he whispered, his voice a croak.

'Aye,' she agreed, squeezing his arm in consolation. 'But even if he wasn't, I'd be leaving anyway. I have to go tonight, back to the mainland. People I love are in trouble. I have to help.'

He stared into the distance as he played, his arms on auto-pilot. '. . . The MacLeod factor business?'

'Aye, that.'

'Will y' be all right?' He looked worried.

'I will.' She squeezed his shoulder. 'But I'll be sorry to leave you, Murdo. You've been a true friend to me.'

'And you're the granddaughter I never had,' he said, looking straight at her, still fiddling, giving everyone a party. Around them a buzz was growing, heads turning, and she knew the word was spreading. 'I wish things could be different to what they are, but at least I'll always have something to remember y' by, lass.'

'Aye, you will,' she smiled, glancing at the fob watch. 'You can keep me close. And I'll never forget you, Murdo. Any time I dig a potato . . .'

He laughed merrily at her joke and she rose to standing again as people began to approach.

'Just remember . . .'

She looked back.

'Everything fares well in the end,' he said as he moved to his own music. 'And if it's not well, then it's not the end.'

Forty minutes later, she leant against the outside wall of the small building and stared up at the sky with wet eyes. The first stars were peeping and a few red deer grazed off in the distance, munching loudly on the grass and raising their heads every few moments as the revellers danced and whooped into the evening. She had slipped away unnoticed in the end, congratulated on her escape.

There was a community here and there were kind-hearted, good people who might have grown to become friends. But she thought again of Mary's wicked letter, and picked up the bicycle without looking back.

She had lost everything, as she had always known she would – but Flora had once promised her that a wave would rise on quiet water and it was her turn now to get something back.

Chapter Thirty

Mhairi stood on deck as the ferry docked in Oban, waving back at Effie in the crowd. Her heart soared at the sight of her old friend, still just a strip of wind in her trousers, shirt and woollen vest, her long pale blonde hair flying loosely about her face.

'Oh!' Mhairi cried, hugging her as they were finally reunited. 'You came!'

'The second I got your letter. I was worried you would get here before me.'

It wasn't only the tinkers who had helped her get away in the end – it had taken a village. Murdo had given her the coins for the ferries, Mrs Buchanan had packed up food from the tables for her journey and Jessie had persuaded her to write two notes before she left the rèiteach, with the promise that he would personally make sure they made the first collection the next day. One was to Effie, asking her to meet her here; the other was to her parents. Her instinct and only thought had been to run to Donald, but Jessie had wisely pointed out that her parents would need to be informed the wedding was off before they set off on their own long journey.

Effie put a hand to Mhairi's cheek. 'You're white as a sheet! You look exhausted! Have you slept at all?'

She shook her head. 'I just couldn't.' It had taken two days to get here. She had cycled from the village hall to Leverburgh, past the golf club and following the road as far as she could; desperation had made her fearless and it had been late when she'd reached the port, the moon hanging high in its cradle as the harbour cats hunted. She had long since missed the last ferry and had had to curl up on the nets and wait for the next day to break. 'I felt like I'd never get here. Until the ferry actually left, I truly feared I'd be stuck there for always.'

'Has it been terrible?' Effie whispered.

Mhairi blinked, holding back her tears. 'I almost killed him, Eff . . . He found out about Donald.'

Effie's hands flew to her mouth. 'But how?'

'He read Mary's letter. She's taken the baby and deserted Donald; she told me I'm welcome to him.'

'Oh god!'

'Alexander went mad. It was just like that night with you and Mathieson all over again.'

Effie paled, the memories still too vivid for her to brush off. She was quiet for several moments, able to imagine the scene all too well.

Then she clasped Mhairi's hands. 'You're safe now. You know that, don't you? It's over.'

Mhairi nodded slowly, although her body didn't seem to believe it for she was still jumpy and watchful, trusting no one. She looked back at her friend, hardly daring to ask the question. 'And Donald . . . ? Have you been able to see him?'

'I went as soon as I got here this afternoon. He's in low spirits, I can't tell you otherwise; but he'll rally now you're here. I know he will. You're all he could talk of.'

'Really?' Her heart felt like it had been stopped in a state of contraction ever since she'd read Mary's words – arrested. Abandoned . . . 'Will you take me there right now? I need to see him.'

'We can't,' Effie said with a shake of her head. 'They're closed now. No visitors. There's nothing that can be done tonight. It has to wait till the morning.'

Mhairi stared at her in disbelief. No! That couldn't be. She'd travelled solidly for thirty-five hours, only to have to wait another night?

Quickly Effie looped an arm through hers and began drawing her away from the water's edge. 'Come – the best thing we can do now is get you into the warm. We need to keep you strong. You can't help him if you're dead on your feet. What you need is a hot meal and a soft bed.'

Mhairi's body sagged even at the words. She was more tired than she could process, but she hadn't thought ahead to what would happen once she got here. 'Where . . . where will we go?' she asked, bewildered as she looked around them for the first time. This town was foreign to them both.

'It's all arranged. We've got a room at the Royal Hotel.'

Mhairi stopped walking and looked at her in fright. 'And how will we afford that?'

'Don't worry, it's all taken care of,' Effie smiled, patting her hand and leading her on again like a reluctant pony.

'But . . .' Mhairi's eyes swept over her friend in confusion. When had Effie become this sophisticated woman of the world, staying in fancy hotel rooms and . . . She took in her friend's clothes suddenly, seeing the sharp cut and expensive cloth of the tobacco wool turn-ups. Effie was still herself, but somehow fine-tuned.

They made their way through a set of tall limestone pillars and double arched doors into a hall lit by sparkling chandeliers. Mhairi stopped walking again, her mouth open-ing in awe as she took in the unexpected opulence; even the clubhouse at the golf course couldn't compare to this.

'Come, it's this way,' Effie smiled from the bottom step of a wide, turning staircase, looking perfectly at home. She held a key in her hand. '. . . You know, you look so pretty in that dress.'

Did she? It had felt so fine the first time she had put it on. She had stood in her bedroom in the boarding house and tried to capture her reflection in the small mirror above the sink by standing on the chair. But so much had happened since then – she had almost killed a man; made friends with tinkers; robbed a party of its purpose; slept under the moon . . . It was filthy and no doubt stinking, maybe even stained or torn. She checked it blankly, thinking of Evabelle's kindness in making it for her. What would she think if she could see it now, little more than a rag?

They walked down a long corridor that had paintings on the wall and fine tables polished to a shine, chairs set at intervals lest anyone should need to suddenly take a rest. Mhairi had never seen the like before. Mrs Buchanan's lodg-ings had been a distinct step up from the life she'd known at home – and at Hollow Farm – but this hotel was almost like a king's palace.

Effie stopped outside a door and slid the key into the lock, opening onto a room that was the size of her old home. Mhairi walked in, eyes like saucers as she took in the sight of a posted bed with fabric hangings, a desk, more chairs and huge windows fronting onto the square.

'Effie!' Mhairi breathed, turning slow circles as she tried to take it all in. 'I don't understand . . .'

Just then, there was a knock and a door in the far wall opened. A tall, blonde man came through with a hesitant expression. Mhairi knew exactly who he was; he seemed to shine somehow, as if his bones had been polished, his skin buffed. Flora had been right when she'd called him a sun god.

'Mhairi, this is Sholto,' Effie said with a shy smile, her eyes bright as they connected with his and for a moment, Mhairi felt herself cast out of their sphere.

'Mhairi, at last. Our meeting has been a long time in coming,' he said, coming straight over with his hand outstretched for hers; but as he took it, he kissed the back of her hand. 'I was sorry not to make your acquaintance earlier in the summer. Effie has told me so much about you. I hope we shall become firm friends.'

Mhairi could only nod as she remembered that he was a lord. A lord was kissing her hand.

She looked at Effie. A lord was kissing her best friend. More than kissing? She glanced again at the door that linked this room to another, remembering Flora's warnings in Glen Bay – but those conversations seemed to belong to another time, as well as another place. How much had they all changed in these few short months?

'Poor Mhairi's exhausted,' Effie said over her continuing silence. 'She's been travelling for two days to get here and I don't think she's slept, or even eaten, in that time.'

'Well, then, we must rectify that straight away,' Sholto said, springing into action and crossing the room to pick up a telephone. He slid a hand into his trouser pocket as he waited, completely unaware of the striking figure he cut; he was like a cheetah in a room of stray cats. An earl's son, a gentleman – even James Callaghan paled beside him. 'Hello, yes. This is Lord Sholto. Can you bring up a pot of tea – the Lipton's I ordered in – some soup, sandwiches and . . . what's the cake today . . . ? Yes, a slice of that as well please . . . The Caledonian Suite, that's right . . . Thank you. Goodbye.'

Mhairi stared at Effie. A feast was coming, just like that? He hadn't even had to leave the room to order it, much less climb a cliff or wring a neck?

'Mhairi, come and sit down, you're awful pale,' Effie said, leading her towards the bed. It was vast, dressed with a tartan blanket and plumped-up pillows. Mhairi didn't think she should make it messy but Effie jumped on it first with a sudden laugh, deflating the puffy pristineness of it and making Sholto grin.

'Why don't I draw a bath for you, Mhairi?' he suggested. 'Then once you've eaten, you can go straight to sleep. Everything always looks a lot better after a solid eight hours of shuteye.'

'Thank you,' she murmured, aware he must think her dumb or ungrateful, but words wouldn't come to her throat. Exhaustion had her in its grip; she'd been frightened for so long these past weeks that the notion of being able to stop and relax was hard to accept.

She caught him throwing a wink at Effie as he turned and left the same way he'd come. Mhairi sank back against the pillows and curled up on her side like a prawn. Effie did the same beside her, the two of them blinking at one another on crisp cotton sheets.

'He really loves you,' Mhairi said quietly.

Effie nodded, seeming to soften at the words. 'And I love him.'

Mhairi watched her friend as she plucked at a feather quill peeking through the pillow. She had never seen her like this before – all her restlessness gone. She seemed content, peaceful, fully in her body for once. 'Does anyone know?'

'Only my father.'

'Not his parents?' Mhairi remembered the countess's conversation outside the golf club.

'Not yet.'

'So . . . where will you be sleeping tonight?'

Their eyes met in girlish kinship, then Effie's skittered towards the door in reply. Mhairi nodded. 'But you know the risks you're taking?'

'I do. But in our eyes, we're already married . . . We jumped the broom together.'

Mhairi gasped. 'You did?'

'Aye. We were actually on our way to tell his parents we wanted to be married – you know, formally – when the police came to the house and arrested Weir.'

'Oh, Eff,' Mhairi whispered, hardly able to believe their bad luck.

'Aye. Sholto wanted to go through with it still, but I made him swear not to say a word, not until this all goes away.'

They fell quiet again, sinking back into memories that disturbed them both; St Kilda still had them in her grip. '. . . And what does he know about that last night?'

Effie's eyes flitted again to the door. 'Not much. Only the early part. I'm trying to keep him out of it as much as I can. None of this is anything to do with him. I don't want him involved.'

But from what Mhairi could see, he already was. It had been Effie and Sholto's obvious and unstoppable attraction to one another that had tipped Mathieson over the edge in the first place – and the fallout had affected all of them, Mhairi included. It was why they were all here now, in a strange port none of them could call home.

'The police have pictures, you know – of how they found the body,' Effie said in a hushed voice.

Mhairi blinked, feeling a sudden chill in her own blood. 'They do?'

'Aye.' Effie bit her lip. 'The whisky bottle was there, of course; and the knife and the rope. But also the brooch – it was on the ground beside him.'

'The brooch?'

'The one Donald gave you.'

Mhairi nodded slowly, feeling her heart rate speed up. 'I see.'

'Do you?' Effie was looking at her with a concerned expression. 'It means it could place you at the scene. You need to be aware of that. They'll ask about it when they question you. They're questioning everyone.'

'Uh-huh,' Mhairi murmured, feeling frightened.

'We'll need to warn Flora, too. She was wearing it when she came into the village with her shawl at her waist, and if I saw it, someone else might have noticed as well. Why would a MacQueen girl be wearing a McKinnon brooch? She'll need to have an answer ready for that. You could maybe pass it off as your mother's brooch, but it would still place you at the murder scene; do you understand? So how did it get there? That's what you have to think on. I don't want to frighten you, but you have to give them a story that turns attention away from you and Flora.'

'Uh-huh,' Mhairi breathed.

'I've been thinking on this ever since they showed me the picture and the police don't seem to know you had the brooch in your possession – you and Flora. That's the good news and hopefully it will stay that way . . .' Effie bit her lip nervously. 'But it means the person it implicates is Donald.'

'Implicates?' Mhairi repeated. She had never heard the word before.

'It's something Sholto's solicitor says,' Effie explained. 'It means it can show that he was involved. In the same way the stolen book Mathieson gave to me implicates me by giving me motive. That brooch was Donald's mother's, which he gave to Mary when they married, of course, so it indicates that either Donald or Mary was at the scene, unless they can prove otherwise.'

Mhairi lay very still, trying to take it all in. 'But Mary and Donald have the perfect cover story.'

'Well, Mary does,' Effie said with a hard look. 'As far as the village knows, she had just had a baby that night, and that's what the police will be told by everyone they ask. No one will point a finger at *her*. But when I went to see him today, Donald said Mary had told the police she didn't see him for several hours after midnight.'

Mhairi felt herself pale. '. . . What?'

Effie bit her lip, nodding fearfully. 'It means he has no alibi – no way to prove where he was when the killing happened. The whole village will vouch for her, but she won't do the same for her own husband.'

Mhairi felt her brain speed up as the case against her lover began to stack up. A brooch belonging to him was found at the murder scene . . . He had motive ten times over . . . And now he had no alibi?

'Then we need to make Mary tell them he was with her!' Mhairi said urgently. 'She either says he was with her or we'll threaten to expose her! She has as much to lose as the rest of us. More!'

'But it's not as simple as that,' Effie said gently. '. . . Mary's gone.'

'Aye, I know, so she said in the letter, but we'll just find her. She can't have gone far.' Her voice trailed off as she saw her friend's expression. '. . . What is it?'

Effie bit her lip. 'Sholto and I thought the same thing, so we went round to their address after we left Donald. The neighbours said she had come into an inheritance—'

Inheritance? Mhairi frowned, feeling an immediate uneasiness.

'Mhairi, she's set sail for Canada.'

Canada? The word had a recoil to it, making her blanch as her mind immediately conjured a vivid image of Mary on the boat, the baby in her arms and a setting sun glowing golden on their faces as they sailed west. How could she do this?

A knock came at the door and Effie got up to answer it. 'Thank you,' she said quietly, standing back so that a uniformed waiter could roll the trolley into the room, china and silver cutlery jangling.

Mhairi watched from the bed, blankly wondering how it was that her friend could look as if she belonged in this grand room, when she herself didn't even look like she belonged in her hand-sewn dress. Only the night before last, Mhairi had been cycling for her life on a stolen bicycle. She had fallen off countless times and once she had even fallen into a hedge on a too-sharp bend. And all the while, Effie had been in a room like this with a man like that. She had found her happy ending, of sorts; she was with the man she loved, even if it was in secret.

But Donald was in a prison cell, implicated, abandoned and alone.

And only Mhairi could save him now.

Chapter Thirty-One

The rain had come in, great sheets of water falling like silver filings and pooling in dark puddles in the square. Mhairi, wearing a mackintosh Effie had borrowed 'from the house' and brought along for her, watched the droplets bounce as she stood within the row of limestone pillars. Inside, Sholto was paying the bill. Her discomfort at accepting his charity had been relieved somewhat by the fact that her presence provided a cover of respectability for him and Effie – in a way, she had done them a favour.

A doorman swung open one of the arched doors and Effie came through; she was wearing her brother's old tweed jacket, but paired with her new sharp pair of trousers, it somehow looked – what was that foreign word? Sheek? She was still herself – her hair brushed but not styled, bright skin but no make-up – and yet an air of refinement was creeping in, lingering about her like a spritz of perfume.

Perfume. Ambergris. Donald and Frank . . . Mhairi's mind sank back into horror, just like that.

'Mhairi?' She felt a hand on her shoulder, Effie smiling back at her. 'Are you still tired?'

Mhairi nodded, even though she had never had a better night's sleep in her life. She had felt cradled by clouds, her body endlessly heavy like she was made of lead, a pleasing vacuum in her mind. If she had dreamt, she didn't remember it.

She watched the people walking past with their heads bent, some with umbrellas, the pinkish-brown sandstone buildings sulking into deeper tones. The door was swung open again. 'Hope to see you again soon, your lordship,' the doorman said, doffing his cap as Sholto walked through. His gaze swung to Effie, then to her, and back to Effie again; the two of them instinctively smiled at one another, unaware of the invisible membrane that surrounded and held them apart from everyone else, like a mother-of-pearl sheen.

Mhairi looked on disconsolately. She had had that once. She had been loved in that way. Effie's life had fallen together, while hers had fallen apart. It had never been more broken.

Sholto looked out at the dreary weather, scanning the grey skies. 'Hmm. We shall need some umbrellas,' he said, turning back to the doorman; but Effie put a hand on his arm, stopping him.

'You're walking with two St Kildans,' she smiled, a tease in her eyes. 'We're not afeared of the rain.'

He chuckled, seemingly so ready to laugh. 'Quite,' he grinned back, turning up the collar on his coat. 'Shall we, then?'

Effie stepped out first, turning her face skywards to feel the raindrops on her face, making the point, as Mhairi and Sholto followed after.

'Is it far?' Mhairi asked, feeling another rush of nerves. Everything she had endured these past few days had been for this coming hour. It felt as if her entire life had sharpened to a point, this point.

'Nowhere's far here,' Sholto said, coming to walk on her far side on the edge of the pavement. 'It's a pretty small place.' He glanced across at Mhairi. 'How are you feeling?'

'. . . Nervous.'

'That's quite understandable, but try not to be afraid. I've secured the services of a solicitor. Gibbons, he's called,' Sholto said, his head down as they walked, oblivious to the stares he elicited from the people they passed. 'He's not our usual chap who manages my family's affairs, even though he's the best. Effie was adamant he had to be independent, I'm afraid.'

'Yes, for the sake of your family's reputation,' Effie said, speaking across Mhairi as if this was a continuation of an ongoing debate. 'They mustn't be dragged into this.'

Sholto gave no reply, but it was perfectly plain to Mhairi that he would be willingly dragged into anything after Effie.

'I spoke to him about your proposal at breakfast. Unfortunately he can't get here in time as he's in court this morning,' he continued as they walked. 'But he was very clear that if you are going in voluntarily to make a statement, you say only what you want to say and nothing more. If they start asking questions – which they may well do, as you'll be on their interview list as well – you're not to answer anything without legal counsel present. You say "no comment". Do you understand?'

Mhairi nodded.

'Good. You're making a statement to provide an alibi for Donald, not being interviewed yourself. It's an important distinction.'

'Aye, I understand.'

They walked on in silence, Mhairi feeling daunted by what she had to do. What Donald's own wife wouldn't. Hadn't.

They walked through shallow puddles, the paved roads always firm underfoot no matter how hard it rained. Her heart was thudding like a drumbeat; she wanted to both sprint there and tear away back home all at once. They passed along narrow streets, past shop windows displaying shoes and bacon and books and lipsticks, and she remembered a day back in the summer when Flora had described all this as they were plucking the birds in Glen Bay. That had been just before all hope was lost, when everything had irrevocably fallen apart. But life could fall back together again, couldn't it – as it had for Effie and Sholto?

They came to a stop outside a large villa, a deep blue sign by the door with POLICE in white lettering. 'We're here already?'

'Oban's really not a big place,' Sholto murmured.

Mhairi stared at the thick walls and frosted glass windows of the police station – it looked austere and impenetrable. The front door was open and she could see a uniformed officer standing behind a wooden counter, writing in a ledger. As if sensing her gaze, he glanced up, taking in the sight of her for a moment – pale-faced, thin, straggly red hair, lilac-and-green patterned dress beneath an oversized raincoat – before looking down again. He probably thought she had just lost her cat; he could have no idea exactly how much she had lost. No one could. She was covered in scars, but they were invisible to the naked eye.

'Are you ready?' Sholto asked her.

Last night and for the previous two days before that, all she had wanted was to get here, but now that she stood on the threshold she was gripped by a paralysing fear. What if she made things worse? Effie had told her about the brooch but she didn't know what else they knew.

She gave a small nod.

'Just remember what Gibbons said: say nothing more than the minimum,' Sholto reminded her, leading the way. The policeman glanced up again, straightening sharply as he took in the distinguished bearing of the tall gentleman; Sholto seemed to wear his distinguishment the way soldiers wore medals.

'Good morning, sir.'

'Good morning. I'm the Marquess of Dumfries, Lord Sholto. My solicitor, Mr Gibbons, has arranged for Miss MacKinnon here to provide a statement – specifically an alibi for Donald McKinnon on the night of the twenty-eighth of August.'

The policeman closed his ledger and opened another book. '. . . Miss Mhairi MacKinnon?' he said after a moment.

'Exactly so.' Sholto turned back slightly, presenting Mhairi to him.

'Very good, sir. Will Mr Gibbons be present during the statement?' The policeman's gaze travelled over their disparate party.

'I'm afraid not; he's in court this morning. But he says it's a straightforward process.'

'In principle, sir.'

Sholto stiffened, not liking that reply. His response prompted a flash of panic down her spine.

'If you'd like to follow me, Miss?'

'We'll wait here for you,' Effie said as Mhairi glanced at her fearfully.

She was led through a door and into a narrow corridor that had doors leading off on both sides. All the doors were closed and the passage was cold and damp as if deliberately derelict, deliberately bleak.

The policeman opened the door to a room on the right. 'If you'd like to wait in there, miss, someone will be with you shortly. Take a seat.'

Mhairi walked into a small, square room. It had only a table and two chairs in it, and a narrow window set high in the wall. The walls were unpainted plaster with cracks running along them and an electric lightbulb dangled from the ceiling.

She gave a shudder as the door was closed behind her. She immediately felt trapped, even though she was here voluntarily, and she tried to think of Effie and Sholto waiting for her in the reception, ready to go again.

Time seemed to shift tempo, dragging and becoming sticky; it felt an age before she heard footsteps in the hall again. She turned around, her breath held as the door was opened and another policeman entered. He was older and thick-set, with epaulettes on the shoulders of his jacket.

'Miss MacKinnon,' he said with an abrupt nod. 'I'm Sergeant Blackford. I'll be taking your statement today.'

'Hello, Sergeant,' she murmured, watching him come over with a thick file in his arms. She waited as he arranged his paperwork for a few moments – her anxiety rising – before he finally leant back and took a proper look at her.

'You're Miss Mhairi MacKinnon, formerly of St Kilda?'

'That's right.'

'What is your current address?'

'Well . . . my family were relocated to Lochaline, but I have been on Harris for the past few weeks. I was supposed to get married there, y' see, but . . .' She stopped herself, realizing that even in these first few moments she had already said far too much. This policeman didn't need to know what she had endured on Harris. She drew back. 'Number two Lochside, Lochaline,' she said quietly. She watched his pen move across the paper, innocuous spidery markings that could change a man's life – keep him locked up or set him free.

He looked back at her. 'So what was it you wanted to make known, Miss MacKinnon?'

She opened her mouth to speak but there was a small lag

between the will to talk and the ability to do it. '. . . I'm here to provide an alibi for Donald. Donald McKinnon.'

'Is he a relative?'

'No, he was a neighbour and . . . f-friend on St Kilda.'

His eyebrow kinked slightly at her hesitation. 'And how old are you?'

'Just turned nineteen two months back.'

'I see. Go on . . .'

Mhairi took a breath, knowing that what she didn't say was as important as what she did. 'Well, I understand Donald's wife is unable to provide an account of his whereabouts after midnight, the night before the evacuation—'

'The night of the murder, aye.'

Mhairi swallowed at the clarification. 'She told you she had just had her baby . . .' she said carefully, choosing her words with the utmost precision. 'And couldn't leave the cottage. She said she didn't see Donald for several hours.' She swallowed again. 'But she could have been sleeping?'

'Miss MacKinnon,' he said in a disapproving tone, setting down his pen. 'If you've come here to offer conjecture about what Mrs McKinnon may or may not have been doing in her own home—'

'No,' she said quickly. 'I don't know what Mary did in those hours; I don't. But I do . . . I do know what Donald did.' She looked down at the desk, knowing her next words would change his fate – and hers, too. Their secret, or at least part of it, would be revealed. And yet, what choice did she have?

'Well?' he prompted as she sank into hesitation.

'. . . He was with me.'

A long silence stretched out. 'Donald McKinnon was with you?'

She nodded, unable to look at him.

She heard another sigh. 'I'm afraid I shall have to ask you to be fully transparent, for the avoidance of doubt. What do you mean when you say he was *with* you?'

She rubbed her lips together, closing her eyes. 'I mean we were being intimate.'

'You were being intimate,' he repeated with an incredulous look. 'His wife had just had a baby and you were being intimate?'

'Yes,' she whispered, hardly able to bear the shame. 'But it's not like you think. His marriage is dead in all but name. We were in love.' She remembered his letter. 'Are. We are in love.'

'I see.' Scorn dripped from the words. Another silence stretched as he wrote in his file, pressing harder on the pen now. He looked back coldly at her again, like she was something he had found under his shoe. 'So you allege you and Donald McKinnon were being intimate together between the hours of midnight and three when the murder took place.'

'I do.'

'And where were you with him, exactly?'

'Where we always were – in our nook in Glen Bay.'

His right eyebrow twitched. 'Glen Bay is where the deceased was found.'

'Yes. It's a big glen.'

He continued writing. '. . . Nook, you said?'

'Yes, just past the Amazon's House.'

'Why there?'

'It's remote and private. No one ever had cause to go that far.'

'So you were there because you were sure you could be together without anyone seeing you, despite the activity on the island that night?'

'It was largely in the village that everyone was busy, but yes.'

He laced his fingers together, his elbows spread wide. 'And can you provide any evidence backing up this claim that you were together?'

She blinked. Did she need evidence? Who would willingly choose to dishonour themselves like this? 'How would I do that?'

The eyebrows went up. 'Did anyone see you together, for instance?'

'No. It was dark, everyone was busy getting the last bits settled before we got on the boat in the morning.'

'So you have no actual proof supporting this claim that you were intimate with Donald McKinnon?'

She frowned. 'Well, no—' She had been braced to be shamed, but to not be believed . . .

'And therefore no way to corroborate this story that he was with you between the hours of midnight and three a.m., when the murder took place?'

'None other than my word.'

He stared at her with hard, unforgiving eyes. 'Miss MacKinnon, why should your word be good?'

'Because it's true.'

'So you say. But you are also telling me you're a woman who would be intimate with another woman's husband, hours after she had a baby. It hardly speaks to good character; in fact, I should say it holds you up as dishonourable and dis-reputable. Without proof I daresay your word wouldn't hold up in a court of law. No jury would be prepared to accept your account as the truth.'

Mhairi felt tears spring to her eyes as the public scorn and reprobation that Mary had predicted would rain down, finally fell. A tear dropped from her lashes onto the table. '. . . You don't have to approve of me, or what I've done,' she said in a hushed voice. 'But that doesn't change the fact that this is the truth and Donald is innocent.'

The sergeant watched her for several moments before leaning forward.

'Miss MacKinnon, you are still very young. You may well believe yourself to be in love with this man. You may believe him to be innocent and think you're doing the right thing in coming in here and providing him with a cover story that can be neither proved nor disproved. But before you sign your name to this frankly shameful account, you should be aware that the case against the defendant is strong. He had clear motive and, in the absence of a credible alibi, clear opportunity. We know he publicly quarrelled with the victim over stock prices—'

'But everyone quarrelled with Mathieson over that!' she protested, the words bursting from her in a rush. 'He wouldn't give us a fair market price! Donald was just the only one who did anything about it!'

'Calm yourself, please,' he said, raising a hand.

Mhairi bit her lip, trying to swallow back her desperation, but she could feel the red flash agitating in her blood at this sergeant's condescension, his cruelty . . . his presumption he knew about them and what had happened that night, when in reality he knew nothing.

'We also know that Donald McKinnon fought with Frank Mathieson on Boreray last spring, resulting in a nasty head wound to the defendant.'

'Exactly! Frank attacked him!'

'The Crown will argue it was a reprisal against the defendant's underhand business tactics. You see, we know all about his trips to Harris, undercutting Mr Mathieson.'

'That was perfectly legal. Our rent obligations had been

met; Donald was just selling the surplus,' she argued, her eyes flashing up to him and away again.

'Perhaps. But – what was far less legal – we also know the defendant stole an item of great value from the victim, selling it on the black market and pocketing himself a small fortune. It was a sum worth fighting over, quite possibly to the death.'

Mhairi stared at him, her heart pounding hard as words clamoured in her throat, demanding to be heard. Sholto had told her the solicitor had advised not saying anything more than the minimum, to avoid incriminating herself – or even Donald further – but she couldn't let these falsehoods stand. She had been there. She knew the truth.

'The ambergris never belonged to Mathieson, any more than it did anyone else,' she said in a low voice, seeing his surprise that she knew to what 'item' he was alluding. 'The whale exploded in the bay and the men went out to harvest what they could before it sank. Mathieson was the only one who knew what it was or what to look for. He smuggled it onto the island, pretending it would be a cure for his mother's gout, and paid me a shilling to turn and cure it every day, when he knew all along he would get over a hundred pounds for it! Donald simply sold it from under him, before Frank could sell it from under us. We were all thieves, if that's how you want to see it.'

The policeman's mouth drew into a flat line as he watched her closely. 'Miss MacKinnon, we have an item that definitively places the defendant at the scene of the crime.'

It was supposed to be the death knell to her protestations but she felt herself grow calm at the mention of it. 'You mean the brooch?'

Effie's warnings last night sounded in her mind – *How did it get there? That's what you have to think on* – but she had yet to compose a story. She wasn't supposed to say too much, none of this should be discussed here without the solicitor, and yet for as long as she didn't speak, Donald would remain locked up in here.

'If that's what you're saying makes him guilty, then you need to arrest me because it places me at the scene, not him,' she said boldly. 'It was Donald's mother's, and then his wife's when they were married. But it's mine now. He gave it to me.'

His eyes narrowed. 'And why should it be yours, if he had given it to his wife?'

The truth surged again, wanting to be heard. She swallowed. '. . . I needed it for fastening my skirt. The waist had become too tight.'

She watched as his gaze openly travelled over her slim frame. There was confusion in his eyes, but suspicion too; theories starting to emerge, falling back . . .

'You're saying the brooch held up your skirt?' he clarified carefully.

'Aye.'

'Because you were . . . outgrowing it?'

She paused, then nodded, seeing how he circled ever closer to the nub of the truth.

'Why were you outgrowing your skirt?'

'I was pregnant.'

The eyebrows twitched again. 'I see. And Donald McKinnon was the father?'

The question offended her – who else could it possibly be? – but she simply nodded.

There was a long silence. 'Did his wife know?'

'Oh aye, she knew all right,' Mhairi replied, her gaze averted towards a crack on the wall. She had been there at the conception, a not-so-holy trinity.

'And . . . ? Were you all to live happily cheek by jowl with your new babies? Explain to me how that was going to work.'

She heard the sarcasm in his words and had to bite back her anger. '. . . Donald wanted us to be a family, me and him. His marriage was over, Sergeant, and he had come to terms with that. His wife hated him, believe me, and he was convinced the evacuation was a gift for them both to start afresh. He sold the ambergris before Frank could do it and the money was supposed to help us start a new life together, over here; for Mary too. He wouldn't have just abandoned her.'

'So Donald McKinnon was going to leave his wife for you?'

'Aye.'

His eyes narrowed and she saw a satisfied look come into them. A mistake had been made. '. . . But you said just now that you moved to Harris to get married – whereas the McKinnons came straight here to Oban.'

She blinked as she realized her nervous error at the start had cost her. No comment, Sholto had said. 'Our plans changed,' she said in a small voice, but she had a sense of beginning to run downhill, momentum at her back even as she tried to slow her legs.

'Why? What happened to change your plans so dramatically that you went off to marry someone else?' he queried, tapping his pen against her Lochaline address. 'What happened to your fresh start?'

Mhairi blinked rapidly several times, holding back tears, her body held now in a state of suspension. Words wouldn't come. Only memories. Only horror.

'N-no comment,' she whispered. Her only protection.

He frowned at her sudden evasion, watching her even more closely as her sorrow surfaced. She squirmed, wanting to leave now but knowing she couldn't. Donald needed her. There was no one else who could save him . . .

A loud silence opened up but the police sergeant appeared to feel no compulsion to fill it. She kept her gaze averted; she was certain he would read everything in her eyes if she looked up, even though it was unguessable, a horror too great to imagine.

Suddenly, as if something had occurred to him, he began rifling through the file, stopping on a certain sheet and reading it through several times.

What . . . ? What had happened? What had she done?

She watched his eyes swivel beneath the lids as he read the same lines over and again, his finger pinned to one specific spot on the page. He looked up at her with a sharp focus. 'Miss MacKinnon, when was your baby born?' he asked in a new tone.

It was all over.

Her heart closed down like a bird's wings in roost. It was the very question she had prayed he would not ask. She knew she mustn't answer it.

No comment. No comment.

It would unlock further questions that, as yet, had no ready answers – at least, not for the police. It would open up a new line of enquiry that seemingly they hadn't yet considered and give them another name for a suspect. It would free Donald – but at what cost?

No comment.

No choice. Donald had motive and opportunity. They were going to turn the lock and throw away the key if she didn't speak.

'Miss MacKinnon, I'll ask you again – when was your baby born?'

Slowly, she looked up, offering a silent prayer for forgiveness. '. . . Three weeks before the evacuation,' she whispered.

Lightly, his finger jabbed the sheet of paper before him. She already knew what he was going to say. 'The census taken on your arrival to the mainland states there was only one baby – a boy, born the night before . . .'

'That's right.' She felt the terrible truth push towards the surface at last. Demanding oxygen. Air. Everything her baby hadn't. Tears shone in her eyes, that whistling silence still a scream in her ears. 'My wee girl was stillborn . . .'

His expression changed and she saw something like pity flicker briefly across his face.

She looked away, knowing she didn't deserve it, knowing nothing mattered now anyway. It was all coming out, the whole dreadful truth. Everything she had tried for months to keep secret would be known. And not just by her neighbours – but by the whole world, once the pressmen caught wind of it. 'It was my fault,' she said stiffly, even as her voice split. 'I helped with the lambing when I shouldn't have done . . .' Her gaze drifted to a distant place and she remembered Flora's frightened look that hot, fateful afternoon. She had realized the risk long before Mhairi. '. . . Donald was devastated. We both were.'

He nodded a few times, as if in sympathy. 'I see,' he said, setting down his pen carefully. 'And that's why he decided to stay with his wife and child instead,' he supplied.

Putting words in her mouth.

Mhairi blinked, registering his mistake immediately, though he seemed unaware of the misstep. She couldn't believe, for once, her good luck. She had given him the truth, just not the whole truth. Her last secret was still protected.

She didn't dare to respond straight away. She must tread lightly, she knew . . . 'That night was our final chance to be together,' she said carefully, allowing her words to run up to his and simply knit together with his assumption. 'Whatever you think of us, Sergeant, we had loved each other for a year but lain together only once in that time. That night was our second and last time. We thought we would never see one another again. Frank Mathieson wasn't in either of our minds.'

She spoke with the conviction of someone with truth on their side, and they stared at one another for several long moments. The policeman blinked first. He picked up the pen again and she watched him write down her words.

'And that's it?' he asked finally.

'That's it.'

The sergeant pressed his lips together, his pen held rigidly in his hand. She could see him thinking hard as he flicked back through the pages, rereading other notes and frowning. Had she done enough for Donald? Too much, or not enough? Several times she opened her mouth to say more – to impress upon him Donald's innocence – but she closed it again, knowing any extra words risked muddying the waters. She must not push her luck. His assumption had derailed an unstoppable unravelling of the facts, but it was down to his error, not her lie. The story, such as he knew it, fit as far as he was concerned and she had only to steel her nerve and go along with it. There was a chance they might get through this after all.

He gathered everything up, pushing his chair back so that the feet scraped harshly along the floor, making her wince. Mhairi's eyes followed him, her heart threatening to leap from her chest, as he headed for the door. Still she said nothing.

'Stay here.'

How much time passed in there? An hour? Two? The door opened and a moment of silence whistled in as composite images seared onto her brain – handcuffs on wrists; sunken cheeks and wild hair – but those eyes that loved her so well settled upon her like blue moons. They hadn't changed at all.

She ran towards him with a sob. 'Oh, Donald! What have they done to you?'

He lifted his arms in a sealed loop above her head and held her close to his chest. It was as if none of the past month had happened. In an instant they were back on Hirta, the wind at their backs, kissing in the grass. Free. His heart thudded against her ear, his arms like walls around her, and she felt again as she always did with him – protected, safe and adored.

The sergeant cleared his throat, intruding on their bliss, and she felt Donald draw back, releasing her from his arms, his head dropping as if he remembered only now their predicament. 'You shouldn't have come here, Mhairi,' he said in a low voice, prudence winning out over passion.

'I had to. I couldn't leave you here! If Mary wouldn't speak the truth, it had to be me.'

There was pain in his eyes as he looked back at her. Open alarm. '. . . What have you told them?'

She blinked, afraid of his fear. Had she done wrong?

'She's said just enough to cause reasonable doubt for you,' the sergeant said, coming to stand between them. 'But quite possibly enough to incriminate herself.'

Mhairi flinched.

Donald immediately tried to step towards her. 'No, it wasn't her. It was m—'

The sergeant held up a hand, silencing him. '. . . *Before* you say something you might regret too, and waste valuable police time with a false confession,' he said in a warning tone, 'you should know that right now you're both free to go, pending further enquiries.'

Donald's eyes widened as the sergeant reached for his keychain and began to unlock the handcuffs. 'We are?'

'But you're not to leave the area, else your rich friend out there will have a big hole burnt in his pocket. He's footed a bail sum that would hurt even his coffers. Do you understand?'

'Yes, officer,' Donald murmured, his gaze coming back to Mhairi. She saw a flicker of relief – momentary hope – begin to simmer in his eyes as he rubbed his wrists and flexed his hands with newfound freedom.

The sergeant opened the interview room door and led them down the corridor, his heavy boots sounding on the concrete floor as Donald reached for her hand and kissed it. Together, they walked behind him towards the exit.

'Right, well; like I said, we'll be in touch,' he muttered as they stepped into the reception hall. Beyond, pale sunlight glowed beyond the doors as the rainclouds fell back like tired soldiers. Effie and Sholto looked up with wide eyes; they had been waiting for hours now.

Sholto rose first, seeming to understand the protocol. 'Shall we, then?' he asked, waving towards the open door where freedom lay.

Mhairi looked up at Donald and smiled. Their future was still so uncertain, this happiness so fragile – but they were together for now, with good friends by their side and the prospect of a fresh start winking just a few steps ahead of them, almost catchable. It was more than she had ever dared to dream of during their stolen hours. Not so much a happy ending as an imperfect beginning, but she would take it – for a patch was always better than a hole.

Acknowledgements

As I sit here typing this, I have written twenty-four books to date, but *The Stolen Hours* without doubt has been the hardest to write. Any author deciding to brave the challenge of a series loses a few nights' sleep worrying if they can pull it off, but add in a remote, dying way of life from a hundred years ago and the anxieties mount. I'll be honest, it took me a while to really get to know Mhairi and Donald. If you could have seen the first draft of this book – and thankfully my editor and agent were the only ones who ever did – you'd be stunned at the contrast to the characters and story now in your hands. The editing pain was real! But sometimes it goes like that – you have to take your time and get to know them, as you would any stranger; it can't always be rushed. I was also still very emotionally attached to Effie and Sholto and it was difficult returning to St Kilda and not living with them!

Then there's the obligation to pick up threads set down in *The Last Summer*, tie them in here and set down new ones for the coming books. I love the logistical mental challenge of it, but it means the story doesn't quite have the narrative freedom of a standalone (which is challenging for a prolific author like me, used to the autonomy of my plots), although what you lack in that regard, you make up with a familiar landscape and characters who are already like old friends. I hit upon a phrase in this book which I really liked – captured tornadoes – and which I think applies well to each woman in the series: be it Effie, Flora, Mhairi or someone else, each character is a force of nature trying to spin out into the world, but she's been grounded, still stuck in St Kilda and a past that won't quite let her go. I hope now that we're two books in, you've got a distinct sense of each young woman.

Those of you following me on Instagram (@swannywrites) will know it took two attempts to get to the islands this year and I've heard of others who have tried unsuccessfully a dozen times. Even in this modern age, St Kilda remains beguilingly aloof and remote, so imagine how much more isolated it must have felt a century ago with only steam and sailing ships. One thing to bear in mind while reading the books is that, even though the action is set in 1929 and 1930, in many ways the lives the St Kildans were living were more akin to those seen in the 1870s. Understanding the social mores of that time is crucial and it does mean sometimes being confronted with behaviours and mindsets that seem alien or even cruel to us. Anyone who's read *The Last Summer* will recall the shocking scenes with the dogs as the islanders left; I remember very well my own horror when I first read about it and it took quite a lot of digging to establish why they did what they did, as it wasn't explained and it wasn't immediately apparent to me when we no longer have (paid) dog licenses in the UK. I didn't understand that this was their only humane option, and even now that I do, it's still a tough read.

Ditto in this book, there are gruesome scenes but not, I hope, sensationalist ones. I did my research thoroughly – this time a deep dive into the whaling industry in the Outer Hebrides. It was fascinating, if tragic, and important not to be forgotten from our recent history. Those were different times with different needs but the impacts have been devastating and long-lasting, with whale numbers still nowhere near what they once were.

I also had to learn about crofting in much greater detail, and should you have any interest at all, I cannot recommend highly enough the Crowdie and Cream trilogy by Finlay J. MacDonald – the author's memoirs of a childhood set in the Hebrides of the 1930s. When I tell you I laughed out loud at the dry wit and the turn of phrase, then fell silent at the sadder scenes . . . With wonderful pathos and humour, Mr MacDonald makes a lost world feel so relatable.

Should you ever find yourself on the Isle of Skye, do head to the Museum of Island Life near Portree. It's actually a collection of restored stone crofts with great agricultural artefacts and so many collected stories. I had to be dragged away by my long-suffering parents who were desperate to find our ancestors' headstones in the nearby cemeteries! We're as bad as each other . . .

There are always so many people to thank for getting these books out to you. Pan Macmillan have been my publishers since my first ever book, *Players*, and they are tireless in their efforts to make sure what you receive from me is the very best version of itself. The team is large and with me name-checking them twice a year, they're pretty sick of my gratitude, but they know who they are and I would like to thank them once again. Special mention though really must go to Gillian Green, my editor. She has had her work cut out propping me up through the various drafts as we inched our way towards the finish line, but she has been tirelessly optimistic and resolute that we would get there, and I believe, finally, we have; it really doesn't feel like a forgone conclusion that you'll have a good book when you're mid-edit with loose ends and clunky characters, so to have a calm and concise steer is invaluable.

Huge thanks are also due, as ever, to Amanda Preston too: my agent and general superhero, she always knows exactly when to call or take me out to lunch so I can stop being a writer for a few hours. Again, we've been together since the beginning of my career and the trust, support and friendship is just invaluable.

Finally, The Fam – my beloveds, my *raisons d'être* – thank you for feeding me, walking the dogs and the hugs that you know keep me going. It's all for you.

The Secret Path

'Deliciously glamorous, irresistibly romantic!'
Hello!

An old flame. A new spark. Love can find you
in the most unlikely places.

At only twenty, Tara Tremain has everything: she's a trainee
doctor, engaged to Alex, the man of her dreams. But just when
life seems perfect, Alex betrays her in the worst way possible.

Ten years later, she's moved on – with a successful career and
a man who loves her. But when she's pulled back into her wealthy
family's orbit for a party in the Costa Rican jungle, she's flung
into a crisis: a child is desperately ill and the only treatment
is several days' trek away.

There's only one person who can help – but can she trust
the man who broke her heart?

The Hidden Beach

'Novels to sweep you away'
Woman & Home

Secrets, betrayal and shocking revelations await
in Sweden's stunning holiday islands . . .

In Stockholm's oldest quarter, Bell Appleshaw loves her job
working as a nanny for the rich and charming Hanna and
Max Mogert, caring for their three children.

But one morning, everything changes. A doctor from
a clinic Bell has never heard of asks her to pass on
the message that Hanna's husband has woken up.
But the man isn't Max.

As the truth about Hanna's past is revealed, the
consequences are devastating. As the family heads off
to spend their summer on Sweden's idyllic islands, will
Bell be caught in the crossfire?

The Spanish Promise

'The perfect summer read'
Hello!

The Spanish Promise is a sizzling summer novel about
family secrets and forbidden love, set in the
vibrant streets of Madrid.

One of Spain's richest men is dying – and his family are shocked
to discover he plans to give away his wealth to a young woman
they've never heard of.

Charlotte Fairfax, an expert in dealing with the world's super
rich, is asked to travel to the troubled family home to get to the
bottom of the mysterious bequest. She unearths a dark and
shocking family past where two people were torn apart by
conflict. Now, long-buried secrets are starting to reach into the
present. Does love need to forgive and forget to endure?
Or does it just need two hearts to keep beating?

**'A beautiful setting and steamy scenes –
what more do you need?'**
Fabulous

Set on an idyllic island, *The Greek Escape* is the perfect
getaway, bursting with jaw-dropping twists
and irrepressible romance.

Chloe Marston works at a luxury concierge company, making
other people's lives run perfectly, even if her own has ground to a
halt. She is tasked with finding charismatic Joe Lincoln his dream
holiday house in Greece – and when the man who broke her
heart turns up at home, she jumps on the next flight.

It doesn't take long before she's drawn into the undeniable
chemistry between her and Joe. When another client's wife
mysteriously disappears and serious allegations about him
emerge, will she end up running from more than heartbreak?

The Rome Affair

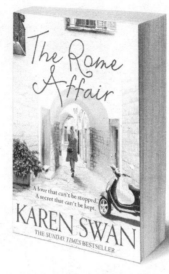

'Enthralling and magical'
Woman

The cobbled streets and simmering heat of Italy's capital are brought to life in *The Rome Affair*.

1974 and Viscontessa Elena Damiani lives a gilded life, born to wealth and a noted beauty. Then she meets the love of her life, and he is the one man she can never have. 2017 and Francesca Hackett is living la dolce vita in Rome, forgetting the ghosts she left behind in London. When a twist of fate brings her into Elena's orbit, the two women form an unlikely friendship.

As summer unfurls, Elena shares her sensational stories with Cesca, who agrees to work on Elena's memoir. But when a priceless diamond ring found in an ancient tunnel below the city streets is ascribed to Elena, Cesca begins to suspect a shocking secret lies at the heart of the Viscontessa's life . . .

Summer at TIFFANY'S

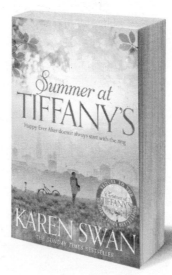

'Glamorous, romantic and totally engrossing'
My Weekly

A wedding to plan. A wedding to stop.
What could go wrong?

With a Tiffany ring on her finger, all Cassie has to do is plan her dream wedding. It should be simple, but when her fiancé Henry pushes for a date, Cassie pulls back. Meanwhile Henry's wild cousin Gem is racing to the aisle for her own wedding at a sprint, determined to marry in the Cornish church where her parents were wed. But the family is set against it, and Cassie resolves to stop the wedding.

When Henry lands an expedition sailing the Pacific for the summer, Cassie decamps to Cornwall, hoping to find the peace of mind she needs to move forwards. But in the dunes and coves of the north Cornish coast, she soon discovers the past isn't finished with her yet . . .

There's a Karen Swan book
for every season . . .

Have you discovered her winter stories yet?

www.panmacmillan.com/karenswan